THE LIES OF OUR FATHERS

Jonathan Mark

"If any question why we died. Tell them because our fathers lied."
(Rudyard Kipling)

Authors Note:

The Lies of our Fathers is the second novel in a trilogy. Although the story is stand alone in many respects, it is recommended that you read The Last Messenger first. There are many references in this novel to events that happened in the first novel which may confuse readers without prior knowledge.

Cast of Main Characters

11ᵗʰ Century AD

Sir Peter de Valognes - Lord of the Manor, Tigan, Essex.
Robert de Valognes - Son of Sir Peter, Knight of the First Crusade.
Akila - Muslim woman from Antioch.
Masood - Oldest son of Akila.

21ˢᵗ Century AD

Richard Helford - MI6 Officer.
David Helford - Father of Richard.
Becky - Richard's girlfriend.
Rowena - MI6 – Deputy Head of Middle East desk.
Amira Al Marami - CIA officer.
Harper - CIA officer.
Nadia Zabor - Saudi General Intelligence Directorate officer.
Maia Zevi - Israeli Mossad officer.
Ali Abu Mantazi- Brigadier General of Iranian Revolutionary Guard.
Mohammed Albitani - Colonel of Iran Revolutionary Guard.
Ayatollah Arif ibn Amaswari - Expert in Islamic studies.
Fatima - Professor of Islamic Studies University of Tehran.

Abbreviations

IRG - Iranian Revolutionary Guard.
MEK - Mujahidin-e-Khalq, - the warriors of the people.

Prologue

Antioch, Turkey. AD 1098

'We will storm the city before nightfall.'

I am too weary to laugh. I've been staring at those impregnable walls for five months, freezing through the cold winter nights, my stomach aching with hunger, watching my men die a slow painful death.

The Romans knew what they were doing when they built Antioch.

Every day, I've marvelled at the sheer scale of its defences. A fortress that would defy the largest of armies, where the walls were too high to climb and where the natural world mingled with man's ingenuity to repel any attack from the sharpest and fittest of men. When the sun comes up, I've huddled up close to the dying embers of the fire and studied every inch of the walls snaking along the Orontes River and climbing towards the mountains of Staurin and Silpius. I've counted every one of the sixty towers and wondered what chance we had to win this siege. It is two years since I arrived in Calais from England before beginning my journey to the Holy Land. Two long years of fighting, not just the forces of Islam but also pestilence, disease and starvation. We are a rag bag army, severely depleted but driven on by the belief that God was on our side. But what if God supported the Arabs and not us. What if God decided that we were strangers in a foreign land? What if God decreed that we should be slaughtered?

After all, we worship the same God.

The man who is talking to me and my fellow knights is Raymond of Toulouse. However cynical I am, he deserves to be heard. In January, those of us who were left had resorted to eating dogs and rats to survive another day, but this man gave us hope. When British ships arrived in Latakia and St Simeon, he took some men to the ports to

1

unload the much-needed provisions. They fought off bloody attacks and ensured the materials we needed to carry on with the siege were delivered to our camp. Our morale has been raised but I remain sceptical about how we will penetrate these formidable walls.

'A traitor has been caught and killed,' said Raymond.

The sound of shocked voices ripple through the crowd of assembled knights.

'By whom? I was not aware we had a traitor.' I said.

Raymond hesitated. 'None of us here was aware. Our knights did not catch the traitor. He was killed before I had a chance to interrogate him. For this reason, I don't trust the source of the information we've received.'

'If you don't trust the source, then why are we discussing it?' I replied, irritated that he thought we could attack with unverified intelligence.

'He's not a Frank, not one of us, which is why I'm nervous. It was Bohemond of Taranto who advised me of the traitor's death,' said Raymond, pacing the line, shifting his eyes away from my intense gaze. 'The excuse was the anger of the mob who craved revenge for the traitor's treachery. There should have been more discipline but, as I have said, these men are not Franks.'

Raymond didn't like acknowledging his rival, an Italian of all people, who had come up with a plan superior to his own.

'We must accept the words of Bohemond whether we like them or not.' Raymond continues to speak with remarkable authority, such that the knights listen, hanging on every word he utters. 'A traitor was feeding information back to our enemies and if we don't act soon, our chances of winning will be diminished.' He pauses for effect and looks at the tired soldiers in front of him. 'God is calling us into battle and if we don't answer his call we will be slaughtered.' Raymond speaks with the eloquence of a *leader and I like his readiness to lead. It is the mission I no longer have the stomach for.*

'We cannot rely on the disunity of our enemies.' Raymond continues. 'The traitor has been instrumental in providing the Sultan of Baghdad with cause to send an army to defeat us. A Sunni army is on its way. The traitor has alerted our enemies that we cannot sit out this siege indefinitely. If we don't attack now, we will be easily beaten when the army arrives.'

The hours of the day pass slowly. I wonder whether the traitor is genuine or are we walking with our heads held high straight into a trap? In truth, we would attack whatever the outcome. I'm prepared to die. It might even be a blessed relief. My father, Peter de Valognes would be proud that his son Robert had died a hero.

The sun is falling in the sky when we approach the city's south eastern ramparts. It is a quieter section of the walls which are not well defended. Why did we not see this weak point before? It may be a trap, but our options are limited. We must try or we will be all dead when the Sultan's army arrives. I watch as a small band of Behomond's men peel off with ladders and begin scaling the walls. But where is their leader? Not leading from the front, that much is certain. If he can send his men to their deaths and protect his own life, then I fear the worst possible outcome.

I need not have worried. The small postern gate near us opens. Men spill into the city. Bugles sounding and chants fill the air.

'God wills it...God wills it.' A marauding cry of my fellow crusaders which I no longer believe to be true.

What does God will?

What I see when entering the city is too horrific to describe. The city streets are flowing with blood and no one is spared. Women, children, the old and infirm are being hacked to death in vast numbers. There is little resistance. I try to avoid this indiscriminate murder and take my leave down a small side street. A mistake.

A man is charging towards me screaming. 'Allahu Akbar.'

His sabre swings above his head, ready to bring it down on my skull. I stand my ground parrying the flashing blade with my shield. In one clean movement, I run the man through with my sword, piercing his heart. As I pull the blade from the man's chest, I instinctively slit his throat, giving him no chance of survival. As the man falls, I hear another scream, this time from a woman.

It would have been easy to kill her, but I cannot slay a helpless woman in cold blood. She kneels, ignoring me, spreading her hands over the dead man who must be her husband. There is no time for guilt. There are more voices rushing towards us. "God is great. God is great,' they scream in unison, the same words cried by my attacker in Arabic, a mob lusting for blood and justifying their actions because they think God approves. If they see this woman weeping over the corpse of an Arab, they will kill her and probably me too for trying to protect her life. We must escape. With only seconds to spare, I lift the woman off the ground. She screams in protest, but I know I must save her.

'Come' I say in the broken Arabic I've learnt on our travels. 'I will not hurt you.' I shout.

'My children,' she wails, waving her hands wildly.

There are two boys hiding under an arch, no more than seven or eight years old. 'Come.' I bellow again to the boys and their mother is also beckoning them to follow. The city is a maze of alleys, deliberately designed to confuse the invader. My instinct is to take those streets which are too narrow to pull a cart which lead downwards, knowing that they'll lead to the walls. The noise from the crowd seems to be fainter but for how long? The Arab woman is calmer, so I put her down and trust her to follow me. Her boys stick close, showing no signs of fear.

We arrive in a small square with a Christian church dominating the space. I can see that the slaughter has reached here and moved on, leaving rivers of blood in its wake. The woman is hysterical, weeping at the carnage before her. She covers the boys' eyes with her hands, but it is already too late. There are at least twenty bodies lying in the square, some are decapitated, and the heads sit on marble plinths for all to see. A red stream trickles down the church steps. None of the dead are Arabs; they must be Greek Christians. They are killing their own because they lived in peace with the Muslims. I look up to the sky in despair and see the moon rising behind the buildings to the right of the church and remember that this must be south east, where the smaller undefended postern gate can be found. I put my arms round the shoulders of the woman, in a hopeless attempt to console her. I point in the direction of the moon, trying to express the urgency of our predicament. 'We must go,' I say with a firm but gentle voice and move quickly away.

At the edge of the square, I notice one of the bodies is a priest lying facing the heavens. As we pass, I hear him groan. I turn and look down, gesturing to the woman and children to keep moving. The holy man is clutching an icon in one hand and a book in the other. The wooden cross round his neck is soaked in blood from a deep slash to his belly. Kneeling, I realise that he will not live more than a few moments but at least I can give him some comfort in death. He is muttering what little sounds he can muster which I cannot understand. His hands lift towards me, while he stills holds the icon and the book, and he calls out again. This is the last thing he says. His eyes close and his hands fall to his side, blood trickling from his lips, the book and icon spilling onto the floor. A vermillion pool is forming around the priest and I see it spreading towards the book which I now see is a Holy Book judging by the cross embossed on its cover made of animal hide. I pick it up for no other reason than wanting to save it from damage and follow the woman and her children.

We find the smallest gate and as I hoped it is no longer manned. In a second, we are out of the city and heading towards the river. There are few people about as all the able-bodied men are killing within the city walls. There is a cave that I know down by the river which I believe will protect the woman and her children until I can bring them food. There seems a strange acceptance on the woman's face. She knows I killed her husband but now she has only one concern to protect the lives of her sons. She recognises that I'm the only one able to help her and she seems to acknowledge what I have done so far. I hold her hands and say sorry. Her eyes are the colour of lapis lazuli; they appear to reflect what little light seeps into the cave. A smile flickers across her lips, a recognition perhaps that I killed her husband in self-defence. The oldest of the two boys looks up to me and clutches my hand. I'm still holding the icon and the bible in my other hand. I bend down to his level and stare into his eyes. I ask his name. My Arabic will not stretch to anything else. The woman hears my words and speaks.

'Masood... His name is Masood.'

'And what is your name?' I ask.

'Akila.'

I hand Akila the icon, placing the bible inside my tunic. 'I'll bring food.'

She nods her approval. I step out into the sunshine and return to the city.

Chapter One

Libyan Sea, August 22nd, 2005.

She heard the rumble first, like the after sound of breaking thunder. A noise growing in pitch, closer to the boat, almost touching the horizon.

Then she saw it. A flash of light like a shooting star swooping across the sea, groaning as if it might explode. She cut the lights and watched, tracking balls of fire as they passed overhead. The growling became a scream; four comets streaking flame before vanishing into the night.

She wanted to warn them. In less than one minute they'd all be dead.

Silence. The waves lapped gently against the side of the boat.

The flash came first, and then the explosion lighting up the darkness. Then another and another and another. Her mouth fell open, frozen with shock.

She knew they were going to die and did nothing.

A gust of wind out of nowhere. The sea swelling in response to manmade destruction. She grasped the rail, steadying herself as the waves rushed under the boat. Then silence once more. Dead calm waters.

It was over.

'Now you know what bastards they really are,' shouted a voice from behind.

She swung round to face the voice, reaching for her Glock lying on the table.

'I should kill you,' she said quietly, staring at the man; his arms and legs securely cuffed to the ships rail.

'May I ask why?' The man spoke in a crisp English accent, nothing like a terrorist. A man who was going to die might have been scared. But he just stared blankly at her, indifferent to the barrel of the gun pointing in his direction.

He was in his sixties, tall with thinning grey hair, a little too long for a man of his age. Handsome in a dignified way; she could see where Richard got his looks. His face tanned and lined looked tired, even upset.

'Because you're a threat to US National Security.'

'Since when did that matter to you? And besides, we had a deal. Get me into Iran you said, in return for your freedom. That's what you care about and...' he hesitated and looked intently into her eyes. 'And my son...you care about my son.'

The woman's olive skin did not blush easily, but inside she knew that David Helford was right. She did care about his son, but did she care enough not to want to kill his father when he ceased to be useful. Nothing should deflect from her mission to get into Iran and begin to negotiate with the moderate factions of the Iranian government, to tell them that sanctions would be lifted if nuclear weapon development ceased. It was a secret mission which did not have the approval of the US government. It was a mission that could easily end her life, but she had no fear of that outcome. If it was the first tentative steps towards peace in the region then it was worth doing whatever the personal cost. The death of her family in the car bomb in Cairo would not have been in vain. She pondered the reason for their murders. Orthodox Christians killed by Al Qaeda in retaliation for the massacres of Muslims by Christians in the 11th Century. In their minds the need for revenge will never end. It was why President Bush had used the word Crusade as a symbol of the war on terror. A stupid thing to do which escalated the conflict. Her memories shifted to the face of her husband lying dead on the mortuary slab. His face disfigured by the bomb set off by a disillusioned young man who thought he was fighting Jihad. Her husband was a Sunni but rejected the version of Islam which bore no resemblance to what he'd read over and over again in the Holy Koran. She'd told him of the days when

Sunni and Shia would be united, and he had just smiled and said.

'Inshallah." If God wills it.

Chapter Two

The Island of Folegandros. One day earlier.

Richard Helford leaned over the deck rail of the ferry, squinting at the light as he retrieved his Ray Bans from his jacket pocket. The wind had dropped allowing the sun to envelop the sea and the sky until it mingled as one sheet of burning orange. The flames of sunset were a vision of hell not beauty. If he'd been starting a holiday, it might have been different. Like the first time he visited Folegandros when only nine years old. He learned to swim in the shallow waters, watching the ferries dock at the port of Karavostasis.

His reasons for coming here this time were not hedonistic. He'd read the Iliad on the long journey from Piraeus, looking for justification about what he was about to do. He'd read the poem many times but today he concentrated on Hector and his father Priam. He cast himself as Hector – a son determined to make his father proud. Priam returned that love as any father would do. Except his father was no Priam. The world wanted him dead. If he didn't do it someone else would. He tried so hard to hate him, not without justification, but with the gun pointing at his father's head, he didn't know whether he'd have the guts to pull the trigger.

The ship rounded the edge of the island losing the blinding light of the sun behind the mountains. The port came into view. Whitewashed buildings lining the shore reflecting the dying light. The ability of Greek ferries to turn in tight spaces fascinated him. He watched on deck as the ferry charged at what seemed like full speed up to the jetty and then at the last moment, the Captain swivelled the ship into reverse so that its rear gangway could be lined up.

Before it anchored, the ramp was already coming down, playing a happy tune, Chopin he thought, to warn people on the quay of its descent. Two of the crew threw ropes out to waiting bystanders to hitch the vessel and within a few minutes, the cars and lorries laden with food supplies were disembarking. He walked off the boat, as other lorries, cars and people were lining up to board. The port officials blew their whistles and for a moment he enjoyed the organised chaos of the arrival forgetting that somewhere on this idyllic island his father was waiting for him.

The ferry departed and the tourists who had arrived dispersed, climbing into hotel minibuses heading up to the main town of Chora. He'd not booked a hotel because he wasn't certain where his father might be on the island. He was not even sure his father was still here. Darkness descended on the village and the harbour lights flickered into life. He sat down on a wall and watched the water gently lapping the small beach - the surf illuminated by the white light of the moon rising in the sky. He remembered the holiday all those years ago, feeling happy because it was the only time, he'd felt part of a family. When GCHQ had tracked the call that his father had made to Becky from the island, he made the connection to that wonderful holiday. The man he had to kill was the same man who taught him to swim. Like Carlos the Jackal, he could see his father assuming mythical status - *The Silver Fox*. A grey haired sixty-three-year-old deceiving the world and most of all deceiving his son. It was the indifference that really got to him. His father was indifferent to killing.

Ever since he got back to London and spoke to Becky, he'd regretted losing her, all because he needed to find his father. Or was it? There was something about her which had changed. She no longer loved him, but it felt more than just a relationship breaking down.

Stray cats distracted his memories. Two scraggy felines were milling round his feet, tails up, rubbing scent on his trousers. It was as if the cats were telling him he belonged to this tiny island. Raising his eyes again he caught the silhouette of a few houses that lined the beach and the faint sound of bouzouki music announcing the existence of a taverna. There were only a few tables occupied. He decided to eat there and think about what to do next. On the other side of the jetty, a steep bank led up to a series of buildings and what looked like a hotel. He'd go there and get a room.

'Do you want a taxi?' a woman's voice spoke from behind, in heavily accented English.

Richard swung round, startled that he'd allowed this woman to get so close without noticing. She was about his age and reminded him of someone he couldn't place. She didn't look Greek or a tourist, too overdressed for the heat of the night air. Another man stood beside her, his face looked tanned and lean, a two-inch scar clearly visible under the harbour lights.

Not the kind of strangers to take a ride with on a moonlit night.

'I'm alright, thank you,' he replied with his best untroubled smile.

The man with the scar waved his hand. A grey Mercedes appeared out of the shadows, reversing rapidly until it reached where they were standing. The rear door opened before the car halted.

'Get in,' the man shouted, shoving him towards the open door.

He fell headfirst into the car, as it moved off at speed. The aroma of leather upholstery mixed with the woman's French perfume triggered his memory. The smell reminded him off Dinah Zevi, the woman his father killed.

His captors were Mossad. They kill first and ask questions later. The gun digging in his ribs wasn't for show.

The car ascended the winding hill towards Chora, only a few kilometres away. The streets were narrow and with the houses tightly packed together, there were few places where a car could go. It was a maze of whitewashed buildings with steps leading up to coloured doors and wooden verandas. Slowly, they followed the road until they reached a small square and stopped. The road had reached a dead end.

Who the fuck told them he was here? Rowena was the obvious choice, sucking up to Mossad, like a paid-up member of their fan club.

'Get out of the car and stick close. Try something and you're history,' Scarface muttered.

On one side of the square was a wall protecting onlookers from a sheer drop into the sea hundreds of feet below. He looked up at the cloudless sky. On a hill side above the town, a large floodlit church with a zig-zag path winding towards it shone like a beacon in the night.

'Get a move on.'

They made their way up a narrow path, taking only a few minutes to reach a slightly wider street where the houses were more tightly packed in terraces, two floors high on both sides. The main entrance of each house was on the second floor with steps leading up to it.

He felt the gun again, not on show, but there all the same. There were lots of tourists but no protection. Mossad didn't worry about such things. They'd kill him if they had to. Scarface pushed him in the back towards a narrow staircase, leading to one of the houses.

Inside, the decorations were simple. There were shelves of terracotta pots, a table, a few chairs, and a computer in the corner. There were lots of books spread around which Richard noticed were on religious subjects. A book on the history of Islam caught his eye.

'Your father has been hiding here,' said Scarface. 'I want to know where he is now.'

'I don't know,' he replied. 'I know no more than you. How did you find this place?'

'The woman your father killed found it for him. A place to escape from the CIA and everybody else. I'm told that he loved this island. We wanted him to work for us so we got him this place so he'd feel he had to help us.'

'You know it was self-defence, don't you? She was going to kill him.'

Scarface raised his hand to silence Richard. 'He's a murderer. Apart from Dinah Zevi, he killed an Israeli citizen – Abel B Multzeimer, a billionaire with great importance to our economy…He also killed another one of my colleagues. We will kill him because we can't trust anybody else to do it, least of all *you*.'

'Have you talked to MI6?'

'It doesn't matter who we've spoken to, ' Scarface replied curtly. 'Your father deserves to die and MI6 support us in our action. If you don't know where your father is then why are you here?'

'I had some information, but it was all very circumstantial.'

Scarface sat down on one of the chairs in the room and pointed to Richard to sit. 'Dinah recruited him after he fell out with the CIA. We smuggled him out of New York after 9/11, thinking that your father's friendship with the terrorist Abdul was worth pursuing. Abdul was close to Sheikh Zabor, one of our key targets, an enemy to Israel even though the Americans were convinced he was a great guy. Maybe something to do with the way he spent his billions in the US.'

'I know you assassinated the Sheikh. My father didn't help. Zabor was blown up by an Israeli F15,' said Richard. 'One of yours I think.'

The Israeli stopped and using his mouth, pulled out a cigarette from a crushed packet of Camels that was lying on the table. The Merc driver struck a match and lit the cigarette before lighting one for himself. Swirls of tobacco smoke filled the tight confines of the house to the evident disapproval of the woman who opened the door, stepping nearer to breathe in the cleaner night air.

'I'll take it from here,' the woman said, speaking with an assured authority, interrupting the older man. She was in charge. The woman reminded him of Dinah. He was sure of it.

'After we trained your father in Haifa,' she said turning away from Scarface who looked like he was going to explode. 'He became a very effective operative in Iraq. We thought he could help us take out Sheikh Zabor. What we didn't know at the time was that he'd switched allegiance to Al Qaeda. That's why Dinah Zevi was ordered to kill him.'

He shifted in his seat. 'Look, if my father is still on the island,' he said in a conciliatory tone, 'I know he wants to see me. But if he knows you're here, he's not going to show his face. I need to be left alone and I'll ask around. If he lived here in this house people will know whether he is still on the island.'

Scarface leaned forward, grabbing him tightly by the wrists. 'If you double cross me,' he snarled. 'You're a dead man, is that clear?'

He tried to stand up, but he was no match for Scarface.

'Let him go,' said the woman, firmly. It had the desired effect. The vice like grip loosened and blood rushed back into his fingers.

'I'll find him if he's here. Let me go back to the port where it's quieter. If my father is looking for me, he'll be watching the ferry arrivals. He may already know I've been picked up by you. I suggest you stay put here and enjoy the sunshine.'

The woman nodded agreement 'I'll drive you,' she said.

As they drove back down the hill to the port, an awkward silence filled the car. He studied the women's face as she drove. It was the fierce eyes, blonde hair and tanned features that reminded him of the woman his father killed. Her hair was cut short, unlike Dinah, which accentuated her high cheek bones emphasising the resemblance between the two women. Although the road was empty of other cars, she stared forward overplaying the concentration required to keep the car on the road. 'You remind me of Dinah,' he said. 'At least how I remember her face. I didn't know her.'

The woman didn't reply.

'You know I've been instructed to kill my father. I could save you the trouble,' Richard continued, deciding that if he kept talking the woman would say something. 'He is an embarrassment to our security services…He's an old man for pity sake and yet he is running rings round us.'

The woman spoke. 'We trained him well.'

'I suppose that was Dinah's doing. She had some kind of hold over him.'

'It was more than that. They fell in love…I know.'

'How do you know?'

The woman stopped the car just short of the port and turned to face him. There was sadness in those fierce eyes. 'Dinah was my sister.'

He didn't know what to say. 'I'm sorry,' he muttered feebly. 'We'll find him.'

'I don't blame your father,' she replied. 'Dinah was going to kill him. It was self-defense. It's the system I blame, kill or be killed, protecting the Jewish right to a homeland on the West Bank. It is an intractable problem unless we live in peace together. I think your father saw that. I joined Mossad to fight fire with fire, following my sister's lead. She was older than me and I worshipped the ground she walked on. Now she's dead, I don't know what's right anymore.'

'You must miss her. I'm sorry it had to end like this. What's your name?' he asked.

'Maia…It means close to God. Ironic don't you think?'

'If you don't want to do this then why don't you leave

Mossad?'

She ignored the question. Instead she turned to face him. 'How could you kill your father?'

He averted his eyes. 'If I'm honest, I don't know I could. There's no love lost between us. He's never been a son to me.'

Maia pulled a card out of her pocket and handed it to him. 'Here's my number. Call me if your father gets in touch. We'll do the rest.'

He took the card and got out of the car. He moved to lean against the open window, expecting some final words but she accelerated away without saying anything else. He sighed and started walking towards the hotel, following a light up a steep path to the reception. He had faint recollections of the hotel being where he'd stayed all those years ago; the building seemed bigger than he remembered but maybe tourism was expanding, and the owner had built an extension. An old woman sat at the reception, glued to a portable television. She looked up with annoyance that he might dare interrupt her favourite television programme. He exchanged greetings in Greek and gave her his British Passport, not his real one but still undetectable as a forgery.

The old woman glanced briefly at his passport and checked her booking list before returning her attention back to the TV. 'We already have a reservation for you,' she muttered.

'Are you sure?' he asked.

'That's you, isn't it?' said the woman pointing to his alias name - *Peter Marchento* on the booking sheet. Only MI6 personnel knew about his false passport and only Rowena was aware of his visit to Greece. A thought occurred to him. 'When was the booking made?'

'About a week ago,' the woman replied, turning to get the room key from its cubby hole. 'There's a message for you.' The woman handed Richard an envelope.

The message was short. He read the words over and

over.

The Church of Christos, Angali

His father had taken him there, all those years ago, leaving his mother at the hotel. The name Angali stuck in his mind even after so many years. It was a sweltering hot day and he remembered they'd walked a long way. They stopped at the church and looked down over the bay. 'It means embrace,' his father had said. 'The beach of Angali.' Without warning the older man had knelt to his level and hugged him tightly. How could he forget that name – Angali? A word burned in his mind because his father had embraced him in that spot for the last time.

The next morning couldn't come soon enough. Sleep had eluded him for most of the night and when he finally succumbed, the noise of the early morning arrival of a Sea jet hydrofoil forced him to open his eyes. He'd spent the evening eating alone - souvlaki, fried potatoes and horiatiki – a Greek salad with an enormous piece of feta cheese laced in olive oil and oregano. Although the food was excellent, he could only think about what he should do with his father when he found him. He drank retsina with a splash of Sprite to lighten his mood. He couldn't allow Mossad to murder him in cold blood, but equally as important, he couldn't let his father go free with all the mayhem that would cause. Bleary eyed, he flung back the shutters and felt the heat of the early morning sun revive his senses. He showered quickly and stepped out onto the balcony to survey the scene. The hydrofoil had already left, leaving a trail of white wispy water in its wake, driving a wedge though the glistening blue sea. The hills that towered round the port showed just how barren the island was, dry to the bone due to lack of rain, parched to a grey sandy hue by the ferocious sun. Against the dreary rock, the whitewashed buildings shone in the blinding light, festooned with red geraniums and purple bougainvillea.

This was no place for killing, he decided.

Breakfast was served overlooking the port where he could see the bus coming down the hill. He drank a watery orange juice and cut two huge slabs of hard cheese to place between fresh bread still warm from the oven. Wrapping his sandwich in a napkin, he slipped it into his pocket to be eaten on the bus. A cup of lukewarm syrupy Greek coffee gave him the shot in the arm he needed to go and find his father.

The bus took him only part of the way. After borrowing a map from the hotel, he realised he would need to get off and walk if he was going to reach the Church of Christos. As the bus trundled through Chora, packed to the rafters with tourists, he sat low in his seat, hoping that Maia wouldn't notice him peering out of the bus. The driver came to a halt about a mile out of Chora, pointing the path out to Richard. He thanked him and stepped into the burning sun sheltering under an olive tree while he worked out the route to the church. An eerie wind blew, barely moving what little foliage existed buried between gaps in the rocky landscape. The path was easy to spot, defined by carefully matched stone, each one shaped to create a mosaic that must have been thousands of years old.

After about twenty minutes walking, the little chapel came into view. It stood on a high outcrop deliberately chosen for its views overlooking the vast expanse of blue sea below. He was in no doubt he was in the right place although his memory of the chapel was faint if not completely nonexistent. A shiver of anticipation surged through his body. He hesitated, reluctant to move forward, uncertain what to say if his father appeared. He listened but could hear nothing but the wind blowing hot air, like a hairdryer, directly in his face.

The ringing sound shattered the silence. He jumped, thinking his ears were playing tricks, but when he listened more intently, there was no doubt; a phone was ringing in the undergrowth, a few feet in front of where he was standing. He waded into the gorse, cutting his fingers on the thorns, following his ears but unsure where to look. The phone stopped ringing.

'Shit,' said Richard out loud. He sucked the blood from his bleeding hands and looked around. 'Where is it?' He tracked back surveying the area where he'd heard the sound. It had to ring again.

But nothing came.

In desperation, he shouted at the wind. 'Where the fuck are you?' He raised his hands and turned a full circle. 'I picked up all the signs. The phone call from the island. I remembered you took me here as a child.' He was saying all he wanted to say to his father, face to face, if only he could see him.

The phone rang again. He collected himself and concentrated, sure he was close. The sound was a matter of feet from where he stood. A rock, camouflaged by gorse, appeared to be the source and when he blinked at a ray of sunshine catching, what could only be, the phone's screen, he knew he'd found it. Desperate to reach it before it stopped ringing, he clambered through the undergrowth, tearing his jeans in the process, before he managed to grab the phone.

'Did the Israelis give you anything?'

Despite preparing himself for the moment, he was shocked to hear the clipped English tones of his father's voice once more.

'There was only the woman in the team who gave me a phone number on a piece of card, that's all.'

'Was her name Maia?'

'Yes. She knows who you are.'

'Have you got it with you?'

'Why? Yes.' Richard retrieved the card from his pocket. It was abnormally thick.

'Oh shit,' he said ripping the card in two. 'There's a

tracking device concealed in the card.'

'Listen to me, Richard. Take the device towards the chapel and leave it there. They are on their way. I knew Mossad would find me, given time.'

'Where are you?'

'I'm near…I wanted to see you just one last time and say goodbye.'

'Where are you going?'

'Iran. They'll protect me. I've already given them the scroll.'

'Iran is an enemy of the West.'

'Exactly, that's why I'm going there. It's the only place where nobody will try to kill me.'

'You what?' Richard's eye widened in disbelief. He clenched his fists. 'You mean, I've come all this way on a wild goose chase while you help out our enemies. I thought I could hear you out and recover the scroll.' Richard felt his voice tail off. He could barely speak.

'And then what?' There was irritation in his father's voice. 'Were you going to kill me when you understood?'

Richard ignored the question. 'I could take you back to London. What are you hoping to achieve, if you don't come with me?'

'Truth.'

'You're a banker - what do you know about truth?'

'That's why I left. I want a purpose in my life before it ends. The CIA betrayed me which is why I ended up in the arms of Mossad. But now even they want me dead.' He hesitated, 'And even you want me dead, Richard. Iran is the only place where they'll listen.'

'But they are bent on the destruction of our way of life.'

'That's Western propaganda. It's not true. I've sent the scroll to a professor of Islamic Studies in Tehran. She's very excited. It's evidence that there was a conspiracy to exclude The Gospel of Barnabas from the Bible. Muslims have long held the opinion that the Gospel is authentic but have been unable to prove it.'

'Until now,' interrupted Richard.

'Exactly,' his father replied. 'They just need to find the Gospel in its original text. Everybody says the Gospel is a forgery because the copy we have dates to the sixteenth century. The scroll gives them hope that such a version of the document really exists.'

Richard ground his teeth, shaken by what his father was telling him. Of all the places for the document to end up, Iran was the worst. Getting it back would be impossible because the propaganda value to the Iranians would be priceless. 'All that noble stuff about seeking truth does not justify killing people, does it?' said Richard. 'How could you stick that knife into Dinah Zevi's stomach and not be affected by your actions?'

An audible sigh came over the phone line. 'Oh yes, I was affected. Big time. I regret it and should have let her kill me…if only to end this sorry mess.'

His father sounded distressed. 'So why don't you give yourself up now?' he said quietly.

'And what good would that do? They'd lock me up and throw away the key. Or maybe, they'd kill me. I'd rather them murder me than be left to rot in some prison.'

'So why did you bring me here if you couldn't give me back the scroll?'

'To remind you of the good times we had together.'

'Bullshit, you can't buy someone's love with a two-week holiday. What about all that time afterwards?'

'I wanted you to be tough…and look you've succeeded.'

'But you still haven't told me where you are?'

'I'm here…not far away. I knew they'd come to the safe house in Chora, but I've friends who helped me hide.'

'I've come here to take you back and if you don't…' Richard felt his throat go dry. He hesitated.

'Or else you're going to kill me. Is that it?' his father

replied calmly. 'Now listen to me Richard. It won't be just me who gets killed if Mossad find me. Get off this road before they arrive. Take the other path that leads south east. It will take you to Livadi. About half a mile down that path, you'll see a group of large boulders. Immediately opposite is a narrow path, very overgrown, leading down towards the sea. Follow that path. But make sure you're not followed.'

Richard cut the call and ran to the church, tossing the tracking device into the bushes without stopping. He turned back up the hill, continuing to run, driven by the urgency in his father's voice and a certainty that Scarface and Maia might appear at any moment. The path his father had described was easy to find. He stopped and looked around for any sign of the Israelis, smiling to himself that his luck was holding but still feeling uneasy. It almost seemed too quiet to be true.

The track down to the beach was barely visible, dropping steeply over rough hewn rock punctuated by thorn bush. Richard descended slowly, becoming more uncertain whether he'd found the right path. When he reached the bottom, the way opened out into what appeared like a steep crevasse. He cursed, refusing to believe that he would need to go back. In desperation, he scrambled over the loose rock that covered the floor, looking for some way out that would take him to the sea.

There was nothing.

The frustration he'd felt earlier, when his father failed to show, returned with greater force. He stared at the phone screen, willing a signal to reappear, but it remained dead. He threw the phone onto the floor, venting his anger on the mobile's plastic casing. 'Where the fuck are you?' he said, loud enough to hear his voice bouncing back off the cliff walls.

'It's a good hiding place, don't you think?'

Chapter Three

The Island of Folegandros, Greece. August 21st, 2005

Richard swung round and saw his father. Nothing like an international terrorist, he was barefoot and stripped to the waist. Water dripped off his body, like a castaway who'd been swimming in the sea to catch fish rather than a Mossad agent trained to kill jihadists. The very idea seemed too ridiculous for words.

They were a few feet apart but Richard remained stuck as he watched his father move closer to him. 'I…I think we need to talk,' said Richard, his voice shaking with emotion.

'We do, but may I hug you first?'

Richard didn't reply, remaining passive as his father wrapped his arms around him.

The older man released his hold and stepped away before continuing to speak. 'I know you're angry with me and of course you have every right to be, but I do love you Richard. I've always loved you.'

Richard almost believed him, not because he wanted to forgive. His father had adopted a pose; his head bowed and his shoulders dropped, as if in an act of contrition. But, it was something much deeper that fueled his anger, outweighing any compassion he might feel for his father's situation.

'This has nothing to do with love,' Richard replied, his expression hardening. 'It's about betrayal.' The earlier composure had gone and the man he was looking at looked like a frail old man rather than a hunted killer. Richard felt nothing except numbing disbelief, unable to separate love and hate. 'Why did you stand by and let Abdul kill Andreas? Why did you abandon Mother without so much as an explanation? How could you stick a knife in the woman you once loved?' Richard rattled off the questions with increasing ferocity without waiting for answers. 'How could you stand by when those tourists were murdered at the lake?'

'You think I haven't asked myself those questions? I regret all the suffering I've caused for something which I believed to be right. I want to end this conflict between the religions. It makes no sense.'

Richard shot a glance at his father. 'Do you honestly think your actions will make the slightest difference? You are deluded and now you've lost the scroll to Iran. We should just own up to this fuck up and move on. Come back with me to London.'

For a moment, Richard thought his father might actually agree to his request.

'It's not that simple. I can't spend the rest of my days in a jail. I need to help find the Gospel of Barnabas before the Saudi's do.'

Richard turned away from his father's stare. He found it hard to look at him.

'The only way to the beach, where a boat will rescue me, is by swimming, which is why I'm wet and undressed,' David Helford said. 'That pool over there leads to the sea…you can't see it from here because you need to swim under a rock. It's what makes this place so private…but enough of that… we need to talk and I think it's best if I start from the beginning.' He stopped and looked around for somewhere to sit, perching himself on a large rock before continuing. 'We're safe here, but it is only a matter of time before they'll find us. Before I go. I've got to tell you everything Richard, because we probably won't meet again.'

Richard nodded and found another stone to sit on. He could not face his father head on; it was all too raw. He'd given up any chance that his father would come quietly back to London.

David Helford spoke in the measured public-school

tones which seemed so untypical of the man's unkempt appearance. 'When I was working in New York, I became obsessed with discovering the truth behind why my father - your grandfather- died in Crete during the war. As I learned about the existence of the scroll and finally met Callidora in New York, I realised that this ancient document outed a lie that had existed for centuries; a lie that undermined the very importance of Islam. The last straw came when I saw at first hand the methods used by the CIA who failed to act on my tip off about 9/11. How I was silenced in Vienna when I tried to give the tape to the 9/11 Commission, a tape which showed that the President knew about the pending attack. When I was smuggled out of America by Dinah, I didn't know that they wanted me to pay for their assistance by training to be a Mossad agent providing intelligence and being part of an off the grid hit squad in Iraq.'

'But why would they do that?' Richard interrupted. 'I mean you are hardly ex SAS are you?'

A small smile crept across his father's lips. 'You're right of course but I had something they wanted which was a way into Abdul and more importantly to Sheikh Zabor.'

'Maia told me that last night. You could have refused to help them.'

This time the smile broke into a laugh. 'Now I know you're joking,' his father replied. 'I knew that Mossad were just as bad as the Americans with their underhand tactics but Dinah was very persuasive. Mossad don't take no for an answer. They provided me with protection from the CIA and got me out of the US, when every bastard CIA operative was looking for me with orders to blow my fucking brains out.' The older man stood up and grabbed Richard's arm as if seeking approval for his actions. 'The CIA were trying to kill me. Don't you understand?'

'But if you are pro Islam then why would you agree to kill terrorists whose cause you support?'

'I don't support terrorism in any form. I support peace

and truth , redressing the balance. The Sheikh was a terrorist providing funding to the 9/11 hijackers. He is guilty and I want to show his methods do not work…that's why I cooperated with Mossad and killed Al Qaeda terrorists in Iraq.'

Richard was speechless. His father was honourable and trying to do the right thing and yet the naivety of his mission was astounding.

David sat down again and laughed. 'You think I'm a stupid old man and maybe you're right.'

'You are an embarrassment to the world's intelligence agencies. That's what you are.'

The old man sighed and focused his stare. 'Look at me son, when you get older, you are that much nearer death, you can take more risks. If I come out of this having achieved some good then maybe I'll have won your respect. All I want is some understanding between the Arab and the Jew, some understanding between Shia and Sunni. I want them to see the other persons point of view and to look forward not backwards.'

There were tears in his father's eyes and Richard for a moment wanted to believe him.

'Go on,' he said.

'Imagine my shock when I heard you were also in Iraq and might recognise me. I arranged for you to be watched so I knew where you were at all times and could stay well clear. While we were watching your movements, we stumbled on a plot to kill you which was being arranged by Harper, the CIA guy you were working with. I discovered that the suicide bomb that killed your bodyguard was a deliberate attack on you to flush me out. The CIA guys of course had no idea I was in Iraq working right under their noses.'

Richard's stomach tightened. 'Are you telling me - Harper set me up?' It all made perfect sense because when the plot failed, Harper was giving him the cold shoulder.

The CIA man must have been responsible for getting him sent back to London and Rowena must have been under more pressure from the Israelis courtesy of his father's intervention. Richard remembered something Rowena had told him. 'Hold on a minute…that can't be right,' he said.

David glanced back in Richard's direction, a bemused look on his face. 'Why?'

'Because the boy who tried to blow me up had a motive.'

'What motive?'

'We were holding his brother Masood. I think you know who I mean.'

The expression on his face was a mixture of surprise and shock 'I didn't know that Masood was in Iraq.'

'Yes. You knew him didn't you?'

'I did. He was interested in my view of the world. We were friends.'

'Is that why he was following me on the underground when the bomb went off that killed him?'

David nodded. 'He was doing me a favour. I wanted to make contact with you.'

'It was no coincidence that Masood gave me the icon.'

'No. But Harper knew nothing of my friendship with Masood. He just wanted to kill me and didn't give a shit about people like Masood and his brother being caught in the crossfire.'

Richard grunted in disbelief. 'What a bastard.'

'Dead right, they're bastards...sending a boy to his death like that and for no reason. They were also party to the torture of Masood, trying to get information about Abdul. Bloody waterboarding…fucking barbaric bastards.'

His father using the word *torture* hit Richard hard. He'd never witnessed any of the torture but he'd heard the screams and seen the evil in Harper's eyes as he'd emerged from the cells. He knew it was going on and was ashamed.

His father looked again at him. There were tears in his

eyes. 'I know I'm crazy, Richard. It's just…'

'Just what?' said Richard maintaining a hard, unimpressed tone.

'Just appalled by the devious, sadistic tactics of the Americans and the Israelis. I wanted to help the Islamic cause. I didn't want to be a terrorist…no way.'

'Your crazy to think any of this will make a difference. You're an embarrassment to the SIS…Just give yourself up for my sake if not for your own.'

David ignored Richard's plea and continued. 'I was keen for the scroll to be seen and the truth revealed. I thought it might lead to peace or at least a greater understanding that all the major religions originate from the same source of Abraham.'

Richard sighed, frustrated by David's single minded stupidity.

'You are mad to think that you can change the course of Middle Eastern politics with your heroics,' said Richard. 'The world doesn't work that way…For a start, it doesn't explain the conflict between the Sunni and the Shia branches of Islam. It doesn't explain anything.'

'But if we can find the real Gospel of Barnabas referred to in the scroll then it is a game changer. If we can prove it's not a forgery, it will verify the authenticity of the scroll.'

Richard shook his head . ' Let's suppose that the Gospel of Barnabas *is* authentic, and Jesus *did* refer to someone greater than him as being the Last Messenger of God. It won't make Christians become Muslims. It'll just incite Muslims more, that a Christian text was withheld which proved the supremacy of Islam,' he replied, becoming increasingly frustrated with his father's logic. He found himself shouting to drum his point home. ' Don't you see, for fuck's sake? The bottom line is that the various religions are cultural manifestations of the same thing. It won't work. Why can't you get that into your thick idealistic skull?'

David listened intently. He even nodded in what appeared to be a halfhearted acceptance of his son's argument. Neither man spoke for several seconds then without warning his father's countenance changed. 'I'm going to Iran,' he said firmly.

Richard pulled out his Glock and pointed it at David. 'I can't allow this to happen, I'm taking you back to London.'

A smirk crept across David's face. 'And how do you propose to defend me against the Mossad hit squad on the island?'

Richard had no idea. 'We could take them on together. There are more of them, but you know their tricks.

'Yes. I do. But we wouldn't stand a chance.'

It was already too late. Gun shots came out of nowhere. Bullets bouncing off the rocks. David sprinted towards the edge of the crevasse, drawing fire as he scrambled towards the pool. Richard needed no second prompt, he lunged to the left, firing two rounds from his Glock, enough to pin the shooters down for a second while they ducked his bullets. David took his chance diving into the water. Richard moved fast, racing from rock to rock before firing again. Scarface was quicker, coming at him with full force, felling him with the skill that only Mosaad provides. With choreographed efficiency, Scarface rolled clear and the junior, who'd been driving the Merc took over, pinning him down, brandishing a switch blade protruding close to his jugular.

A volley of rounds pumped into the water. Maia bellowed orders, stopping the firing. The grip loosened on his neck. Junior rolled off him, still clutching the knife and holding a pistol in his other hand. 'Get up,' he said, spitting out the words.

'Where is he hiding?' Maia shouted.

'You saw him,' said Richard pointing to the pool. They looked away for a split second. Long enough. He ran, following his father in one swift movement. He caught a glimpse of Maia, pointing her gun, but not firing. His head broke the surface and he kicked hard to go deeper. The weight of his clothes hindered his descent, vaguely aware of a bullet zipping passing his head.

But there was only one bullet.

If they'd wanted to kill him, it would have been easy.

Disorientated, he swam towards the light. The colour changed to a dazzling azure blue as the sky penetrated the sea, changing its hue. Looking upwards he could see the sun. Surfacing, he breathed large gulps of warm air. He was in a larger cove bobbing around in the choppy sea which bashed up against the rocks. A narrow channel directed him out into open water. The salt stung the back of his throat as he swum for all his worth. Out of the corner of his eye he could see Scarface catching him with every stroke, however hard he pushed. Ahead, there was a small beach and not much else. There was no sign of his father, but the shore was the only place he could go. As soon as he could get his feet on the ground, he ran, splashing through the surf until he reached dry land. Scarface caught him as he staggered over the sharp pebbles. He couldn't run and collapsed as the Israeli tackled him. 'Where is your father?' he screamed.

The next thing he heard was a loud crack. Scarface toppled forwards. He pushed the limp body to one side and stood up. His father was clutching a large rock, looking down at the man he had just hit. 'One down - two to go,' he said with a smile, looking as if he was enjoying the chase. 'We need to hide,' he continued. 'Maia will be sending a chopper.'

'And our friend here will come round,' said Richard pointing at Scarface laid out on the sand.

They walked towards the edge of the beach and were confronted by a sheer cliff face. He followed as David felt his way along a sloping escarpment at the base of the cliff until he disappeared through a gap in the rock, barely wide enough to squeeze through. It opened out into a small cave, which shielded them from the sky and the sight of choppers. 'They'll be here before my boat takes me to freedom. I've got to go now.' He grasped Richard by both hands. 'I hope one day you'll understand me.'

He didn't wait for Richard's reply. His son watched as the older man ran towards a small fishing boat leaving the cove. He fumbled for his gun to stop him but he'd lost it when he'd dived into the water. Anchored only a few metres from the coast a larger vessel, one he'd seen before, dominated the horizon - *The Istanbul Star*. The distraction diverted his attention for just a few seconds but enough for him to lose sight of his father. He strained his eyes expecting to see him swimming towards the vessel but there was no sign.

He looked back towards the horizon and the larger ship. If he could see it, so could Mossad. *The Istanbul Star* was no hiding place. It was a floating coffin and that was exactly where his father was heading.

He waited for what seemed like hours, listening to the waves. No breakers. Just gentle ripples of water running over the pebbly beach. The soothing noise comforted him, and he fell asleep watching the glistening waters.

He awoke to the stabbing pain of a gun barrel, digging into his ribs. He opened his eyes and stared at Maia.

'We have no further need of you....' She turned away from his gaze and said, 'And neither does your father.'

Chapter Four

London, UK. August 26th, 2005.

'How do you know he's dead when you've got no body?'

Richard stared blankly at Becky and nodded. 'I don't know,' he said quietly. 'I'm just trying to say to you that it's over with my father. I just know I want to be with you at the birth of our baby…do you think I could come in? Just for a few minutes to talk about it.'

Becky stared over his shoulder, looking from right to left up the street. It was early, and commuters were rushing passed on the way to the station. Some smiled as they passed and other's even said hello. Becky pulled the cord of her dressing gown, nodding an embarrassed acknowledgement of the child she was carrying rather than some half-hearted effort to preserve her modesty.

'I've got to go to the doctor for a checkup, so I haven't got long. You're lucky to catch me.'

'It won't take long.'

Becky stepped aside, and Richard entered her flat. He tried not to notice the general mess of dirty dinner plates and flowers dying in their vase.

'Can I do anything to help tidy up a bit…while you're out at the doctor's?'

'You didn't come to be my house maid,' said Becky, maintaining her stern unwelcoming voice. She didn't look pleased to see him.

He tried to hug her, but she pushed him away.

'I want to believe it's over with your father,' she said. 'But you had no body after 9/11 and you still don't have a body…. I'm sorry I just don't believe you when you say it's over.'

'I'll pack in the job. Will that convince you?'

Becky sighed. 'You don't seriously expect me to

believe that as well.' She let out a cynical laugh. 'You are your father's son. Interested in danger and addicted to a devious world. Only you are not as good as him at playing silly games. You could no more settle down to an office job or play the dutiful father than your father could towards you. You've got to face up to the reality of our situation. The chances of us working out as a couple are zero. I've thought a lot about it while you were away.' She looked at her watch. 'Is that the time? I've got to get ready.'

While Becky dressed Richard stacked the dishwasher and picked up the flowers from the vase. A card became detached from the bouquet and fluttered down to the floor. He put the flowers in the green bin outside the back door and coming back inside, picked up the card.

He read the words . *'Thanks for a lovely dinner last night - H xx'* He put the card down on the breakfast bar and felt a pang of jealousy in his gut. To take his mind off the message, he swept the floor and wiped down the worksurfaces. It wasn't like Becky to be untidy.

'Thank you, ' she said.

He had his back to her when she spoke. When he turned and saw Becky dressed, ready to face the world, he noticed something different about her. Before now, she would have spent hours preparing for the grand entrance, but this time there was minimal show. The pregnancy had changed her beauty from an image of calm efficiency where nothing in her appearance was out of place; the way her tussled hair fell dramatically on her shoulders and her Dior makeup captured a woman with what seemed like sculptural beauty. The woman he could see now was real, not manufactured; the earth mother; a woman with a soul. He'd always found Becky more attractive without makeup and now the hormonal changes created a woman with a flawed appearance he admired even more. 'You look wonderful,' he said, which he noticed registered a look of approval on her face.

'I don't feel wonderful,' she said. 'I feel like a waddling duck.'

'Let me take you to the doctor and then maybe we can have some lunch.'

'No, I can't. I've got to go to work. Not on maternity leave yet.'

They walked to the surgery together and barely spoke. He wanted to ask about the card on the bouquet but didn't know how to phrase the question. When they parted Becky grasped Richard's hand.

'Take me to dinner,' she said. 'Call at seven. We need to talk.'

He took her to Luigi's restaurant on Clapham High Street and laughed as she tucked into a mound of tortellini. It took several minutes before she stopped eating and looked at Richard, blushing when she burped.

'Pardon me, my appetite has increased to obesity levels... I must be carrying triplets.'

Richard acted horrified and Becky laughed. She'd been drinking water but picked up Richard's glass of red wine and drank a large mouthful.

'You shouldn't be drinking alcohol,' Richard scolded.

'For God's sake Richard, please don't lecture me. The odd glass won't matter.' She wagged her finger in a playful way and Richard winked. 'No more I promise,' she grinned.

Richard was finding it hard to be jovial. He twisted spaghetti on his fork, focusing on the plate in front of him. Anything, rather than look into Becky's eyes and tell her that he was sure his father had escaped death once more. When he stole a glance, he could see Becky had picked up on his uneasiness.

'He's not dead, is he?' she said.

'The official explanation is that he has died. I can't tell

you how.'

'Did you kill him?'

'No of course not.' He shifted uneasily in his chair and poured some more red wine. 'I think he's fled to Iran…I cant tell you how they think he was killed. It's secret.'

'But you don't believe it.'

'No, I don't.' He noticed she seemed relieved.

'You've never told me what your father has done which is so awful that people want to kill him. All I know is what he told me when he rang and tried to tell me you were in great danger and I should get you to leave the spying game.'

Richard stared back, grinding his teeth, he stabbed his food. 'He did what?' The disbelief on his face was theatrical because he knew about the calls. GCHQ had advised him with transcripts.

'He called me a few days before you got back,' Becky replied.

'When exactly did he call?'

'If you mean the last time, it was about a week ago.'

'And you haven't heard from him since?'

'No.'

Richard looked round the restaurant to see if they were in earshot of anybody. Fortunately, the tables on each side of where they were sitting were empty.

'Did he ask you to do anything for you?'

Her eyes shifted away from his stare. She was hiding something. She let out a nervous laugh. 'What sort of question is that?' She stood up, glaring at the people in the restaurant who looked up from their own meals. 'If you won't talk to me and tell me the truth then I might as well go home.'

He didn't like to see her annoyed. He lowered his voice and spoke, covering his mouth a little to prevent lip reading. 'Please sit down. I'll tell you what I can,' he whispered. Becky sat down again , taking another gulp of

Richard's wine.

'Officially he is dead,' he said looking round the restaurant once more. 'But I think he's alive. It's only my opinion…and besides what's important is that my father is no longer a threat to our relationship, whether he's alive or not…' He put his fork down and took hold of her hand, this time his eyes found hers and he was pleased she did not look away. 'You know something …pregnancy suits you - you look more beautiful than ever,' he said trying to deflect the subject away from his father.

'Don't change the subject,' she snapped. 'There's no chance our relationship is going to survive. I'll let you see the baby and be a father but I want to move on Richard. I can't stand all the lies...you think you love me but you don't.'

It was almost a relief to hear her say this. He thought there was a part of her which wanted to be with him and give it a go, but the other side always won over.

'There's no chance for us if I change?'

Becky smiled and took hold of his hand. 'I've done a lot of thinking while you were away. It's like I said before. You're not the marrying kind. The fact that I want to end it with you does not mean I don't care for you.' She hesitated. 'Truth is…truth is I don't love you anymore. There you are…I've said it.'

'I know you don't but what's changed?'

'Everything has changed.'

'I don't understand what's different.' He said that for effect because he knew she was right. The last time she'd rejected him, he hadn't really accepted it might be forever. Something had indeed changed and the fact that she was carrying their baby made no difference.

'I want our baby to know it's father…I'll pay my share.'

She was still holding his hand, but her face told him it was over. Her face said sympathy and not love. 'Are you going to tell me what's going on?' she said.

He wanted to tell her everything, but knew that it must remain a secret. 'I'm not allowed to say anything …you know that Becky…I'm bound by the Official Secrets Act. Besides, if it's over between us why do you care?'

Disappointment spread across her face. She pulled her hand away. 'You've told me some things,' she said, ' Like what happened in Iraq…so why not the whole story?'

'I'd like to tell you, but I can't…I'm sorry…and besides…' Richard's voice tailed off as something caught his eye on the other side of the restaurant. There was a man eating on his own four tables back from where they were seated. He looked like he was engrossed in a book but the ear-piece linked by wire to his phone could mean he might be listening to their conversation.

'Besides what?'

He hesitated. His thoughts raced, trying not to look over towards the man in case he noticed that Richard had spotted him. He forced a smile and looked back at Becky. 'It's nothing. I just got distracted…Eat up all your pasta because you've got tiramisu to follow…Remember you're eating for two or is it three? '

'Don't patronise me Richard…I can read you like a book. Something is bothering you.'

'Those flowers that were dying, I noticed they were sent by H who I assume is a man.'

She glared at him. 'It's none of your business who they were from. You don't own me.'

He tried to stay calm but anger was getting the better of him. 'I need to know who you are seeing because there are people out there who want to get at me by hurting you.'

Becky shrugged and laughed nervously. 'I had a visit from an admirer - somebody who saw me at that Foreign Office bash you took me to. He took me to dinner. Asked me some questions about you, asked were we an item?'

'And what did you say?'

Becky hesitated. 'I said no… He was rather dishy.'

'Are you deliberately trying to hurt me? What did he want to know about me?' He raised his voice causing a few heads to turn, once more. The man he'd noticed had stood up and was walking towards their table. Richard recognised him but couldn't put a name to the face.

'Hello Richard,' said the man. His accent was Irish New Yorker.

Becky swung round and Richard saw her face light up. 'Harper,' she said, 'Please join us.'

The penny dropped, Anger welled in his gut and flash backs of the bomb in Iraq flickered before his eyes. He spoke. 'No don't, Harper. Piss off. And if you bother Becky anymore I'll beat the shit out of you…I thought you were my friend.'

'Richard, what are you saying?' said Becky, a bemused expression on her face. 'You can't speak to Harper like that.'

'Not here, Becky.' He turned to Harper. 'Are you going to go?'

Harper held his hands up in a gesture of mock surrender. 'Okay…Okay.'

Richard eyes followed Harper as he left the restaurant. The waiter saw him stand up and came over to ask whether they were ready for dessert. He nodded, not really listening, sitting down, his eyes fixed on Becky who also looked in Harper's direction, He noticed a disguised smile creep across her lips as Harper turned to look back before going through the door of the restaurant. When the dessert arrived, Richard pushed the chocolate cream of the tiramisu round his plate, his appetite gone. He didn't want to taste anything sweet when the memory of Harper made him bite his lip, irritated that he couldn't take him outside and finish it, there and then. He continued to stare blankly at the dessert on his plate, unconsciously using a teaspoon to extract some chocolate.

'Don't ever see that guy again?' he said.

'Don't tell me how to run my life? I'll see who I want to.'

'I have my reasons for telling you this. This man is bad news.'

'Stop treating me like a child, Richard.'

'You have to trust me Becky…that's all I can say.'

The tiramisu felt bitter in his mouth as they ate their dessert in silence. A gulf was opening up between them and Richard didn't know how to close it. In desperation, he spoke, 'Aren't we going to talk about names for our baby? I like Robert.'

'And if it's a girl?

'Er…how about Rachel? There's a biblical link to Rebecca so it ties the baby to her beautiful mother.'

Becky leaned forward and took hold of the lapels of Richard's jacket, planting a kiss firmly onto his lips. 'That was a lovely thing to say,' she said. 'I'm sorry about Harper. I was feeling lonely and he came along and was a real gentleman.' Her voice had mellowed, and her annoyance seemed to have melted away 'If it's a girl she'll be Rachel - no question.'

The pleasure in seeing Becky warm to him once more was far outweighed by the nagging concern about what Harper was up to, or whether his father was out of his mind for good - dead or alive. His brain ticked over in the background while he continued with the small talk about babies on autopilot. The meal could not end soon enough. 'I need to get you home,' he said.

The restaurant was only a few minutes' walk from Becky's flat. They walked in silence. There was still a rift between them which was only occasionally bridged by talk of their child. He held her hand. His grip was so tight she cried out.

'You're hurting me Richard.'

'I'm sorry - I was lost in thought,' he said releasing his

grip.

'Still thinking about Iraq?'

'That's it.'

Richard broke into a run. Becky had no choice but to follow as he still held her hand.

'What's the matter Richard? Why are we running?'

'I'll tell you when we get back to your flat.'

Reaching the flat Richard froze. He put his finger to his mouth.

'Give me your keys,' he said. Becky stared at him, looking terrified but still obeyed. Richard turned the key, and put his hand up to block Becky entering. He put his finger to his mouth. The first thing he noticed was the breeze. One of the windows was open. Whoever had been in the flat had already left.

A shiver ran down his spine and he signalled to Becky to wait at the front door once more. Nerves tingled as he pushed the door, cringing as it creaked. If there was someone there, they'd know he was coming. He waited for the reaction, but nothing happened. Remaining on his guard, he entered the hall and stepped into the lounge. The drawers of Becky's filing cabinets were open, and papers taken out, strewn on the floor. He scanned the contents; the normal stuff of life; bank statements and utility bills. He flicked through the papers but didn't know what he was looking for. Something big. A bank statement caught his eye; dated two weeks ago there was a credit of £3240.65 with the description *FX*. On the same day, £3000 was paid away into an international account. Taking out a pocket Canon digital camera, he photographed the entries with the IBAN number of the outgoing payment. He scanned the room, hoping to find compelling evidence. A copy of an edition of the Gospel of Barnabas lay on the desk. He picked the book up and realised that it was a translation of the sixteenth century forgery. There was nothing else.

He sighed. Turning to leave something caught his eye. A green light flickered on Becky's answer machine indicating a saved message. He pushed the playback button and waited to be shocked.

The caller was familiar, but it was still a shock.

The sound was poor, but the man's voice was unmistakable.

His father had called again. Becky had lied to him. Plain and simple.

Chapter Five

Antioch, Syria. AD 1098

4th June 1098

Our success is short lived.

The Christian army I foolishly joined on a mission of madness, only survived because Islamic tribes refused to unite and destroy their common enemy.

But that is changing. Kerbogha, a general from Mosul with a fierce reputation, has forty thousand troops from Syria and Mesopotamia assembling outside the gates of the city. We are outnumbered by two to one. We have no choice but to barricade ourselves within these bloodied walls and await our fate. We've held Antioch for just one day and now the boot is on the other foot. At least, Akila and her sons will be safe with their own kind. They will not need to rely on this disillusioned knight. It will be me that is needing food, not them.

14th June 1098

All our exits are blocked. Our hunger becomes more desperate as each day passes. Nearly two weeks with only a few morsels of food. Today, there is hope that God has not forsaken us. A peasant by the name of Peter Bartholomew has been digging at the Basilica of St Peter. He is convinced by God's grace to search the site. He discovers a small metal shard which he is saying is a remnant of the Roman lance that pierced the side of Jesus while he was on the cross. How does he know this? He claimed that an apparition of St Andrew had revealed to him the exact resting place of the lance. The Franks are desperate to believe in something and I've seen improvement in morale. They believe that the discovery of

43

the lance is a sign from God that he approves of their mission and will protect them. However great the odds are stacked against us; they believe that the Christians will prevail. The Muslims also believe that God is great. Allahu Akbah they shout. Is that not a shout to the same God that we Christians pray to? Is there only one God?

28th June 1098

Our hunger is now so acute that we have no energy to fight. But fight we must. It is better to die here on the field than to succumb to the agony of starvation, a slow and painful way to meet God. The Bridge Gate is opening and through the gap I can see the line of Muslim soldiers waiting to confront us. Their numbers are already diminishing as volley after volley of arrows are raining down on their front line. I advance quickly surrounded by my fellows, motivated by a passion and belief which the Muslims could not match. Enthused by the divine inspiration of the Holy Lance and helped by the superior strategy of our leader Bohemond. I cut a swathe with my swords. A larger blade to do the damage and a smaller weapon to run my adversary through. My eyes are blurred with the splashes of blood that drips from my sword and smears my battle dress. As I swing, I turn on all sides, so I miss nothing. The killing is indiscriminate and brutal. Our opponents are young and inexperienced. Within no time I can see they are retreating.

A boy is staring at me. A boy who today became a man who would not give way and escape. I shout, 'yarkud' which I think means run, but he stands steadfast. His sword catches the sunlight and our eyes meet. I see beauty in those eyes. A perfect face begs me to stop. Not in words, but in the image that he projects - an image of immaculate beauty. There is a message in those eyes - a message of love not hatred. Why are we killing each other, the eyes seem to say?

I do not listen to the message and swing my sword. That beautiful face raises into the air departing from his young muscular body. His comrades are in retreat and at that moment I vow to kill no more. This is not my country. I can no longer kill in the name of God.

My exhaustion is complete. I sink to my knees and weep. My tears mingle with the blood splattered in my hair and staining my cheeks. I am so ashamed I want a stray warrior to strike me down just as I have done to this beautiful boy. Something compels me to look up. A blinding light forces me to shield my eyes, but I cannot look away. The boy is smiling at me, summoning me to join him.

There is silence now. No more screams of terror and pain. No more shouts of anguish. All I can hear is the breeze. Our troops are chasing the retreating army. I cannot believe that we have won but win or lose I want no part of it.

I've killed a beautiful boy.

My bloody sword is thrust into the ground and I am kneeling as if waiting for execution for my sins. Yes, they are sins. There is no redemption from God to justify this slaughter, not even if His Holiness the Pope says so.

God has told me to stop.

Something touches my cheek. I raise my eyes slowly and see it is Akila's son - Masood. He hands me a small piece of bread soaked in water. I eat the bread slowly, glad of the liquid to help me digest the food in my aching stomach. Masood takes my hand and begs me to follow him. We wind our way down the hill towards the banks of the river. I'm unsure whether I've been seen or not. But I no longer care. I don't know why I am following him. Am I dead, walking into the next world? My steps are more akin to a stagger, like a drunkard full of ale. Fatigue saps what little strength

45

I have left. My sword is weighing me down, dragging in its scabbard. Every time I trip, it is harder to stand again. When I stumble once more, I can no longer move. I roll over and blink at the sun. The heat comforts me before a shadow blots out the rays. A soft hand strokes my brow. and I know before I open my eyes that Akila has come to me.

Chapter Six

London, UK. August 26th, 2005

'They don't appear to have taken anything,' said Becky, visibly distressed that someone had violated her personal space. 'But they've searched my bank statements. Are you going to tell me what this is about?'

Richard decided that he must tell her something because with all the calls from his father, and her contact with Harper, she seemed to be up to her neck in the whole thing. 'Ok, I'll tell you but never speak to anybody, especially my father.'

Becky saluted, in mock seriousness.

'The guy Harper that you saw while I was away is somebody I know from my time in Iraq and is probably behind this break in. He's CIA. I think he's been tasked to find my father and thinks that I might know where he is. What I don't understand is why he thinks *you* might be able to help?'

'It can't be Harper.'

'Why? Who else could it be?'

Becky looked sheepish and turned away walking round the flat checking again if anything had been taken. She was hiding something. After a long pause she spoke, 'I think my phone must have been tapped,'

'Why not Harper? You seem sure it wasn't him.'

Becky shrugged. 'Harper asked me whether your father had been in touch. He also told me he knew you in Iraq. He's on our side and had no reason to break in to my flat. We were friends.'

'Don't you think that was strange? A guy turns up at your house unannounced and starts asking you questions about me and my father. It's not the most obvious way to impress a woman like you?'

'Yes, I did, but when he told me he knew you in Iraq, I was keen to know more as you wouldn't tell me yourself.'

Richard was taken aback that Becky could be so devious. 'So, you knew all the time who Harper was?'

'Yes. I just wanted to know more about you and what you were going through.'

Richard turned to look at Becky. 'And now you know, you've decided to dump me.'

His blunt response troubled Becky. She dropped her head and refused to catch his eyes. 'We can still be friends. I still want you in my life because of our baby.'

That sense of relief he'd felt earlier continued. At that moment he realised the two sides of his life could never go together.

'I'm not much good at this secret life. In fact, I'm bloody useless.'

'Then give it up…give it up.'

Richard knew he couldn't, at least not now. 'Give me some time,' he said.

'It's ok. It's done now. Forget it…make me a cup of coffee.'

As far as Richard was concerned it was far from done. The credits to her bank account were worrying and why was she reading a copy of the gospel of Barnabas? He decided not to ask. The only person who had mentioned the Gospel was his father, evidence that she was doing something for him. He must have told her about the Gospel. If he spoke about that now, it would aggravate the situation which he didn't want to do. But however hard he tried to reject the notion; he could not trust her. She was hiding something from him. It had to be Harper, who broke into her flat, maybe to lead him off the scent, creating some sort of diversion, but what? He watched her slump down on to an armchair. resting her hands on her stomach, feeling the small lump growing inside her. 'I blame it on my hormones. But it's also what your father said about you which worried me.'

Richard brought the coffee in and sat down opposite. 'What did the old bastard say?'

She sipped the coffee and pursed her lips, choosing the words. 'I don't want to upset you, he said he was looking forward to seeing you in Greece,'

'And? Go on.'

'He advised me against marrying you. He said that when he telephoned before he was worried for you and wanted you to get out of the business and marry me and live happily ever after.'

'But?'

'His opinion has changed, and he has decided that you are too much like him. A loner...' Her voice tailed off and she looked away.

'What's it got to do with him? He knows nothing about who I am. What else did he say?'

She bit her lip. 'He said you were a killer who one day would end up with a bullet in your head. He didn't want me to suffer.'

What surprised Richard was that he didn't feel anger. Sadness seemed more appropriate because he knew his father was right. He couldn't play the dutiful husband and father, no matter how much he wanted to do the right thing. 'Maybe he's right,' Richard said in a whisper. 'I'm sorry.' He stood up and walked towards the door. 'Will you be okay on your own? You can come back to my flat if you want?'

'Stay here tonight Richard.'

They got undressed silently. She didn't try and cover herself up, but he couldn't look at her. He felt like a doctor seeing his patient naked. A cold separation of the senses existed between them, something clinical and impersonal. He lay beside her but didn't touch her. He listened to her breathing and lost himself in his thoughts. He felt sick he would never be able to marry Becky. Despite his acceptance of that fact he still wanted to kill Harper, plain and simple. These murderous thoughts did not shock him anymore.

Next morning, he telephoned Rowena and told her about Harper's approach to Becky and about the break in.

'The CIA know your father is dead. The Israelis killed him when they sank *Istanbul Star.*'

'He's not dead and I think Harper knows it, even if the CIA don't. The Israelis may have sunk the ship, but my father's not stupid enough to go and hide in it. He knew he'd be a sitting duck and knows what the Israelis are capable of. When I saw him in Greece, he told me he was going to Iran.'

'Iran. He's gone to fucking Iran. Tell me you're joking.'

'I'm not joking.'

'The Israelis will be spitting blood when they hear about this.'

'They shouldn't have let him escape. I was there. It's not like Mossad to let someone like my father slip through the net.' Richard hesitated. There is something you should know. Dinah Zevi's sister Maia was there. Looks like she's got a conscience despite what happened to Dinah.'

'Maia was there?'

Richard noticed a softening of Rowena's voice. 'You know her?'

Rowena didn't answer which told Richard that she did know who Maia was.

'If your father gives them the scroll it will a diplomatic coup for Iran and disastrous for us. The Americans will be fucking crazy. Why am I only hearing this now?'

'Because you weren't interested. For now, we need to find out what Harper's up to. Can you check if the bastard is still on the CIA payroll? I think he's working off grid.'

He made Becky breakfast- scrambled eggs on toast, a yoghurt and coffee with more buttered toast and marmalade. He sat down at the table while he drank tea and watched her devour the meal. 'Hey,' he laughed. 'Put toast on your marmalade.'

'My appetite is enormous. They'll need a crane to lift me when the baby's born. Aren't you having anything yourself?'

The attempt at banter was strained. 'I'm not hungry,' he said with an apologetic grin.

It was a relief when his phone started ringing. For a moment, he stared at the mobile flashing and buzzing like a beacon on the table.

'Harper doesn't work for the CIA anymore. He's freelance,' said Rowena. 'He's being doing consultancy work in Manhattan. Advising senior staff on security.'

'He's not in New York. He's in London. We need to pick him up for a chat. What does the CIA make of him being in London? Do they know?'

'I don't suppose they do or even care. He left in a cloud of recrimination, some job he did for the Saudi's involving a shit load of money.'

Vauxhall Cross - Headquarters of MI6. August 27th, 2005.

'Has anybody had any luck finding where Harper is in London?'

Rowena looked annoyed by the question. 'As if we haven't got better things to do with our time. To be frank, Richard, as you let your father run off to Iran, I'm wondering why I continue to waste my time with this investigation.'

Richard sighed, 'I know, I know, but you owe me.'

'I don't owe you anything,' Rowena replied, flicking through some notes she'd taken. 'You're lucky he wasn't hard to find. He was spotted at Stansted airport, boarding a plane to Cyprus; the Turkish north - not the South. Why on earth would he want to go there?'

Richard thought for a moment. 'It was something my father said to me about finding an authentic Gospel of Barnabas. The gospel in existence is a known forgery but that doesn't mean that the words within are not genuine. Barnabas was born in Cyprus. Maybe he thinks that there is a real copy of the Gospel of Barnabas in Cyprus. If he finds it, he can lure my father to come and take a look. It's the missing link which will give credibility to the scroll we found in Crete.'

Rowena raised her eyes in Richard's direction. 'You may have a point. Something has come up which may be connected.' She scrolled through pages of material on her computer. 'Come and look at this.'

Richard walked around Rowena's desk so he could see her computer screen.

'We've got this,' she said. 'It's a bit of a longshot, but it may be relevant.'

Richard peered at the images flashing across the screen 'What does it say and where did it come from?'

'It's being broadcast from Dubai, '

Rowena stood up and let Richard have access to her keyboard. He read each individual page, which provided intelligence analysis, before reading the transcript of the press statement out loud.

'The *Words of the Faithful* decree that until the Gospel of Barnabas is taken into the Holy Bible as a legitimate record of the life of Isa, who the Christians call Jesus, there will be no peace between religions...' He looked across at Rowena 'Do we know who this group is?'

'We're working on it. This is a new one on us. We're trawling the internet, and, now, it doesn't look as if they've been involved in terrorist activity. But one thing I'm certain about is that they don't look like a back-street operation. They have funding…lots of it.'

Richard scanned the screen, reading quickly. 'It says here that the group Words of the Faithful are run by women with indirect jihadist connections...that probably means they've got terrorist husbands.' He scrolled down, looking at the photograph of some of the rallies they'd had, mainly in European cities. There was not much interest in their activities as they were poorly attended. One in Barcelona and others in Seville, Marseille and London.

'Did we do any covert monitoring of the London rally?'

Rowena tapped out a search on another terminal. 'What was the date?'

Richard looked back at the screen where the Internet photos were posted of the London rally in Hyde Park. 'They've been tagged as August 19th - one week ago.'

Rowena continued to type. 'There's nothing…we probably didn't think it was worth the time.'

Richard compared the photos and quickly picked up that there were women who appeared at all the rallies. Most had covered their faces but there were two that just wore a black chador veil. One of the women seemed to be familiar, as if he might have seen her before, but the face was so blurred he couldn't be sure. He captured the images into a file and flicked them over to Rowena. 'Can we blow these pictures up…See if we can make a match?'

Rowena looked at the pictures 'It will take a bit of time to process.' she said. 'Bloody system is brilliant but takes its time to trawl through the data. I'll get back to you.'

It took an hour before the results came back. Richard spent the time reading up on what was known about Barnabas and where he'd been. Paul and Barnabas had spent some time in Antioch before they fell out. Barnabas' cousin John Mark was the reason for the argument. Richard made a note to find out more about this disagreement.

Rowena rushed towards Richard, waving papers in the air. 'We've got a match,' she said. 'Nadia Zabor former husband of Sheikh Zabor.'

'The same Sheikh, assassinated by Mossad.'

'The very same. It makes sense, even if she doesn't play the fundamentalist, her dead husband wanted to buy the scroll.'

'Sounds like I need to meet Nadia. I'm going to Cyprus and maybe Harper will lead me to her.'

'There is something else you should look at.'

Rowena handed Richard a large picture. The face on the shot was very grainy but the familiarity had turned to something more certain. He was looking at a picture of Becky. The copy of the Gospel of Barnabas in her flat made sense.

'What the fuck is Becky doing in a rally about Islamic rights?' Richard said.

'Are you sure it's her?'

'It's her alright? I need to go to Cyprus and take her with me.'

He noticed Rowena was uneasy. She leaned forward onto her desk and put her head in her hands. 'I don't want you taking Becky. She is not part of the Service. You know that.'

'I'll pay her expenses. The Service won't be charged a penny. I'll even pay my own flight if that makes things easier.'

'Good idea. Don't charge any of the trip to us. I haven't the budget for jollies to Cyprus. Do it in your own time. I still don't want Becky to go.'

Richard scowled at Rowena. 'Becky maybe useful in the light of that picture. We could do with a holiday before she is too pregnant to travel.'

It was Rowena's turn to pull a face. Richard wondered whether she approved of him fathering a child. There was something about Rowena that did not suggest happy families.

'This baby thing, you know it won't help your career in the Service.'

Richard saw red. 'What I do is my business…but if you must know, we're splitting. She thinks I am too much like my father. You've got nothing to worry about. I am staying in the Service. You'll not get rid of me that easily.'

Rowena's face told him she was pleased by his news. He wondered whether she was jealous of his relationship with Becky. The idea that Rowena might fancy him was strangely appealing although he couldn't quite get his head round why that may be. Sleeping with the boss was tantamount to sleeping with the enemy.

He left the room and called Becky. 'Fancy a few nights in Kyrenia in Northern Cyprus. It'll be nice to catch some sun before your bump gets out of control.'

Becky didn't sound too thrilled at the idea and immediately smelt a rat. 'Why are we going there? Why the North and not the South of Cyprus or Majorca or the Greek islands.?'

Richard decided to be honest. 'I would have thought it would be obvious to you. I've heard your lover boy has gone there…I want to know why you were seen at a rally for Words of the Faithful and why you've been reading the Gospel of Barnabas. I assume you know St Barnabas was born and murdered in Cyprus.'

She didn't respond.

'Do I take your silence as a yes?'

'Yes. I'll come.'

As they drove to the airport, Richard questioned Becky why she would want to get involved with Words of The Faithful.

'I met one of their leaders. A woman. She told me that conflict between the Christian West and Islam was caused by the way scriptures have been manipulated to create division. The suppression of the Gospel of Barnabas was an example. That's why I was reading it.'

'How did you meet her?'

'She came and sat next to me in a café.'

'Didn't you think that was strange?'

'No. I talk to strangers all the time. She really impressed me, talking about the invasion of Iraq. How misguided it was.'

He was distracted by her fidgeting, tugging at the seatbelt, as if it were dangerous rather than for her own protection. Taking his eye of the road, he caught her nervous expression. An unconscious reaction that he'd been trained to recognise. She was lying.

'It wasn't a random meeting. She targeted you.'

'It's not true. It was me who wanted to meet. Knowing you'd been in Iraq I wanted to know more. She was the first Muslim woman I'd ever talked to. After chatting for ages, she invited me to the rally in London and as I wasn't doing anything I went.'

Richard checked his mirrors and pulled onto the hard shoulder of the motorway. They were fifteen miles from Stansted Airport. He reached for a leather bag on the back seat and retrieved a photo. It was black and white and blurred as a result of being enlarged. He handed it to Becky.

'Is this the woman you met?'

Becky stared at the photo while Richard watched her expression. There was a flicker of recognition. 'I can't be sure, but I think it's her,' she replied.

'The woman is Nadia Zabor, former husband of Arab billionaire Sheikh Mohammed Zabor Bin Hitani, who was known to fund terrorism and who was assassinated by the Israelis.'

Becky's mouth dropped, shocked but no sign of surprise on her face. 'I didn't know,' she said, pretending to be concerned.

'There are a lot of things you don't know Becky. If you don't want me in your life and you don't approve of my search for my father, then why are you getting involved? You're pregnant for God's sake. These are bad people. '

'But your father has involved me '

'I know and I am angry with him for involving you...in fact anger is too gentle a word for what I feel about him right now. The truth is that this whole thing is a bit of a side show as far as the Middle East is concerned but Western agencies don't want the historical facts to be used as propaganda by Iran...And while we are talking about him.' He hesitated not sure about what he wanted to say.

'What about your father?'

'He was right to call me a bastard.'

'He didn't say that.'

'But he implied it...I haven't told you everything but at least you understand why we are chasing my father.'

'But your father is trying to reveal the truth not supress it? Just like the ladies of Words of the Faithful. Surely that is the best policy and not so hypocritical as yours? And another thing - Harper is on your father's side. I think that's why I talked to him.'

'Take it from me,' said Richard. 'Harper is not a friend of my father.'

Becky slunk back in her car seat. Richard fired up the engine and they drove on towards the airport. They were just pulling into the car park when Becky spoke again.

'Let me see if I've got this right. Your father has the scroll in Iran and if they find an authentic Gospel of Barnabas, they'll have enough evidence to say that the Gospel was supressed from the Bible in Nicene when books were being selected. That these documents confirm Jesus is acknowledging that there was a prophet to come after him. It could only be Islam which suggests that the Holy Koran is the last word of God, more important than The Holy Bible.'

'Yes. You've got it. That's why Western intelligence agencies want it stopped and for the evidence to never see the light of day.'

Richard parked the car in the short-term car park by the Radisson hotel, a short walk to the terminal. He switched off the engine and stared blankly through the window.

'What's up Richard? You look worried.'

'He turned to face her. 'I don't think you should come with me to Cyprus. Harper is a nasty bit of work who is capable of physical harm. I can't risk that with you. You've got to think of the baby. It's a long journey because we've got to fly via Turkey because of the sanctions in the North. It will be very tiring for you.'

'I want to come,' said Becky firmly.

'Like I said, it could be dangerous and the last thing I want is to put you and the baby in harm's way.'

'But I can help you with Harper. He likes me.'

'I'm sorry Becky...Harper doesn't give a shit about you. He's a bastard, plain and simple.' Richard handed Becky the keys to his car. 'Take the car back I think it's the right thing. Only I wish I'd reached that conclusion before we set off.'

He tried to take hold of her hand, but she pulled it away and turning fumbled with the handle to the passenger door. Frustrated, she turned back to face him, her hands were shaking and her face tight with anger. There were tears in her eyes and her voice was breaking with emotion. 'I don't care if you never come back.'

'The tears had turned to sobbing. Richard got out of the car and walked round to open the passenger door. 'You've got to believe me…it's for your own safety,' he pleaded. 'I don't want you getting hurt.' He tried to put his arms round her as he opened the driver's door, but she pushed passed him.

'Don't touch me,' she shouted.

Richard leaned forward and grabbed the car door. He couldn't let her go like this. 'You've got every right to be angry,' he squirmed, embarrassed by his about turn.

'Then let me come with you,' she pleaded. 'You owe this to me.'

Richard banged his hands on to the car in frustration. 'OK…OK…you can come' He turned to face Becky. 'I'm worried about our baby, that's why I don't want you to come but I can't stop you if you insist.'

'I do insist. I'm not an invalid. I can make my own decisions about the risks.'

They had to rush to get to the check in desk before it closed. One hour later, he sank back into his seat on the aircraft and looked at Becky. They had hardly spoken since their arrival at the airport. He knew he should apologise.

'I'm sorry,' he said. 'I shouldn't have tried to exclude you from this. Please forgive me. I just don't want you to get hurt and besides, you said yourself you don't want me in your life.'

Becky squeezed his hand and forced a smile. 'It's my hormones. I shouldn't have shouted like that. I know this is not easy for you.'

He surprised himself how good it felt to have her by his side, but he still wondered whether he would regret allowing her to come. The nagging doubt that Becky was holding something back continued to linger in his mind. Perhaps he was exaggerating how dangerous Harper was. Instinct told him to hold back, but part of him, the part he didn't like, the part he'd inherited from his father, wanted to use Becky as bait to lure Harper into a trap and find out what the fuck he was up to. He was disgusted with himself for even entertaining the possibility.

Chapter Eight

Kyrenia, Northern Cyprus - August 29th, 2005.

Finding Harper wasn't going to be easy. His only hope, apart from meeting him by chance, was to use GCHQ to eavesdrop on all calls in that part of Cyprus. The CIA still used Cyprus to help with US propaganda and so it was easy to persuade Rowena that such an exercise would be a good use of the listening post on the island. Fortunately, the station chief hadn't been told about Harper's Langley connections otherwise the outcome might have been different. While Richard waited for news, they looked for a suitable hotel in the popular tourist destination of Kyrenia, deciding that it was as good a place as anywhere else to begin his search. The hotel overlooked the horseshoe harbour crammed with fishing boats but their room, situated at the back, had a view of air conditioning units and a glimpse of the mountains rising above the concrete. At least the sheets were clean, but the rest of the room needed refurbishment. It didn't look as if it had been touched since the Turkish occupation.

'James Bond would never stay in a shit hole like this,' he said, trying to lighten the mood between them which had remained strained throughout the flight.

Becky did her best to appear impressed. 'This is fine.' she said bouncing up and down on the bed with a mischievous wink. She seemed genuinely pleased to be here and that made him suspicious.

They were both exhausted and Becky slept almost immediately, putting her arm loosely round his neck. He wanted to sleep but however hard he tried, he couldn't. Something nagged his mind with increasing urgency. Why had Becky been so keen to come to Cyprus? Previously she had not wanted to be part of his life. She'd criticised him in his efforts to find his father. He wondered whether she'd told him all there was to know about her meetings with Harper. He continued to mull this for at least an hour, tossing and turning in his efforts to get comfortable. At last sheer fatigue got the better of him and he lapsed into a deep sleep.

Next morning, he decided to visit the Monastery of St Barnabas, which was near Salamis, over an hour's drive away.

'I'll stay by the pool and relax…I need to, for the baby's sake,' she said, echoing his words at the airport.

'Of course, you must. It's just I thought you were interested in the Gospel of Barnabas.'

'I won't find anything in a pile of stones or an old monastery.' She shifted her eyes away from his gaze and pulled down her sunglasses to cover her eyes. He couldn't help noticing that she appeared distracted.

'Salamis was a Roman settlement, the place where Barnabas was imprisoned and executed. The Monastery is nearby and is only a few metres from his grave. It would be a nice day out.'

'You go,' Becky replied. 'Surely somebody will pick up Harper's scent soon. I don't see the point of traipsing round a ruin.'

He must have driven for at least thirty minutes lost in his thoughts. His security status had allowed a Glock 19 in his luggage which he found himself unconsciously caressing in his pocket. His mind was hardly on the road, harbouring thoughts about how he would like to see Harper's brains spread across the hotel lobby. As he drove on, he continued to think about Becky and what she was up to. The payments across her bank account and the way her eyes had lit up when she'd seen Harper didn't look good. The outskirts of Nicosia were looming when his doubts got the better of him. He drove onto a roundabout and without a rational decision set in his mind, kept turning the wheel until he'd come full circle and was heading back to Kyrenia.

Arriving back at the hotel, he went straight to the pool. There was no sign of Becky. In a wave of panic, he raced up to their room to find it empty. Maybe she'd just gone for a walk down to the port, he told himself, trying to stay calm. He decided to head in that direction, running down the steep hill by the castle. Halfway down, he stopped to catch his breath by a low wall where he could see for the first time a view of the little horseshoe harbour. He used his binoculars to scan the tables in the many restaurants lining the quayside. He saw them in a fish restaurant, laughing and joking. The enjoyment on their faces made him look away, too much to stomach. She'd lied to him again, knowing where Harper was all the time. What was even more disturbing was that he wouldn't be here now if he'd trusted her implicitly. Spying on them through binoculars made him feel like a sad jealous stalker. Convinced they would be there for some time; he decided to visit the Castle and climb up to the battlements where he could watch them from a less obvious vantage point.

After about forty-five minutes they left the restaurant and headed back to their car in the public car park high above the old port. They were in a black Ford Focus saloon which had seen better days but was not going to attract any attention. His car, hired from a local dealer in Kyrenia, was a newer VW Golf that smelt of tobacco smoke and grated every time he changed up to fourth gear.

It was easy to keep their car in his sights as they negotiated the streets of Kyrenia. As the road began to climb out of town, the distance between the two cars widened. The road was becoming steeper as they wound their way up the mountain towards Nicosia. Richard cursed the VW Diesel engine as it laboured against the gradient of the road. He lost sight of them several times as sweeping bends negotiated the sheer rock faces on either side.

As the road became straighter, he expected to see them. But somehow, he'd lost sight of their car. Swearing out loud he swung the VW into an abrupt U turn. Holding his breath, horns blared, and tyres screeched, but somehow he managed to complete the manoeuvre without incident. Glancing in his rear-view mirror the shaking fists of other drivers amused him. He swore in defiance and focused on the road, accelerating back the way he'd come. There was an exit road about a mile away where he would have crossed the oncoming traffic had he seen it on the way up the hill. It was now on his near side and harder to miss. Becky and Harper must have managed to leave at the junction without stopping because, if they'd been delayed, even for a minute, he would have caught up and seen them waiting when he went passed. Reaching the turning, the sign pointed to St Hilarion; a Crusader castle, perched on the rocky peaks, nothing like the Norman castles in Britain. It was a fairy castle. He'd heard that Walt Disney may have used it as a model in Snow White. Glimpses of the castle confirmed the story might be true, but it was the last thing he wanted to think about as he climbed the steep narrow road, praying he wouldn't drop over the edge. The blue waters of the Mediterranean seemed surreal as

But there was still no sign of their car.

His heart sank, unable to figure out where he might have lost contact. He slowed the car and looked upwards. The first thing he noticed was the silhouette of what appeared to be a military soldier standing on a crag. As he got nearer, he saw that it was a metal sculpture introducing him to barbed wire fencing and a real soldier guarding an entrance to what looked like a Turkish Army base. The soldier locked onto his gaze and ushered with his rifle for him to keep moving. Richard drove on, stopping the car when he reached the perimeter of the base. He parked outside a solitary round tower, well clear of prying eyes. He could see the castle walls and battlements, visible hundreds of feet above. They seemed to trace the outline of the landscape and in doing so become part of the terrain, as if Mother Nature had built the castle herself. The air conditioning worked overtime. Retrieving the binoculars from the passenger seat, he opened the door. The searing sun scorched his unprotected skin, catching some of the scars he'd picked up from the bomb. He swung the glasses around the landscape, raising his vision towards an imposing white building which he guessed to be part of the base.

He didn't have time to linger.

Three soldiers surrounded him, pointing rifles directly at his head. A jeep with more soldiers screeched to a halt. Before he could even shout, his hands were twisted behind his back and cuffs clicked round his wrists. He didn't struggle. They nudged him with their rifles towards the jeep and he saw no reason to resist. It was a short hop to the military entrance and a shorter one to the cell.

There was no air in the cell and only a little light coming from a small window high up and unreachable. Even though the room appeared to be sealed, insects had found their way in. He lay down on the pallet bed and tried not to think about Becky. That wasn't easy. The boards on the bed were hard and unforgiving; impossible to relax on, which was a relief as he had no intention of relaxing. His mind raced over everything that had happened. He remembered the murders at Lake Sikonas, the killing of Andreas, the meetings with Rowena, Amira and Becky - women in his life who seemed so distant from who he was. His father continued to loom over all these events. A millstone wasn't the right word. His father was a leech ready to suck out any capacity he had for love, life and doing what was right. If his father was in Iran who was going to get to him? He almost understood his logic. If all the Western agencies are after you, why not go to the West's number one enemy? Several hours went by before they came for him. Guards brought him food and water and did not speak. He asked why he was being held but they did not answer. As the hours passed, fatigue began to overtake frustration. He began to doze and dream. The face of Abdul burnt and the shock on Dinah's face as she breathed her last, haunted his mind. All these images kept returning in his dreams as if on an ever-repeating loop.

When he awoke, he tried to think straight. The jumble of thoughts consumed him so much that he jumped when he heard the keys turning in the lock. Two armed soldiers led him across a quadrangle, still handcuffed. As they walked, Richard was struck by how many plants were dotted around the base and many were in bloom. There were swathes of purple bougainvillea, orange hibiscus and red geranium; bright colours which lifted his spirits. The soldiers led him into another building on the opposite side of where his cell was situated. The contrast could not have been starker. Marble floors and four Doric pillars propping the building's domed roof, appearing out of place in an army base. In the centre, a woman, dressed head to toe in a black chador, also looked alien to such an opulent environment. She sat behind a large marble desk supported by three naked carved marble figures. She looked up at him and Richard noticed her expensive makeup.

'The Three Graces, in case you're wondering, Mr Helford. The building was built by your countrymen, but I suspect this table is French,' she said. 'Just because I'm a Muslim does not mean that I cannot appreciate Western art, however decadent.'

'It's rather vulgar,' said Richard. 'Built at a time when officers dressed in red frock coats.   Let me guess, you must be Sheikh Zabor's fifth wife, Nadia.'

'You are well informed Mr Helford. But let me now ask you a question. Did you know that I'm a widow? Did you also know that my husband was murdered by the Israelis who were tipped off by your father?'

Richard hesitated. 'Yes, I did know. Your husband was funding terrorists. That's why the Israelis killed him because the Americans wouldn't.'

Nadia eyes widened, shooting Richard an approving glance. 'Your honesty is admirable Mr Helford.'

'Cut this crap and tell me if you have my girlfriend?'

A small smile crept across Nadia's lips. 'All in good time,' she replied. The chador gave a tantalising view of her face but everything else remained hidden. He remembered Amira dressed in a similar way when they first met, the moment he told her about the death of Masood.

'I never actually met your father, but I will call you Richard instead of Mr Helford as I hope we can be friends.

'You've already converted Becky to your cause so why not me?'

'Your girlfriend is bright, well informed and we have a common interest, so it goes without saying that we got on well. You are right about my husband, but my approach is different. I am a Muslim not a terrorist.'

'The Words of the Faithful.'

'Exactly. Battling against Western materialism will achieve nothing. If Islam is going to be a force in the world, the conflict between Shia and Sunni must cease. It is the cause of all our problems, and it is why the people of other religions are dominating Islam. Your girlfriend was impressed by my arguments.'

'So, she has told me, but I suspect your motives are different.'

Nadia smiled. 'I wanted to meet you because of your father. He discovered the scroll on Crete with the new revelation of Saint John of Patmos. It will reinforce our case to unite Islam against Western materialism.'

Richard scoffed. 'Hold on a minute. I discovered the scroll. My father stole it and went off to Iran. But leaving that aside, I agree with your objectives. They are just misguided and have no chance of succeeding. It's too deep routed. It goes back centuries.'

'Please forgive me for my incorrect statement. The fact is your father has the scroll and therefore stopping him is a big ask. It's a mountain to climb, but I believe that the scroll will lead us to the ultimate truth.'

'It proves nothing because if Barnabas has correctly reported the words of Jesus, it does not mean he is referring to Islam which was not even thought about when he wrote his Gospel. Besides all that does not help the Shia Sunni conflict.'

'The Iranians have the scroll, thanks to your father, and we will find the Gospel. One document will not work without the other.'

'That's all very well, but you can't get away from the fact that the existing copies of the Gospel are proven forgeries. You can't say they are authentic unless you can prove that the words you read date back to the first century when Barnabas wrote the Gospel.'

'But that doesn't mean it didn't exist,' Nadia exclaimed. 'It's an acknowledged fact that Pope Gelasius banned the gospel in the fifth century AD. He couldn't ban it if it didn't exist in the first place. That's two hundred years before Islam so how could disaffected Muslims write the gospel if Islam hadn't been started at that time. We need you to convince your father that we've found the original Gospel. Tell him that the original manuscript was found in Salamis here in Cyprus where St Barnabas was executed. Who knows, we might even find the original.'

Richard sighed. 'Even if I could convince my father, which I doubt, you can't honestly believe that the Iranians will want to ditch the conflict between Sunni and Shia because of the Gospel, even if it is proven to be genuine.

Do you think that the festival of Ashura will be abandoned? The martyrdom of Hossein, married to the Prophet's only child, Fatemeh is celebrated at that festival. It's ground into the Shia psyche. They will never give it up, not in a million years. According to Shia belief, they are the true descendants of the Holy prophet. That belief will never be erased. They will not forget everything that has happened over the centuries and they are certainly not going to forget the million dead in the Iran Iraq war. Nothing will change until the Saudis and Iranians agree to bury their differences and actually talk to each other.'

'That is precisely my point. Maybe the Gospel will give them some common ground.'

Richard grinned. 'St Barnabas was known as the great encourager. The apostles changed his name from Joseph to Barnabas to reflect this great quality. He was a motivator and would approve of your efforts. So well done. I hope you're right...I really do... but even if you are, it won't change anything.'

'Why not?' Nadia protested.

'Because the Christians and Jews will continue to deny that the Gospel is legitimate whatever you say. These religions are too embedded in the culture to be upended. Besides, you say you are not a terrorist, but your proposal will provoke violence among religions. I guarantee it.'

'Please stop,' Nadia said putting her hands over her ears. He could see the frustration in her eyes. She knew he was right. He was reassured because it showed she believed in peace and was prepared to face the reality of the situation.

She signalled to one of the guards waiting at the entrance. The door swung open and Becky entered. Behind her a man was being dragged into the room by two guards who held him up while his legs trailed along the ground. It was Harper. His shirt ripped and his face bloody and bruised, eyes swollen, the lids shielding his injured eyes, closed and discoloured.

'People you know I think,' said Nadia.

Becky let out a cry when she saw Harper's injuries. 'What have you done to him?' she asked, looking at Nadia. 'I thought Harper was on our side?'

Richard gasped. 'Our side?' he said sharply.

Becky glanced at Richard. 'You already know I've joined Words of the Faithful. I will fight for their aims and be on their side.'

'This is not about sides,' Richard said, exasperated that she was talking as if they were enemies.

Becky ignored his comment, continuing to stare at Nadia.

'You can never trust a man from the CIA. We had to test his resolve. His commitment to our cause,' Nadia replied.

'Harper deserves this,' Richard intervened. 'But I don't. What do you think you are doing Becky? Trying to get information out of me so you can help Nadia. You knew where to find Harper all the time and you led me on while you were screwing the man who tried to kill me in Iraq.'

He had Becky's attention now. She didn't deny his accusations, but her fierce glare said it all. Their relationship was over.

'That's just it' she replied curtly. 'You haven't told me everything have you? What about the innocent people you were torturing in Iraq?'

Richard's anger bubbled over. 'He's lying. What's the bastard been telling you? Do you honestly think I could do such a thing?' He peered at the ground, feeling he wanted to break something, unable to look her straight in the eye.

Becky stepped forward before the guard pulled her back. She wriggled free from his grip and ran towards Richard.

'You've changed. You're not the man I fell in love with. It's the lie I can't stand.' Tears streamed down Becky's face and Richard swallowed hard. 'I joined Nadia to be part of your world, to understand how stupid it all is. I realise now that you're turning into your father,' she said, pointing to Nadia. 'She stands for peace and so does Harper.'

He noticed Nadia's face beaming with pleasure, pleased by Becky's praise. 'Whatever my father told you, it's not true,' he said. 'And even if it is true, which it's not, Harper is just as bad as me if not worse, working for the CIA. You are being manipulated. Can't you see that?'

Becky let out a cynical laugh. 'Exactly whose being manipulated here? Harper resigned from the CIA because he couldn't stand the lies, but I don't see you resigning. I just don't believe you anymore.'

Richard sighed 'I'm not sure I believe myself anymore.'

The guards pulled her away from him, but their eyes met. He couldn't make her out. 'Whatever you do, I don't want you bringing up our child with that heap of shit,' he said nodding in the direction of where Harper was trying to stand. He glanced back at Nadia and thought she must be enjoying his argument with Becky.

'What do you want from us?' he asked Nadia.

Nadia stood up and took Becky by the hand, directing the answer to Richard's question to Becky. 'Your differences with Richard will not help our cause. I want you to help me find the Gospel.' She turned to face Richard. 'I want you to join my organisation just like Becky has done and help me recover from Iran what your father stole. We'll hold Becky in nice surroundings. A house arrest I think you English call it. She'll be able to relax and top up her suntan while you and I talk. It will be a holiday for her.'

He watched as the guard led Becky away. 'Why do you want her out of the way?'

Nadia turned cold, frowning at Richard. 'I'm sure you would like to kill Harper,' she said. 'We don't want Becky witnessing what you are capable of …killing I mean.'

He felt uneasy with her reply. It seemed like she was evading a truth. A guard, right on cue came forward holding the Glock 19 pistol Richard had brought with him on the plane. He handed the gun to Richard who just stared straight at it without moving.

Nadia taunted him. 'Take the pistol…go on. Where is your strength of purpose?'

Richard took the gun and stared straight at Nadia. She nodded her approval. He checked whether the gun was loaded and flicked the safety catch, levelling it squarely at Harper's head. For a moment he enjoyed the fear in Harper's eyes.

Richard said, 'Give me one reason why I shouldn't kill you.'

Harper raised his head slowly and spoke in a whisper. 'I may not have killed you in Iraq, but I've managed to fuck with your head.' His fierce eyes invited Richard to hit him.

The pistol whip knocked Harper on to the floor. Richard aimed the barrel of the gun but could not pull the trigger.

'I asked you a question,' he shouted. 'Why shouldn't I kill you?'

'Because we are on the same side. I'll help you find the gospel and I'll stay away from your girlfriend.'

'Why would you do that?'

Harper lifted his head and looked at Nadia. 'Because she promised me a million bucks if I found it.'

'This is true, what he says,' said Nadia. 'I've had him knocked around a bit to see if he is genuine. I believe he is. I'll pay you the money instead of him if you find the Gospel. If you work together, I'll pay you a million dollars each.'

'I would never work with him however much you paid me,' said Richard nodding towards Harper.

'There are factions within the CIA who want to support the Saudi's and others who want to help Iran,' said Nadia. 'The president has been persuaded that after the disaster unfolding in Iraq, we need to open up a covert line of discussion with the Iranians about lifting sanctions, re-establishing relations with Iran after all these years. We want to use their interest in the Gospel as a way in. The agent working on this is somebody you know.'

'Who do I know?'

'Amira.' Richard's hold on the gun faltered when he heard the name. He remembered the last time he saw her on the Thames embankment. Always a mystery. she'd told him she was leaving the CIA.

'Amira is in Iran?'

'Yes.'

'But that's where my father is hiding.'

'He helped Amira get into the country.'

'I thought my father was a wanted man. How come he's helping Amira?'

Nadia intervened. 'Your father is like me, Richard. He believes in peace within the confines of Islam. If the Americans want to resume talks with Iran, then he's going to help because it's what he wants.'

'Your father is a pain in the arse,' Harper said under his breath.

Richard lifted the gun back again and moved closer to Harper. 'I still don't get it,' he said. 'It's just some religious document thousands of years old. What difference can that make?'

Nadia spoke. 'I think I should explain.' Richard lowered the gun, flicking the safety back. He caught Harper's sigh of relief. Carefully, he placed the gun on the marble desk and stepped back. 'Go on,' he said.

Nadia sat down again behind her desk. 'About twenty years ago, the grave of St Barnabas was robbed. A journalist investigating the incident was found drowned shortly after he had revealed that the original manuscript of the gospel had been taken from the grave of the saint. In the year 2000, the Turkish authorities recovered a text written in Aramaic, the language spoken by Jesus and his followers. The text, believed to be the document stolen from St Barnabas' grave, is held in the Ethnography Museum in Ankara. Before my husband was killed, I had been working in the background to gain access to the text. It has taken many months to persuade Mohammed Al Shisani who is Professor of Islamic art at the Museum to talk to me. I've kept the details secret, but the Israelis did me a favour and got rid of my husband, I am now at liberty to speak. The professor told me that the document dates back to the 7th Century and is written at the time when the Islamic faith was becoming established. There's no doubt in the professor's mind that the document has been altered by Mohammed's followers. It does not undermine the Christian case. It is just another forgery like the newer Italian and Spanish versions which date back to the 16th Century. What is interesting about the document however is nothing to do with Barnabas. It explains why the Turks have not allowed the document to be openly viewed.'

Nadia stopped and told Harper's guards to leave. When they were alone, she spoke. 'The gospel has a postscript, believed to be written in the hand of the Holy Prophet. It decrees that the line of succession, after the Holy Prophet's death, should be succeeded by his blood family and not some intellectually superior consensus leader favoured by the Sunni tribe. It is the justification for the Shia case, that they represent the true religion of Islam. That is why the document has been supressed by the Turks.'

'But it's dynamite to Iran?' Richard said.

Nadia continued. 'Harper has told us that some in the CIA thinks it will be a good thing if the evidence in this version of the Gospel gets out. They used to be worried about the scroll but, without definitive proof from the genuine Gospel, which is written before the birth of Islam, it is useless. They will even discredit the scroll found in Crete as a forgery.'

'So, you want to find the genuine document?'

'Yes, but I also want the Iranians to see the version in Ankara.'

Richard laughed. 'There are two problems with what you are saying. First, we'd have to steal this gospel from the museum in Ankara and second, you are a Sunni. Why would you want to help the Shia case?'

'I am not supporting the Shia case anymore than I am supporting the Sunni case. There are Sunni's in Iran and some support for Al Qaeda. I am only interested in promoting a modern and progressive view of Islam. Just because I am a Saudi does not mean I support Wahhabism which has wide support in my country. It is an ultra-conservative, austere doctrine which encourages a literal interpretation of the Holy Koran. Wahhabism supports a world that existed in the 7th century and takes no account of our lives in 21st century. I am against it.

He stood with one hand leaning against a column feeling the cool marble surface. It helped him think. He walked back towards Nadia, still seated at her desk. 'Okay, so you've got a grand plan to help promote peace among Muslims,' he said leaning over the desk. 'You and the CIA have common aims; you both want the Ankara document sent to Iran. For their part they want it as an olive branch for negotiations on sanctions, but they also want it as bait to kill my father. In your case, you want to promote the case of Islam and make the Muslim world reject extremism

Nadia smiled and touched Richard's hand. 'Yes, yes…If the Shia win the argument of succession, it will encourage the majority to focus on the real issue which is the supremacy of Islam as an extension of the existing faiths. Mohammed came after Jesus, but they are all part of a continuous stream of belief in God. They are not alien religions to each other, but Islam is the greatest because it is the last.'

'So, who is going to rob the Museum?'

'You are of course.' Despite the chador, Richard could see her face clearly. It sparkled with anticipation as if they were approaching a level of understanding where he might be able to trust her.

Harper was listening intently to all this. 'Please let me sit down,' he groaned. 'Your cronies have done my legs in.'

Nadia got him a chair, placing it close to Harper. He was about to sit when Richard kicked the chair away forcing Harper to collapse onto the marble floor.'

'Shit.' he shouted. 'What you do that for?'

Richard leaned over and grabbed Harper by the shirt. 'Because you are a fucking shit…that's why…screwing the mother of my baby and setting up that kid in Iraq who was trying to kill me.' He kicked Harper in the stomach and enjoyed his groan of pain.'

Harper lifted himself to his knees and crawled up to the seat. This time Richard allowed him to sit. Their eyes locked together in mutual hatred, but Harper spoke first.

'You know Becky told me about what your father said. You are too much like him - a fucking headcase - I'm just sorry we didn't kill you in Iraq.'

Chapter Nine

The road North of Acre, Palestine. AD 1102

I saw the cloud of dust in the distance. A shimmer of sand blurring the horizon. As it came nearer, I heard shouts; a battle cry from Arabs hunting out Christian pilgrims. There must have been twenty horsemen attacking fifty or more, but the odds were deceiving as many of the Christians were women and children. We watched waiting for our moment. My men were Fatimids who over the years, since I left the Crusaders, had grown to respect my fighting abilities. This was a band of Muslims who supported Fatima, the Holy Prophet's daughter. The Arabs fighting the Christians were from the Abbasid caliph of Baghdad. They were as many imposters in Palestine as the Christians. My men hated the pilgrims but hated Sunni Muslims more. I waved my hand and we charged.

As we drew near, I could see the Sunnis decapitating the Christians with brutal savagery, showing no mercy to women and children. They must have killed over half of the pilgrims before we reached them. The Christians fought valiantly and inflicted casualties but were no match for their enemy. The victims of the slaughter were my people and yet I felt nothing. It was nearly three years since I had deserted the Crusade and now, I was one of them. A Muslim, an enemy of the Christian Crusade. We cut a swathe into their line and with better horse skills began to butcher the marauding gang. Within minutes, the Sunnis had retreated.

The visitors stared at us in disbelief that they were still alive, but fear rather than relief remained in their eyes. I dismounted and spoke in French.

'Bring me your leader.'

An elderly man dismounted from one of the horses still left standing. I could see he had been in the battle. His tunic was torn and his face bloodied. He glanced at me and then walked slowly towards the pilgrims lying dead all around him. He found one and knelt down crossing himself and wailing openly. My men were growing impatient, but I bid them stay silent and allow the group to pay their respects to their dead. After several minutes he stood up and came up to me. 'My name is Saewulf. Why do you speak French?'

I ignored the question 'Where are you heading and what is your business in Palestine?'

'We come in peace,' said Saewulf. We need your leave to bury our dead and then we will be on our way. We came to Palestine to follow in the footsteps of Jesus Christ, to visit holy shrines in his memory. Now we have seen. we must return to our homeland. We are heading for a boat that leaves from St Simeon. From there we sail to Cyprus.'

A boat. A chance to leave the Holy Land. My mind raced with the possibility. Cyprus is the home of St Barnabas. It is his book that I found in the hands of the dying priest in Antioch. It is his book which gave me a reason to convert to Islam. I can wear the head scarf and take Akila into my protection, treating her sons as my own, but I could never be an Arab. My heart leapt that, as a member of this Christian band of pilgrims, I could at last find a way to leave after three long years.

'You must come to my camp tonight and meet my wife and sons.' I said. 'It is too dangerous on this open terrain. From here, I will provide protection until you reach your boat.'

Yes, I married Akila, whose husband I killed in self-defence in Antioch. It was Akila who introduced me to the band of fighters who protect a small Muslim village east of Acre. With her two children, Masood and Mohammed, I learned to live the simple life and melt into the landscape

78

and away from my fellow Crusaders who I had grown to loathe. I read the Holy Koran and worshiped Allah with other Arabs living in the village. At first, I communicated to them through Akila. I drew pictures in the sand and got my message across. Masood used to laugh at my pictures, but he saw how much his mother relied on my presence. My moment of acceptance came one night when I came back from farming in the fields and found three tribesmen attacking Akila. I realise now that it was a deliberate ploy to test me. Many of the Arab men in the village would have been happy to see me die. I fought the three men together and killed them all. It was at that point I was accepted but never completely trusted. I learned later that the men distrusted Akila because she belonged to the Druze sect. These men chose to deny she was a real Muslim even though she regarded the Holy Koran with great reverence and read it every day.

Druze is a particular brand of Shia Islam. It seems very private and accepting of all religions. It was Akila who persuaded me not to destroy the gospel I received from the dying priest in Antioch which remains sewn into my tunic. After converting to Islam, Akila taught me that Islam in many ways is a religion similar to Christianity. It is what caused me to renounce being a knight of the Crusade. It is true that I deserted because I no longer wished to kill in the name of God but Akila told me that we were all children of God. Being a Druze, she loves all people and is quite content to learn from other religions. The Holy Koran is my only source of comfort. There are times when feeling the gospel against my chest, I resolve to destroy it despite what Akila says, but something holds me back. God is preventing me from destroying the gospel. It was that same God who instructed me to board Saewulf's boat to Cyprus. Akila and her sons were pleased to come with me, but the men I'd commanded did not shed any tears. My approach had always been to avoid conflict and live in peace, but my men chose to confront the Crusaders and drive them out of Palestine.

I would never have made the trip to Famagusta had I not saved the life of the pilgrim Saewulf. It was a calling from God. My destiny was to be with an Englishman with a Viking name. A holy man who showed me the right path.

Chapter Ten

Bellapais, Northern Cyprus -August 30th, 2005.

The food was good without being exceptional, but that didn't matter because the restaurant was situated in a beautiful location, opposite the floodlit ruins of the gothic abbey of Bellapais. The setting overshadowed culinary expectation. Outside, on a warm sultry evening, he could hear violins playing Vivaldi in the Abbey grounds, just a few feet away. As darkness began to fall, he could see the twinkling lights of Kyrenia, lining the coast. A bright star was already visible, Venus he thought, but it might be Mars. On a perfect night like this, he was surprised how little he thought of Becky. He knew she was safe, but the way she had jumped at Harper sickened him. He was becoming reconciled that it would never work between them but knew he must protect her whatever happened, for the sake of the baby if for nothing else. Her friendship with Nadia also troubled him. There was an understanding that seemed to be more than idealistic. In this moment, he was happier looking across the table at Nadia and felt some regret that in such a romantic setting they were sharing a table with another man.; a priest, no less, dressed in a long black cassock. His hair was long and bushy, black with streaks of grey, woven into a long scraggy beard. His eyes were sharp, alert and startling, shining like sapphires through a mop of silvery curls.

'May I introduce Father Christos Alonissos,' said Nadia. 'He has been corresponding with the Professor I told you about at the Museum of Ethnography in Ankara.'

'I was.' corrected the priest. 'He is no longer sending me messages.'

Richard could see from the concern on Nadia's face that she was not aware that the Professor has ceased contact. She picked up her phone and clicked the speed dial. Richard noted the number was high up on her contact list. She spoke in Turkish which he could not understand but the tone of her voice gave away her anger at the news. After cutting the call, she spoke in a low voice, looking around to see if anybody was listening. 'Father Christos is right.' she said. 'I pay a lot of money to get access to this sort of power. Money speaks. That's why I'm able to conduct my meetings with you in an Army barracks because I paid off the right man. My access to the Professor involved payments on account, but the Professor has been removed from his post without explanation. Somebody has talked.'

'I assume stealing the Barnabas text is now out of the question. We could never get in without help from the Professor.' said Richard.

Nadia didn't answer. It made him wonder whether her anger at the loss of contact with the Professor was more to do with her orders being disobeyed rather than concern for the professor's safety. He continued to stare at Nadia, his eyes locked onto her gaze.

'We will get the document for you to take to Iran,' she said. 'I promise.'

'There is another way,' interjected Father Christos, speaking in Greek which Richard could just about understand.

'What's that?' said Nadia now also speaking in Greek.

'Find the original text.'

Nadia laughed. 'If I knew where it was. There are no clues.'

Father Christos did not have time to answer as the waiter appeared to clear the starter course. When this was done, more waiters surrounded their table with great ceremony, delivering the mains with a flourish as they lifted the lids off each meal simultaneously and then wasted more time topping up the drinks. Nadia had a grilled bream and asked for Perrier. Richard and Father Christos both chose rump steak washed down with an Argentinian Merlot. Nadia fidgeted with her fork as she waited for the waiters to leave.

Alone again, the old priest continued speaking. 'My conversations with the Professor at Ankara were very fruitful. The text in Aramaic in his possession had aroused his interest in the life of Barnabas. The stolen document the Turks had recovered also included some parchment - just fragments, but interesting as they date back to the 11th century. They must have been stolen from the Monastery of St Barnabas archives. The fragments involved correspondence between a father and his son written in Arabic. It refers to Barnabas visiting Antioch. It also discussed a holy scripture in the possession of the Bishop of Antioch being truly the authentic word of God. One of the fragments are signed Masood.'

Hearing the name was a shock to Richard. It was ingrained in his mind and flashed him back to that moment on the bombed-out train. He almost choked on his food and took a sip of wine to help him swallow. Nadia noticed his reaction and looked at Richard.

'Does the name mean anything to you?' She filleted her bream with precision but also with aggression.

'It's just that I met somebody with that name…but it's nothing…a coincidence.'

'Masood is a common name. Why would it have such an effect on you?'

Richard looked at Nadia, wondering whether he could trust her. He noticed the irritated tone in her voice. There was something not quite right about this woman with a conscience who just happened to be married to one of the world's richest men who was responsible for funding so many terrorist acts. He hesitated to go over the issues in his mind. 'I'll tell you later, but we should let Father speak first.'

Nadia nodded, looking at the older man. 'Please continue, Father,' she said. a little too loudly causing a woman on the next table to turn around with a disapproving glance.

Father Christos continued at the same speed as before. 'I decided to examine the archives of the Monastery myself and see if I could find more documents that might relate to these fragments held in Ankara.'

'And were you successful?'

'I would not go as far as that, but I did find something.'

Nadia sighed at the priest's procrastination. She raised her voice. 'What did you find, Father?'

'I found a journal written in French which I must assume was written by someone with connections to the Christian wars in Palestine. The man writes about Islam as being a religion of equal importance to Christianity and that there was no justification for the wars with the Arab people. The link is the reference to a young Muslim called Masood. The journal also refers to a gospel recovered from a dying priest in Antioch.'

'There is no reference to what he might have done with the gospel?' said Richard.

The old man's eyes lit up. He took a large gulp of red wine and swallowed a piece of steak, chewing it slowly, enjoying the suspense and the attention he was getting. 'When the knight arrived in Famagusta, the rulers were Byzantine. Although they were united with the Christians in the fight against Islam, they didn't really trust each other. The knight was ideal because he was a deserter from the Crusader cause. '

'What's that got to do with finding the Gospel of Barnabas?' said Nadia becoming increasingly irritated.

'Patience, my child…it is because of his counsel, the Byzantine ruler gave him many privileges. At first, he lived with monks in St Hilarion but later he had his own villa near Salamis and not far from where they discovered the Barnabas tomb.'

'How do you know this?' said Richard.

The knight is mentioned many times in documents preserved in the archives of Famagusta. His name was Robert de Valognes, living in England, but a Frenchman from Normandy who came to England after the Battle of Hastings. Robert is recorded by the monks of St Hilarion, travelling in the footsteps of Barnabas, visiting places like Paphos and Tamasos in Cyprus and also places in Turkey including Lystra and Iconium.'

'Okay,' said Richard. 'What you are saying is that there is evidence that the knight was interested in Barnabas, but if Robert the knight had the original gospel, why didn't he shout about it from the rooftops. I mean Barnabas was big news in Cyprus. The knight would have been feted as a hero by the people because Barnabas was the patron saint of the island. It would be a miraculous find.' Richard stopped to swallow some food. 'And another thing,' taking a sip of wine before continuing. 'Don't forget they found a handwritten copy of the Gospel of Matthew in his tomb. The handwriting is believed to be the work of Barnabas himself, although God knows how they knew that.'

Nadia eyes widened at the points Richard was making. 'Why would Barnabas not be buried with his own gospel, if one existed?' she said, her irritation had turned to frustration that they were getting nowhere.

'Simple,' said the priest. 'Because it shattered the illusion of Barnabas the encourager, offering a different narrative to the one everybody knew. Barnabas was a mediator who settled conflicts and a new controversial gospel would shatter that belief in him shown by the common people.'

'It is possible that the Gospel of Matthew found in the tomb was just a cover up. I've read that some think the

Gospel was indeed written by Barnabas. Do you agree?' asked Richard.

'It is possible,' the priest replied.

'We are no further forward?' said Nadia, slamming her glass down on the table, forcing the bubbles of her water to spill on to the pristine white tablecloth.

'What we are missing is the complete journals of the knight,' said Father Christos. The fragments we do have were found at the unexcavated villa that belonged to the knight.'

Richard groaned, 'we haven't time to go on an archaeological dig.'

'I will get people onto it straight away.' said Nadia. 'We may find something.'

'That doesn't help...I need something to take to Iran.'

Nadia leaned forward across the table. Her lips parted mouthing her words silently, leaving Richard no choice but to lip read. 'Like I said...I'll get you the Ankara document.'

'How?'

'If I offer a big enough sum, my contacts will steal the document and give it to you. You'll need to travel to Turkey as a tourist and take your girlfriend with you.'

'Why do you have to involve Becky? She shouldn't be anything to do with this.'

'Because you will look more like a tourist if you are a loving couple. A man on his own will stand out.'

Richard laughed. 'You saw our disagreements; she's not interested in being with me anymore.'

Nadia stood up and shook Father Christos' hand. 'Goodbye Father,' she said. 'We will, with your assistance, start digging at the villa.' She turned to Richard. 'You'll bring her round.'

Father Christos looked upset that Nadia was calling a halt to their dinner because they hadn't eaten dessert. He shook Richard's hand and left the table, muttering to himself. As Richard watched the old man leave, he caught the sight of a man looking in their direction. As their eyes met, the man looked back towards his dinner guest who was also male. Richard took in both men's features. Mediterranean looking, not Arab, thirties, a thick black hair, leather jacket, shirt, tie: they were identically dressed except for the colour of their shirts and the pattern on their ties. They looked suspicious, but it was too obvious.

He nodded in their direction to Nadia. 'Your people, I think. Correct.'

Nadia glanced over in the direction of the men and glared. 'Yes, they are my security…useless though they may be. 'She sighed and signalled to the waiter for the bill. Turning to face Richard, she punched out a number on her phone. The message she gave the caller was clear even if the content was undecipherable. Nadia knew how to give out orders. She finished the call and spoke. 'Your girlfriend will be delivered to your hotel in the next hour. You better go there and greet her. I'll send tickets for your direct flight to Ankara tomorrow…From there you'll join an organised tour from Tehran. That will be your excuse to visit Iran. Your girlfriend will not be needed to accompany you into Iran'

'What are you going to do with the American – Harper?'

'I am arranging for him to be smuggled into Iran. Americans are not welcome so crossing the border won't be easy but that's his problem. He will be there to assist you in Iran when you recover the scroll from your father.'

'I'm not working with Harper. I don't care what you say. He's hardly going to get me a meeting with the Iranian president, is he? He's a liability. It would be like walking around Iran wearing a suicide vest with no control of the detonator.'

Nadia laughed. 'I take your point. But he will assist you when the going in Iran is dangerous, which it will be.'

'Getting across the Turkish border with a document stolen from the Museum in Ankara will not be easy, but I don't want Harper holding my hand. While I think about it, who's going to arrange visas? They could take months to be granted.'

'All that will be arranged but you will not take the original document, just a facsimile. The original will stay at the museum.'

Their voices remained low, but Richard was sure they were being watched, A sixth sense or paranoia, he didn't know which. He just knew.

Chapter Eleven

Ercan airport, Northern Cyprus - August 31st, 2005

Their conversation was stilted, punctuated by long silences. Richard tried asking about her meetings with Harper but got nowhere.

When they arrived at the terminal, she broke her silence. They found a seat away from the check in area and he bought her coffee. She bent her head, holding the coffee in two hands as if she were warming herself. 'I let Harper into my life because I wanted to understand you -what you did in Iraq' she said. 'But Nadia had contacted me through him. I didn't meet her in a café. That was a lie.'

'I was just an observer in Iraq…I was never party to any torture,' he replied. 'They wanted me because I spoke Arabic.'

'But you helped the Americans with rendition. If you observed, then you were just as guilty. Some of them will have ended up in Guantanamo.'

'That may be true. I may have been party to the crime, but Harper was up to his neck in it so why favour him and not me? He was at the centre of the whole thing. We worked together, but I was just a translator. He was stringing the poor bastards up.' Richard tensed his knuckles, trying to subdue the anger burning in his stomach. 'What sickens me Becky is that you thought this guy was better than me. He was using you to get at me. Don't you see that?'

Becky stared into space refusing to look Richard in the eye. 'I know I was stupid. I guess my hormones were all over the place, with the pregnancy, and when your father warned me against you, I was clinging to anything that might explain whether I loved you or not. He was very charming towards me and I was lonely.'

'I watched you with him and you seemed happy together. Did you sleep with him?'

Becky said nothing. Her mouth was wide open, feigning shock. He regretted asking but he detected a hesitancy in her voice. If she had he was not sure whether he could continue as before with the idea in his head that Harper, the man who had tried to kill him to get at his father had slept with the mother of his child.

'Er…of course not.' she said. 'How could you think of such a thing?'

It was that small delay, no unequivocal denial that told him she was lying. He didn't believe her and that concerned him even more. He already regretted bringing her to Cyprus. The truth was unpalatable. He'd used Becky to flush out Harper, knowing that she'd try and make contact.

Becky changed the subject. 'It's a pain we have to go to Istanbul before going onto London.' She squinted her eyes, focusing on the departure screen. 'Oh shit, it looks like we've got to wait three hours before it leaves.' She sighed and scanned the departure hall for somewhere to sit, which was away from people eating food from the cafe.

'We're not going to Istanbul. We're flying to Ankara. You are involved now Becky, so we've got to see this through together. Nadia wants us to pick something up. I'll get you on the next flight to Heathrow as soon as it's done. I promise.

'What are we picking up?'

'Just a package- some documents …not drugs or anything silly. London knows what I'm doing.' He lied as he had not been in touch with Vauxhall Cross and didn't intend to.

'Can't you do this on your own? Why do you need me?

'Nadia thinks we will be less obvious as a courting couple.'

Becky let out a cynical laugh. 'Some chance of that. 'How long is this going to take?'

'I don't know how long … a few days or maybe just a day.'

'If it's for Nadia, then I'll do it. Although I'm due back at work.'

'You can phone in sick. There is really nothing I can do.'

Ankara - September 2nd, 2005

They'd been in the city two days and was surprised she did not complain.

'If Nadia thinks this is important, then we must do it,' she said.

She allowed them to sleep together out of necessity. They'd been allocated a double-bedded room and needed to continue with the pretence that they were young lovers. They slept with their backs to each other and did not touch. Occasionally, they would smile sweetly when someone complemented them on Becky's pregnancy. He felt terrible that it had come to this.

Richard wanted to hold her in his arms to break the wedge of distrust that had been driven between them. His suspicions about her motives didn't seem right because he'd never had cause to doubt her before. Despite all these doubts, he couldn't quite accept that it was over between them. Once he tried to kiss her forehead, but she turned her head away. He watched as she drifted into sleep admiring the small bump where his baby lay cocooned in her womb.

At the beginning of September, the nights were still hot and sticky. Their air conditioning unit bumped and crashed pumping lukewarm air into the room. The noise did not stop Becky from falling into a deep sleep, but it was not so for him. After tossing and turning, sweat dripped over his whole body, he got up and pulled on a t shirt and jeans and climbed the stairs to the roof top bar. He ordered a beer and stared over the city. Even though it was late, Ankara, like any other capital city, was buzzing with life. He could see for miles the swirling vehicle lights racing along the main thoroughfares and there in the middle of the city, the Kocatepe Mosque, every bit as large as the Blue Mosque in Istanbul, bathed in light dominating the skyline. Ankara was a very different place to Istanbul, lacking the history dating back from the beginning of time, nor did it benefit from the cooling breezes which blew off the Bosphorus separating the waters of the Black Sea from the Sea of Marmara. There was no East West division here. Ankara was Turkish to its core.

A man was standing by his side. He did not speak but Richard was certain it was his contact. The art of the drop was not something Richard had any inkling about. He'd never done one before, so it was hardly surprising. *Learn on the job.* Rowena's words echoed in his ear. He stood up and allowed the man to brush passed him. He apologised for his clumsiness in schoolboy Turkish and it was over.

Back at his room Becky was still sleeping. There were two tickets to the Museum of Ethnography in the envelope that had been stuffed into his inside jacket pocket. There was also a postcard of Ataturk's mausoleum with 11am scrawled across the back. Richard thumbed through his guidebook and found that the handover would take place in the crowded museum entrance hall in front of the tomb of Ataturk. Even though his body had since been moved to its final resting place, tourists flocked to see it. The Turks revered Ataturk and treated him like a God, so he was sure it would attract a lot of visitors and make the exchange easy to execute. It all seemed straight forward. They'd be back on a plane to London before the day was done.

He found it even harder to sleep now that he knew things were going down. Nadia had given him a brown leather briefcase to take to the rendezvous. He should put it down at the preferred spot and wait for a switch to be made.

Ankara - September 3rd, 2005

They arrived at the museum with time to spare. It was another hot day and climbing the hill to reach the entrance exhausted Becky. He found a seat where they were shaded by the building.

'It's less than one hundred years old,' said Richard. 'It looks older. Sultan Ottoman style at the peak of their power. But that statue over there gives it away. It's Ataturk riding his horse, the founding father of the Turkish Republic.'

She wasn't interested. Her expression said it all – bored, blank and irritated.

'I'm sorry,' he said with a sheepish grin. 'It'll be over soon, and we'll be on the plane back to London - I promise - I'm sorry to put you thorough this.'

The clock moved closer to eleven. 'It's time we went inside,' he said, holding out his hand to help her stand. Inside, as he predicted, there were lots of tourists milling around the tomb of Ataturk taking photographs. He pulled out his camera and began snapping. She looked done in.

He put the briefcase down by his foot and continued to take pictures. The crowds jostled for position. She was visibly distressed.

But he did not stop taking photographs. He had to maintain the pretence of being a tourist for a little longer.

'Smile,' he said looking at the viewfinder. He noticed a small hint of a smile but nothing else. His eye remained fixed on the camera's viewfinder looking at her image.

Something changed in her face.

He saw her eyes begin to roll and her legs were buckling. Rushing forward, he caught her before she hit the floor. A woman in the crowd screamed, causing commotion among the tourists surrounding Becky.

The museum staff were quick to react. One official shouted orders in Turkish before turning towards Richard.

'Lady. Hospital. Quick,' he said in English. The man's voice was urgent, but his face showed no signs of shock, as if he knew what was wrong with Becky.

Her colour was changing - white like a corpse. It was serious.

'Oh my God Becky, please God - No - speak to me.' He held her tightly, as if someone might steal her from him. Her body was limp in his arms.

Barely conscious, she struggled to speak. 'Nadia – Tell Nadia. I failed.' She was gasping for breath. 'They stabbed me.'

'Who stabbed you?'

She did not answer. Her eyes closed and her breathing was less desperate. Leaning closer, he saw a cut in her clothing – difficult to spot over her patterned floral dress. A red stain confirming his worst fears. A small blot as if her body had been scratched by a thorn, not a big hole, more a prick. The bleeding had already stopped. 'It'll be okay,' he said. 'It'll be okay.'

The ambulance took only minutes to arrive. The medical team moved with swift efficiency, but he could see the concern on their faces. In the ambulance, the vomiting started. Retching like he'd never seen before. The nurse wiped her face and moved her head so she wouldn't choke. He held her hand and prayed. It seemed so normal - a pregnant woman fainting in the heat of the sun.

But she hadn't fainted. He waited what seemed like ages but in reality, was barely thirty minutes before a doctor appeared and told him that Ricin poison was not normal. The quantity forced into her bloodstream was untreatable. She would not survive, the doctor said. Death in thirty-six hours at the most. Sedation was all they could do to smooth her passing. He could do nothing but wait and cry. He wanted to kill himself.

A British embassy official called Smelton arrived to assist him with the Police interrogation. 'I'm really sorry about this. She's getting the best possible care but it's not looking good. The Police will want to ask questions and may be a little abrupt, not very sympathetic. We just have to help them as best we can.,' he said.

The police fired off questions, which Smelton translated. Richard stared through them, dazed and not taking anything in. Smelton repeated each question but it did no good.

'We were tourists,' he pleaded. 'Why would anyone want to kill my girlfriend, my pregnant girlfriend?' When he said the word, he wept. She hadn't died but he knew it was only a matter of time. He wept so much that the policemen handed him a tissue, seeming to be sympathetic, contrary to what Smelton had said.

The wait seemed endless. He held her hands and hoped for the miracle he knew would not come. She died in the middle of the night when he was sleeping. He'd dozed off and her grip had slipped away from his. Waking, he grasped her hand and held it to his cheek. It was taught and cold.

'I can't even stay awake. I can't even do that right,' he shouted, loud enough to bring the nurses to the bed side. The sense of utter failure engulfed him, like a dark thunder cloud about to break in a torrent of tears.

He lost all track of time and when Smelton appeared once more, he didn't want to speak. 'I'm sorry for your loss,' the civil servant said, forcing a reassuring smile. 'Life goes on, but don't worry I know who you are.'

He wanted to rip his stiff upper civil servant lips away from his sickly smile. Smelton did not look particularly worried that a British citizen had been murdered on his watch. His suit was ill fitting and the sweat on his brow and shirt befitted a man who had reached the end of his Foreign Office career. 'Don't worry. We'll get you back to London.'

'Don't worry…You are telling me not to worry?' Richard's voice was loud and Smelton put a disapproving finger to his mouth. 'You can stuff your finger up your arse.'

Smelton ignored Richard's abuse and continued as if nothing had happened. 'We need them to drop the case and release the body. I'll arrange it,' he said, leaving the room.

There were no windows. Just a table and two chairs and a fan whirling on the ceiling. Richard clocked the worried look on Smelton's face as he left. It wasn't going to happen, not easily. Becky had been murdered and the Turks would realise it was a sophisticated hit. The police had confiscated his phone and were looking through the last pictures he'd taken of Becky. Maybe the killer was on the photos.

He needed the time on his own. He'd tried to be calm in front of Smelton without success. The diplomat's holier than thou manner really pissed him off. He could no longer distinguish between the conflicting emotions of rage, anger and grief. He banged his head against the wall and cried again. His fingernails dug into the plaster. His anger was focused on Nadia. What was she doing involving Becky? They were working together, and he couldn't figure out why. He had no idea where the briefcase was and what it contained. He beat the wall again for even thinking that way. He'd lost Becky. He'd lost the child she was carrying. His child.

Nothing else mattered.

He sat down at the table and laid his head down on its surface. The breeze from the fan blew across the back of his neck and he remembered how Becky used to massage it and relieve his aches and pains. Her spirit was with him now and she smiled. Not like the faint smile he'd seen in his view finder before it happened. This was a perfect smile. A smile that refreshes the soul. A smile of forgiveness and a smile of love.

This changed everything. He no longer needed to decide about his future because he no longer had anything to live for.

He no longer feared death.

How could he manage the guilt he felt? How could he look Becky's parents in the eye when he was to blame for their daughter's murder?

Him. Not the Service. Not his father. Not even the killer.

Him. He was to blame and only he could make it right.

Chapter Twelve

London, Vauxhall Cross- September 9th, 2005

'How did you persuade the Turks to bring Becky's body home?'

Rowena shuffled the papers on her desk. It appeared aimless, as if she were buying time while she chose her words with great care. She wore glasses which he'd never seen before. It shielded her eyes and established distance and authority. He noticed slight smudges on her mascara hiding behind the glasses. He thought she'd been crying. He looked at her and saw her mouth quiver. Mouthing words that didn't come out.

'Before I answer your question, I'll say two things.' she said at last, removing her glasses. He could see her eyes were red and watery. She had been crying. She noticed him looking and put the glasses back on. At last she spoke. 'First, I'm really sorry about what has happened to Becky. Second, you can't blame the Service. I may have authorised the trip to Cyprus but there was nothing about you going onto Ankara.'

Richard felt his stomach tighten. 'Listen Rowena...I'm not blaming the Service. I contacted Nadia – you know - Words of the Faithful and paid up member of the Saudi intelligence services. She wanted us to go to Ankara. I blame her for Becky's murder. I thought she was on our side.'

He noticed Rowena's reaction to the mention of Nadia's name. She lifted her eyes and appeared shocked. 'Whoever it was doesn't matter,' she said after a prolonged pause. 'That was no reason to involve Becky and take her with you. She was pregnant for God's sake and you put her in danger.' Her voice was cracking, and he could see she really cared.

Rowena stood up and paced the room, retrieving a bottle of water from the fridge in the corner of her office. 'It wasn't easy,' she said. 'We had to bring in the Foreign Secretary and call in a favour at the highest level.' She broke the seal on the bottle and drank several large mouthfuls before continuing. 'The Turks have enough terrorist problems of their own. Once they'd satisfied themselves that Becky's murder was not related to the Kusadasi minibus bombing that happened in July, they were glad to leave it to us.'

'Have they told you how she was killed?'

'Ricin, a poison tip like that umbrella killing by the Bulgarians in 1978…bloody primitive, but effective.'

'Yes – that's what the Turks told me. Cold War stuff. Are the Russians sniffing around? Sounds like something the GRU would come up with.'

'It's possible, but we haven't picked up anything yet. This looks like terrorism to me dressed up a bit to make it look like the Russians are involved.'

'But this is Becky they killed. Why her?' He mouthed more words, but nothing more came out.

Rowena swivelled her chair, out of his line of sight, unwilling to catch his gaze. 'Becky was poking her nose into stuff, but I don't think that was the reason why they killed her. We've entertained the possibility that it was a revenge killing because you killed Abdul,' she said. 'We've looked at the photos you took of Becky and ran a check on the faces in the background. Nothing came up. Your briefcase was empty by the way. They'd forced the lock.'

The shock that the documents he'd expected to find had gone hit him hard. The trip to Ankara had been compromised and Becky had died in vain. His throat was dry. Sweat dripped down his forehead. 'Oh my God,' he whispered under his breath. He stood up and paced the room. *Whoever did this was seeking revenge. He had to find Nadia.*

Rowena noticed the shock on his face. 'What was in the case, Richard? I need to know.'

'It was supposed to hold a facsimile copy of the Aramaic Gospel of Barnabas. It dates to the seventh century AD and has been doctored by Islamic followers. I am advised that it presses the case for the Shia interpretation of who was the rightful successor of Mohammed. The Turks are keeping it under wraps as it undermines the Sunni case. I was going to use it as a peace offering to get access to my father. None of this matters anymore, now that's gone.'

'I'm sorry,' said Rowena. 'You will never understand how sorry I am.'

He turned towards the door. 'I've got a funeral to go to.'

'Wait Richard. Please don't go. Of course, I care for Becky. You will never know how much this hurts me. I feel responsible. But we need to focus on finding who did this to her.' Her voice was breaking, but she stood up and wiped her eyes. She took a gulp of water and continued to speak. 'The murder of a British citizen raises the stakes in this investigation. We need you to find out what is going on and whether this is connected to your father being in Iran.'

'Murder of a British citizen. Is that what you are going to call it?' He glared at Rowena, noticing how distressed she really was and refusing to be moved by any of her expressions of sorrow. He wanted to vent his own anger with himself onto Rowena, so she suffered as much as him.

Rowena's eyes narrowed. She leaned across her desk and stared back with a new sense of gritty determination. 'I'll give you all the support you need to get the bastards who did this. There you are. Is that language good enough for you?'

'Perfect.' He muttered, shutting the door to her office as he left.

North West Essex-September 9th, 2005.

The funeral was in the country, a sleepy North Essex village. A perfect English setting, alien to the scene of Becky's murder. Thatched houses surrounded the village green, elegantly defaced by a wicket cut for the cricket team; abandoned deck chairs on the boundary and at the edge, a Norman church, whose tower nestled among ancient oaks. Richard stood among the gravestones and watched the coffin being carried into the church. He didn't normally cry in public, but seeing Becky's mother, father and brother Edward walking behind, heads bowed, was too much. His stomach churned and the tears poured out dripping on to the Order of Service sheet, soaking the smiling image of Becky, so innocent looking back from the page. The more he thought about it the more he decided that it was his fault she'd died.

The service followed the traditions of a lost world, the green and pleasant land with poetry readings from Donne and Wordsworth and the rousing finale of Blake's Jerusalem. The eulogy read by Edward with bitterness, talked of being cruelly deprived of his sister's love before her natural time to leave this world. He spoke of how hard it was for his parents to lose a daughter while they continued to live. The words flowed without looking at his script. Every word known by heart and fixing his gaze on Richard, leaving no doubt who he blamed for the murder. His piercing stare locked onto him; a guided missile that was programmed to destroy everything in its path.

And he was right. Richard hated himself because of the way he used Becky to get to Harper. She died because of his selfish pursuit of his own agenda. And yet, despite all his grief, he could not get away from the fact that Becky was hiding something from him at the time of her murder. Nadia had the answer. It was the last thing she said. Why would she suddenly become interested in Harper and the Words of the Faithful? It was totally out of character. She never showed any interest in world affairs or religion and suddenly she was lining up with Saudi women who wanted a different approach to the troubles in the Middle East.

After the service, Richard hung back so he could be last to leave. As he stepped out into the sunshine, he saw Edward had broken away from the procession and was heading in his direction. The mourners continued to walk slowly to a quiet corner of the cemetery where a grave had been dug and flagstones removed.

'Why is my sister in that box and not you?' Edward said, grabbing Richard by the lapels of his suit and pushing him up against an oak that stood in the churchyard.

'I wouldn't blame you if you hit me...I don't know why this happened Edward, but I understand how angry you feel... I'm truly sorry that Becky's lost her life because I wasn't tough enough. I blame myself and I won't rest until I find her killer...I swear to God I'll get the bastard who did this.' He swallowed hard trying to hold himself together and fighting back the tears.

Becky's father, seeing the confrontation had signalled to the vicar to wait and came over. He took hold of Edward's arm and spoke softly. 'Come on Edward. We need to lay your sister to rest and then we can talk.'

Richard stood back and let Becky's close family hear the last rites as she was lowered into the ground. The tears continued to fall in a torrent of grief and when it was over, he just stood and could not move. His whole body seemed burned to the spot in that little churchyard with the smell of wild honey suckle and butterflies flitting from flower to flower. It was Becky's mother who stirred him from the trance he was in. She just came up and wrapped her arms round his neck. 'I don't blame you Richard,' she whispered in his ear. 'She was impetuous and wanted so much to be involved in your world. Finance never suited her.'

He pulled away so he could see her eyes and realised they were Becky's eyes he was seeing. It was Becky's scent he was smelling. 'It is my fault,' he said softly. 'I swear I'll find out who did this and bring them to justice. Thank you for being so understanding. I don't deserve it.'

The two other men in Becky's life, her father and brother looked on at the comfort offered by her mother. Richard stepped forward and faced the two men. 'I won't let you down.' he said.

Edward moved closer and put his hands-on Richard's shoulders, tears in his eyes. 'What did she die for? We have a right to know.'

Becky's father came to his aid. 'He can't say anything Edward…National security…he's bound by the Official Secrets Act.'

'Bullshit,' Edward shouted. 'What could my little sister be involved in which has anything to do with national security…It's all crap and a waste of her life.'

Richard looked away embarrassed at his own silence. A moment passed and then he turned back to face them. 'Are you aware that she had made some new friends in the last couple of months and began to take an interest in Middle Eastern politics?'

Becky's mother said. 'She took a call once from someone.'

'Do you know what they were discussing?'

'I asked Becky, but she wouldn't say who it was…I remember some of her words which I thought sounded strange.'

'What did she say …It may be important.'

'She said that she was uncertain whether she could spy on them. They were not bad people.'

'Do you know whether it was a man or woman she was speaking to?'

'I think it was a woman.'

'What's that got to do with Middle Eastern politics?' Edward said.

Becky's mother raised her eyebrows and stared into space. 'Oh, nothing like that. It was just that I've never seen her speak with so much intensity…Stupid really but I suppose it was a mother's intuition.'

'Intuition about what?' said Richard.

'I can't put a finger on it.' Becky's mother fidgeted with her necklace, trying to articulate what she felt in her bones was right. 'There was something about the caller which transfixed her. Almost like being brain washed…or…'

'Or what?'

'Or she was in love? I know that sounds stupid. She loved you, Richard.'

'It's kind of you to say that but I didn't deserve her love,' Richard said, wiping his eyes with a handkerchief. 'You've been very helpful. Thank you.' He hugged Becky's mother and then faced the two men once more. He repeated his earlier words. 'I won't let you down…I…I promise.' With that he turned and walked away feeling their eyes burning into his soul.

A taxi was waiting to take him to the station, but he changed his mind and decided to visit his mother who lived only a few miles away on the outskirts of the next village. He was not sure why he'd come except that the familiarity of the house was comforting. The flower beds at the front of the house were well tended and that reassured him that his mother had not sought refuge once more in the whisky bottle. Initially, when she heard his father was alive, she'd relapsed but recovered quickly. He'd been shocked and pleased by her response one day on the phone when she said, 'Your father can go and fuck himself...I don't care anymore.'

He found her sitting in the garden dozing in the afternoon sun. For a moment, he stared at his mother and was pleased with what he saw. Her hair was smart, and any traces of grey had vanished. Her make-up was no longer smudged and the shirt and skirt she was wearing was not stained like it had been when he'd last visited the house just after the London bomb. He decided to let her sleep, going into the house to make tea. Inside, the house was better organised and just like the front, the back garden was immaculate and a riot of colour. As he carried the tray, the rattling of the china cups woke her. She started and then seeing Richard smiled. 'You've been to the funeral?' she said, wiping her eyes. Her reading glasses had fallen onto her lap and the book she was reading had fallen awkwardly onto the grass.

'Yes, I have. Understandably, they are all terribly upset, and I blame myself.'

'I blame your father,' she replied. 'If it weren't for him pretending to be James Bond, none of this would have happened.'

'I saw him in Greece. Remember that island we used to go to when I was small -Folegandros.'

'Of course, I remember, that was the only happy time in our marriage.'

'I tried to get him to come home and face the charges laid against him.' He hesitated and looked at his mother. 'I tried to get him to come and see you...I know you miss him.'

'It's too late...I don't want to see him anymore.' She gestured at her garden. 'I'm getting my house in order and the farm. I'm enjoying life...I don't need him.' She winked. 'I've even had a date.'

Richard was pleased. 'That's great news. Who is the lucky man?'

'Someone I met a long time ago when your father was here? He's a nice man. Very handsome. American…Jeb Butler.'

Richard's face dropped, remembering the name from Athens. He was CIA. 'I'm sorry to say this but I don't think you should see him again.'

The colour drained out of his mother's face. He could see she was displeased. 'I'll see who I want to. Nobody is going to tell me what to do…not even you Richard…I've done with all that.'

'It's just that he is probably trying to get at you in the hope that he can find father - he's a wanted man.'

'Your father can look after himself…I don't care anymore,' she said with a defiant stare. 'Do what you like Richard. It won't make any difference to me.'

Although he wanted to protect her, he could see where she was coming from. It was almost a relief to hear because he didn't need to worry about his mother anymore. She was all he had left and now that Becky was gone, he felt a strange kind of liberation. It was not a liberation that he wanted. If no one loved him then he need no longer fear for his safety. He had no one to weep for him.

Seeing his mother had been a coping mechanism which was no longer available in his cold, uninviting flat. His grief lingered beneath the surface never quite emerging into the open. Today, seeing her coffin lowered into the hole in the ground, everything he'd been hiding from bubbled to the surface. He'd bottled it up and now alone in his flat with her presence all around him, the aching pain in his gut became too much to bear. Everywhere he went he could feel and smell her presence; her perfume in the bathroom, her special muesli in the food cupboard, the trashy novel she'd been reading on the night before the bombing. It was several weeks since she'd been in his flat, but those weeks had changed nothing. It was all here.

He was still weeping when his phone rang.

'You think it was me who killed her, don't you?'

He recognised Nadia's accented English straight away. 'You were the only one who knew where I was going. You demanded that I take Becky with me. Why did you do that unless you wanted her killed?'

'I swear in the name of Allah, I had nothing to do with her death.'

'Just before she died, she said tell Nadia I failed – Was she working for you? Why did you want her to go to Ankara with me?

'I've got enemies too,' said Nadia. 'I need to explain.'

'Where? Are you in London?'

'There's a park in the City - Postman's Park - it's called - off King Edward Street. There are some flats overlooking the park. Come to flat seven. Can you come now?'

Richard looked at his watch. It was just after 10pm and he wondered whether he was walking into a trap. Problem was he didn't care. It was worse not knowing.

I'm on my way…It'll take forty-five minutes at least to get to you.'

Chapter Thirteen

London, King Edward Street – September 10th, 2005

The block was in darkness when Richard arrived and the gates to Postman's Park were locked. He rang the bell for apartment seven and waited, turning his back on the glass entrance door and staring at the office buildings across the road, still brightly lit even though the workers were no longer at their desks.

The entrance buzzed, but there was no voice on the intercom. He pushed the door and went inside using the fire exit to find his way to the first floor. Warily, he looked out onto the landing and listened. There was no sound from any of the other flats. Number seven was only a few feet from the exit. Before knocking, he put his ear to the door but could hear nothing. His hands shook, adrenalin kicking in, but this time not out of fear. His hold on the gun tightened. Leaning on the door a little more, he noticed it move.

It was open, only a couple of inches, but just enough to see the flicker of a shadow. He rammed the door hard against the internal wall expecting someone behind. A groan told him his hunch was right. He threw all his weight at the door again, this time a hand fell into view holding a gun. He lunged, yanking the hand backwards against the door. The gun fell to the floor and in one movement he was in the hallway pointing his own gun.

The man he'd hit was not dressed for armed combat. He wore a traditional bisht cloak and ghutra head dress. Around his waist was a dagger with an ornate jewelled handle and curved blade. Not the type of dagger to be used in anger.

'Get up,' Richard shouted. 'Where's Nadia?'

The man glared at Richard. 'I am Sheikh Ranjhirad, a senior official of the Saudi Monetary Authority who will claim diplomatic immunity if you lay any charges on me. I am here to take my sister Nadia back to her family in Riyadh.'

'And I refuse to go.'

Richard turned in the direction of the voice. Nadia was leaning against the wall. Her face was swollen where she'd been slapped. Last time he'd seen her she was wearing a chador and now her dress was short and sophisticated. Her veil revealed all her face and she wore make up, everything that was an anathema to the Saudi culture she represented.

'This man is not my brother. He calls me sister in a tribal way. He thinks that my actions bring disrepute onto my family. He wants me to renounce my freedoms and return to Saudi Arabia.'

Richard pulled the man up by his cloak and thrust him against the wall. 'Did you do this?' pointing at Nadia's bruised face.

'She deserved it. She is nothing more than a whore. Look at the way she dresses.'

He spat at the floor in Nadia's direction and turned back to face Richard, who tightened his grip. Their eyes were only a few inches apart. The Saudi studied Richard's face with an accusing stare, trying to unsettle him 'I know who you are,' he said. 'There is no corner of the earth where you'll be able to hide. You are the killer of Abdul and responsible for the murder of Sheikh Zabor. You will pay by execution. It is too easy to murder you with a bullet. You will be killed like a true kafir and beheaded.' He spat out his words with venom catching Richard on the cheek. Saliva ran down his chin. Richard lifted his fist, but Nadia stopped him, rushing forward and grabbing his wrist.

'Let him go,' she said. 'He is no use to you.'

The Sheikh laughed. 'If you kill me, someone else will find you with blood on your hands.' He turned to look at

Nadia. 'You are insulting your family and the family of Saud. If you continue with your campaign you will die by stoning. The treatment of a whore is all you are good for.'

Richard released his grip, unnerved by the threats but deciding to take Nadia's advice. While still pointing his own gun, he picked up the Sheikh's gun and tossed it over to Nadia.

'Please don't kill him,' she shouted. 'He didn't kill your girlfriend.' There was a firmness in Nadia's voice which worried him. It was as if she was on the Sheikh's side.

He turned towards her while still pointing the gun at the Sheikh. 'He's threatening to have me executed and you want to let him go.'

'Arresting him will achieve nothing. As he said he will claim diplomatic immunity.'

Richard shrugged, lowering the gun slowly. 'Piss off before I change my mind.'

He watched as the Arab left. When he'd gone, he turned to face Nadia, still holding the gun. 'You sent Becky to her death. You insisted. Becky told me to tell you that she'd failed. What was that all about? What was Becky doing to help you?'

'I persuaded her that it was very important to get the Ankara bible. It was the key to peace. She was doing this for me not you. But I didn't know she was going to be killed. I swear I had nothing to do with it.'

'Then who did? You said the Sheikh had nothing to do with it.'

Nadia didn't answer. She stood up and went to the kitchen ignoring his gun. He followed her and watched as she retrieved ice from the fridge and put a compress on her face. She poured herself a glass of water from a bottle on the coffee table. She sipped allowing trickles to run down her chin. Her makeup barely disguised the bruises across her cheeks. He noticed the quality and elegance of her veil,

Black silk embossed with Arabic symbols which he did not recognise.

'I know who killed her. I just don't know their motives,' she said.

Richard could not disguise his anger. He kicked out at the coffee table sending the water flying. 'If you knew then why did you allow it to happen? Becky trusted you – God knows why. You must have known we were walking into a trap.'

Nadia leant forward and picked up the bottle that was spilling water onto the floor. 'I didn't then but I do now. I'll tell you everything I know.'

'Okay, I'm listening. It better be good.'

'Ever since Sheikh Zabor was murdered there has been a campaign in Saudi Arabia by my family to get me to return home. I'm a woman and in Saudi Arabia women are given no freedoms. We are not allowed to drive a car and cannot go out without being accompanied by a man.'

'Yes. I know this,' said Richard impatiently. 'What has this to do with what happened to Becky.'

'I have a rich family and most of them are followers of the Wahhabi doctrine within Islam. You know what that means.'

'I do. It's repressive. Not true Islam.'

'Yes. You're right. It promotes Jihad. Most of all, it takes away the fundamental human rights of women…I will not stand for that.'

'I repeat, what's that got to do with Ankara and the Gospel document?'

'My family have connections with the Taliban and Al Qaeda.'

'You think they were behind the murder?'

'Sheikh Ranjhirad told me that my other uncle - Raashid infiltrated my security and that's how he knew who you are? They are out to get you and the killing of your girlfriend was just the start to make you suffer. It's only a matter of time before they kidnap you and then you are a dead man.'

Richard sighed. He could feel his blood pressure rising. The killing of Abdul would follow him around for the rest of his life, like a fatwah where there was no escape. 'So, have I got this right? You think you were responsible, indirectly for Becky's death?'

'I knew nothing of their plans but since I heard about the killing, I have been using my contacts to find evidence. My Uncle Raashid will certainly provide finance using networks in Bosnia to channel funds to the killers. I have spies in his entourage and have obtained this information.' She stood up and went over to a briefcase, retrieving a large envelope. She spread the pictures out on the coffee table. Richard picked them up one by one.

'They have been recovered from the cameras in the museum. The Turks know who did this but are saying nothing.'

Richard looked at the images with an increasing degree of horror. He could see himself taking photos of Becky. There were two men directly behind her. Several frames had been blown up so the faces of the men directly behind Becky could be clearly seen. Although, there was no picture of the needle another picture showed Becky's face change and the men are right up against her. He cursed himself for missing their attack. It all seemed so obvious from the pictures. He'd need to check his own camera and see if the same faces appeared. At least that would confirm that they were genuine.

'Where did you get these pictures?'

'I have contacts inside Turkey who are open to bribes.'

'These people who take the bribes are the same people who said they'd provide the facsimile copy of the Gospel.'

'Yes, but I don't know who they are. There is a go between in the Turkish government.'

'Do you have a name?'

'He is an official in the Turkish embassy in Tehran - Doctor Mensur Shabak.'

Richard made a note of the name and then looked at the photographs once more. 'Did...' He looked at his note. Did Dr Mensur Shabak know who these men are?'

'Yes, he did.'

'Who are they?' said Richard.

'They are Iranian Revolutionary Guard. Mohammed Ahmed Bakirati is a senior officer in the Qods unit as is the man beside him who is called Hossein Mahmood. They work for a Brigadier General Ali Abu Mantazi.'

'Hang on a minute...this doesn't make sense...Why are IRG officers carrying out Saudi financed murder missions? They are supposed to be enemies.'

'There are groups of Al Qaeda in Iran supported by the IRG. They have a common interest in destroying Israel. These leaders of the IRG do not bring the Sunni Shia differences into play.'

Richard stared at the photographs, his hand shaking with anger. The photos brought back the vivid horror of those few seconds when he'd lost Becky.

'This is not the same group who we are trying to open negotiations with to lift the sanctions?'

'Correct....That's the government and the clerics who are kept in power by the IRG. The problem is that there are different factions and rivalries within the IRG which cripples the government and prevents meaningful reform.'

'And the Saudis want the talks to fail.'

'Yes, that's right. If Iran improves relations with Western powers, it weakens their own position.'

'What do you want to happen Nadia?'

'I don't want revenge for the deaths of Al Qaeda jihadists. You were bringing a document out of Turkey that I asked you to retrieve. Why would I spoil that by murdering your girlfriend?'

Richard pondered her reply. What she was saying seemed to make sense, but Nadia may have been pretending her motives were good. He just couldn't be sure. 'The Americans and I assume the British, want to foster mistrust and cause a fissure within the Revolutionary Guard. If the Guard folds, then the revolution will topple with it.'

Nadia nodded. 'Maybe, but not the Saudi government.'

Richard put his head in his hands and tried to make sense of it all. 'Memories of Abdul's final moment flashed through his mind. Nobody saw him kill Abdul. He'd reported it of course to Rowena, but the only person who saw him was Amira. She even pumped two bullets into Abdul, just to make sure he was dead. She would have reported it to her bosses in Langley.

Then it came to him. 'Harper,' he said out loud.

'What about Harper?'

'He's in the mix somewhere…I can smell his dirty work.'

'What you say is possible, but Harper is only about making money and is nothing to do with the wider impacts of the scroll falling into wrong hands.'

'If it wasn't him then it must be you who is responsible for Becky's murder.'

Nadia scowled, flashing an indignant hurt expression across her face. 'Why would I show you the killers and tell you my plan if I had ordered Becky to be killed. Besides what influence do I have over the Iranian Revolutionary Guard? Like you said, they are the enemies of Saudi Arabia.'

Richard sighed. He knew she was right.

'I need to find those men and find out who is paying them.'

Nadia took him by the hands. 'Those men killed your girlfriend to declare revenge on the murder of Abdul. They want you to suffer.'

'But how did they know I was in Ankara. Only you knew that.'

'Somebody must have been following our conversation. The Sheikh who was just here knew a lot about what was going on. It must be somebody on my side, but I will never know or be able to prove who was responsible for the murder.' Look at me Richard. I would never harm your girlfriend. I'm not a terrorist. I'm really sorry for your loss.'

He could not fail to notice the sincere expression on her face. Nadia's attention shifted away from Richard's gaze. He decided he would get GCHQ to monitor the calls of Sheikh Ranjhirad who had just threatened to have him beheaded.

Nadia had noticed Richard's intense gaze. 'As you can see from the bruises on my face, I have enemies who don't approve of me - a mere woman trying to unite the factions of Islam. My enemies are from my own tribe and hate the Shia. They are friends of Abdul and the Taliban and Al Qaeda and the disaffected troops of Saddam Hussein's army who have been allowed to run riot since the invasion of Iraq. These people want to make you suffer and eventually die. It's not me. '

Richard thought for a moment. He was inclined to believe Nadia and focus all his attention on stopping Harper, who he was sure was mixed up in this somewhere.

'You said Harper was still in Cyprus, looking for the Gospel, I want to talk to him alone.'

Nadia's expression changed and she blushed.

'He's gone and I don't know where.'

'Gone...' Richard shouted. 'He can't have just gone.'

Nadia nodded, holding her head down. 'I'm sorry, we let him go...not deliberately.'

The disappearance of Harper was a cause for concern. After seeing him torture prisoners in Iraq, Richard didn't like the guy. Maybe he would do him a favour and kill his father. Richard sighed, 'I've got no reason to go to Iran except to find the killers of Becky. If I had the original Gospel of Barnabas, I'd have something to trade.'

Nadia put down her ice pack and went over to a table where she picked up a sheaf of papers. 'I've only just received this from Father Christos. He has discovered some more of the knight Robert de Valognes' journal in the archives at Famagusta. It is a treasure trove of material which nobody had bothered to translate because it was filed with manuscripts from the monks of St Hilarion. We may not have the Ankara version of the Gospel, but we can show that there has been real progress in finding the Gospel of Barnabas in its original format, not some doctored Italian or Spanish translation which has all the hallmarks of a forgery.'

Nadia put on white gloves and picked up a document from a tube sitting on the table. Richard could see immediately that it was old. A rolled document on papyrus. 'This is the latest extract from the journal which proves the Gospel did exist.'

'How did you manage to get your hands on the original?'

Nadia chuckled. 'It was easy to steal it. Nobody looks at this stuff in Cyprus and Father Christos is a holy man so beyond question, especially if US Dollars are involved.'

'It's good that you've got the original, it will impress the Iranians if I can give it to them.'

'Yes, that's exactly what I want. You can take this to Tehran as a gift to assist with talks on better relations with the West. But you should also use it to get close to your father.'

Richard looked at the document and nodded approvingly. 'This is pretty impressive, but how am I going to get into Iran with this tucked under my arm?'

'I expect your friends in high places will be able to arrange something, through…what do you call it...the diplomatic bag?' She picked up a small leather bag which was lying beside her on the sofa and after rummaging retrieved a memory stick. 'This has all the documents that Father Christos has recovered. It will be easier to view if you show others on your trip. There is an Ayatollah Arif ibn Amaswari, he is a committed academic on Islamic studies in Tehran university. Please commit this name to memory. You should give this memory stick to him and only him – is that clear?'

'How will I find the guy?' Richard asked, pacing the room, trying to get his head round what needed to be done.

'Don't worry, the Ayatollah will find you.' Nadia replied.

Nadia's motives sounded genuine, but he didn't trust her. She let Harper go for starters. But he didn't care. It wasn't a good enough reason not to go into Iran. If he could deliver the document and help Amira win over the trust of the Iranians, the world would be a better place. If he went in as a diplomat, they would follow him everywhere, but it would be easier to see his father. He also needed a visa which would take at least three months unless he had diplomatic status. He couldn't wait that long. He needed to go now.

Chapter Fourteen

St Hilarion Castle, Cyprus. AD 1103

I am homesick for England but leaving Akila and her children, Masood and Mohammed, who I have grown to love as my own, would be an impossible burden. Just being with them makes me realise how misguided the Crusade is. But that is not the only reason why I cannot return to my native land. If I go back my father will disown me for bringing dishonour to his family. I will be tried as a coward and will most likely be executed for desertion. It is better for everyone if I die here. The monks of St Hilarion do not know about my Muslim family on the island and would also not understand how a Knight of the First Crusade would have such a family. I keep Akila and the children hidden away in Girne where they can lose themselves in the crowd. I visit at night and stay until morning, sometimes longer if there is nobody about who might reveal my secret to the monks.

I am treated with suspicion, but the monks have recognised my ability with a sword and have hired me to build a militia to protect them from marauders. They've seen Crusader ships sail by the island and fear that one day they may invade. They think I am a lonely disillusioned knight who is prepared to reveal the whereabouts and intentions of my former friends, but I would never betray my people. I have no disagreement with them. It is the principle that the Christians have some divine right to destroy the Arabs in their native land. That is what I can no longer sanction. My paymasters assume I am best placed to marshal resistance and repel an attack. They pay well for my services and in doing so give me the means to feed my family.

With no sign of invasion, the militia is rarely called into action, usually to resolve local disputes. Most of my time is spent training the men and organising rotas for guard duty which, as the commanding officer, I am not called upon to do myself.

My days at the castle are spent studying the beautiful gospel I was given by the dying priest in Antioch. To think I almost destroyed it, had not Akila made me realise how wonderful a book it is. For the first time I have seen the words of Jesus in a new light. Not the warmongering of priests of the church promoting a holy war but a message of peace to all men. Jesus would never have supported the Crusades. The gospel dates back to the First Century and was written by a man called Joses - a Greek derivation of Joseph. The author writes with passion in his own hand, how he knew Jesus of Nazareth and how he was given a new name by the Apostles of Christ. They called him Barnabas, the encourager. The opening pages are written as a memoir with justification for the Gospel which follows. Barnabas is referred to many times in The Acts of The Apostles but there is no mention that he might be an Evangelist. As I read the memoir, it becomes clear to me that Barnabas is deeply troubled by the failure of his relationship with Paul. At the start they were inseparable. It was Barnabas who encouraged the Apostles to accept Paul as one of their own when he had his conversion on the road to Damascus. But Paul is rejecting everything that Barnabas has done for him by refusing to accept the words he has written. In my opinion the Gospel is a legitimate record of the life of Jesus, written by a man who was there witnessing his sermons first-hand, unlike Luke. This book is ready to take its place alongside the other Gospels but why is this work singled out for exclusion.

Barnabas describes the argument he had with Paul in great detail and explains that it started over the cousin of Barnabas - John Mark - who had accompanied them on their tour of Cyprus. When the younger man returned suddenly to Jerusalem on family business, Paul accused John Mark of weakness and would not let him return to the mission. This angered Barnabas, but it was the Gospel which was the real reason for their separation. This is not recorded in the Acts because it would have caused a devastating split in the early years of Christianity. I can see that the differences in this text would cause problems, principally because Barnabas did not see Jesus to be the Son of God. He agreed that Jesus was a prophet who said that he was not the last messenger of God. Other prophets would come after him whose message was just as important. I immediately thought of the prophet Mohammed and turned to my Holy Koran to study the references to Isa who is Jesus. I can see many similarities to the teachings of Jesus and Mohammed. When I was in the desert with other Arabs, I found solace in the Holy Koran but that did not mean I would abandon the Holy Bible. Both Holy books have equal value. Barnabas writes that the rejection of his text by Paul was solely to do with the idea that spreading the word of Jesus had to be universal and final and suitable for all men. To suggest that there was someone coming after Jesus would only weaken the power of his teachings and discourage people converting to Christianity. Barnabas continued to be understanding and accepted Paul's point of view. His Gospel would never see the light of day much to his disappointment.

I have found a truly historical document of great importance. It could contribute to peace being declared between the Abrahamic religions.

Chapter Fifteen

Tehran, Iran - September 15th, 2005

For some days, it had been uncertain whether Richard would be granted a diplomatic visa as an unknown professor of Islamic Studies from Wolfson College, Cambridge. The Iranian embassy wanted proof and the leaders of The Faculty of Divinity at Cambridge were refusing to play ball. The forged documents that were eventually produced were a rushed job and he was convinced they would see them for what they were - crude forgeries. He started thinking about how he would enter illegally from Turkey, when, out of the blue, all objections were dropped, and his visa was granted. It was too easy. They must know he was not Professor Lewis Raymond, despite what it said on his passport.

The brown Alborz mountains glowed orange in the early morning sunshine as the British Mediterranean Airways flight descended south west across the city to Mehrabad airport; the glow turning to haze as the grey concrete of the city came into view. Tehran appeared mystical through the polluted mist which hung over the city like a gossamer sheet absorbing the sun's colour. As he stared out of the window at the bleak buildings below, he surprised himself that he was not scared, despite his false passport and worry that his visa had been granted too easily. The sudden change of heart, from a state of hostility at every turn, to his visa nodded through with consummate ease, unheard of according to the Foreign Office, could only mean one thing. It was an excuse to be thrown into jail before the British diplomats could get to him. Despite the risk, he knew there would be more likelihood that he'd see his father if they knew who he was. It would give him the opportunity to present the pages from the Knight - Robert de Valognes' journal as a peace offering. He felt certain that the clerics would be interested in the evidence that the Gospel of Barnabas existed.

At the immigration desk, the Iranian guard looked at him several times, staring at his passport and then back at his face, scrutinising every detail.

'First time in Iran,' the guard said in broken English.

'Yes, I'm hoping to visit all your wonderful sights - you know Isfahan, Shiraz and of course Persepolis.'

'But why do you come as a diplomat? Why not a tourist?'

'Research.'

'Are you sure you're not spying?' The Iranian guard spat out the words and Richard thought of the Saudi who he'd disarmed at Nadia's flat. He smiled nervously choosing to mumble rather than answer the question directly.

'Answer my question. Are you spying for your country?'

'No,' said Richard, more emphatically this time. 'I'm researching Persian History. I'm interested in how the art of the Mughal empire which conquered India in the Fifteenth century was influenced by Islamic art in Iran.'

'Persepolis won't be much help to you in that period.'

'True, but the art of that time references the greatest era of the Persian empire when Darius the Great ruled over many countries. It would be a shame to miss such a wonderful place.'

The guard grunted agreement and looked at him again leafing through the pages of his passport for the fifth time. 'You've been to Saudi Arabia? Why?'

'My studies do not discriminate between Shia and Sunni Islam.'

The guard wasn't impressed by Richard's confident answers. He pulled a disapproving face and typed rapidly into his computer terminal. Drips of sweat trickled down

Richard's back as he thought of all the details of Professor Lewis Raymond's fictitious life, preparing for the questions to try and catch him out. For a brief moment, the guard looked up from his computer.

'Age...Father's name?'

'29...Father is Peter Raymond.'

Several more minutes passed. Some of the passengers standing behind him, mumbled their irritation at the wait and then moved to another queue. At last, the guard picked up Richard's passport and left him standing, leaning up against the immigration desk. He watched as the guard handed his passport to what looked like a more senior official, who had been standing a few feet back from the desk, surveying the scene. He also examined Richard's passport looking back in his direction with an accusing stare. The senior guard nodded, and the guard returned to stamp his passport.

'Your bag will be searched before you are allowed to meet your driver. Recover your bag from the luggage belt and take your passport to a custom officer. Welcome to Iran.' The officer did not smile when he spoke.

'Don't I get diplomatic immunity from these formalities?' he asked, a little irritated by their attitude.

'Normally yes,' replied the guard but you are British and just like the Americans you are treated differently. The guard stared at him; suspicion written all over his face.

The search of his bags was thorough but revealed nothing. The extract of the journal had gone ahead in the diplomatic bag, hidden between the pages of a London School of Economics report on the effects of sanctions on the Iranian economy.

At last, the automatic doors rolled back, nearly an hour after landing, releasing him into the chaotic crowds of the airport terminal building. A bank of drivers displayed banners with names, some written in Farsi and others in English. He scanned them quickly not wanting to catch any

124

body's eye until he was certain that they were the official person from the embassy assigned to meet him. He scanned the placards again but there was nobody displaying his name - Professor Lewis Raymond. He found a corner where he thought he wouldn't be troubled and waited. Standing on his own was not a good idea. Taxi drivers surrounded him, touting to drive into the City for a low price. Some even offered to change currency. A couple of drivers wrestled with each other to carry his bag. He pulled it away from them shouting *boro ke nar*. He hoped that meant *go away* in Farsi. One of the taxi drivers loosened his grip which was a good sign, but the other held on for dear life. Richard felt flustered as he shouted *No* in English and when a smartly dressed man appeared from nowhere, he was relieved.

'Professor Raymond?'

'Yes.'

'Come this way, I am your driver.'

Richard thought it was strange how the taxi drivers gave up bothering him and he was left alone with the man. Maybe they recognised police in plain clothes even if he didn't.

'I apologise for being late,' the man said. 'The traffic is horrendous. Please follow me. My car is not far.' The man spoke in English with barely any accent.

'Are you from the embassy?'

'Not literally. I work for them as a contractor. I studied English in the United Kingdom before the revolution. Embassy officials are reassured that I am not against your country. Those opportunities to study don't exist anymore.'

Alarm bells were ringing in his head. The man seemed too eager with the explanations. 'Can you show me your contract note with the Embassy?' Richard said, 'Just to prove who you are…You can't be too careful.'

'Of course. It is in my car. I'll show it to you then.'

They entered a covered area with nobody around and only a few parked cars. 'It is over there,' he said pointing to the Mercedes standing alone in a corner. An official car, Richard thought. If he were genuine, the embassy would have sent a guy in a Peykan, car of choice for taxi drivers. Richard looked around for an escape route, but it was already too late. Two men emerged from the shadows without warning. Richard swung round and saw his exit blocked by another man. The man he'd been talking to had changed his tune and drawn a gun. Richard didn't know which one and didn't care. A gun is a gun and this guy knew how to use it.

'Get in.' the man snapped.

Richard obeyed, and the car sped off, not in the direction of the centre or even to the embassy but out of town.

'Where are we going?' said Richard, trying to keep a cool head, despite the pistol prodding him in the stomach.

His captor didn't answer.

Richard stared out of the window and said nothing. They were heading out of town, and the Alborz were no longer in view. They must be heading South, he thought. He had no idea what his captors wanted and who they were working for. The only good thing was that they did not look like they wanted to kill him. The car came to a halt about five kilometres off the main highway. They were surrounded by warehouses which didn't look as if they have seen any activity for several years.

'This is what Western sanctions do to our economy.' said the man who met him at the airport. His suit seemed out of touch with the climate and dirty air of the Tehran streets. It reeked of tailored Western extravagance.

'I like your suit,' said Richard. 'Is it from Saville Row?'

The man glared at him and waived his gun. 'Get out,' he said. 'We are not all barbarians in Iran. Education is important. Our Persian heritage demands it.'

'Does your Persian heritage expect you to wear a Western clothing of the highest quality? Where does it say that in Holy Koran?' Richard asked.

'Not another word,' the man shouted, grabbing Richard by his shirt and hauling him out of the car. The punch came out of nowhere and then another one slamming into his stomach. Richard gasped, winded by the unexpected onslaught; bent double as pain surged through his body. The man stopped him falling and thrust him against the car bonnet. 'For your insolence,' the man snarled.

Richard forced a grin, even though his stomach hurt like hell. 'I thought you said you liked the British.'

The man glared but did not hit him again. Dazed, Richard stumbled along the track supported by two of the goons who had abducted him. Inside, the warehouse was empty and dark. His eyes began to adjust, making use of the glimmers of light escaping through cracked metal roofing which cast pencil thin rays onto the dusty floor. He could just make out the silhouettes of five men at the other end of the warehouse

A power switch was flicked, and fluorescent lights stuttered and flashed into action. His senses seemed to exaggerate the whirring sound of the power entering the light tubes before it was drowned by the marching footsteps of men walking towards him.

'Mr Helford,' said the man in the middle of the group, his voice echoing around the empty warehouse. 'I assume this is the name you'd like to be called and not Professor Lewis Raymond.'

Richard stayed silent and scrutinised the man's demeanour. The first thing that came to mind was a younger Saddam Hussein, except this man had a beard. He wore military uniform just like Saddam but bottle green instead of khaki favoured by the Iraqi dictator. His beard was neatly trimmed with flecks of grey softening the severity of his piercing stare. He held out his hand. 'I am

Brigadier General Ali Abu Mantazi, officer of the Iranian Revolutionary Guard and more recently Vice commander of the Quds special forces... Are you familiar with that unit Mr Helford?'

Inside, he'd felt his stomach churn at the mention of the name. If Nadia had given him good information, then the man standing a few feet away maybe be guilty of Becky's murder. He breathed deeply, trying to calm his racing heartbeat.

'It is the section of the IRG responsible for international covert action. Your boss is Qassem Soleimani, answerable only to the Iran Supreme Leader.'

'Exactly right Mr Helford...You are well informed.'

'I've heard your name before from a Saudi woman.'

'I have no connections with Saudi Arabia.'

'But you all hate Israel so you have something in common.'

'That maybe so but Saudi Arabia is my enemy. My goal is to convince the United States that it is the Saudi people who are spreading terror in the world, not Iran.'

'You'll never do that in a million years. What about Iran's support of Hezbollah? They've killed Americans.'

'Hezbollah is not Iran.'

'I didn't say they were...but you're splitting hairs. Your guys fund them and provide arms through your Quds operation. You've also provided safe harbour to Al Qaeda'

'That is ridiculous. Why would a Shiite state support a Sunni organisation? It's not true?'

'Certain intelligent leaders like al Zawahiri in Al Qaeda were impressed with the Ayatollah Khomeini speeches when he was alive.'

'Western commentators were also impressed with the Ayatollah's speeches, but that doesn't make them terrorists.'

Richard nodded agreement, pleased that his point had been taken.

'Who is this Saudi woman who claims to know me?' said Mantazi, changing tack. His eyes darted around the room looking for acknowledgement from his men that he was in control of the situation. The expression on their faces registered nothing, neither good or bad and Richard wondered whether any of them were trustworthy.

'I didn't say she knew you,' Richard replied. 'I said she knew who you were. 'Her name is Nadia Zabor. She was married to the lately deceased Sheikh Mohammed Zabor bin Hitani, billionaire, loved by America, known funder of terrorism?'

'But not loved by Mossad.' Mantazi retorted. He stepped forward and offered Richard a cigarette. When Richard declined, he lit one himself and waited while the other men took it as a cue to follow suit. Clouds of tobacco smoke drifted up towards the warehouse ceiling. At last Mantazi spoke again through the haze. 'What else do you know about this woman?'

'Do *Words of the Faithful* mean anything to you?'

Mantazi eyes widened, leaving no doubt that he knew who they were. He struck Richard across the face. 'Tell me all you know about this group.'

Richard winced, his cheek burning as the blow caught him unawares. The pain from the earlier punch came back into his brain. He bit his lip and felt the taste of blood on his tongue. 'Nadia, the woman who claims to know you, is funding the organisation. It's set up to challenge Saudi Wahhabism. This woman gave me the names of two men who are responsible for the murder of my girlfriend in Ankara and for the baby she was carrying in her womb. Their names are Mohammed Ahmed Bakirati who is a senior officer in the Quds force as is the man beside him called Hossein Mahmood…I think you must know them. She told me they work for you.'

Mantazi looked worried by Richard's reply. He drew on his cigarette and inhaled deeply. He seemed calmer when he spoke. 'I was aware of a hit in Ankara, but I did not know why or who was the victim. I understand your concern and I apologise for striking you. We need to help each other.'

The change of tone surprised Richard. 'What do you want?'

The Brigadier looked again at his men and some of them nodded as if they were giving him approval. 'I know who your girlfriend's killers are, but they do not work for me,' he said softly. 'They work directly for the clerical leaders of this country.' He hesitated, stubbing his cigarette out on the floor. 'Just like your father,' he added with a wry smile.

'What do you mean?'

'Your father is behind the death of your girlfriend.'

'Where's the proof?'

Mantazi turned to the man standing beside him who handed him a folder. 'Here is your proof.'

His hands shook as he opened the folder.

A single picture showed three men standing in front of a modern cream coloured limestone building which he recognised from a guidebook he'd read on the plane, to be the Museum of the Islamic Era, located in central Tehran. A garden in front was being enjoyed by Iranians chatting in the sunshine. No one seemed to notice the three suited men in deep conversation. He recognised them immediately. Blown up, he could see the faces clearly, leaving no doubt who these men were. The two murderers, he'd seen on Nadia's photo were talking to his father. One of the men was shaking hands with his father. A warm handshake with Becky's killers. Even now, he struggled to accept it could be true.

'Help me recover the scroll from your father and discredit him in the eyes of my leader.'

'Soleimani?'

'Yes.'

'I think you are doing this all by yourself.' Richard sneered still reeling from what Mantazi had said about his father. 'You get caught running your own show and you're finished.'

'That's why I want to win the trust of my leaders by exposing the imposter - your father.'

Richard coughed, irritated by the incessant cigarette smoke. 'I'll help you, but why do you care about the scroll or my father for that matter?'

'Your father is giving the clerics something to be pleased about. He had to stop the Ankara document getting into their hands because it would have undermined the importance of your father's work in the clerics' eyes. Proof of Mohammed's succession is a game changer for the Shias. The scroll and the Gospel become irrelevant. That is why he had your girlfriend killed.'

The logic of the argument was compelling. The pain in his stomach where he'd been hit became more pronounced as if his whole body were reacting to the hatred he felt for his father. He tried to stay focused. 'But why does any of this matter to you?'

'It's the supreme religious leaders that we want to destroy with their pathetic religious wars spoiling things for the ordinary people of Iran. I take these risks because of what they did to the MEK.'

Richard eyes widened. 'The MEK - who are they?'

'These men that you see accompanying me are members of the MEK. The letters stand for Mujahidin-e-Khalq, - the warriors of the people. They were the original organisation responsible for deposing the Shah in 1979. But after putting the Ayatollah Imam Khomeini into power, the clerics around him decided that MEK were a threat. They started rounding up their supporters and killing them in their thousands. Those that were left fled to Iraq and were taken in by Saddam. So incensed were they by their treatment that they started fighting their own countryman – Iranians in the Iran Iraq War.'

'That's an extreme reaction, not what you expect from patriots.'

The Brigadier's anger seemed to have subsided a little. 'I agree entirely …I chose to stay and fight for change from the inside,'

'Do you want to work for the British?'

'The momentary change in mood was gone in an instant. The Brigadier walked forward and was only a foot in front of Richard when he slapped him again, this time it was harder, knocking Richard off his feet.

'How dare you suggest that I would even think of spying against my country. I love Iran and its independence from Western materialism. These fighters are not traitors. They are dedicated to establishing a true democracy in Iran, so I am with them.'

Richard rubbed his cheek. 'I'm sorry if I've offended you. Everything you say is very commendable but how do you think I can help you get close to my father.'

'He'll come to us if we throw him the right bait.'

'What bait?'

'You.'

'How?'

'We will arrange everything. Your father will get in touch with you, but on our terms.'

'Are you going to kill him?'

Mantazi ignored the question, lighting another cigarette. The other men had also been chain smoking making the smoke denser.

'I think you know Amira Al Marami?' Mantazi continued.

'Richard shrugged. 'What's she got to do with any of this?'

'She was sent by the American government to open up a dialogue. The clerics are suspicious of her motives and are holding her under house arrest.'

Richard blinked through the tobacco smog and coughed. 'She's been arrested. How could that happen? She's a diplomat.'

'Not in the eyes of the authorities, they have accused her of spying and the US government are not interested because she is not an American citizen. They are denying that she is on a diplomatic mission. Imagine what the US senate would say if they knew that the US government were talking to Iran.'

'So how did Amira get involved?'

'She came into Iran with your father on the pretence that she was going to assist him with the study of the scroll. She was arrested at Tehran university after your father declared who she really was to one of the Imam's interested in the scroll.'

'Are you saying my father betrayed Amira?'

'Yes. He did it to win credibility, so the clerics knew he is on their side.'

Silence. Richard didn't know what to say. The fact that he might betray Amira showed him even more that he might be responsible for Becky's murder.

'So, you see, your father is capable of anything and must be stopped. He is the only one who seems to be able to get through to the Iranian clerics. In Western eyes, he is an outlaw distrusted by the West and especially Israel. The clerics like his CV because the Israelis want him dead.' Mantazi pursed his lips in a self-satisfied smirk. 'He is an old man like many of the Imams, he's been dealing with. They trust him.'

Richard turned to face the Brigadier. 'You've taken a big risk kidnapping me and bringing me here. If some of your friends in the Iran Revolutionary Guard find out what you are up to then you are a dead man.'

The Brigadier forced a smile, stroking his beard to disguise his tense jaw but unable to hide the worry lines creasing his forehead.

'You're right of course, but I love my country more than my own safety. Help us eliminate your father and we will find you the killers of your girlfriend.'

Shouting from outside the building interrupted Richard, distracting Mantazi and his cronies before he could say more. Two men ran forward into the warehouse, bellowing instructions, picking up the Brigadier in one sweeping movement. Richard's taxi driver appeared and begged him to follow. When they got outside into the sunshine, two Mercedes' were already disappearing in a cloud of dusk.

'Get in,' said the driver.

'What's the problem?' Richard shouted.

'Police…There's a roadblock about fifty metres from where we turned, and a police car is approaching.'

The taxi sped down the track for only a few metres before it lurched sharply to the left, disappearing through scrub land, accelerating through the grey parched grasses of the field they'd entered. The driver didn't take his foot off the accelerator.

'They're following us.'

The Police car was less than one hundred metres behind but did not have the power of the Merc or the strength of suspension. When the field perimeter was reached, the Merc bounced back onto the road and headed further out of town.

'We'll take the next exit and circle back,' said the driver.

The police car was still in sight as they turned off and when another one screeched into view, sirens blazing and lights flashing. Richard knew the game was up. The driver was not yet convinced and raced into a village. People watched from their doorways, holding onto their children tightly, as the car rushed through.

Another police car was parked, blocking the narrow street. The driver hit the brake and Richard held onto the seat, braced for an impact against the roadblock. The car skidded, out of control, its wheels locking, hurtling through the dust. It screeched coming to a halt, inches from the Police car.

Commotion and shouting filled the air as more men crowded round the car. They were both manhandled out of the car and pushed over the bonnet. 'I'm a British diplomat,' Richard said. 'This guy was supposed to take me to the embassy.' The Policemen did not understand a word of his English. He felt cuffs tighten around his wrists and then without ceremony he was thrown into the back of a van. The driver didn't join him.

The cell he was in had shackles draping down the wall, although thankfully he was not attached. Excrement and blood were smeared across the walls and the stink of urine made him want to retch. Some of the walls were scratched where fingernails had tried to break away the crumbling plaster. He'd been strip searched and now shivered in just his underpants. By now, they should have discovered his diplomatic status and called in the big boys in the IRG. He hoped it was only a matter of time before he saw the Brigadier once more with an altogether more confrontational approach than in the warehouse, but strictly for the benefit of onlookers. Maybe that was the plan. Get arrested and arrange a meeting with his father and hopefully Amira.

When the door to his cell swung open, he breathed a sigh of relief. His relief was short lived. The man who turned up to interrogate him was from the Iran Revolutionary Guard. He wasn't the Brigadier.

'I am Colonel Mohammed Hassan Albitani of the Iran Revolutionary Guard ...Your passport and visa says that you are Professor Lewis Raymond and have diplomatic status.'

'That is correct.'

'But this passport is a forgery and so I have no reason to accept your diplomatic status. You are an imposter and a spy in my country.'

'I demand to speak to an official in the British Embassy.'

'Do British diplomats come to Iran with false passports? I don't even know for certain that you are English. You might be an American spy.'

London, Vauxhall Cross - September 15th, 2005

Three thousand miles away in the MI6 building at Vauxhall Cross, Rowena looked uncomfortable. She looked up from her papers at Ray Dunmore, one of the Joint Intelligence Steering Committee bag carriers.

'We've thrown Helford to the wolves.' she said, her voice cracking under the strain of what she'd done.

'The Americans don't give a shit about the Helfords.'

'Do we?' Rowena sighed.

'You said it Rowena. We all stood idly by and let Richard go to Tehran.'

Rowena stood up and paced the floor of her office, stopping briefly to look at the view across the Thames. She always did this when she needed to think.

'But Richard deserves better from us - especially after that awful business with his girlfriend.'

'Do we have any intelligence on who might be responsible?'

'Somebody who has got it in for Helford. This is not a politically motivated assassination.'

'CIA perhaps -you know Harper - he's working off the grid. What about the Saudis?'

'Or Al Qaeda in revenge for the killing of Abdul Alim? We haven't got the resources to do a special investigation. It could be any of them.'

Dunmore turned to leave. 'You haven't mentioned Mossad on your list of suspects. You know how vindictive they can be.'

Rowena sighed. 'The list of David Helford's enemies is very long. And maybe we should add the Service to that list as well and Uncle Tom. I don't think I'd shed any tears if there were news about his demise…Shut the door please.'

Dunmore didn't reply, taking his cue that their conversation had come to an end.

Alone again, she picked up the phone and thought for a moment. She'd wanted to make the call ever since it happened but had not wanted to face the truth or consequences of her actions. Her fingers tapped on the keys slowly, without hitting a number. She hesitated and then punched her handset with more purpose. This time the connection was made, and the phone began to ring.

She exchanged no greetings or pleasantries with the caller. 'When I told you to persuade Helford to go to Ankara, I only expected you to lean on him a little. I didn't ask you to kill anyone, least of all his girlfriend.' She paused to listen to the speaker on the other end of the line. Her face turned grey as she heard what the voice had to say. The shock of the reply startled Rowena. She dropped her phone and watched it spinning on her desk before falling onto the floor. For a moment, she forgot that she no longer held the handset. 'Are you sure?' she said, her voice breaking with the shock of what the caller had said. Realising her mistake, she fumbled on the floor for the phone. The muffled voice was still speaking.

Rowena, at last put the handset to her ear. 'I dropped the phone. What evidence have you got to make the accusation?'

She listened intently to the reply and swallowed hard as she let the words from the caller sink in. The printer on her desk started clicking and whirring into life. She muttered something in response and watched as an image emerged out of the printer.

'Oh shit,' she whispered, leaning back in her chair, her eyes drifted towards the blank ceiling, willing the evidence to go away, before staring once more at the photograph.

'This picture changed everything. She blamed herself for Becky's death. She should have stopped her going with Richard. But this picture revealed something new. Somebody she never believed would be connected. It showed three men shaking hands in a street in Tehran.

She knew that two of the men were Becky's killers, not from the pictures in Richard's camera, but from another set of pictures, which Richard had not shown her. It was the third man that shocked Rowena. The man greeting the killers was David Helford.

Returning the handset to its charging port, Rowena noticed her hands shaking. She sat back down in front of her computer and called back the file of photos. She didn't understand why Richard had kept quiet about his real reasons for going to Iran. It didn't matter because she already had the photos he'd seen, provided by the same woman she'd just spoken to on the telephone.

Nadia.

Chapter Sixteen

Tigan, Essex. England AD 1105

Despite my wish to remain in Cyprus until the end of my days, I have had my dreams shattered by the cruelty of rivalries between religions. God must be punishing me for all the blood I have spilled in his name. My beloved wife Akila and little Mohammed have been murdered in a bloody attack that cut me to the very core. I blame myself for ever thinking that they could be safe on this island where there were so few Muslims. Akila never showed any outward signs of her faith, praying only in private and never wearing a veil. Her children dressed exactly like the other children and Akila, while always modest in her attire, remained indistinguishable from the other women. When the people of Girne saw me take Akila on my arm, they knew that to insult her would incur my wrath. They gave Akila and the children due respect as none dared to cross me. It was a stranger who broke that understanding, a visiting soldier from Constantinople, walking around the market square insulting Islam and the Holy Prophet. If I had been there that would have been as far as he would have gone. It will be to my eternal regret that I was not there to protect Akila's dignity and beliefs. She could not allow the insults to go unanswered. It was her duty to her religion to take the soldier to task and defend her faith. For that she was beaten to death and the people who watched refusing to intervene were just as bad. I had won these people's respect out of fear rather than out of friendship. From that moment, I knew I did not belong in Cyprus and never want to set foot on its golden shores again. It is an island paradise and yet to me it is hell on earth. It is where Barnabas, whose Gospel I carry every day, was murdered by the Romans at Salamis and now it is where my beloved Akila and her son have been brutally slain.

At least the witnesses helped me serve justice on the perpetrator, but nothing will bring my adoptive family back to me. I am cursed and now regret ever taking them away from their native land. I must thank God that Masood survived, despite his efforts to save his mother. It is for Masood's sake that I have come to England, whatever my father may think of me, to face the consequences.

It took nearly ten weeks to reach our destination at Tilbury. From there, it was only two days ride to Great Tey Castle where my father lives. The journey across the sea gave me much time to reflect and consider the meaning of the Gospel in my possession. The murder of Akila left me in no doubt that the Gospel is a priceless manuscript which should be put to good use. It will contribute to the breaking down of barriers between faiths. I will ensure that Akila did not die in vain. If I am not executed for blasphemy I will fight until my last breath to end the Crusades and leave the Muslim people to live in peace. Little Masood is growing into a fine young man who proudly calls me father.

I'm writing this while resting in a nearby inn. I can see the castle in front of me as I stare through the window. The inn keeper is suspicious of my intentions but when I offer him a good rate for his room, he gladly accepts. Masood will share the room with me but now he is sitting obediently by my side, taking everything in of his new home. There is a large grin on his face, so wide, if his mouth stretches any more, I fear it will be torn asunder and split his head in two. A buxom wench passes by my table and tries to lure my attention away from my words. She must have also noted my bag of gold coins on the table. I smile but that is all. I wave her away and return to my thoughts. My attention is aroused by a shadow casting over my page. There are two men standing in front of my table, daggers drawn. As I raise my eyes, one dagger flashes in front of *me, burying its blade into my desk. It lands only a breadth from my fingers and one of the men laughs revealing his few remaining blackened teeth.*

'*Maybe you should share those gold coins around stranger if you want to continue to stay in this village,*' *says the other man, wisely holding onto his dagger.*

'*I don't want to fight you, gentlemen,*' *I replied.* '*Please go away as you are blocking my light and I am trying to write.*'

The men did not step aside. I stood up and lifted the table, flinging it in front of the man with the dagger. He fell backwards, the heavy oak table falling on top of his fat belly. I pressed down with my foot while swinging my sword in the direction of the one who laughed. My blade slashed his cheek missing his neck by a fraction. I never intended to kill them. They were just ruffians with no sense of sword play. It would be like killing a lamb compared to the many Arabs I had despatched without mercy. I still see the face of that beautiful boy I killed on the battlefield at Antioch and it still haunts my soul. Turning, I face Masood and smile with him. The fight with the men raised his spirits.

My assailants leave with their tails between their lily-livered legs. The landlord apologises and brings me another flagon of ale as my other one had spilt when I lifted the table. I drink the ale quickly and catch the eye again of the wench. My loins need a woman but not this one. Besides, I have no time for fornication while Masood looks on. He beamed with approval when he saw me deal with the ruffians and I don't want to shatter his opinion of his father.

We step out into the sunshine and look out at my former home. The castle is nothing spectacular. A single stone tower in the middle of the site, rises above the outer stone walls which shield a bailey and chapel and overlook a moat. The drawbridge is down as if they might be expecting me but that is just hope rather than reality. The position of the castle is hardly strategic, some six miles inland from Colchester, it is a second line of defence from invaders. I was not born when the Battle of Hastings was fought but history shows that the castle played no part in the defence of the realm from William, the Norman, the one they call Conqueror. I never saw myself as being French, despite my name and heritage. My childhood friends were of Saxon origin and not wanting to be left out, I made much of the fact that I was born in England and would always follow those traditions loved by the English. Maybe that is why I never got on with my father who was a proud Frenchman, who worshiped the essence of Christianity and respected the authority of the Pope. I think I became a Crusader to please him rather than any profound affiliation to the cause.

My father was a good man who was always fair with the tenant farmers, collecting dues which was only ever what they could afford. He came over to England after the Battle and occupied this castle, which was a fragile wooden structure that provided a home for cattle and a few simple men but was never a citadel. Now it stands majestic as a result of Norman ingenuity and a great deal of stone.

This castle is where I call home. It is where I can lay down my sword and know it will be there for me in the morning. It is where I will sleep soundly. Whatever my sins are, I long to make peace with the incumbents. I long to see my father again and to explain myself and find forgiveness and understanding. I long to be able to give Masood a secure home.

The Gospel I am carrying will be the foundation of my life from now on. I will start an order which will be dedicated to finding peace between the religions.

I shall call it The Order of St Barnabas

Chapter Seventeen

Tehran, Iran - September 15th, 2005

The Colonel stared at Richard intently. He was nothing like Brigadier Mantazi who reminded him of Saddam Hussein. This Colonel was not as ugly and was built like a soldier should be, tall and muscular with a thick set jaw. His hair was jet black and straight with not a strand out of place including his neatly trimmed moustache and beard. His eyes were sharp and blue and his skin free of pock marks. 'Your friends in the Embassy have sold you down the river, Mr Helford. Isn't that what you English say when you don't want to be so blatant. Betrayal is a wretched word, don't you think? I trust Helford is your name?' The Colonel spoke in impeccable English.

'What do you mean?' replied Richard.

'They are saying they don't recognise you as a diplomat. They do know who you are, which I suppose we should be thankful for. They recognise you to be the son of David Helford who is a guest of the Iranian government, who the Americans and the British want extradited on terrorism charges. To add to the mix, we even see that Mossad want him assassinated. All his enemies are our enemies, so we have a lot in common with your father.'

'So, you won't mind me seeing him then, will you?'

'Have you ever met Brigadier Mantazi?' The abruptness and change in direction of the question took Richard by surprise. His ability to lie was never one of his strong points and now he could only garble a negative response.

The Colonel sank back into his chair and sighed. 'You see. How can I trust you?' he said, his tone hardening. He banged the table that separated them. 'How can I let you see your father when you are lying to me?'

'I don't know what you mean' Richard felt his cheeks warm with the embarrassment of his lie.

The Colonel laughed. 'We know one of his men picked you up at the airport and took you to the warehouse where we found you. We know he also visited the warehouse. I have wanted him removed for a long time and now is my chance and you are going to help me.'

'Have you told anybody else about your suspicions?'

'No, I haven't. To accuse Mantazi is a risky strategy. He is not the type where mud sticks easily, I can assure you. He has many powerful friends among the clerical elite whereas I am only a junior ranking Colonel who covets the job as head of Qods in the Republican Guard.'

Richard shifted uneasily in his chair, feeling the weight of the Colonel's suspicious eyes bearing down on him. 'So, what if I did see the guy, what's wrong with that? He's senior to you and can do what he likes. There must be something else you don't like about him.'

'How very perceptive of you.' The Colonel leaned forward, and Richard noticed his scar for the first time, just below his chin; the long straight line of a knife must have just missed his jugular. 'I believe Mantazi is trying to recruit the MEK to overthrow the Supreme leader and take over the IRG. We believe the MEK are being financed by the Americans. They are looking for regime change via the back door.'

'I suppose it's not surprising that you don't like anybody who helped the Iraqis in the war with Iran. Mantazi told me about the MEK. They were patriots of the 1979 revolution who were betrayed by the clerics. They decided to give Saddam a helping hand.' Richard pointed his finger at the Colonel. 'Judging by that cut below your chin, it must have nearly killed you. I would wager you got that in the war.'

The Colonel let out a booming laugh, putting his hands up in a mock gesture of surrender. 'Right again. I congratulate you. Your observation skills do you credit.' The Colonel stood up and walked around the cell. He put his hands in his pockets and produced a silver knuckle duster which he played with like a set of worry beads.

'You're not going to hit me with that are you?' said Richard eying the Colonel's fist cradling the weapon.

The Colonel laughed again. 'Nothing could be further from my mind. My orders are not to harm you.'

'So, what's the story? What do you want me for, if you're not going to beat the shit out of me?' said Richard with more confidence.

'It's really quite simple. The Americans want regime change in Iran. After the mess up in Iraq they want to be more subtle. We call them the Great Satan for good reason. Over many years they have interfered with our affairs. Had they not funded the Mujahedin and the Taliban against the Russians in Afghanistan, Al Qaeda might never have existed to cause 9/11 and the Taliban would never have become a permanent thorn in Western backsides. If the Americans hadn't helped Saddam Hussein in the war against my country - things would be better. It was not the Iranian people behind 9/11 or any other act of terrorism against the West and yet we are labelled as the bad guy in the Middle East while the Saudi's fund terrorism and the Americans and British supply them arms.'

'But you've funded terrorism against Israel and are trying to build a nuclear bomb.'

'And why not?' said the Colonel briskly. 'The Israeli's have a bomb so why should we not be allowed to counter this threat. Have not all your British politicians argued against those who campaign for nuclear disarmament, that we need nuclear arms as a deterrent and that is exactly why Iran also need a bomb, to deter Israel. We cannot negotiate from a position of weakness.'

The Colonel scowled, clearly irritated by Richard's statement about building a bomb. 'Let me tell you something about the Jews which might surprise you. The Iranian people maybe Muslim but we are not Arabs. We are intensely proud of the past before Islam. We only became Muslims in the 15th Century and our Persian heritage is deeply embedded in our psyche. Our great king Cyrus the Great established the first charter of human rights and recognised that people should be able to follow the religion of their choice. He helped the Jews. If anything, we are more like Jews than Arabs. The Jewish people travelled into Judea from the area of Mesopotamia which we now called Iran. We have never persecuted the Jews and do not intend to do so. It is the Israeli and Saudi governments that we have an issue with as they threaten our national security.'

Richard said nothing, standing silent, absorbing the contents of the Colonel's speech. 'Ok, I see the unfairness and the ridiculousness of the American policy but what do I have to do with it.?'

'I am trying to explain why your father is here in Iran. He knows he is an embarrassment to the Western intelligence agencies. This is why he is trying to help break down barriers with Iran, providing links to the Americans and maybe the British to negotiate a better relationship.' The Colonel stood up and put his hand on Richard's shoulder in a gesture of friendship. 'I am a go between you and your father. He wants you to understand him.' He said with a wry smile. 'We want you to help us stop Mantazi and his MEK rebels.'

The suggestion that he might work with his father repulsed Richard.

The Colonel must have sensed his anger. 'He is not a bad man,' he said.

Richard bit his lip. 'Take me to my father and I will think about cooperating.'

The Colonel stood up and walked to the window, squinting through French blinds which covered the glass. 'We will leave in the next few minutes.'

The two Mercs drove quickly until they entered Vali Asr street which cuts a swathe through Tehran. The road is distinguishable by rows of sycamore trees lining the street, a natural break from the interminable concrete buildings. The car had come to a halt; the road clogged and polluted, there was nowhere to go. Two goons, one on each side, prevented Richard from making a dash for it. They still don't trust him, he thought.

The other Merc carrying the Colonel was some four cars ahead. The driver started his siren to get the cars in front to move aside; a pointless exercise as there was nowhere to go.

He peered out of the window and watched the little guys on scooters who were able to keep moving, weaving in and out of the traffic jam. Women walked past them wearing silk chadors and make up. He wanted to get out and walk, but his escorts were unmoved. In air-conditioned bliss, he was oblivious to the heat and smell of the choking smog. Why would he want to walk?

He had lowered his gaze only slightly when the bomb went off, preventing the blinding flash from catching him head on. The noise of the explosion, muffled by the bullet proof security of the Merc, didn't scare him. He remained calm when the car lifted off the ground and the windscreen shattered without blowing through the reinforced glass. A myriad of cracks spread across the windows, obscuring the view while protecting him from the carnage outside. His senses sharpened, focusing on the sounds exaggerated in the aftermath which lasted a matter of seconds. Car horns blaring and the thudding hailstorm of debris raining down on the car, embedding holes and dents into the steel bonnet. He'd been there before and become immune to the horror of terrorist bombings.

The Colonel's car must have been hit. His two guards opened the door, rushing to help their boss. They were looking in the wrong direction and didn't see the two men on the scooter. Richard saw the pillion holding the AK47, pumping bullets in the direction of the guards. He didn't see them fall because the next bullet came through the glass lodging in the dashboard. He dived sideways in the direction of the opposite passenger door rolling off the seat and lodging himself in the footwell. Two more bullets ripped into the seat leather but mercifully missed. They must be kids, he thought, as he pulled the door handle and rolled onto the street. The firing had stopped but the screaming continued. He was alone. In the commotion, nobody noticed him walk free into the crowd. He could see blood on the sidewalk and the Colonel's car upturned a few feet further up the road. The guards were lying in the road, shot in the back but were moving. He noticed a blood-stained silk scarf hanging from a tree and wondered where its owner was. Women with their modesty no longer protected lay in the streets. People were screaming, and sirens wailed while everybody else looked the other way. He didn't look back, half expecting another bullet to find its target.

He kept walking. The problem was where to go from here. He had no map and no money. The Embassy was the obvious choice, but they'd already denied his diplomatic status. Relations between Britain and Iran were difficult. Harbouring a British citizen with a forged passport was not going to help. He remembered the knight's journal had been sent in the diplomatic bag. That was his lifeline. He also realised that the Colonel's men would know which hotel he was booked in. The Embassy was his only chance. He tried several taxis before one agreed to take him, bribing the driver with the promise of a large tip, even though he had no money.

The British Embassy on Ferdowsi Avenue didn't look welcoming. Metal electric gates blocked the entrance, with mythical unicorn horses at each pillar. The soldiers guarding the entrance, surrounded the taxi. They must have heard about the bomb because they seemed on edge, the two at the front cocked their rifles in his direction while the two at the rear opened the passenger door. The taxi driver was blabbering, clearly nervous and worried when he'd be paid. Richard got out, holding his hands up and went to the intercom. One of the soldiers stepped across his path.

'Stop.' he said, showing his nerves.

'I'm Professor Lewis Raymond. I have diplomatic status,' said Richard.

'Papers,' said the soldier.

'Let me speak to the intercom. I don't have my British Passport to show you.'

The soldier spoke into the intercom. The wait for a response seemed like hours. The taxi driver became more impatient for his fare. Richard wondered if they'd plead ignorance, breathing a sigh of relief as the gate began to move sideways.

The soldiers ran a metal detector under the car and when they were satisfied, gestured to the driver to move the car slowly just inside the gate.

An official was waiting, holding a large envelope.

Richard smiled holding out his hand, but the official didn't take it. 'I want to see the head of station.'

'I'm afraid that won't be possible.' The official's eyes shifted away from Richard's stare.

'What are you saying? If he's not available, then let me see the Ambassador. They know I'm in Tehran.'

'I'm sorry sir, I can't do that.' Richard could see from the official's expression that he was uncomfortable being the bearer of bad news. He handed Richard the envelope.

'What's this?'

'There's money, a phone and the document you sent…and a passport with a Visa. There is also a plane ticket. You've got a week…That's as far as we can get involved - orders from the Foreign Office. You're on your own I'm afraid. We've had questions from the Iranian government about the Professor. We are denying knowledge and confirmed the passport is forged.'

Richard was shocked. But he'd half expected it wouldn't be easy. His cover was blown and from that moment, he was persona non-grata. He got back into the taxi and told the driver to reverse. 'Give me money first,' said the driver. 'Pay me or get out of my car.'

Richard retrieved some money from the envelope and waved a two half million Rial notes at the driver. 'This is yours,' he said. 'Just drive.'

The taxi driver snatched the notes and said, 'Where?'

'The University…Oh and find me a hotel first.'

The car picked up speed, dodging traffic with a series of manoeuvres downside streets. Richard had no idea where he was going but he was past caring. The traffic was nose to tail and scary as the drivers jostled for a few inches of vacant road. He decided not to look out of the window and focus on why the Colonel's car had been hit. If the Colonel was acting alone then maybe another branch of IRG were trying to kill him. It seemed to be no secret that he was in Tehran and some didn't like the clerics sucking up to his father. At first, he ruled out Mantazi's men and then he had second thoughts. Maybe they were trying to take out the Colonel without killing him. An elaborate ploy to put the shits up him. He didn't think he was the target. A professional hit would have found their mark and he'd be lying on a slab somewhere. They were kids on scooters. A smoke screen. It was the Colonel they were after. Mantazi was eliminating his enemies, boosting his position. These thoughts rushed through his mind until he saw the taxi driver making a call on his radio.

'Who are you calling?' Richard shouted.

It was already too late. A Toyota Land Cruiser cut the taxi up. Four armed men were in the back of the truck. There was no flashing stop lights. The familiar bottle green uniforms and matching peaked baseball caps were all the taxi driver needed to see to know what it meant. He jammed on the brakes and ran for his life. The soldiers let him go. Richard saw the van approach from behind. He opened the door calmly and put his hands in the air. The back door of the van swung open. This time they cuffed him.

'No more escapes,' said the IRG officer as he clicked the locks into place.

'How is the Colonel?' said Richard with as much genuine concern as he could muster.

The man he was chained to, raised his eyebrows. 'How should I know?' he said with a sarcastic grin.

Chapter Eighteen

Tehran, Iran - September 17th, 2005

The Colonel was alive. The armour plating on his car had done its job although his impeccable appearance had taken a battering. His neatly trimmed beard had been shaved to administer first aid to his tanned features now blemished by two large cuts across his face. The jet-black hair had been crudely cut to make way for several stiches that ran several inches across the left side of his forehead. Richard noticed the Colonel grit his teeth as he sat down, evidently in pain while struggling to arrange his bandaged left arm, secured by a sling strapped across the immaculate bottle green uniform of the Revolutionary Guard.

'Colonel, I'm sorry for your misfortune. I hope you're not angry that I left the scene,' said Richard. 'They were trying to kill me, not rescue me. I still can't understand how I'm still alive.'

'The fact they failed suggests that they only wished to scare you. It was me they wanted.' The Colonel's voice dropped to a barely discernible whisper.

'They certainly scared me, but you are right, I was a sitting duck in there. God knows how I survived.'

'God has nothing to do with your survival. They were amateurs sending out a warning message. The same ones who killed your girlfriend.'

'Do you know who's behind this?'

The Colonel raised his head and looked at Richard. The pained expression lifted. 'We have two men in custody.' His voice became firmer, adopting the authority of a soldier. 'They will confess, but I am sure they are MEK.'

'Mantazi?'

'Yes, but these prisoners will never betray him. They will be executed, and he will be safe.'

The Colonel stood up and began to pace the small cell, limping slightly from the after effects of the bomb. 'Mantazi and his MEK friends want a freer more American friendly government.' The Colonel stopped walking and, after fumbling in his pocket produced a packet of cigarettes. He put one in his mouth and struggled to light it with his one good hand. Richard looked at the brand – Kish, it said in English, with a dolphin on the crush proof packet. A mild cigarette. Did that reflect the type of guy he was, or was he a paid-up member of the sadistic branch of the IRG? The Colonel noticed Richard looking and pushed the packet towards Richard who shook his head.

'More dangerous than living in your country I think I'll decline.'

The Colonel forced a laugh, wincing as he felt the cuts tighten across his face. He coughed, sending smoke rings across the room. 'You know our newly elected President Ahmadinejad is much more willing to throw relations with America and Britain back into the quagmire. He has no wish to even consider some sort of deal. America is the enemy and always will be as sure as night follows day.' He stopped for a drink of water and sighed. Richard could see that the Colonel was irritated by the discomfort caused by his injuries, not wishing to show he was in pain, a demonstration of weakness in the eyes of the Revolutionary Guard. Sitting down again, the Colonel continued speaking, in between puffs on his cigarette. Richard knew all about the shock you feel after surviving a bomb blast and could see it etched all over the Colonel's face. There was an uncertainty in his actions but somehow, he managed to keep speaking. 'So Mantazi is living in fantasy land if he thinks the Americans will be our friends. The President listens to our clerical advisors and has heard about the Gospel of Barnabas. He has sanctioned statements to the media saying that the latest discoveries in Turkey will damage the Christian religion beyond repair. However, he is not stupid enough to suggest that it proves beyond doubt to be an authentic version of the Gospel, because it does not date back to the first century AD. The fact that you tried to steal the proof to bring to us when your girlfriend was murdered is a point in your favour.'

'Except that the murder of my girlfriend disrupted our attempts to bring a copy of the Ankara Gospel to Iran. Somebody from within Iran stopped this happening. If the President supported speaking out, then why would one of his own people stop it?'

The Colonel nodded. 'You are right, but Iran is a complex web of self-interests and rivalries. Nothing is as it seems. We love a conspiracy.'

'I can add to your conspiracy theories.'

The Colonel's eyebrows raised. 'What do you mean?'

'I have seen photographs of the men who murdered my girlfriend.'

'Where are they?'

'In my suitcase which you took from me. You'll find them concealed in the lining.'

The Colonel punched a number on the cell phone that lay on the table in front of him. When it answered, he leant forward to get closer to the phones mouthpiece and issued instructions in Farsi. Richard guessed they'd be ripping his suitcase apart in the next few minutes.

The Colonel shifted in his chair, pulling faces as he moved. 'The pictures may show who was responsible, but they are just hired hit men. We need to prove that Mantazi is involved?'

Or you...or my father, Richard thought.

'Your father is the key to all this. He must convince the clerics that you know where the original Gospel is to be found.'

A uniformed officer entered the room and placed Richard's case on the table. He handed the Colonel a folder which contained the photographs and a single sheet of paper which Richard could see was nothing to do with him. The Colonel picked up the paper and read the contents, his face turning grey with worry. He then turned to the photographs and sighed.

'Do you recognise these men? Are they the men you have in custody?' asked Richard.

'Unfortunately- no, but yes, I know who they are. They are not easy to arrest.'

'Why not?'

'If these are the killers, they are part of the President's personal bodyguard. They are loyal to the President and only work for him. They are untouchable. If they're the murderers, then the order to kill your girlfriend came from the President of Iran himself.'

Richard's mouth dropped. 'I've been told that these men worked for Mantazi.'

'They may well do that as well, but they are also part of the President's bodyguard.'

'I thought the President was on our side. Why would he want the Ankara document not to get to Iran if he's making statements about its authenticity?'

'He is on our side,' said a voice from behind.

It was a voice he recognised. His father's voice.

His father looked the part, as if he'd been an Iranian all his life. It was almost a month since they'd last seen each other and yet in that short time David Helford had transformed into a different person. The white turban and trimmed beard, greying at the edges and the long black cloak, gave him the gravitas of a cleric. The way he spoke suggested authority, as if he had the power of the President behind him.

Richard did not embrace him or extend any sort of greeting. He pushed the photos across the table towards his father. 'Do you know these men?'

David Helford nodded. 'Yes, I know them, but I did not have anything to do with Becky's murder.'

He stared at his father and hated what he stood for. 'Then find out who was responsible. Becky deserves justice,' said Richard.

Helford did not reply. His son could only see guilt etched into his face.

Chapter Nineteen

Yazd, Iran September 18th, 2005

They left Tehran and were speeding South into the vast desert plains in a convoy of three black military Land Cruisers. He sat beside his father in silence; a million questions going through his mind, gripping the arm rests in a futile attempt to quell his anger. His father often looked over to him; their eyes briefly met, and he was sure his facial expression held nothing back. Richard imagined himself, fingers around his father's neck, squeezing the shit out of him. He knew it would be a stupid thing to do but inside his head, he wanted to believe he was responsible for Becky's murder so he would never have a conscience about killing him. He was tired of his father promises and unrealistic ideals, claiming he loved his son but doing nothing to show it. He was tired of his father interfering with his life at every turn. It was as if he was on some crazy adventure where reason had been thrown out of the window. The Colonel sat in front with the driver and another guard sat beside him. Their vehicle was sandwiched between the other trucks loaded with more Revolutionary Guards. Yes, it was a stupid thing to do but he would do it one day when the time was right. He'd questioned whether he could do that when they met in Greece but now since Becky was murdered everything had changed. He just had to find the right moment to confront him, but they'd never been alone for even one minute. There was another thing that stopped him trying. Becky could not die in vain. He had to settle this once and for all and find the Gospel of Barnabas.

The calming influence of the landscape came to his aid. A wasteland unchanged for thousands of years. A desert, nothing like the golden sands of the Sahara; it seemed like a metaphor for Islamic rule. The grey grittiness of the terrain reflecting the gravity of the clerics while the azure blue skies mirrored the colour of the tiled domes of many mosques he'd seen. His eye wandered towards the horizon where the Zagros mountain range provided some relief from the barren views which darkened his mood.

'On the other side of those mountains,' his father said, appearing to read Richard's thoughts. 'There is a green and fertile plain. Shiraz and Isfahan are like the promised lands.'

Richard did not reply. He'd asked earlier where they were going and had been greeted by silence. The only option was to lose himself in thought. The identity of Becky's killers remained his priority. His father had questions to answer. The logic for the murder was indefensible. She never hurt anyone, but he wondered whether he was the reason. Kill her to get back at him. They'd succeeded. He did blame himself but also wondered whether discovering the authentic Gospel of Barnabas had anything to do with her death. He bit his lip but could not stay silent any longer.

'Why did Becky have to die?'

His father turned towards him. For a moment, he said nothing, but Richard could see he was troubled. 'I don't know,' he replied after a prolonged silence.

'But if those guys are personal bodyguards of the President then he is behind her murder.'

'Not necessarily.'

Richard's anger bubbled to the surface. He'd avoided his father's stare, but the answer made him flip. 'What do you mean – not necessarily?' he said, grabbing the older man by his shirt. 'It was your new-found friends here who did it? Those guys in the photo work for the President. They must be involved which means he is also involved. You've met the President, haven't you?'

His father nodded.

The guard sitting next to Richard pulled him away from his father, squeezing his airways in a vicious headlock. He could see his father watching him suffer for a minute before the guard let go, leaving him coughing and gasping for air. He doubled up, panting and trying to speak. Richard mouthed words, but nothing came out. He coughed and felt his vocal cords twitch in the back of his throat. He tried again and this time he heard his voice. 'If the President's men are behind this, then how can you say he is on our side?'

'Because someone is trying to destabilise the government of Iran. The President would never do that, but the Americans would.' His father remained calm, speaking in a measured tone.

The Colonel, hearing what had been said, turned back to face them both. 'Your father is right. I've been treading carefully. I do not want to arouse suspicion until we are sure who's behind the killing of your friend…if those men are guilty – they'll be acting on instructions.'

'From the President?' Richard struggled to contain himself. He stared again at his father. 'How do you know all this? Since when were you an expert on Iran and speaking Farsi to boot.'

A faint smile crept across his father's lips. 'You remember when you were a kid and I was stationed in Riyadh, I learned Farsi at the same time as I learned to speak Arabic.'

The time they'd spent in Saudi Arabia flooded back into his memory. Richard remembered being lonely with no schoolfriends to hang out with in Riyadh. It was an awful repressive city and in desperation, he'd learnt Arabic. His father changed, working all the time. If he'd succeeded in pinning his father down for a few minutes, he'd try and speak a few lines while his father listened. They weren't happy days, just days of interminable boredom.

'Where are we going?' he said, changing tactics. 'Why won't you tell me?'

'I don't suppose you would have known even if I had told you. We are going to Yazd.'

'Where?'

'Yazd is a holy city but not because of Islam. It is a centre for the ancient religion of Zoroastrianism. It is older than Islam, Judaism and Christianity. Its principles are similar. All the major religions are in its debt. Zoroaster defined the meaning of good and evil.'

'I'm sure it is fascinating but what has that got to do with us?'

'In good time...all in good time.'

It took most of the day to reach Yazd. At first, it just seemed like a modern city, overwhelmed with too many cars before the older city emerged. It was nearly evening, and the coloured domes of Yazd's mosques shone in the copper sunlight, rising above the sandstone shades of peoples' homes. He could see tall wind towers everywhere which he guessed would channel air into the burning streets below, giving the people some respite from the stifling heat. In the centre, soaring above the old city was another mosque distinguished by two oversized but proportioned minarets which dominated the skyline.

The cars headed for the landmark and pulled up in a square. They could travel no further as they were surrounded by mudbrick walls framing narrow passageways. Climbing out of the Land Cruiser, Richard noticed the fear on the faces of people walking in the early evening sunlight. The uniforms of IRG were well known to them. The people were cowering in their effort to avoid eye contact. He noticed women tightening their veils, avoiding the faintest glimpse of a hairline. Both men and women stepped aside as they walked into the maze of lanes. As they got deeper into the labyrinth, the people in the streets melted into the alleyways and disappeared. Nobody wanted to be anywhere near the most hated militia in Iran.

But the guards did not follow, taking up positions blocking the exit routes. They were alone standing under a covered walkway. Despite the crude methods of construction, the arch was symmetrical with natural simplicity emphasised by the materials used. The walls were plain with a textured roughness to the surface, created by straw, mixed in the clay. At one end of the walkway, he could see a carved painted wooden door, dazzling turquoise against the earth coloured back drop of mud brick. He followed his father as they walked towards it. The frame caught Richard's eye because of the Koranic scripts carved around the door. He couldn't understand the words but felt compelled to try and find meaning in the elegant flowing letters. Large metal door knockers hung from each door panel. The knockers were different designs and he wondered why they needed two.

'The other one is for females,' he said, reading Richard's mind once more. 'It enables women to anticipate whether they should wear the veil or not when they answer the door.'

His father took hold of one of the knockers, applying some weight causing the door to move ajar. He pushed it further open before stepping out of sight. Richard followed.

They were in a garden, built with the precision of a draughtsmen. An oasis, providing relief from the sun-bleached clay of the city. An Islamic paradise garden, with geometric water channels trickling passed bougainvillea, scented herbs and trees laden with oranges leading to a central shell shaped fountain surrounded by an intricate mosaic. A tiled roof provided shade on one side. He wanted to linger for a minute or two to absorb the calming effect of the beautiful design, but his father had other ideas, crossing to the shaded area. The walls of the loggia were tiled in bright yellows and blues punctuated by ornate

designs of flowers and birds. It seemed a far cry from the
dour bleak message of Iran's clerical rulers.

A woman appeared at the entrance immediately
opposite. She was dressed head to toe in a black chador.
His first thought was of Becky, appearing like that in
Cyprus, but that memory faded just as soon as it appeared.
He recognised the woman across the yard. He remembered
how he'd first set eyes on her. Not in a Chador but wearing
black; a woman in mourning. A woman mourning for
Masood.

Amira.

The intensity of that first meeting, when he'd told her of
Masood's death, remained vivid in his mind as if it had
happened yesterday; how captivated he'd been by her
presence, how he could focus only on her eyes, lips and
hands.

Just like now.

He moved slowly towards her and seemed vaguely
aware that his father was speaking.

He took hold of her hands. The vulnerability had
returned. There was no more hardness, like he'd seen in
Crete. Her hands were shaking.

'It's good to see you Richard.'

'What have they done to you?' he replied. She bowed
her head and said nothing. He turned towards his father.
His anger returning. 'Is there no end to where you'd sink
to? How dare you betray Amira just to improve your own
credibility with the Iranians.'

'I'm alright.' said Amira. 'It's not your father's fault.'

Her face seemed to be more animated as if she weren't
troubled after all.

'I don't understand.'

'The interrogation was hard because they didn't trust me
at first, but they do now.'

His father spoke. 'We had to let them interrogate Amira.
She agreed to this. There was no coercion. I just had to win

their trust. I told them to bring her here on house arrest. She would help me with a lead I've discovered.'

'But you told them she was CIA.'

'No...That's not true. I told them she was a religious historian studying ancient religions like Zoroastrianism.' The older man stared at his son, concerned that he might not believe his explanation. 'I told them to let her help me. This was a compromise solution. I brought you here so that you can see that she is okay and that she is not imprisoned.'

Richard turned towards Amira. 'Is this true?' he said.

'Yes, it is true. The guards were suspicious. I convinced them that I was studying Zoroastrianism. I told them that I had a theory which might connect Barnabas to this ancient religion.'

'But you're here to try and reopen talks and improve relations with Iran. How does studying an ancient religion help?'

'Because it is a way into their mindset. This is a deeply religious country, ruled by clerics. The existence of the Gospel of Barnabas and the scroll you found on Crete are important.'

'So, you are not under house arrest?'

His father answered the question. 'We have removed the guards thanks to the Colonel.'

Richard opened his mouth to speak when gun shots stopped him in his tracks.

Amira's face changed. It was if the sound of gunfire shook her out of a trance. She turned and raced to the door. 'Follow me,' she shouted.

His father pointed towards Amira. 'Do as she says?' There was urgency in his voice, but no sign of fear. The Colonel appeared at the door; his gun drawn. The worry on his face seemed more real, unlike his father.

'Get out, now.'

They followed Amira down steep stairs which seemed to be going underground. The air became cooler. The first passage they entered opened out into a large dome like structure, as if they were in a giant underground beehive. There were several exits out of the room, not corridors but narrow tunnels. A man was waiting beckoning them to follow into one of the exits. He carried a lamp to lead the way, but there was barely any light and it was a struggle to see where the turns were. There were exits from the central tunnel every few metres. Damp air clawed at his throat and the narrow low ceilings made it impossible to stand straight. The sound of running water teased his senses. Was it getting closer? He breathed in deeply as they turned into a larger chamber. The room appeared to be a hammam, fully tiled, with a bath in the centre. On the other side, he could see steep steps back up towards daylight. His father was shouting in Farsi to the Colonel. Amira looked back at Richard before ascending.

'Who are we running from?' He shouted in the direction of his father.

His father said nothing. They emerged into another courtyard of a different house, less grand than the one they'd left. It was surrounded by rooms on all sides, but the central area was barren of any flowers, unloved and deserted. Although the sun was disappearing, the stifling heat burned his face, exaggerated after the damp cool air of the tunnels. Richard shielded his eyes from the sunlight and followed Amira and his father up some more steps, which were tall, probably twice the height of a normal step. They entered one of the rooms relieved to be away from the sun.

'To keep the scorpions at bay,' his father said.

'Never mind the fucking scorpions - tell me who we're running from...Is it Mantazi?'

'We expected Mantazi to follow but the Colonel doesn't think it's them.'

'Then who?'

'Al Qaeda.'

'What do you mean? There is no Al Qaeda in Iran? They are enemies.'

'Not to everybody in Iran. There are factions of Shia Islam that supported the Mujahidin in Afghanistan.'

The Colonel shouted with increasing desperation into his radio. Interference crackled across the airwaves.

'Will they find us?' Richard said.

'I don't think so,' said Amira. The tunnels we've been through are called qanets. They're ancient water supply systems controlled by gravity. They feed nearly all the houses. Most people think they are filled with water but in the height of the summer supplies are low, so it is possible to use them to pass through. Even if they do find them, they won't know which house we are in.'

His father and the Colonel didn't seem sure they were safe. They argued in Farsi and Richard guessed they were angry that the jihadists had found them. Amira ignored the two men and stared out of the window leading to the barren secluded garden.

'What the fuck is going on?' said Richard, coming between the two men.

His father turned to face him. 'We've got to leave and get help. The Police will have heard the shots. I want you to stay here with Amira where you'll be safe. We'll draw the fire away from you.'

He watched his father open the door and, with gun cocked, move out into the street. The Colonel followed, appearing more nervous than his father, holding a pistol in his one good hand, as the one injured in the blast was still heavily bandaged. When they had gone, Richard bolted the door and walked over to where Amira stood. 'I wish I understood what's going on,' he said. 'I don't know who is on my side.' He stood behind her wanting to reach out and hold her. 'If these are jihadists maybe they want to kill us in revenge for me killing Abdul.'

'Yes,' she said. 'And maybe because I helped you do it - maybe they want me as well.'

Amira took his hand, leading him to a table and chairs at the other end of the room and as far as possible from the door that led to the street. 'Come let's sit here and talk. I've seen the document.'

They were in an alcove which opened towards the garden. The stone walls absorbed the heat of the day, but the sun was already losing its power, disappearing fast, casting shadows across the dried-up fountain in the centre. Richard wondered who once lived in the house which, despite neglect, maintained a timeless elegance.

'There are other pages of the journal which you haven't seen.' he said. 'The knight describes how he recovered the Gospel from a dying priest in Antioch. We know Barnabas spent some time preaching in Antioch with Paul.'

'What else does it say?'

'The dying priest held an icon in his other hand. The knight doesn't say who is depicted on the icon, but it is reasonable to think it might be Barnabas?'

Amira's eyes widened with excitement. 'You mean Masood's icon,' she said.

'I think so, an incredible coincidence I know. It seems very unlikely.'

'Remember I told you in London that Masood and your father became friends. Your father is convinced that the icon proves that there is an original Gospel of Barnabas and that the sixteenth century forgery is a red herring. Your father and I have been searching for more evidence here in Iran.'

'Why would you choose Iran?'

'For your father, it is a question of safety from those trying to kill him, but for me, I am here to find the truth about the Gospel and win trust with the Iranian government by helping them prove the legitimacy of the Shia line. It was something that Masood once said to me about the icon. He said that the artist was Persian.'

'But the Persian empire was pretty big. It doesn't mean it came from Iran.'

'That's true but I found something else.'

'Tell me.'

'The icon isn't first century like Masood thought. It's much later in the tenth century at the time the knight lived. It's reasonable that the icon found by the knight on the dying priest is the same as the icon I have.'

'It's possible,' said Richard, with a sceptical glance away from Amira's excited eyes.

'There is another connection. Masood once said to me that his mother was a Druze and his history dates to the Crusades in Antioch. It was on his father's side that he became a Sunni Muslim.'

It was Richard's turn to be excited. He remembered some of the words in the knight's journal.

'Akila was a Druze.' he said. 'The journal says she was, so it fits. She became the knight's wife after he became a Muslim. It's in the other bits of his journal you haven't seen...She was murdered in Cyprus.'

Amira's excitement faded and she looked down at the floor. She let out an anguished sigh and stretched out her legs. 'The icon meant everything to Masood,' she said, her expression becoming more serious. 'It's priceless, but he would be disappointed to know that it didn't date back to the first century and so didn't belong to Barnabas himself.'

Richard thought for a moment and then spoke. 'So where does all this lead?'

'It's why I'm here in Yazd,' she replied. 'Ever since Masood died, with all that has happened since then, I have decided that the answer to the icon lies within its work of art. Before I came here, I took it to an expert in London. The picture is painted on ceramic tile and the expert dated it to the Seljuq period. There is calligraphy in the picture which is of a similar style similar to Holy Korans' dating to the early eleventh century. It suggests the picture originates from Iran.. But something else confirmed it beyond doubt. The expert separated the painting from its silver case.'

'And what did you find out?'

'On the back of the painting is an inscription. It is a winged bird, like an eagle with a human head of a bearded older man. Something I've seen before on the walls of Persepolis, here in Iran. It is the symbol of Zoroastrian religion. There is also a painter's mark. The expert was able to match it to the author of calligraphy in an ancient Koran held in the museum in Tehran. The painter was from Yazd.'

'But Barnabas never came to Iran?'

'But I think the knight did because of the Zoroastrian symbol I found on the picture.'

'You can find that symbol all over Iran, why here?'

'I think the knight came here. I can only speculate but I think it was to do with Akila's family.'

'But the last record we have shows that he went to England.'

'Yes, it's curious that the journal from England was found in Cyprus.'

'Could he have come back to Cyprus?'

'Yes, but we have no record why he left England or if he did actually leave. I must admit that issue is confusing me.'

'Don't let's worry about that for now. Go on telling me what you found out about the painting.'

'Okay,' Amira smiled. 'This is really interesting part. I have had the painting x rayed and there is another painting underneath.; a more typical Greek style view of the saint.

Richard interrupted. 'So, if there are two paintings then it is conceivable that the second one was added after the knight took the icon and gospel from the priest in Antioch.

'Exactly,' said Amira, her eyes lightening up at Richard's new-found enthusiasm. 'The painting that we see on the icon is Persian. The Zoroastrian symbol proves that the artist may have been here in Yazd because it is the home of the ancient religion. I think the knight came here in tribute to Akila, and had the image changed so it had a Persian rather than an orthodox, Christian image. Although the knight met Akila and her children during the siege of Antioch, I think she was a Persian. Most of the Druze settled in Syria and yet in ancient times there was a small community in Iran because the Druze version of Islam originates from Shia religion.'

'How do you intend to prove your theory?'

'I have been looking into the records here in Yazd of the painter in the hope that I might find a connection. But I've found nothing.'

He sighed. 'A dead end then.'

'Not entirely. I found a story about disaffected Crusader Christians converting to Sufism. There was an increased interest in Sufism in the time that our knight was alive, and he may have come here with his disillusionment with the Crusades. Sufism is a spiritual religion where any elements of egotism are abandoned. Our knight was a beaten man. He wanted to end his days in peace not war.'

'Aren't you clinging on to straws here Amira?' he asked, sounding frustrated. In his mind it was another dead end and he could not disguise his irritation. 'I don't mean to be dismissive of your work because it is all very interesting but since Becky's murder, I don't really care about anything other than finding her killers and doing something about my father once and for all.'

'Doing something?'

He avoided her gaze, looking out of the window. He said nothing. 'My father is a bastard. I hate him. How he has betrayed my mother, his country…' He hesitated. 'You know what he's like.'

169

'He's an idealist and he loves you.'

Richard laughed. 'He no more loves me than Bush loved Saddam. If he loved me why would he get Becky killed?' Richard swallowed hard to keep back the tears. 'You know what really bothers me more than anything.'

'What?'

'I am too much like him. I'm incapable of love and treated Becky badly … just like he treated my mother.'

Amira touched his cheek with the back of her hand. He responded, running his fingers down to her wrist.

'I'm glad you are here,' she said. Her voice was soft and comforting.

He forgot everything at that point. It was like they were suspended in time with no understanding of the danger all around them. 'I'm sorry I got agitated, I just want us to get a lead and you have barely anything to go on.'

'I have belief, Richard. God will look after us if we have right on our side.'

Richard bowed his head in meek acceptance of Amira's calming influence. He hurriedly changed the subject. 'Have you tried to discuss peace with the government yet?'

'No – but my motives are genuine. My studies into these ancient documents were our way in.'

Richard looked away from her eyes. He regretted the offhanded way he had dismissed Amira's research. 'You know my father. Was he involved in Becky's death?'

Amira reflected his sadness. 'I don't know…Your father is a complex character but the idea that he might arrange for his son's girlfriend to be murdered is too horrible to think about. I don't believe he did it. But you can't dismiss the awful things he's done to stay alive.'

There were tears in Richard's eyes when he spoke. 'She was carrying his grandchild.'

The shock on Amira's face told him she didn't know. 'He would never have that on his conscience I'm sure,' she said.

Richard opened his mouth to speak but the moment was shattered by an explosion. The detonation blew the door off its hinges and the surrounding mud walls caved in. They had no time to react. Clouds of dried mud flew through the air. The blast of air knocked them both off their feet. If they'd been behind the door, they would have probably been killed. Three masked men burst through the smoke and dust.

He'd seen them in Iraq, lying dead in the dust after a shootout with the armed forces. Now it was his turn to die. He looked across at Amira, who was unconscious. At least she wouldn't feel anything.

Richard put his hands up and waited for the bullet. Something hit him in the back. The pain was excruciating; his head spinning like a lead weight, his legs crumbled to jelly.

Chapter Twenty

Natanz, Iran- September 19th, 2005

There was no roof on the building. A square stone structure with arches on all sides. Some of the arches had collapsed and he could see evidence of work going on to repair the damage. In the centre of the ruin was a brick-built pit. Flames were flickering from its centre. Four guards huddled by the fire. It might have been a mosque at one time, he thought. He looked up through the arches and up to the sky. The mountain range, framed by the curved walls, could only be the Zagros, because the summer heat had melted the snow on the peaks, suggesting they were somewhere south of Tehran. The night sky was claiming the last minutes of daylight and heat, replaced by the desert cold, penetrated his bones like a virus; his body shivering out of control. He wondered whether it was the cold or fear that made him shake. He tried to move his body a little, pushing his back into the wall he was leaning against. His legs were untied but his wrists were shackled to the wall. When he stretched, pulling his buttocks up a little to relieve the pain in his back, he winced as the straps tightened round his wrists. reminding him of his predicament. Apart from the men by the fire, another guard stood only a few feet away, pointing a gun in his direction, glaring eyes suggesting he would rather kill him now than waste time sitting here doing nothing.

He hadn't seen Amira since they had been snatched in Yazd. The journey had taken several hours, bumping around in the back of a van with no windows. When they stopped to have a smoke or go for a pee, they left him in the van forcing him to wet his pants. He must have passed out toward the end of the journey because he remembered them dragging him through the dust but had no recollection of getting out of the van. At this point they doused his face with water and let him drink. If these were jihadists, they were well informed, knowing exactly where they'd been hiding. The old city was a maze and yet they'd blown up the right house. Somebody must have told them where they were.

He shouted, 'Where have you taken the woman? What do you want of us?'

The guard looked blankly at him and shouted something in Arabic which he thought told him to shut up. It wasn't Farsi which suggested he wasn't Iranian. Two of the other men around the fire stood up and came over. The tallest issued instructions, signalling to the other guard to help him stand up. The moment he applied pressure onto his legs, they buckled under the weight, turning to jelly. As he stumbled two of the guards supported his weight under each arm, enabling him to stand.

The man in charge moved closer and cut the shackles that tied him to the wall. 'Can you stand on your own?' he said in English in a tone that seemed conciliatory rather than aggressive. 'I apologise for the way you have been treated. My name is Zafar. Please accept my deepest apology. This is not the way a Persian would treat an honoured guest, but the men they've given me are Afghans.'

Richard pushed the men away and tried to stand without assistance. As the blood began to flow though his veins once more, his legs seemed firmer. He staggered but managed to remain standing. He looked at the leader and saw a man marked by the ravages of war. His features were pitted with scars, one ran down his cheek bone and curled behind his ear and another ran across his forehead from end to end. His arms were exposed revealing more marks, blotching his skin with the effects of shrapnel wounds.

'The war in Iraq has taken its toll on my beauty.' the man said with a chuckle, noticing Richard staring at his scars. His face widened into a smile revealing teeth overly white and false. 'I am lucky to be alive, not like the thousands of martyrs whose pictures you see lining the streets.'

'It was a terrible war,' said Richard.

'Prolonged by the CIA supplying arms to Saddam Hussein.'

The conversation was unnecessary, but in those short exchanges a rapport built between them. Richard wondered how he learned to speak English.

'Do you know what this place is?' said the man.

'No - is it an old mosque or a caravanserai?'

'No this is not a mosque. There is a mosque behind us.' He pointed to the building about two hundred metres behind them. 'That building is a Sunni mosque, only one minaret instead of two which the Shia's use. You see we argue about everything, even how many towers we should have, so what use are we against our real enemies - the Israelis, the Americans and of course your countrymen - the British?'

'The British did lots of bad things in the past but that is behind us now. Iran should look to the future and not dwell on the past if it is going to succeed.'

'We don't see it that way. Besides, I don't care what happens to Iran. If you were so sincere you would not sell arms to The House of Saud.'

Richard shrugged. 'You are Al Qaeda, that's why you like the single tower mosque. Look whether we have sold arms to Saudi Arabia doesn't really matter here and now. It doesn't explain why I've been abducted and brought here. This is the third time I've been picked up since arriving in Iran. It seems that every faction in Iran either pro or anti regime is after me for some reason or another.'

The man laughed. 'I told you we are always arguing amongst ourselves, but I am different. I have simple needs not related to who rules Iran. Just because I am Sunni in the

Shia state of Iran does not make me Al Qaeda and nor are my friends here.'

'So, what is this place?'

'It's an old disused Zoroastrian fire temple. But we will not stay here. We are taking you to the mosque and then your questions will be answered.'

The name made him think of Amira and the Zoroastrian symbol she'd found on the icon. Now that he was standing, they allowed him to walk freely the few metres to the mosque. They soon reached an open square, laid out for running water with yellow flowers in symmetrical beds. A few people sat under lights which illuminated the garden. They chatted to each other, choosing to look the other way at the sight of the guns the men were carrying. They must have seen it all before, he thought. To be fair, his guards were not threatening, pointing their gun barrels at the ground.

Immediately in front of the mosque was a giant tree, flood lit to make it stand out.

'That tree's older than the mosque which makes it more than seven hundred years.' said Zafar. The entrance was not as ornately beautiful as the mosques at Isfahan he'd seen in picture books but retained the classic symbols of Islamic art with calligraphy adorning the walls and turquoise and blue tiles. Inside the interior was more austere and in need of work. Some of the calligraphy designs were illegible but the elegance of the architecture remained. Richard noted the dome was a pyramid shape which would make it easier to pinpoint where he was if he ever got out of the country. Crossing the courtyard, open to the elements, they entered a large ante room with a ceiling

'Where is the woman?' he shouted.

'I'm here.' said a female voice.

He looked towards the sound. Amira appeared from behind a wall. She was no longer wearing a chador but wore a patterned scarf and long bright blue coat and jeans.

'Hello Richard, these men are my friends.'

Chapter Twenty-One

Natanz, Iran- September 19th, 2005

'I'm sorry, Richard for keeping you in the dark.' Amira's apology lacked sincerity, but he didn't care. She looked at him with her usual beguiling beauty and the innocence he fell for every time. Her smile lacked the tenderness of their previous encounter when they'd discussed the background behind the icon. He wondered whether her frosty response was for the benefit of his kidnappers rather than trying to upset him.

'These so-called Jihadists are working for us,' she said with a smile. 'That's why they speak such good English. They're not Al Qaeda and not out for revenge for the killing of Abdul.'

The relief he felt was tinged with annoyance. 'Did you know they were going to take us?' Richard asked. 'I saw you were unconscious.' His expression hardened but he thought he saw guilt in Amira's eyes.

'Yes, I did know,' she replied, flashing Richard an apologetic glance. 'I must admit the explosion in Yazd was more than I bargained for. A bit too convincing don't you think? We needed to convince your father and the Colonel that we were being attacked by jihadists. We didn't know your father was going to make a bolt for freedom to get help.'

'I thought you were working with my father not against him.'

'I was, but I changed my mind during the interrogation. I was interviewed by an Ayatollah who I want you to meet now. He doesn't speak English, but we have an interpreter to help.'

Two men entered the room before Amira could answer. He didn't need to guess which one the interpreter was. The Ayatollah held out his hand, staring at him through thick lensed, slightly tinted glasses. He wore a black turban and long black cloak over a brown smock. He'd read somewhere that the black turban signified that the cleric was a descendant of Mohammed, albeit several times removed. Most of the man's face was covered by a long greying beard, trimmed without being neat. His forehead was lined with deep set wrinkles suggesting a studious outlook to life.

Richard bowed and offered his hand in return. The cleric took it and then embraced Richard kissing him on both cheeks.

'This is…' said the interpreter, looking nervous in the presence of a religious leader. 'Ayatollah Arif ibn Amaswari.'

The name rang alarm bells in Richard's head. The name that Nadia had supplied had found him, just what she said would happen. He remembered the memory stick sewn into the lining of his jacket.

Zafar and two of his men carried some chairs into the room. Dim electric lights barely illuminated the faded calligraphy adorning the cracked stucco walls. The Ayatollah was the first to sit and with a wave of his hand indicated Richard and Amira should also sit. Zafar lit candles to increase the light available, casting shadows across faces, creating eerie patterns thrown across the floor.

'We have seen the document.' said the interpreter. 'It makes interesting reading.'

Richard removed the memory card from the lining of his pocket and passed it to the cleric. 'This has copies of the other documents we found. It will add to the certainty that the Gospel of Barnabas does actually exist.'

Richard waited for the translator to catch up. The Ayatollah listened, clutching the memory stick, nodding his approval as his words were relayed in Farsi. 'There is also evidence that the gospel discovered recently and held by the Turks authenticates the Holy prophet's wishes, praise be upon him, about the succession. If the document is authentic, and we believe it is, this is a clear view of the Holy Prophet's intentions regarding Shia lines of succession. We were going to let you have this proof when my girlfriend was murdered in Ankara. I have photographic evidence that the persons responsible for the killing are soldiers in the Revolutionary Guard.'

The Ayatollah's face clouded. Indignation was all too evident in the fast-staccato words he spat in the direction of his interpreter who appeared visibly shocked by the barrage of abuse coming out of a mouth of a holy man. 'We are concerned, although not surprised, that someone from our own country would seek to block this truth which our leaders want exposed to the world.' The translation more subdued than the vitriolic outpouring from the Ayatollah's mouth.

'Will you help me find the perpetrators?' asked Richard.

'The Ayatollah is sorry for your loss, but he has no power to influence Iran's leader - not the President, not the Supreme leader. We cannot help you. The Ayatollah is an expert in Islamic studies but has no influence over the government. He is here because he is interested in the historic importance of the documents. He believes that the Gospel…'

Amira interrupted. 'But the Ayatollah *can* help us gain access to documents held in a mosque in Natanz…I don't mean this one, a Shia mosque which exists outside of the town.'

'The painter of the icon?' enquired Richard.

'Yes. You're right. It's dedicated to a Sufi who was both a poet and a painter- a certain Babu Rfhan. It is possible that our knight Robert de Valognes met this Sufi. The Sufi kept a journal of his life and the original is preserved in this mosque. We may find evidence of the knight's visit.'

'If this leads to the Gospel,' said the interpreter after conferring with the Ayatollah once more. 'We will be eternally grateful, but we must carry on with great caution because of those responsible for withholding the Ankara gospel. They are against us and your father is working for these people.'

While they were talking in English, the interpreter conferred with the cleric. After several minutes, the cleric stood up and bowed, leaving the room, followed by his interpreter and two bodyguards.

Amira stood up and pointed to the door. 'Now that it's dark we need to go to the house where we will eat and rest. Tomorrow we'll go to the mosque with the Ayatollah'

Richard stood and then winced as he became aware once more of his back pain. She seemed to read his thoughts. 'I'm sorry for treating you so badly,' she said, showing more concern than she had done before.

'I'm sorry too,' he replied, rubbing his back.

Amira came forward placing her hands on his lower back. A gesture of sympathy but nothing more. 'Your father will have sounded the alarm, the IRG will be looking for you.'

Chapter Twenty-Two

Natanz, Iran- September 20th, 2005

'We're going there?' said Amira pointing towards a barren plain surrounded by grey mountains.

A vast industrial complex was spread out across the stark desert. At its centre, a large spherical structure with adjacent chimney dominated the skyline.

'Natanz,' said Richard. 'That's a nuclear reactor not a mosque. I thought we were looking for a Sufi's journal?'

'We are, but the mosque is in the grounds of the nuclear facility. It's very old and they had to build round it.'

'They're never going to let us go anywhere near their centrifuges. They'll think we're spying.'

Amira smiled and nodded in the direction of the old man sitting in the front of the land cruiser they were travelling in. 'That's where the Ayatollah will help us. That black turban opens lots of doors.'

'But they'll be looking for us after what happened in Yazd. It's not every day that a British guy swans up to Iran's largest nuclear facility and asks for access.'

'The Ayatollah will vouch for us. I don't think the IRG will have circulated our pictures. They'll want to keep the incident secret and the last place they'll think we might be is outside the gates of Natanz.'

Richard wished he shared Amira's optimism.

They were closer now, approaching the first roadblock. A three-metre-high fence with barbed wire separated them from the complex. Lookout posts, strategically placed along the perimeter, threatened trouble. Soldiers manned the towers, watching every move they made. A glint of sunlight reflected from unseen binoculars. Anti-aircraft gun positions defended the entrance.

'You just think they won't know about us...you don't know for certain.'

Amira nodded nervously but said nothing.

The roadblock was crawling with soldiers carrying machine guns. They stopped just short of the barrier while the Ayatollah got out and spoke to one of the guards seated in a kiosk by the roadside. The conversation was heated but then Richard could see the guard making a call. After a few minutes he slammed the phone down and came out of the kiosk barking orders at the guards who had surrounded their vehicle. The driver released the engine bonnet and the rear hatch so the soldiers could carry out their search. A mine sweeper was placed under the chassis and carefully moved around. One of the soldiers waved all clear. The passenger doors swung open and two hands gripped his arms, pulling him out of the car. Amira was treated with more civility as the guards allowed her to get out of the car on her own, respecting her as a woman or was it something else, he wondered?

He stood with his arms stretched and legs apart as an electronic sensor moved over his body. A vigorous hand search followed. They found the passport the embassy had given him and checked every page in minute detail. His Iranian visa received extra attention and the details noted. They took his photograph and then snapped every page of his passport. Nothing was left to chance. He looked to see if Amira was getting the same treatment, but she was left alone which puzzled him more.

After several more minutes they were released, and the barriers lifted. Armed soldiers provided an escort, one jeep at the front and another taking up the rear. The buildings they passed were faceless.

'Just the place to build a nuclear bomb,' Richard quipped.

Amira ignored him, too busy studying the buildings, her brain seemed to be working overtime. 'Shame we can't take photos,' Richard joked, in a feeble attempt to calm nerves. The car came to a stop at the foot of the mountain which rose steeply above them shutting out the light.

The mosque was small by comparison with others he'd seen, lost in a maze of industrial buildings. No aquamarine dome, with only a small minaret in proportion to the size of the building. It merged into its backdrop, using stone hewn from the mountain. The dark dreary nature of the rock gave the mosque an austere appearance reflecting its age. An old imam emerged from the building, his hands outstretched and a big smile on his face. There was no doubt that he knew the Ayatollah and was pleased to see him. They embraced warmly. When the extended greetings were completed, the Ayatollah pointed to Richard and Amira.

The interpreter spoke first. 'Salam Aleikum. The Imam Hossein Abanazi welcomes you.'

Richard and Amira bowed. 'Salam Aleikum,' they replied. The old man smiled through brown stained and broken teeth and, unlike the Ayatollah, his beard was unruly and unevenly cut. Not a single hair dangled from under the white turban suggesting it might conceal a bald head. He appeared older than the Ayatollah but not as senior, in a white cloak to match his head wear. Altogether, right down to the over large glasses he wore, the Imam appeared to care less for his appearance than his relationship with God which, Richard decided, was the opposite of where the Ayatollah saw himself.

Amira secured the veil she'd been wearing and removed her shoes. Richard took that as his cue to remove his own trainers and together they followed the two clerics and their interpreter inside the building.

The apparent small size of the mosque was deceiving because inside it seemed much larger. They passed through the open courtyard and into a larger room crammed with books. There was a manuscript laid out on a desk. The Imam gestured towards it with overplayed enthusiasm. The dim light made it difficult to study the calligraphy, but the Imam was having none of it. He produced a flashlight and shone it across the pages, continuing to talk rapidly, waving his hands as he pointed out features of the text.

The Ayatollah nodded and leaned over until his eyes were a few inches from the manuscript.

'I recognise Sanskrit, but I think it must be Persian. Unfortunately, I have no idea what it says,' Amira said. 'I've given the Ayatollah some magnified images of the icon to assist comparison.'

Richard looked at the interpreter, hoping for guidance on what the two older men thought. He responded by putting his finger to his mouth and looked towards the clerics pouring over the manuscript. In one hand the Imam held the blown-up images of the icon, while the Ayatollah scanned the original text with a magnifying glass, but never once letting up on the intensity of their heated discussion. After a while, they put the images next to the actual manuscript. They stood in silence pondering the two documents and then in unison began a vigorous shaking of their heads.

Amira held the flashlight and watched their deliberations.

After several more minutes, the Ayatollah spoke to the interpreter who said, 'There is no doubt that the icon is the work of the great Sufi poet, Babu Rfhan.'

Amira could not contain her excitement 'That's brilliant news.'

The interpreter remained severe, refusing to smile back. 'There is a problem,' he said.

'What problem?' Amira and Richard spoke together.

'There is no record of the knight ever visiting Babu Rfhan,'

'But if the painting is Babu Rfhan's handiwork, then the knight must have been here,' said Richard.

'Or somebody else brought it to him.'

Their attention was diverted to a shout of triumph from the Imam. He'd been turning the pages of one of his large books. After finding what he was looking for he showed the entry to the Ayatollah. After several minutes, the senior cleric nodded his agreement and spoke again to the interpreter.

'This is the receipt for the painting written in Arabic, but the signature is illegible,' said the interpreter.

Richard thought for a moment and then said to Amira. 'Do you know how Masood inherited the icon? I mean what is the parental line which leads back to the 11th century. Where are the connections?'

'There was nothing very concrete to go on. He inherited it from his grandfather who lived in Turkey…somewhere near the Syrian border…I can't remember the name.'

'It wasn't Antakya by any chance?'

'Yes, that's the name, what's your point?'

'Antakya is the modern name for Antioch where the Gospel was found - just a long shot but worth pursuing.'

Richard's thoughts were distracted by the sight of the Ayatollah holding the memory stick he'd received from Nadia. The sight of the stick in the Ayatollah's hand and Nadia's face in his head made him uneasy. Something didn't feel right.

'He is asking for a computer,' said the interpreter. 'The Imam says that Babu met up with a delegation of religious travellers from Europe in 1109.'

'Does he have a list of who attended?'

'We can ask.'

The answer could wait as far as the Imam was concerned. He was already leading the way down a long corridor. The ceiling changed shape as they walked, becoming more uneven and lower forcing Richard to bend his head. The walls were rough cut and cold to the touch.

They were heading into the mountain.

The sounds of generators boomed in the distance growing louder as they ventured deeper. The air was colder, and the floor was rough, lined with grit that had dropped from the rock's uneven surface. Richard winced as one sharp piece dug into his bare feet. He looked at Amira, blinking at the flickering light, regretting taking her lead and removing his shoes. He still couldn't make her out. Did she know for certain whether his father was behind Becky's murder?

A brighter light ahead and a warmer breeze encouraged them forward. As they approached, the narrow passage widened into a larger cavern with banks of computers lining the uneven rock. Uniformed personnel studied banks of screens and Richard noticed graphics which he thought showed the outlines of centrifuges. MI6 would sell their souls to get access to where he stood now, he thought, and yet what could he do about it?

One of the men stood up and acknowledged the Imam allowing him into the room with the Ayatollah, but a firm hand blocked the path when Richard stepped forward. Neither he nor the interpreter or Amira were allowed to go any further.

'They're going to look at the stick,' said Amira. 'The Imam hasn't seen the documents so maybe he'll be able to make some connections with the Sufi journal.'

Richard retreated but still managed to see what the Imam was up to despite the blocking tactics by the guards. Everything seemed normal as the clerics exchanged ideas.

But things were not normal. A minute change in the Ayatollah's behaviour; a hint of a self-satisfied smile creeping across the old man's face as the memory stick flashed a green light and unloaded its contents onto the

Natanz plant servers. At that moment, Richard knew something was wrong, but it was already too late.

All hell broke loose. Sirens erupted. An ear-splitting noise, made worse by the reverberating sound bouncing around the cavern, caused panic. He covered his eyes from the blinding flashing lights and tried to see what was going on. He could just make out the computer operators frantically working the keyboards of their machines.

The Ayatollah was already pointing the finger in his direction and the soldiers were approaching fast. He looked around for options and when his eyes met Amira's she shot back a fierce accusing glare.

'You're a fool Richard,' Amira shouted as the soldiers attacked him. 'Didn't you check the stick for a virus?'

After that he remembered nothing.

Chapter Twenty-Three

Natanz, Iran- September 20th, 2005

He was a fool.

He had checked the files carefully and decided they were all legitimate. If there had been a virus, why didn't it open on his own machine? If he'd asked the tech boys at Vauxhall Cross, maybe something would have turned up, but he couldn't draw attention to what he was doing. Rowena wouldn't have authorised it.

Sweat seeped from his aching body, remembering nothing after the first punch. They'd beaten him up, that much was certain. In the cloying airless heat he coughed, struggling to breathe. His mouth was bloody and his ribs hurt, but mercifully they had left his face intact. He tried to stand and felt relieved when he could do so despite the pain. Shackles restrained movement, digging into his ankles. Damp and hard, he traced his fingers around the edge of his cell, counting steps. He was in a windowless room, no more than a few feet square. The ceiling was low enough for him to touch. He banged on the wall and waited. It was a matter of minutes before he sank to his knees – exhausted, quickly losing consciousness.

He came round to the sounds of bolts being drawn back. As the door opened, he blinked at the light flooding the room. In the background he could hear the rattle of machine gun fire.

An officer entered, flanked by two soldiers. They looked scared, ducking instinctively when an explosion outside rocked the building. The soldiers left, leaving the officer in a state of panic. He moved closer to Richard, hurling abuse, prodding his pistol hard into his ribs.

'We're under attack. Tell me who they are or I'll kill you.'

'I don't know. I'm helping the Ayatollah, that's all I know.'

'Liar,' said the officer. He pushed the barrel of his pistol up against Richard's chin. 'We shut down the servers for less than an hour, to clear the virus from our systems and that took down our security cameras. In the time our computers were out we were attacked. They must have known what you were doing.' He prodded the gun harder. 'I will kill you, if you don't tell me. Where did you get the memory stick?'

Richard grunted, trying to buy time to think. 'It was given to me by a woman who was assisting the Ayatollah in his research. Her name is Nadia Zabor. She is a Saudi but is rebelling against the Kingdom of Saud. I swear I didn't know the stick had an embedded virus loaded onto it. I also don't know who is attacking you.'

The officer let out a nervous laugh. 'We'll see about that.'

The gun fire was getting nearer. The officer had lost control, waving his gun around with increasing hysteria. He peered out of the door and with an apparent lull in the shooting, signalled to his men who had taken positions outside. They hauled Richard to his feet, undoing the shackles around his ankles so he could walk. They took hold of each arm and pushed him into the open air. His hands remained cuffed but with his free legs he had a chance. The sentry tower was on fire. There were no guards manning their posts. His interrogator prodded the muzzle of his pistol into Richard's skull, pushing him into the line of fire, sheltering behind Richard's exposed body.

'We'll see if they are on your side, shall we?'

But was he their man? The bullets showed no sign of abating. There was no price on his head, no room to barter. They'd kill him anyway unless he acted now. He jerked backwards, stamping on the Iranian's feet, throwing all his weight into his stomach. With one movement he swung his cuffed hands into the officer's face, running for the cover of a nearby building. The adrenalin of fear counteracted the pain in his legs. Shrapnel peppered the floor around his feet, drawing sprays of sand and grit into the air. He could move no further without certain death.

Even though he had cover, the bullets continued to fly, carving pit marks into the wall. He was still exposed to Iranian's gun. They were separated by the drive way between the buildings, by no more than twenty feet. There was nowhere to go except to continue to run.

But the bullets from the Iranian's gun didn't come. Looking round, his captor was lying face down in the centre of the road. A sniper's bullet.

They could have killed him just as easily. Richard decided. Instead, he'd been subject to scare tactics; wild machine gun fire aimed to miss. The sniper was on his side after all, but he couldn't be sure. There was a plastic trash bin lying on the ground. He stuck out his leg and managed to roll it nearer where he could pick it up without inviting more shooting. He kicked the bin and waited for the hail of bullets.

None came.

Slowly, Richard stepped into the open with his hands up, starting to walk towards the mountain. He focused on where he thought the gunman was hiding, looking for a glint of sun reflecting off a gun barrel. The desert wind pounded his face and the blistering heat accelerated the sweat glands in his body that were already working overtime, reacting to the fear he felt. An eerie silence descended on the nuclear base. Without warning, fighters, dressed in tribal jihadist clothing, moved out of the shadows. He saw soldiers lying dead at every corner, their blood mingling with the sand. Two of the jihadists pushed him forward, prodding him with their weapons to move closer to the mountain entrance. It didn't feel like he was free. They entered a tunnel, where the lighting had failed. A siren blared; a signal that they were being attacked, but already too late. The computer operators he'd seen earlier, were being rounded up and it was obvious the jihadists were in control of the base. This time he was not excluded from entering the inner sanctum. They led him into a chamber towards a metal door at one end. A Jihadist brought one of the computer operators over to where they were standing and shouted at him to open the door. The operator pleaded ignorance. The jihadist became hysterical, waving his pistol at the operator who continued to shake his head. The impasse was broken when a shot rang out and the operator crumpled in a heap on the floor. Another operator was brought forward and this time the message got through. An entrance code was tapped into the lock and the door swung open. The jihadists grabbed the man who had revealed the code and pushed him through the entrance. He was too scared to resist.

The corridor they were now in was much narrower than before. There was no light and only a torch to guide them. The smell of damp and cold stale air seemed a long way from the heat outside. In the gloom he could see stalactites on the roof. It was as if the tunnel was not part of the overall complex. It felt as if he was walking into a dungeon.

He couldn't have been more wrong.

At the end of the tunnel another door had already opened. Stepping through, he gulped at the fresher air and the shock of what lay below them. They were standing on a parapet, looking down on a warehouse. It was impossible to see whether they were still in the mountain, but he could see the roof was held up by giant concrete pillars. The building housed a large transporter truck which carried a single missile which must have been over thirty feet long. Huge metal doors were whirring as they rolled back, revealing a desert plain. A blast of warm air blew into the building and sunlight flooded in. The jihadists pushed him towards some metal stairs which would lead to the floor below. As they reached the bottom, one of the transporter engines fired up, pumping grimy diesel fumes in an acrid cloud. The truck began to move forward slowly towards the opening door.

A voice spoke. 'You are looking at Shahab 3B ballistic missile with a range of over two thousand kilometres, capable of hitting Israel.'

Richard recognised the voice, but it was not who he expected to hear. He'd assumed that Brigadier Mantazi would be behind the raid.

He had not expected to hear the voice of his father.

Chapter Twenty-Four

Natanz, Iran- September 20th, 2005

While his father stood calmly, the Colonel looked agitated, barking orders to his men. He wondered why they were dressed in the khaki combat uniform of the Qods force when the attackers were all jihadists. The Colonel tapped numbers into a terminal, nodding with approval at the results on the screen before turning to face David Helford.

'I have the codes,' he said. 'We need another five minutes before we can fire the missile and then we need to get out of here before IRG reinforcements arrive.' He looked at his watch. 'Their ETA is fourteen minutes from now…I've called them in. They know the base is under attack. We need to be ready to meet them.'

Richard glared at his father. 'What the fuck are you doing? Why are these men dressed as Qods and the guys outside - jihadists?'

David Helford sighed. He replied in a cold official tone, not like a father would speak to his son 'We're setting up Mantazi to help the Supreme leader overcome an internal struggle within Iran…The men inside this room have not been seen by any of the guards and operators who are still alive…Anybody who did see them is now dead…As far as they are concerned, the men who attacked them are MEK insurgents. When the IRG arrive, they will be sure that the raid was orchestrated by the MEK and linked to Mantazi.'

Richard couldn't believe what he was hearing. 'You are fucking crazy. Why would you of all people want to do this? Mantazi is not here. How do you think the IRG are going to make the connection?'

The expression on the older man's face changed. He paused and switched his stare away from Richard. 'That's where you come in.' he said.

'Me...What do you mean?'

'We supplied pictures of your meeting with Mantazi. It shows Mantazi gave you the memory stick which caused the virus which enabled the raid. You will be in this room when they arrive. They will arrest you as a spy working for MI6 with the mission to engineer regime change by firing a missile on Israel.'

'You bastard...You know Mantazi didn't give me the stick.' Richard lunged at his father but was stopped in his tracks by two soldiers. They pulled him clear. He continued to struggle, bristling with anger. 'So, you want to kill me just like you had Becky killed,' he yelled.

'You won't be killed.' Helford replied emphatically.

'How do you know that?'

'Because the Colonel and I will be with the rescue party. I promise you... but you will be imprisoned. The evidence doesn't have to be compelling in Iran...We just have to steer the clerics in the right direction.'

Richard let out a cynical laugh. 'Since when have any of your promises to me ever been kept? They are lies.'

David smiled, 'The Lies of Our Fathers. I remember those lines from Kipling. If any question why we died. Tell them because our fathers lied.'

Richard could not hide his disgust. 'You don't seem to be able to take anything seriously do you?'

'Okay, Okay. I understand why you wouldn't trust me, but right now you have no other option.' His father appeared hard and unforgiving. 'You've got to believe me. Sometimes extreme measures are necessary to move forward.'

'You're crazy.'

David ignored the comment. 'Come and see the launch,' he said.

194

They followed in a Land Cruiser directly behind the truck which moved away from the hangar and began trundling along a runway. By the time it had stopped it must have been a quarter of a mile from the complex. David and the Colonel got out of the car and signalled to the driver. He moved quickly, cuffing Richard to the steering wheel. His father came back, poking his head through the open window.

'I'm sorry to do this. We want to show the regime that I am prepared to do anything to win their trust, even the elimination of my own son. You will provide the evidence which will convince them.'

'You bastard.'

'You may well think I'm crazy, but I'm in this up to my neck and know that Iran is the only place for me to be safe.'

'To save your own skin you'll sacrifice me?'

'That's not true.' He said nothing more. He stopped and put on his sunglasses to look at the spectacle a hundred metres from where they were standing. The missile launch was being prepared. Slowly, it was being hoisted by a hydraulic lift in the same way as a crane might be raised up to face the sky. After several minutes, the missile, painted a murky mustard yellow, stood up right and alone in the bleak landscape. The flag of Iran was painted on its side.

'Ready to fire.' The Colonel shouted.

David nodded agreement.

A cloud of rocket fuel fumes was submerging the missile. A deep growling sound reached his ears, followed by a blow back of hot desert air. He shouted once more at his father, but he didn't know whether he heard or not. The older man was staring with wonder as the missile rose into the air.

'Murderer,' Richard yelled. 'The deaths of thousands of Israelis will be on your head.'

Chapter Twenty-Five

Natanz, Iran- September 20th, 2005

The Israelis' got to Richard before the IRG. The Jericho II missile hit the warehouse with pinpoint accuracy, sending a fireball hundreds of feet into the air. If he'd believed in God, he might have said it was a miracle that he survived, but the truth was more banal. It was the Land Cruiser he had to thank. They'd left him helpless chained to the steering wheel. The force of the explosion blew the car further into the desert. It rolled over like a skittle hit by a bowling ball, but the vehicle did not break up. When the Land Cruiser came to a halt, he was upside down and still a prisoner. He waited for the fuel to ignite, cursing his father for ending his life. Closing his eyes, he tried to imagine Becky. She was smiling and holding a baby – his baby. He wept and waited.

It seemed like an age before they found him. He must have passed out once more because when he came round, he was undercover, in what looked like the mosque he'd been to before. There was no sign of Amira or the Ayatollah. The Imam who had shown them the records had also disappeared. All he could see were men dressed in green, bottle green to be precise and he knew only too well what that would mean.

He hadn't seen the man in charge before. He must have been over six feet tall, grey hair and tanned rugged features. All these IRG soldiers had grey hair, bleached by the sun and a never-ending war. The man was shouting at his father.

The Colonel was also there, standing next to him, impassive, while his father was interrogated. 'What's he saying?' Richard whispered to the Colonel.

'He wants your father to question you and if necessary, kill you if you don't cooperate.'

The Colonel was right. His father approached him with some reluctance, holding a pistol.

Richard raised his head slowly. There was a remoteness in his father's face. A distance which seemed to suggest that they had never met before. He'd tried to kill him once, strapping him in the Land Cruiser, so why not finish the job?

He spoke. There was an unsettling formality in his voice. 'You came to Iran under an assumed name - a Professor Lewis Raymond. Is that Correct?'

'Yes.'

'Your embassy has disowned you and refused to acknowledge your diplomatic status?'

'Yes.'

'Are you a Spy?'

'No. I am a son looking for his father.'

The older man paused. His words had registered the distance between them. The Colonel filled the silence with a translation back to Farsi.

'But we know you work for the British intelligence services.'

'If you know, then why do you ask?'

The shock of being slapped by his father, surprised him. Why should he care? It just added to the hatred that already existed.

'Do not be insolent and answer the question.'

'Loosen these ties first or my hands will drop off.'

The Colonel looked at the ties and signalled for them to be cut.

The feeling of blood rushing into his fingers was a welcome relief. Of course, he could have wrung his father's neck, gun or no gun but that didn't seem like a good idea.

The leader was not so trusting. He shouted at one of his men and the ties were reapplied, a little looser but this time he was secured to the chair by his hands and ankles.

'So how did you meet Brigadier Mantazi?' His father continued.

'He found me.'

'Did he give you the stick which caused the virus?'

'Yes,' He lied, which was what his father had told him to do. It seemed like the only sensible option to comply with their stupid scheme.

The Colonel translated and Richard watched the man in charge. There was a ruthlessness in his eyes that worried him. It was not over yet.

His father moved away and exchanged a few words with the other man. Seeing his opportunity, Richard whispered to the Colonel.

'Who is this man?'

'Mohammad Routani...He works for the President. He is also looking to overthrow Mantazi, but I don't think he trusts your father.' The Colonel looked worried.

Richard realised why.

Routani was remonstrating with his father and the Colonel. He was trying to place the gun in his father's hand and kept pointing to where he was sitting. Richard didn't understand Farsi, but the body language explained everything. Routani wanted his father to kill him.

A test of loyalty.

He watched in horror as his father seized the gun. The Colonel stepped back as David Helford advanced three paces to be sure of his aim. Slowly, he raised the barrel and tightened his finger on the trigger. Richard noticed his hands were shaking and with one glance at his face, he could see tears in the older man's eyes. For a second, he thought his father was not going to kill him. Something changed. Fear changed to determination, his father gripped the gun with two hands and fired.

Richard closed his eyes. He heard two more bullets find their spot, but he felt nothing. The first thing he saw was the smouldering barrel of the Colonel's gun and his father rushing towards him. He must have swung his gun at the crucial moment because Routani lay on the floor, a bullet hole in his forehead. The Colonel had killed the two soldiers assisting Routani.

'Quick. There are hundreds of soldiers outside,' his father said. 'We will march you out under gun point and commandeer one of their trucks.'

Outside, A lot of the soldiers were distracted, putting out the fire. The warehouse had completely gone including the men inside. The missile had carved a huge crater in the ground and destroyed many other buildings in the complex. Other soldiers were preoccupied with the task of securing the area around the facility. Nobody took much notice. They spotted a truck with a lockable van used to take away prisoners. The Colonel shouted at the soldiers loitering by the vehicle and keys were provided.

David forcibly pushed Richard into the back while the soldiers watched as the Colonel fired up the engine. They stopped a few minutes later. He listened as voices argued and then he heard the locks being opened to the van door. Two guards peered inside. He stared back, trying to look scared, as they shone a torch in his face. The Colonel shouted at the soldiers. He caught the word British and the sentry in charge nodded in agreement. They shook hands and then the door slammed shut once more. He breathed a sigh of relief when the engine sprung back into life and began moving off at speed. It would not be long before Routani's body was discovered.

They drove for an hour before he realised, they'd slowed down and were turning. The vehicle groaned as a lower gear was selected. Its speed dropped as they struggled upwards. They were climbing. It was sweltering and the smell of diesel more noticeable as the engine strained to the challenge of what was surely a steep road. Richard could stand it no longer, with his tied hands he banged hard on the metal facing the cab. They continued moving but when he shouted and hit the metal even harder, they stopped.

When the door opened, he almost fell out of the back.

The Colonel greeted him. 'What do you want?' he said.

'I need a drink before I die of thirst. And cut the ties, they're fucking killing me.'

'There is no water in the cab. We are also thirsty. We've tied you in case we're stopped by the police.'

'It's too late for that, they will be searching by now and no doubt with choppers. They know what vehicle we are in and it is only a matter of time before they find us.'

The Colonel nodded and cut his ties. 'You're right. Get out. We're going to abandon the truck.'

Richard's stood up and swallowed hard trying to find some moisture in his parched mouth. He blinked in the sunlight and tried to refocus. There were dozens of almond trees lining the flat land on one side of the road before it sloped steeply into a forested ravine. The air seemed thinner and mercifully cooler. The sun was lowering in the sky.

The Colonel climbed back in the cab and reversed the vehicle until it was at a right angle to the road. He drained the fuel tank to stop it igniting when it fell.

'An explosion will make us easier to spot from the air,' he said.

All he had to do was put it in neutral, let off the handbrake and over it would go. His father stood a few feet away from the truck, staring at the sky, and ignoring his son's gaze.

The truck began to roll forward. The Colonel stayed in the cab, waiting until the last moment, then jumping clear. Richard stood in silence, watching the fall, the weight of the engine tipping it forward. It fell a hundred feet before hitting a rock. The impact flipped it over as it continued to bounce down the mountain ravine. It crashed against fallen boulders, breaking up as it made its descent into oblivion.

A cloud of dust and debris drifted upwards before subsiding. When the truck came to a standstill, tall trees obscured the wreckage.

'What now?' said Richard.

'We walk,' said the Colonel.

Trying to find some shelter from the prying eyes of helicopters would be impossible. They'd seen none so far, but it was only a matter of time before the Iranians worked out where to look. After ten minutes walking, feeling exposed, they came to an area littered with rocks broken away from the mountain. There was a narrow cleft which hid them from the sky until nightfall.

Richard flopped down against a rock, far enough away to avoid his father. Staring up to the sky, he could see only a chink of fading sunlight escaping through the rocks. From sweating buckets, he began to shiver as the warm stone around him began to cool. The Colonel was near enough to hear him speak.

'Shooting those guys was not a good career move on your behalf. Thank you.'

The Colonel smiled. 'It will work out for good in the end, you'll see.'

'But your plan to discredit Mantazi backfired, big time.'

His father replied from a recess which prevented Richard seeing him. 'Killing off Mantazi was not our goal…It was gaining trust with the Supreme leader. That's what counts.'

'But what about Routani? That wasn't part of the plan. Was it?'

'No. It wasn't, but that doesn't mean Routani is loyal to the Supreme Leader? The IRG are fragmenting with everybody watching their own backs.'

Richard stood up and saw his father standing in a small crevasse a few feet away. He walked over and looked at him. 'You know, I will never understand your stupid games. Besides from nearly killing me – your son, you don't have any moral compass, whatever you may say. How can you justify launching that rocket and killing hundreds if not thousands of Israeli citizens?'

David Helford laughed. 'There's no risk of that. The Israelis have some of the most sophisticated missile defence systems in the world. You saw how quickly they retaliated. A single missile has no hope of getting through their defences. I would be surprised if it even reached Israel.'

'You don't know that for certain. Just because you are on Mossad's hit list does not give you a free reign to murder innocent people.'

'I've told you. No innocent people have been killed. I'm sorry you had to suffer. I thought the Israelis would respond but not that quickly. It was as if they knew all along what was going to happen.'

'Well thanks very much then…and while we are at it thanks very much for not killing me back there,' Richard sneered. 'Thanks for nothing.'

'You're welcome.'

The Colonel intervened. 'We will leave very soon.'

'Where are we going?' said Richard.

'You'll see, in good time,' the Colonel replied.

It was not quite dark when they set off. The Colonel led the way with him next and his father taking up the rear. Walking was harder because they didn't have a torch. It was also getting much colder. Lack of water didn't help but he was pleased that with the day cooling he was sweating less. Falling over the edge was the biggest danger. He kept his hand out feeling for branches or rocks which he might grab if he slipped.

His father was not so careful. He heard the cry but didn't see him fall.

Leaning over the edge, the Colonel shouted downwards. 'Are you okay? How far have you fallen?'

David Helford groaned. 'I think I've twisted my ankle. I can't see anything.'

His voice seemed close, but Richard could see nothing. The Colonel struck a match, but the flame barely penetrated the darkness. 'How far do you think you've fallen?' he said again.

'Maybe twenty feet, I'm not sure,' came back the reply.

'I'll climb down to you. Hang on.' said the Colonel.

'Leave me here. Don't waste time. I don't think I can walk I'll be a hindrance to you. Keep going to the rendezvous. Come back at dawn.'

Richard turned to face the Colonel. 'How long?'

'It's probably about five miles. I didn't want to risk driving any further and being spotted.'

There was a certain attraction to leaving his father in the hope that he might die, and all his problems would go away. But there were so many unanswered questions. He wasn't ready for him to go just yet.

'I'll wait with him …You go and get help,' said Richard.

The Colonel lit a cigarette. The glowing tip provided some illumination of his worried face, still marred by the cuts he'd sustained from the attempt on his life.

'Okay, but don't do anything stupid. You need your father to get us out of this.'

Richard wondered whether the Colonel was right. For all his festering suspicions, for all the betrayals, for all the frustrations, something inside wanted to understand. The Colonel pulled out a hipflask and after taking a swig, handed it to Richard. 'It's not alcohol, but it has a kick, cinnamon, spices and a few chilli flakes. It's very warming. Your father might need it.'

Richard smiled and sipped the flask, coughing when the chilli bit the back of his throat.

'That's good. Thanks. Who needs alcohol?' Richard quipped, but the Colonel didn't respond. He ground his cigarette butt into the ground and turned to leave. Richard grabbed his arm.

'Who are you going to meet?' he asked.

The Colonel hesitated before speaking. 'The Ayatollah who helped you get into the facility. He will be with Amira. They're expecting us.'

He was relieved to hear Amira's name because he thought she'd betrayed them.

'That's great news,' he said, still suspicious of how she had managed to evade capture.

'She's playing a double game,' the Colonel said, refusing to elaborate as he began walking along the path. Richard watched, quickly losing sight of him in the darkness. Turning, he knelt and peered back over the cliff edge. He shouted down into the void where his father was lying.

'The Colonel is gone. I'm coming down to get you.'

'Wait until light,' his father said. 'No sense in you hurting yourself as well.' His voice was strained as if he was in pain.

Ignoring the pleas to hold back, Richard lowered his legs over the side of the cliff and fumbled around to get a foothold. He couldn't see anything. It was all a question of feel and hope for the best. Shrubs were growing horizontally from the incline which he grabbed hold of. Carefully he tested his weight on the branches to see if they would support him. Satisfied, he lowered himself down, hoping there would be more solid ground below.

His father called out. 'I think I can make out your silhouette. About another ten feet to reach me.'

Richard lunged, holding the branch with one hand, he let it take his whole-body weight as he floundered, trying to grab something that he might cling on to. The branch roots were beginning to tear away from the rock. The imminent fall, made him swing more, catching a shrub that was protruding from the rock face. He let go of the branch, grabbing the plant with both hands, wincing with pain as thorns pricked his skin without mercy.

'You're just above me...There's room for two. Five more feet.'

The space that had broken David Helford's fall was not large. Richard could just make out the hazy shape of a person, propped against the cliff as he lowered himself onto firm ground.

'Over here.' His father whispered from the same direction, confirming he had not imagined the shape. The black night allowed no other means of recognition and no facial expressions which might have registered the pleasure or otherwise on his father's face, seeing his son's attempt to help him. Richard knelt, feeling carefully around the edge of their refuge, to establish how much space they had to spare. He decided they were on a stone ledge, jutting out away from the cliff face.

'I wouldn't take a leak if I were you... or swing a cat,' he joked; a nervous reaction to being this close to his father when there was nowhere to run. 'My guess is there's a big fall below. Certain death.'

'Isn't that what you would like?'

'What do you mean?' Richard knew perfectly well what his father was saying but preferred to pretend ignorance.

'I'm an embarrassment and you think I had Becky killed.'

'I'm listening,' Richard replied curtly. He passed the flask in the direction of his father's voice. 'The Colonel gave me this. It'll relieve some of your thirst and help against the cold.'

It was a slow and clumsy process giving and retrieving the flask. Their fingers touched a few times, a moment of intimacy which Richard fought himself not to accept. 'Give me a reason why I should believe you didn't do it...I've seen a photograph of the killers.'

'I wasn't responsible for Becky's death. How many times do I have to tell you? If you choose not to believe me that's your problem.' The older man's voice was firm but sounded sincere. 'It's true I spoke to her about a few things including telling her to break up with you. I said you were too much like me to play happy families.'

'Thanks a lot.'

Richard wanted to see his father's expression, but the darkness was too great. Even if he did see, he was not sure he would know whether he was telling the truth or not. His father was a good liar. He felt a leg, move closer to his own. His instinct was to move away but he left it there for reasons he couldn't quite understand, just as he couldn't understand why he was down on the ledge comforting his father.

For a moment, they sat in the darkness in complete silence. Richard agonised over what to do next, feelings going round and round in his head.

At last the old man spoke. 'They were pretty angry with you, I had to kill Routani to stop him killing you. He wanted me to do it.'

'And if he had killed me, it would be your fault as you set me up?' Richard replied.

His father shuffled his leg once more, trying to get comfortable. 'This bloody ankle hurts like hell and I'm cold.'

They were both cold and there was nothing they could do about it except drink the Colonel's flask. He passed it back to his father.

'Thanks,' the older man squeezed Richard's hand which felt strangely comforting. 'I would never have killed you and I'm sorry I hit you back there.'

He didn't want to thank his father and said nothing in reply.

'Look I know you think I'm mad, but I've told you before, Iran is the only place where I feel safe, although

God knows it's a dangerous place. The ordinary people are nice, and the women are beautiful.'

'You're an old man who shouldn't be thinking about chasing women or terrorists.'

'You may be right, but I don't want to die in prison in the West. When I see how I've been treated by the West, it is little wonder that Iran has won my sympathy. The British and Americans have been fucking around with Iran for centuries. Look at the history books and tell me how is it that we sell arms to Saudi Arabia and Israel but do not allow Iran to defend itself? It's seen as the aggressor in the region and yet it's not the perpetrator of terrorism against the West. It only commits these acts in the region against its enemies.'

'But in return for fucking up its own people. It's a game they can't afford to play,' Richard said. 'The Ayatollah should talk to all parties and reach a consensus.'

'The Gospel of Barnabas will change everything. I think we are close to finding it. My vision is for it to lead to peace in the region.'

Richard laughed. 'You can't possibly believe that. Iran is a shithole full of liars and cheats fighting each other. It can't speak with one voice. It won't work.'

'The Ayatollah I am helping is committed to stable government. What is wrong is the approach by the leaders? Khomeini ranted and raved about the evil West and the clerics continue, while persisting with the fight against Saudi Arabia and the Sunnis. They've learnt no lessons from the Iran/Iraq war. The Ayatollah wants to build support to topple the regime and rule Iran with peaceful reconciliation offered to the Sunni majority in the Middle East. No more proxy wars around the region. Talk to the Saudi's for God's sake is what he says but no one is listening to him.'

'You think the Ayatollah is a good man, but he is also an old man and the Sunni/Shiite conflict has been going on for hundreds of years; it's not going to end here.' He looked at his father and for the first time saw a slight outline of his features.

'We need the Ayatollah to get us out of this mess. There is no doubt that the dead men responsible for the raid will be identified as MEK but not necessarily linked to Mantazi. We will say we escaped after being taken by the MEK who killed Routani.'

Richard thought for a moment and then took another swig of the Colonel's flask before passing it to his father.

'Your story sounds pretty weak if you ask me.'

'Maybe, but we'll have to take that risk so we can get out of this fucking country.'

'I thought you felt safe here.'

'Only because there's a price on my head everywhere else.'

Richard rolled away and stood up. He didn't like this cosy chat with his father. It made him feel uneasy, dispensing too much good will. 'If you didn't kill Becky then who did?'

'Al Qaeda.'

'You think it was a revenge killing for the death of Abdul? Why didn't they just kill me? Why Becky?'

'They'll kill you in due course but not until they've made you suffer over the loss of Becky and your child. They want you to blame yourself. Don't forget Abdul lost his daughter in an American bombing raid in Afghanistan in 1998.'

'Maybe you're right.'

'There is one thing that worries me about that conclusion.'

'Those men I met, if they did it, then they are not Al Qaeda. Something is not quite right.'

'They did it alright, no question.'

They sat in silence for several minutes. His father was the first to break the impasse. 'Who really gave you the stick which caused the virus?'

'Nadia gave it to me; you know she was married to the late Sheikh Zabor at the time he was hit by Mossad.'

'I know the name, but I don't know anything about her and why she is caught up in internal Iranian politics. Is she Iranian?'

Richard sighed, surprised that his father did not know Nadia was a Saudi. The cold blurred his thoughts. He shivered, pondering his next question. 'What's troubling me is that if you don't know Nadia, how did you know to attack the facility when their systems were down when you didn't know anything about the stick?'

'The Ayatollah must have known, he told us to go in.'

Richard said nothing. He welcomed the chance to try and think through what had happened. It seemed that Nadia was working with the Ayatollah but then maybe Amira knew some more. Maybe that is all to do with this idea that the Ayatollah wants to talk to the Saudis.

'I wish I knew what the fuck was going on.'

His father did not reply. He whispered his name but still no answer. He could hear his breathing, slow and deliberate. He was asleep.

Richard lay awake and looked up at the sky, a thin layer of cloud was clearing, revealing thousands of stars emitting tiny flickers of brightness as the milky way wrapped its sparkling white shawl across the heavens. There was no moon, but his eyes were beginning to focus on their surroundings.

Chapter Twenty-Six

The village of Amadifan, Iran- September 21st, 2005

The Colonel returned at first light with reinforcements to help the two men back up the cliff. They brought a beat-up Peugeot which was parked on the road not far from where they dumped the truck over the mountain.

Richard watched his father struggle back up the hillside. The Colonel led him to the car, his arm round his shoulder. They walked slowly in earnest conversation. Both men looked worried.

'What's up?' said Richard.

'I didn't see the Ayatollah or Amira when I arrived at the village,' the Colonel said. 'I was told they were not there. I think it's a trap, but we'll go anyway. They won't kill us. We are too valuable to them.'

The village was silent but not abandoned. Fresh hay stacked up against a wall for animal feed and the smell of smoke in the air suggested somebody was here. The usual pictures of martyrs from the war hung from poles at intervals. The images had begun to fade and the flowers which adorned some of the shrines to a lost son or brother had shrivelled and died. They got out of the car and began walking along a narrow-deserted street.

'A few more metres and we'll be at the house where I borrowed the Peugeot,' said the Colonel, still supporting David with his arm.

A man moved out of the shadows. 'You guys looking for something.' The voice spoke with the unmistakable drone of a New Yorker.

They swung round and stared at a man dressed like a Mujahidin and nothing like a Wall Street banker. This man wore a black turban and beard with a Kalashnikov, slung by a leather strap, over his shoulder. The calling card of a jihadist except for one thing. The man's face was white, which could not be disguised by mud used as camouflage. First impressions might have suggested a committed Jihadi, but the man's eyes gave the game away. They were as blue as the sky above and the voice was American.

It was Harper.

The beard did not hide a mocking smile. The man who had tried to kill him in Iraq, who most probably fucked the woman he loved, who might even be responsible for her murder was standing a few feet away taunting him. More fighters had emerged from the alleyways, armed and looking like they wouldn't hesitate to kill them all, given half a chance.

Harper approached Richard, shoving the barrel of his gun into his chin. 'You should have killed me when you had the chance,' he said.

The American turned away from Richard's defiant stare. He pivoted, swinging the butt of his rifle into Richard's stomach who fell backwards, clutching his midriff, landing hard on the crumbling stone. 'Father and son, together. What a surprise. I thought you two couldn't stand each other.' Harper sneered.

David rushed forward, as if his ankle pain had gone, colliding with Harper in a textbook rugby tackle. Harper was younger than David and more agile swinging his left boot into David's groin as he fell.

'Stop.' Another voice, but this time it wasn't American. The man pushed through the crowds of fighters. 'Stop.' He shouted again. The response from the soldiers was immediate. David was manhandled off Harper and made to stand. His legs were weak, and he fell to his knees. The soldiers pulled him up once more. David yelled in Farsi, leaving no doubt he was in pain.

'Brigadier Mantazi, fancy meeting you here,' said Richard, sitting up, rubbing his stomach where Harper had struck. Out of the corner of his eye he noticed the Colonel, shocked at the sight of the man he was trying to usurp.

'The pleasure's all mine,' Mantazi replied. 'Especially as you've brought your father along.'

Mantazi issued orders to his men to take Richard, David, and the Colonel to the mosque. He had dispensed with his IRG uniform and now wore the clothing of the men around him. A thick belt of bullets was strung from his left shoulder to his right hip. His turban was tied formally, and his beard had been allowed to grow and become more unruly since Richard had first seen him in the warehouse. He could see the men respected Mantazi's leadership.

'Won't they be missing you in the Revolutionary Guard?' Richard asked.

Mantazi chuckled. 'Nobody will miss me. My boss is too busy fighting proxy wars outside of Iran to know what I'm doing.'

They removed their shoes and entered the prayer hall which was covered with carpets. The Mihrab alcove, which indicated the direction of Mecca, was immediately in front of them, carved in stone in an exotic floral design. Mantazi led them into an adjacent room and sat crossed legged on the floor, bidding the three men sit down in front of him. Harper came in and stood behind where they were seated. Mantazi, bellowed orders to the guards and they withdrew, closing the entrance behind them.

Richard shifted his position slightly so he could see Harper. The American fidgeted with his gun which made him nervous.

'I apologise bringing you here, but this is the only place we can speak without hindrance.' Mantazi looked directly at Richard, refusing to engage with his father and the Colonel. 'I must admit I'm surprised to see you working with your father when we know he arranged for your girlfriend to be killed. We have conclusive proof.'

'What proof?' said Richard.

'Mantazi produced a photograph from his pocket and handed it to Richard.

It was the same photograph Mantazi had shown him in the warehouse when they first met. A photograph Nadia had chosen not to give Richard. A photograph which made his blood run cold. His father shaking hands with the men who had murdered Becky.

He was pleased to see the photo again and get the chance to confront his father. 'What is this?' he said, thrusting the photograph into his father's hand.

The older man glanced at the image 'That proves nothing. For a start, how do you know these men were responsible for the murder of Becky?' He looked at his son. 'It's a lie, don't believe him.'

'I've seen photos of the same men in Ankara at the time Becky was killed. It's true, you met the murderers.'

'I can prove it's not a lie,' said Harper. The smirk on his face had just got wider.

Richard looked at Harper. 'Go on.'

'You've seen the photograph and we know your father met the killers. Listen to this recording.' Harper held up a small Dictaphone and switched it on. There was no doubt the voice on the tape belonged to David Helford. He was speaking in Farsi.

'What's he saying?'

'I'll translate for you,' said David. He paused while the tape recording continued. 'I'm telling the Ayatollah Arif ibn Amaswari that I've offered Becky money to keep her quiet.'

Richard remembered the money in Becky's bank. 'Why did you pay Becky?' he shouted.

'To shut her up, but I didn't give those guys instructions to kill her.'

Harper snorted with contempt, 'That's what you think…Shall we ask the guys who did the deed to explain who put them up to this?'

Mantazi shook his head, 'We are not exposing the killers,' he said firmly.

'Are you telling me that the men who murdered Becky are here in this room?'

Mantazi laughed. 'No, they are not here.'

Harper grimaced, angry that his moment of glory was lost, but Richard had heard enough. He glared at his father.

'You've admitted you paid Becky off…so why? You owe me an explanation.'

David Helford was no longer animated. His face had turned ashen grey. His expression appeared apologetic, even contrite. 'I don't know how to say this,' he replied, quietly.

'Go on…' The rage in Richard's gut was no longer in control. He thought he was going to explode. 'Tell me why you tried to pay her off?'

'I didn't worry about giving Becky money because I| thought it would benefit you somehow. I was concerned that she could have slept with the guy who was trying to kill you.' His eyes wandered towards the smirk on Harper's face confirming what Richard always knew.

David continued, looking more worried with every word he spoke. 'Becky told me she slept with Harper and he let her see the CIA file on me. It revealed a lot of secrets which I didn't want you, or anybody else for that matter, to find out.'

'What secrets?'

'That I've worked for the Iranian government since 1980, since shortly after the Revolution. It's why the Americans want to kill me. Its why Harper wants me dead. But I never sold secrets to Iran. My role was to expose US hypocrisy. I paid off Becky because if you knew you would feel obliged to report it to MI6. I didn't want to put you in that position.'

Richard could not believe what he was hearing. He turned to the Colonel. 'Is this true?'

The Colonel nodded.

Richard stared at his father. 'You were working in the City in 1980. How could you work for Iran when you told me you tried to warn the President about 9/11?'

'Of course, I warned the President that 9/11 was a Saudi plot. It had nothing to do with Iran. The 9/11 terrorists were enemies of Iran and the US. I used to travel to Tehran with my bank in those days. That's how I met the Ayatollah.

'You met Khomeini?'

'Yes.'

'Which is why your voice carries so much weight with the Clerics?'

'Yes.'

'But you also worked for the Israelis?'

'As a double agent.'

'What about your love for Dinah? And you used to kill jihadis for a living. How could you love someone and stab them at the same time?'

'I only killed Sunnis never any Shia. It's a dirty game. It's devious and self-serving. These are the qualities you need in the spying game.' David's expression and tone became more sombre. 'And Dinah was self-defence. She was going to kill me when she realised I was working for Iran.'

'Enough,' Mantazi interrupted. 'This is not the time to discuss the integrity of David Helford.' We have other matters to deal which are more important.' He turned to the Colonel. 'Your little plan to attack Natanz with my men has failed. We know you killed Routani and I have fifty men dead because of the raid. Routani was trying to establish a link to me and you shot him dead. You silenced any suggestion that I was behind the raid.' He paused and coughed, raising his left hand slightly. 'I suppose I should thank you for disposing of the evidence, but the Supreme Leader will want someone to blame.' The last word came out louder than the rest. He lowered his hand.

The bullet hit the Colonel side on, entering his brain through the right ear. Half his head was blown away, splattering bits of brain across the Persian carpet.

The smoking gun belonged to Harper.

Richard recoiled in horror at the sheer brutality of the execution. He wanted to be sick. 'You bastard.' He jumped up, launching himself at Harper.

The American stepped backwards and cocked his gun. 'Another step and I'll blow your fucking brains out as well.'

'I thought he was one of the good guys,' Richard shrieked. 'A friend…. you've killed him in cold blood.'

Mantazi's men grabbed Richard and pulled him away. He glanced across to his father, expecting some reaction but the older man, sat impassive. 'Are you satisfied now?' said Richard. Their eyes locked together, and something connected between them. His father was simmering, fighting an undeniable rage to do something.

Mantazi looked down to where the Colonel lay, disdain rather than an expression of pity, immune to the savagery of Harper's action. He turned to father and son. 'The Colonel has been killed because he knows what I'm doing to save Iran. He will betray me. He is my enemy and must be eliminated.'

'What does that make me?' said David. 'The Colonel was just following my orders.'

'It makes you the enemy.' said Harper.

Mantazi glared at Harper. 'Shut up,' he shouted. 'I tolerate you because you supply me with arms and money from your government. It doesn't mean I like you.'

The impact of the rebuke made the American step back. Richard noticed his mouth open to speak and then close responding to a signal from the Brigadier who was directing his men to remove the body.

David Helford was not silent. He spoke with a firm unwavering voice, like someone who did not fear for his safety. He stepped closer to Harper until his gun was almost touching his chest.

'I'll tell you who I'm the enemy of...enemy of fucking America that's who I am...And that's why you want to kill me. You've killed the Colonel so why not just get it over and blow my head off.'

'Don't worry, I'll kill you when the time is right because you are a traitor.' He spat on the ground, registering his distaste.

David Helford didn't appear worried, quite the reverse. He was becoming more animated. 'Don't you see,' he continued, turning around to face Mantazi. 'Harper finances your fun and games because it's in America's interests to see the leadership of Iran fail. You're his pawn and he won't give a shit if you lose.'

Mantazi was listening intently and saying nothing. He had lifted a gun and was pointing it directly at Harper. 'I am not going to let you kill him. This man's enemies are Iran's enemies.'

Harper was seething. For a moment he pointed his gun at Mantazi, but then thought better of it as two of the Brigadier's henchmen appeared out of nowhere, pouncing on him. He struggled but they disarmed him with ease.

Mantazi spat at the ground, looking pleased with himself. 'This should give us an even better chance to consolidate my power when I present an American spy to the IRG generals.' They watched as Harper was dragged out of the room. Mantazi turned to Richard and struck a more conciliatory note. 'The trouble with Americans,' he said with a coy smile. 'They think everything revolves round money. Harper thought I would always want his money and therefore as long as he was writing the cheques, he thought he was safe.'

Richard was relieved Harper was no longer a threat, but his anger had not subsided. 'What will you do with him?' he said.

'Execute him for spying, what else?' Mantazi replied. To have killed the Colonel as the ringleader of the attack on Natanz and captured the American who he could blame for funding the operation was a stroke of good luck he hadn't anticipated.

Much that Richard hated Harper he didn't want him thrown in a jail or even executed for spying. 'Harper's important,' he said. 'He knows where the murderers of my girlfriend are.'

Mantazi looked irritated by Richard's outburst, raising his voice. 'I am no longer interested in who killed your girlfriend. As I have already said, my priority is to find the Gospel, not worry about disagreements with your father.'

'You told me you wanted to discredit my father. The Ayatollah and Amira don't trust him either. Take me to them and we will find the Gospel of Barnabas and deliver it to you, without his help,' Richard replied.

'That will be done,' Mantazi replied. 'I blame the Colonel for the attack on Natanz but your father is also to blame. We will need to deal with him later.' He pointed at David with his gun. 'The Ayatollah and the woman - Amira have gone back to Yazd. An army escort will meet us fifty miles from here and take the prisoner back to Tehran while we head to Yazd.'

David Helford listened quietly to what was being said. 'You forget I have the scroll that was found on Crete. You will never convince the supreme leader without my help.'

Richard glared at David. 'That scroll belongs to me. I found it.'

David Helford turned his back on his son and said nothing.

Fifteen minutes later, three Land Cruisers were speeding South along a dusty winding road, laden on each side by pistachio trees bulging with nuts. Women were out in the fields, in brightly coloured chadors, harvesting the crop, oblivious to the convoy speeding by. They were heading down the mountain pass to the main arterial motorway that runs through the desert, when the road, without warning left the plains of trees behind and entered a narrow gorge with steep rock cliffs on both sides. Richard was watching out of the window when the IED hit the car in front. It was a mild explosion but enough to blow the lead truck onto its side.

Harper hadn't run out of options.

The lead car, lying crippled, was the one holding Harper. The men emerging from behind the rocks, guns blazing, had one thing on their minds; a determination to set the American free.

Chapter Twenty-Seven

The Zagros Mountains West of Isfahan, Iran-
September 21st, 2005

The men in the lead truck that carried Harper didn't stand a chance. A hail of bullets picked the guards off one by one as they tried to return fire. With these men down, the jihadis rushed forward and pulled the American from the burning wreckage. Another bunch of killers attacked the truck at the rear of the convoy which managed to resist before two grenades blew up under their vehicle. Two of the guards who survived the explosion tried to escape. Their clothes were on fire as they leapt clear, rolling in the dust, desperate to put out the flames sweeping across their bodies. The jihadis looked at their helpless efforts before calmly shooting them and ending their misery. In the seconds that this took to play out, in middle of the convoy, Richard, David and Mantazi could only watch in horror. Stray bullets dented the armour plating of their Land Cruiser, but it was clear to Richard that they were not going to kill them. At least not now. Harper took control, barking orders to the men, pulling the captives out of the undamaged truck. The driver got out without being pushed, remonstrating with a jihadi. He must have known him, thought Richard, but that didn't seem to matter. The gunman hit the driver in the ribs with the butt of his rifle, who fell on his knees, shouting for Allah.

Harper stared at Mantazi, with undisguised loathing, in no mood for polite conversation. 'You'll get no more money from the US Government. Nobody, not even you Brigadier, will ever double cross me.' He paused, walking round the three men, prodding each one with the Glock he'd been supplied with. 'Of course, I knew you would fuck with me,' he boasted. 'In this shitty country money speaks, even after the fucking revolution, capitalism still rules.' He chuckled, enjoying his own joke. 'I took contingency plans and sprayed these guys with enough dollars to make them kill their own mothers if I asked them to.'

Harper swung round and shot the driver through the head and then through the chest to make sure. 'Just to show I mean it.' He spoke with a sickening nonchalance and disregard for what he'd just done. The jihadis didn't protest at the brutality of Harper's act. They might have even respected him more because they understood ruthless leaders. Richard watched Harper step over the body, carefully avoiding the pool of blood building around the corpse. He may have hated his father but not even he was capable of indiscriminate violence. He was a dangerous idealist who had to be stopped. Harper was a psycho who didn't give a shit about anything but himself.

Harper was warming to his message, enjoying making them squirm. 'I'm not stupid enough to kill you Brigadier, although I would have been pleased to blow you away. You are much too important to the US government to do that.' He turned his gun on David Helford. 'But you...' He raised his voice to an almost hysterical pitch. 'If I do nothing more before I get out of this fucking country, it will be to kill you both.'

The smoke from the burning wreckage and circling vultures, ready to pick over dead bodies, made the task of spotting them from the air so much easier, but Harper seemed relaxed about that possibility. The sound of engines made him look up. A convoy of 4x4 trucks was racing towards them, leaving a trailing cloud of dust in its wake. Harper's rescuers brought their vehicles out from hiding places in the trees and waited for the others to catch up. When the motorcade arrived, Harper dismissed a contingent of men, handing out bundles of US dollars removed from the lining of his jacket. He shook hands with the men and smiling, they drove off, cheering at their new-found wealth.

'Bastards.' Harper shouted at their vehicles as they pulled away, leaving Richard in no doubt that the American's smiles were false. The new escort operated with less swagger and more military efficiency, quickly marshalling the captives into separate trucks. They were dressed as Iranian soldiers in khaki fatigues. Richard went with Harper and three other guards, one who drove and the other two sat on either side.

The transport had seen better days; the standard terrorist issue-Land Cruiser replaced by black Nissan Titans. The powerful five litre engine handled the rugged terrain with ease, lifting dust and grit into the air, laying down easily discernible tyre tracks, easy for anybody wishing to hunt them down. They were avoiding the straight central highway that ploughs through the Iranian desert on the road to the Gulf or across the border to Afghanistan. Richard reckoned they were heading South, albeit by a roundabout route. He hoped they were heading for Yazd, but it was impossible to tell. For the first few miles, Harper didn't speak, sitting at the front with the driver. Richard sat in the back flanked by the two guards. The noise of the road drowned the sound of Richard's voice, but he kept asking until Harper relented and turned to face him.

'She said to me that she didn't sleep with you…Did you?' Richard asked.

The self-satisfied smirk on Harper's face didn't convince Richard. 'Wouldn't you like to know?' he sneered. 'Your father thought she did because Becky told him she had. He wasn't best pleased that some woman was shitting on his son.'

'But you didn't, did you?'

Harper frowned. The troubled expression confirmed Becky had remained faithful. Richard was relieved but, in his mind, he felt ashamed that he could be worried about himself when Becky had lost her life while he'd been allowed to live. He wondered why Becky would have said she slept with Harper when she didn't. Maybe she just wanted his father to go away and this was the best way to do it.

'I tried to get her into bed, God I tried, just to get back at you for not dying in Iraq. She was also pretty fucking attractive.' Harper spoke with a lustful smile that irritated Richard. 'I was really pissed off that my scheme to blow you up failed and your dad got away once again. It fucked up my career which is why I gave her the CIA file. I wanted you to see it so you could understand everything about your fucked-up dad. The file was going to be the last straw after everything he's done to you. I felt sure you'd want to blow his brains out. The CIA, MI6...' He paused and caught Richard's eye. 'And *you* wanted him dead.' Harper spoke slowly and directly at Richard. 'It's time to call in that debt and take him out.'

'I don't owe you any debt, I owe you a bullet in your guts.'

Harper laughed loudly. 'What a prick you are. You want to be an intelligence officer and play with the big boys, do you? Well I'll tell you Langley and Vauxhall Cross need to know you can be trusted. To take out your father would secure that trust. Any allegiance to your own flesh and blood, a fucking traitor, would make you a shit not a spy. Killing him would end that association.'

'But you could have killed him back there.'

'Not in front of Mantazi...Your father is a decorated hero in Iran. He's given them so much intelligence on Israel. He won't sanction the killing of your father. I'd be signing my own death warrant.'

Harper turned away and looked out of the window. The convoy had entered a small valley surrounded by steep mountains rising on all sides. The road had become rougher forcing the trucks to move at a snail's pace. Ahead of them, an ancient sand coloured fortress, dwarfed by the stark backdrop, looked as if it was hiding from the world. It might have been a caravanserai had this place been a likely trading route, but Richard doubted whether there had been any camels within one hundred miles of here. The Nissans screeched to a halt in front of a tall wooden gate. The doors opened and the trucks pulled into a central courtyard. One of the walls to the building had been destroyed and in between the space several tents had been erected.

Harper was the first to get out of the truck. The reception committee he'd been expecting didn't materialise. His cocky demeanour disappeared fast as soldiers crowded in on him. They grabbed him before he could pull his gun. 'What the fuck are you doing? You'll pay for this,' he shouted, but none of the soldiers answered.

Richard, David and Mantazi, after getting out of their trucks, stood a few feet away from Harper who was surrounded, soldiers watching his every move.

'What is this place?' Richard asked.

His father was the first to answer. 'It's a Christian monastery built in the 11th Century,' he replied, surprising Richard that he knew anything about it. 'It's a ruin now but the Ayatollah has been leading the excavation. It was destroyed in 1125AD when Shia tribes killed the monks and stole all their treasures,' His attention was drawn to the people emerging from the interior of fortress. 'Except the monks hid their manuscripts,' he added.

Amira was standing next to the Ayatollah in the shadow of one of the ruined towers. She remained still as the old cleric moved forward to face Mantazi. He may have been diminished in size in front of the IRG officer but his voice and tone more than compensated, showing who was in charge. He bellowed at Mantazi and at one stage slapped his face while gesticulating at Harper.

'He doesn't like you,' David shouted at Harper through the barrage of guards that surrounded him. 'He doesn't approve of Americans or your dirty money. The Iranian people will decide who rules them and not the Great Satan.'

The Ayatollah finished ticking off Mantazi and proceeded to shout more instructions to the soldiers.

David continued to translate. 'He wants Mantazi to go back to Tehran and clear his name, telling the authorities how his convoy was attacked by MEK rebels and the American was freed.'

'The whole rescue of Harper was a set up to create a credible back story. Harper didn't know he was being double crossed yet again.'

'So why does Harper get to stay with us?'

'It's an insurance policy, maybe a bargaining chip if things go wrong. Americans always have propaganda value in Iran.'

Mantazi came over to see them and held out his hand. 'Goodbye to you both, if you find the Gospel then Iran will be forever in your debt…I think the Ayatollah is correct. I need to keep a low profile after what happened in Natanz. It is a shame that I cannot take Harper with me, you will need to watch him.'

'But what about him?' Richard pointed accusingly at his father. 'Where is the evidence that he was behind the murder of my girlfriend?'

'He denies it and my conclusion was based on the existence of those photographs showing your father with the killers. If he denies it, then I believe him. Inshallah, your father is an honourable man.'

Mantazi walked past Harper on his way back to the truck. He turned and told the soldiers to move aside so he could face Harper. 'Iran is a great country with a history that stretches for thousands of years. We cannot be bribed into submission. Whatever you may think.'

Harper grunted but did not answer. Mantazi stepped back and stared as the soldiers tightened their cordon. He got back into the Titan and the gates opened as the vehicle's engine started up. A burst on the throttle, and he was gone. Richard watched and wondered how he would ever manage to escape Iran without Mantazi's help. Amira seemed more confident than he was. She was coming towards him smiling and dressed in Western clothes, her only concession to the country she was in, a silk scarf patterned with flowers acting as her veil. It was a far cry from how he'd seen her in Yazd. He'd learnt that Amira would always amaze him. She was a woman of contradictions, from the demure Muslim woman in black chador to the tanned self-assured CIA agent capable of killing at will. She was flanked by two soldiers on either side. Her smile turned to serious as she faced Harper and pointed to him.

Harper grunted with disgust as the soldiers took away his gun and began to march him away. 'The United States Government has a price on Helford's head. You have a duty to see that order is carried out,' he protested to Amira as she walked away.

David Helford could not hide his contempt for Harper. It was his turn to milk Harper's discomfort. 'Lest you forget Harper, you are not in California now, you are in Iran and there are many people, not just me, who would like to kill you. I support Iran because of hypocrites like you.'

Richard noticed his father's expression as the soldiers took Harper away. Once again, his emotions swung from hate to something a little more positive. These conflicting emotions worried the shit out of him. There was going to come a time when he needed to face up to the man. He didn't like the word – kill. It seemed so final and unsuitable for a son to want to do to his father.

Amira looked at Richard, her smile had returned to greet him. 'I've discovered that the Ayatollah knew about the virus and is in contact with Nadia,' she said.

'A Shia cleric in contact with someone in Saudi intelligence, pull the other one,' Richard replied and then he remembered the Ayatollah's expression in the cave the moment the virus was discovered. 'Are you sure?'

Chapter Twenty-Eight

The Zagros Mountains West of Yazd, Iran- September 21st, 2005

Amira didn't answer him, beckoning David and Richard to follow her. They went into the building and along a passageway open to the sky. The floor in front of them had been dug away revealing a hole with steps leading down below ground. They descended slowly following a small flashlight that Amira was holding. At the bottom, a labyrinth of tunnels led off in various directions, but fortunately she knew where she was going. A short distance further and the tunnel opened into a room. She flicked the switch of a generator which triggered lights, revealing a space packed to the roof with hundreds of scrolls and dozens of large books.

'This is a treasure trove,' she said. 'The monks were Syrian Christians who came here to escape persecution. The monastery was only recently rediscovered. The valley is hidden and rarely visited. Nobody realised how important it was until the Ayatollah got involved. The interesting thing about the documents is that they are focused on the study of God rather than a particular religious doctrine, be it Islam, Christianity or Judaism.' Amira picked up one of the scrolls, blowing away the dust before undoing a leather tie and unrolling the papyrus document. 'I can't read this, but I can see by the illustrations that it's discussing the Holy Koran. The paintings are showing scenes from the prophet's life without depicting his image. Don't you think it's strange that Orthodox Christians are writing about the Holy Koran?'

Both men nodded without comment. Amira turned and led the way back to ground level. Reaching daylight, she walked briskly in the direction of one of the tents where they found the Ayatollah pouring over a large illustrated book embossed with gold and decorative art. He had a young woman with him, dressed in black. They were engaged in earnest conversation but looked up when Amira started speaking.

She pointed at the woman talking to the Ayatollah. 'This is Fatima who speaks Aramaic and is a professor at Tehran University. She also speaks English.'

Fatima held out her hand to Richard and smiled. 'Please excuse my traditional dress. I don't normally dress like this, but I do it out of respect for the Ayatollah.'

Richard returned the smile. 'This is a wonderful place and so much to learn.'

Amira asked Fatima to join them and after the Ayatollah signalled his approval, they all sat down on cushions while they waited until tea was brought.

Fatima spoke in clear unaccented English.

'Your English is impeccable,' said Richard.

Fatima smiled again. 'I studied in Oxford at the institute of Islamic studies. Let me tell you what is going on.' She waited while a soldier served the tea. She took a sip and then continued. 'The Ayatollah is sifting through each book and scroll even though they are almost exclusively Christian,' she said. 'The discovery of this place made him want to seek new ways of ending the conflict in the Middle East. He contacted the Saudi woman -Nadia through her organisation *Words of the Faithful*. Both believe that there must be reconciliation between Shia and Sunni if peace is to be possible. The Gospel is the key. Only then will Islam be able to thrive in a less violent way. Jihad should be a thing of the past as all religions should coexist peacefully. It's what I'm working for as well.'

'But the Americans and the Israelis have other ideas. They prefer - what's that saying?'

'Divide and rule,' said David, interrupting Fatima's flow. 'They are concerned that if Saudi Arabia and Iran are allies it will be an unstoppable force in the region and against Western interests. The last thing America wants is for the two main Middle Eastern powers to be best buddies.'

'That's not the issue,' Fatima replied. 'This is an academic question about the origins of religion. The Ayatollah thinks that these wonderful documents will reveal something which might encourage Iran to stop being so insular. He is a visionary and he is also a lone voice among the clerics and in great danger if he is found out. His problem is that many of the manuscripts are written in Aramaic, which he doesn't speak. He's been taking the books and scrolls in small quantities to the Tehran university for analysis which is where I come in. He's made some remarkable discoveries.' She took a sip of tea before continuing. 'These are documents which show Christian monks reading the Holy Koran and showing an interest in Ahura Mazda, the good god of Zoroastrian religion. It shows religion evolving to meet different community needs but still essentially being the same thing, that is the worship of a superior being who they called God. In ancient times Iran was the hotbed of religious thought, such as the spread of Manicheism into Christianity promoting the idea that all sexual relations were sinful unless they were for the purpose of procreation. In other words, sexual intercourse was a necessary evil.'

'What's that got to do with Barnabas and the Gospel?' said Richard.

Amira indicated to Fatima that she would answer. 'Because the Ayatollah has found something else which links Barnabas to this place.'

'You think Barnabas came here? No way. We know he didn't go anywhere near Iran.'

Amira smiled, 'No, not Barnabas, St Thomas the doubting apostle. We've got proof that he came here while he was on his way to preach the Gospel in India. He wrote letters to Barnabas. These letters are a revelation because Barnabas states that he disapproves of Roman dominance of the church. He states clearly that he has fallen out with Paul and that is because he cannot accept that Jesus was the Son of God. Barnabas says Jesus was a prophet and not the last messenger.'

'That's an incredible discovery but without the real Gospel we are no further forward,' said Richard. 'We know the knight didn't come here so we won't find the Gospel that he recovered from the dying priest in Antioch.'

'It's true what you are saying,' Amira continued. 'But we have had a breakthrough.'

'Go on,' said Richard, who was beginning to get excited.

'When the match was made with the icon and the Sufi artist in Natanz, the Ayatollah remembered something he'd seen written in some notes in a book he'd taken from here. The notes were written in the same hand as the person who had signed the receipt for the painting that the Imam showed us. He showed me the book where the annotations were made, and I confirmed it was the Gospel of Thomas written in Latin. It is the same text as that found on Crete and as part of The Dead Sea Scrolls haul found in Egypt at Nag Hammadi. The Gospel of Thomas is subversive in that it makes Jesus into a more mystical character and not one which would fit well with the Christian view of God. The pronouncements are reminiscent of Sufism. There were many versions of Christianity that veered away from Rome. Thomas ideas in his Gospel did not work anymore than those of Barnabas which is why they were both blacklisted.'

'All this is very interesting but where does that get us?' said Richard, frustrated by Amira's enthusiasm which was leading them nowhere.

'Let me finish,' Amira said, irritated by Richard's continued scepticism. 'This Gospel of Thomas was studied by a Muslim scholar who came here to study with the monks. We've confirmed he is the same person who signed for the painting.'

'What do you know about him?' said Richard.

'He is a Syrian who was fascinated by the relationship that Syrian Christianity has with the Gospel of Thomas. The book is annotated with his notes and comments on the letters between Barnabas and Thomas. Even though he is Syrian and a Muslim, he is writing in Latin. The discovery that the painting in Masood's icon was completed by a Sufi artist in Yazd has drawn the link between the Muslim studying here and the icon in Masood's possession which I am sure is the same icon found with the Gospel by the knight. The writing is the same, we are sure of it.'

'So, who is this monk? What's his name? Can we connect him to the Valognes family?'

Amira beamed with excitement, handing Richard a parchment. 'We've found the accounts of the monastery and several books of guests who have stayed here over centuries. This is a list of people staying in the monastery at the time that our student is studying around 1125AD. The records are written in Farsi, but Fatima has discovered a name which reads Masood Valognes. He must have taken Robert de Valognes name.'

Fatima interjected. 'Valognes is not a name that converts easily into Farsi, but it is remarkably close, and Masood is of course quite a common Muslim name.'

Amira pointed to the name on the parchment. It meant nothing to Richard. His father leaned over and looked at the writing. He shrugged. 'It means nothing to me. I may be able to speak it, but I can't write it.'

Richard felt certain that Fatima would not make things up. She was a serious academic. The icon in Masood's possession was the same icon handed down over the centuries. Now there was another strong link to the knight. For a moment all the troubles with his father disappeared and a feeling of elation lifted his spirits. He looked at Fatima and grinned, noticing the sparkle in her eyes. She was as excited as he was. He turned to hug Amira. 'This is fantastic. It is unbelievable that you've established the link to the man I saw dying on that London Underground train back in July. Akila's son came back here to seek the truth.'

'Let's hope we'll find a clue revealing where the Gospel ended up.'

'Are we sure that Masood didn't bring the Gospel with him?' said Richard. 'It's amazing to think that Masood, the knight's adopted son has been here in this monastery. How long will it take us to go through all the books?'

'We've already done that and drawn a blank. I'm sure the Gospel is not here.'

'It must have stayed with the knight in England?'

'You're right, but we don't know where.'

The shelter of the mountains drew the darkness in like a curtain. The air moved from blistering heat to icy desert night. Richard shivered as the sudden temperature change took its toll on his bruised body, still aching from the beatings he'd taken since arriving in Iran. The soldiers lit fires and began preparing a meal of lamb stew in a pomegranate sauce. It smelt good and pangs of hunger tugged at his empty stomach. He couldn't remember the last time he'd eaten a proper meal. Moving closer, he allowed the warmth of the fire to penetrate his bones and warm the blood in his veins. The therapeutic effect of the extra heat made him feel much better. There had to be something here which would help find the Gospel. If it was in England, he needed to know where to look. He looked over the leaping flames and saw his father in deep conversation with Amira. Deep in thought, he didn't notice his father and Amira approach.

His father spoke first. 'Mantazi has bought some time for us, but it won't last for ever. We need to get you and Amira out of the country, and she wants me to come with you.'

'But you said Iran was the place where you want to die.?'

'It is, but I need to prove to you I was not behind the killing of Becky, so I'll come and face the consequences back in London. I'll find out who did this, whatever the consequences for me.'

He seemed sincere and a part of Richard wanted to believe him but no more than the other half that wanted to call him a liar.

'And how do you propose to do that?'

'I don't know but I'll think of something.' His father no longer looked concerned by the prospect of spending the rest of his life in jail for spying. On Greece, it had been a different story, but he seemed to have changed. The weariness in his eyes suggested he'd lost his willingness to fight. He paused and looked at the flames. 'I helped Iran because I disapproved of the way they were being treated by the West. I was trying to put an end to hypocrisy but look where that got me. I have been very naive to think I could change the world.'

'Whatever you think about what you've done doesn't convince me that you had nothing to do with Becky's murder,' said Richard.

'Somebody played Becky, let her get in too deep and then fed her to the wolves.'

Richard didn't answer at first. There were too many likely scenarios and the most convincing involved revenge for the killing of Abdul. He grabbed his father's shoulder and swung him round. 'You at least admit you know the men who did it. So, who are they connected to?'

'I met them, but I don't know who they are except to say they're bodyguards of the President. I don't think they could have been working for the President when they carried out the hit because he wanted to see the document you were trying to retrieve. The meeting I had with the killers was intended to make me look guilty. The photo was a set up.'

'By whom?' Richard said, in no mood for conspiracy theories.

Amira interrupted. 'I think your father has a point. Circumstances are forcing us to get out of Iran and that kills off any chance of improving diplomatic relations. Somebody is trying to scupper this and it's not in the President's office.' Amira didn't look as relaxed about leaving Iran as David Helford. 'I accept that we have to get out of Iran for our own safety, but we can't leave until we've found the clue that might lead us to the Gospel. It must have stayed in England, but we don't know where.' She held her hands to the fire and Richard caught the lines of her face in the flickering light. 'Why do you think we found the knight's journals in Cyprus?' she asked.

'Because Masood brought them with him on his return to Persia.'

Amira nodded in agreement. 'I think you're right but that tells me that he would only have the journals if he had inherited them after the knight's death in England. Assuming this is true then Masood would have nothing to stay for. He must have left England to find his mother's Druze family.'

'That makes sense. We need to go over all the annotations in the Gospel of Thomas, there must be something to help.'

Amira frowned. 'I wish I were as optimistic as you. If the knight were dead and buried why would Masood want to leave clues?'

'Let's look now,' said Richard. 'Is the Gospel of Thomas here?'

'It is in the Ayatollah's tent where he is now,' Amira replied. 'I've looked and I can't see anything, but you can try.'

Richard turned in the direction of the tent, 'Save me some stew,' he said with a smile.

The Ayatollah was in one corner with Fatima going through another text.

She smiled again when she saw Richard and he thought how beautiful Iranian women were. Although the chador covered up her femininity, her eyes were made up, emphasising the brilliant whites of her eyes, which sparkled in the dim light. 'What can I do for you?' she said, her lips parted revealing a perfect set of teeth.

'The Gospel of Thomas, can I have a look at it'

'Of course, I'll bring it to you.'

Richard was surprised how small the book was. Fatima also carried another small manuscript which was tied together by cord. 'These are the notes of the scholar Masood,' said Fatima. He has referenced them to the sayings in the Gospel.'

'Sayings?'

'Yes – sayings. The Gospel is not a life of Jesus like the other Gospels. It is a document which reputes to be the sayings of Jesus. Some of them are quite intriguing and do not seem to be the same voice as Jesus words as recorded in the other more recognised Gospels…Please wear these gloves while you look, they are very old.'

Richard sat down at a table by a lamp. The Ayatollah had decided to retire. Fatima came to join him. 'I suppose that if the Gospel of Thomas is subversive then that explains why Rome decided it was a fake.'

She nodded. 'That's true, but many more enlightened scholars think it is genuine.' She sat down beside him, and he smelt her perfume mingling with the night air. 'Is there anything I can do to assist you?' she said. 'You will need help with the translation.'

'That's kind,' said Richard. 'You must be hungry.'

'Hunger means nothing when there is so much to find in these documents. It will be my life's work to study them. They are amazing and reveal so much we don't know about the various sects and tribes. I am intrigued by the Parthians who ended up in India probably with St Thomas.'

'Another time,' said Richard, turning the pages of Masood's notebook.

'He's written the notes in Latin, which is unusual. I'll translate for you' said Fatima.

Richard's attention was distracted by some drawings which accompanied the notes. There were several detailed sketches of plants.

'These are Pistachio flowers, pollinated by the wind so don't need to be colourful to attract insects, but these are almond blossom which are much more attractive,' said Fatima.

'He's a talented artist.'

Richard turned the page and saw another drawing of a group of trees. 'You won't find these in Iran,' he said.

'No,' Fatima smiled. 'I remember these from my time in Oxford…Oak trees.'

'Why would he draw oak trees? I mean he will have seen oak trees in England but why here?'

'I think he is making a visual comment about the text in the Gospel… it says…*in paradise there are five trees that do not change between summer and winter and their leaves never fall. Anyone who comes to know them will not die.*'

'But oak trees drop their leaves and he is referring to evergreen trees like Cypress.' Richard stared at the drawing. 'There are only three oaks trees here and the text refers to five.' There was something familiar about the way the trees were grouped in a triangle, but he could not remember what it was.

'He is referring to paradise and possibly death of someone he loves.'

'His mother died in Cyprus just like Barnabas. Could that be the connection with the trees?'

'It's possible but we believe the knight had also died so it is possible he is mourning that death in these words'

'I agree…Do you see the next quote from the Gospel that he's written below the picture.' Fatima translated the quote.

There will be five in one house. Three will oppose two. Two will oppose three. The father will oppose his son and the son will oppose his father. And they will stand up and they will be alone.'

The words rang in Richard's ears, thinking about his own disagreements with his father but the significance of the *five trees and two will oppose three* troubled him. He turned to face Fatima. 'Something is troubling Masood in these drawings,' he said.

'I think his relationship with his stepfather – the knight- is important because the word alone refers to someone renouncing worldly things and being alone with God.' Fatima looked down at the text, her finger running over the words. 'He has quoted again from the Gospel of Thomas:

Jesus said recognise what is in front of you, and that which is hidden from you will be revealed to you. Nothing that is hidden will fail to be displayed.'

'He's trying to tell us something.'

Fatima's eyes lit up. 'Yes…He knows that he will never go back to England and he now knows that the Gospel of Barnabas is important. If he had known about the letters between Barnabas and Thomas, then there might have been a reason for him to have the Gospel with him, but he doesn't want to blatantly tell us where it is out of respect for the knight – his stepfather.'

Richard beamed and touched Fatima's hand unable to control his excitement. 'So, it might be buried with the knight? We need to find the tomb and disinter the body.'

Fatima smiled. 'I think you're right, go back to England and find the tomb.' It was her turn to take Richard's hand and squeeze it. 'Promise me, you'll find the Gospel and bring it back to me…to this place where it belongs.'

'I want to find it; I swear I'll try.' He thought for a moment and looked directly into Fatima's eyes. There was a goodness and clarity in this woman unlike Amira – who was full of contradictions. 'Why do you think the Gospel belongs here?'

'It's a hunch that there is something here that connects the Gospel. I don't know what it is. It was just that there is another quote from the Gospel in Masood's notebook. It says:

Split wood, I am there. Lift up the rock I am there.'

'What does that mean?' Richard asked.

'There was once a wood here, just outside the walls, you can still see the roots where the trees once were. It is divided by solid rock which splits the wood. I can show you.'

Richard didn't answer, he was flicking through Masood's notebook, looking for something which might explain all these quotations. There were several detailed drawings of trees, none of which were oak or Cypress. There was also a drawing of a settlement. Small thatched huts were built around a circle. There were dense trees around the clearing where the huts had been erected, suggesting that it might be in a forest. On the next page he saw a picture of a church where Masood had repeated the words of St Thomas.

'Recognise what is in front of you,' he said.

'Yes, please do,' said Fatima with a wink. 'We should go and see the remains of the split wood.'

Richard nodded. 'I'll follow you.'

'We can go out through the gap where the wall has collapsed, it is just on the other side.'

Fatima picked up the lamp and he followed her out of the tent. The broken rocks where the wall had fallen were difficult to cross and he stumbled as he made his way across the crumbling stone. Fatima seemed surer footed, despite her chador. The blackness of her cloak blended into the darkness and he struggled to see her despite the lamp. A voice cried out. It was not a female voice.

'Helford.'

Richard clenched his fist; the intervention by Harper took him by surprise. He strained his eyes, trying to adjust to the darkness and the direction of the voice.

'Fatima, where are you? I can't see anything.'

He stumbled again and then he saw him.

Harper had escaped.

Chapter Twenty-Nine

The Zagros Mountains West of Yazd, Iran-
September 22nd, 2005

'Don't fucking move one more inch or I'll blow little miss Chador's brains out.'

The lamp Fatima had been carrying was on its side on the ground, its light illuminating Harper's desperate face. He held Fatima by the neck, a pistol pressed into the side of her head. She looked terrified.

Richard raised his hands above his head. 'I'm unarmed. I'm not going to shout. Let her go Harper and we can talk about what you want.'

'I want a vehicle and safe passage out of here to the Gulf and a high-speed boat to take me across to Oman.'

'And I want to know about Becky's murder in Ankara. If you tell me, I'll help you.' Richard hated Harper but he needed to find out whether he should hate his father more.

'How do I know you won't double cross me again?'

'I was nothing to do with that. You've got to believe me.'

Richard kept walking forward.

'No fucking further.'

He stopped and listened. He could see them only a few feet from him. He knew Harper would not hesitate if he thought he was threatened.

'Look Harper...Amira and myself are leaving tomorrow and my father has agreed to go as well and face the music in Britain. We all need to get out of Iran. You can come too. Just let Fatima go and we'll talk. The Ayatollah will use his influence to get us out of the country.'

Harper released his grip. Even in the poor light he could see the relief on Fatima's face. She rushed to Richard, who took hold of her hand and felt it shake, her palms perspiring even in the cold night air.

'Thank you,' she said.

'Wait with me here. 'said Richard. 'I'm sure this won't take long to resolve.'

He turned back to face Harper. 'How did you escape?'

'Money always works in this fucking place. How do you think I did it?'

'But you haven't got enough dollars to get you out of the country - have you? Tell me what you know, and we'll help you, but you're not going to kill my father.'

Harper walked closer to Richard, still brandishing the gun. He glared at him, suspiciously. 'I ought to kill you now like you should have been killed in Ankara.'

Richard's eyes widened. 'Are you telling me, they should have killed me and not Becky?' He almost howled with guilt that he might be responsible for her murder.

'Yes, but your father stopped us killing you. He didn't want you dead, but somebody had to die to stop the Ankara gospel getting to Iran. That only left Becky. You know I told you that your father has been working for Iranian intelligence. That means he works for the Qods, led by Qasem Soleimani. The Ankara Gospel could strengthen the Shia hand in terms of the succession dispute between Shia and Sunni. Soleimani wanted it back here in Iran but your father didn't.'

'But if he worked for Soleimani then why would he defy him?'

'Your father is a fucking idealist; he wants peace in the Middle East. He wants it more than his loyalty to Soleimani. He reckoned that if Shia Islam had the upper hand it would only incense the Saudis and make them even bigger enemies than they already are. That's why the Turks are supressing the contents of the Ankara Gospel. Nadia's motives were different. She sent the virus to set back the nuclear programme but also give the Ayatollah a chance to consolidate his position with the supreme leader.'

'How's he going to do that?'

'By identifying Mantazi as an enemy in league with the dead Colonel, even though they are sworn enemies. It's like killing twoo birds with one stone. There will be a purge and Mantazi will be executed for terrorism. The Ayatollah's standing with his fellow clerics will shoot up for unearthing the conspiracy. He will be seen as a potential leader.' The gleam of satisfaction on Harper's face said it all. 'That's why the Ayatollah sent Mantazi to Tehran but instead of being greeted as a hero, he will be thrown into prison and executed after a show trial.'

'So which side are you on Harper?'

The American didn't have time to answer. The first bullet hit Harper in the right hand. He yelled in agony; blood gushed from his wrist. The pistol flew out of his hand, spinning into the air.

'Step away from Harper, Richard,' His father was clutching an AK and moving forward. Even in the darkness, the gun was unmistakeable. His finger was on the trigger and his other hand supported the barrel of the rifle.

Harper let out a cynical laugh. 'Those Mossad guys gave you great training, that was a fucking good shot.' He looked at Richard and muttered under his breath. 'See what I mean,' he whispered. 'Your bastard father is still trying to cover his tracks.'

Richard's dismay must have been obvious to Harper because the American looked satisfied that he'd made his mark. He didn't hear his father's voice. It felt distant.

'I've no time for jokes, step out of the way Richard.'

Richard turned around with his back to Harper and faced his father's gun. 'No, you're not going to kill him. You'll have to kill me first.' Soldiers were surrounding the area, shining lights on the scene. 'He's coming out of Iran with us so he can testify against you for being behind the murder of Becky.'

'I didn't do it Richard…I swear. I've told you. Who are you going to believe me or Harper? His story is fiction.'

'I don't believe you. I am going to see that you face justice. The truth is all I care about. You're not going to kill Harper unless you kill me first.'

'Put the gun down, David.' Amira said. 'We've got a lovely stew that needs eating. We're all going to relax and get some sleep, and tomorrow the Ayatollah will get us across to Oman. Whoever was responsible for the murder of Becky will have to answer for it when we are out of the country.'

David continued to point the gun and Harper laughed, a cynical humourless laugh, he raised his hands above his head and clapped - a slow unappreciative handclap. He didn't struggle when the soldiers surrounded him. The smile continued but his eyes were closed, averting the dazzle of the spotlights. Richard sighed as they led Harper away. He turned to Amira.

'Harper was arrested by the Ayatollah's men. How are you going to persuade him to let Harper go?'

'He'll agree. He wants rid of Harper just as much as we do.'

Richard nodded and wondered whether taking them both out of Iran was a good idea. Who should he believe? A murdering devious bastard like Harper or his father, a traitor to his country and to his family.

Fatima stood alone a few feet away having recovered the light she'd lost. 'You must be in shock,' he said softly. 'I don't suppose you still want to show me what we came out here for in the first place.'

Her smile was less confident than before, and her hands were shaking. 'It was scary, he is a bad man. You are not like that.' She took a piece of paper out of her pocket and handed it to him. 'This is my email. It's a US mailbox that can be used via the University of Tehran network. I'll write to you if I find anything about Barnabas.' She smiled, 'I'd like to keep in touch, not easy in our blessed Republic.'

'You are very kind.' Richard realised he was shivering.

Fatima put her arm around his shoulders. 'I'm not the only one in shock. You're a good man, I know it,' she said.

The compliment made him feel good. 'Show me the rock that lies between the split wood.'

'It's here.' She turned her lamp onto the rock that was next to him. It must have weighed several tons.

'We'll never move it.'

'I don't believe we need to, see how it is split. This rock was put here by man and not nature.'

Richard stood up and stared at the boulder. It was round and curved in the most unusual ways, like a Henry Moore sculpture made by nature. The split was not wide enough to hide anything; his fingers barely penetrated the crack. 'Can we drive a chisel in and open the split a little further? See if anything his hidden.'

Fatima laughed. 'That would be a major job and we haven't time to do it. I think we should go and eat.'

Richard nodded. 'I think we must.'

Chronic fatigue was taking its toll on Richard. He tried to think but his mind was blank. The words of St Thomas echoed in his brain. *Recognise what is right in front of you. The father will oppose the son. Nothing hidden will fail to be displayed.*

They went back to where the food was being served. It was delicious and Richard ate like it was the last meal he would ever eat. Maybe it was the food that made him remember. Whatever it was, the memory came to him without warning. He remembered where he'd seen the oak trees before. He seen them on the reverse of the icon – three oak trees in a triangle.

He didn't need to split the rock. The answer was already there.

Chapter Thirty

The Straits of Ormuz, the Persian Gulf, Iran- September 23rd, 2005

It was still dark when the jet boat moved out of Bandar Abbas harbour. The Straits of Hormuz were dangerous for such a small boat, surrounded in a cramped shipping lane by many oil tankers. As Richard's eyes adjusted to the darkness, he became aware of black hulking shadows of metal passing close by, causing the boat to rock uneasily in the swell. On the journey to the port, they'd remained out of sight in the back of a van. Nobody talked and when the drivers stopped at check points they were let through without ceremony. Their hiding place was basic and would have been spotted had the soldiers or police chosen to carry out a search. Richard decided the Ayatollah's influence must have stretched far and wide through this beleaguered country. He had plenty of time to reflect on where to look for the Gospel as the long journey to the coast passed in considerable discomfort. The castle visited by the knight in England was the last recorded location. That would be the first place he went to but before that he needed to resolve the more immediate problem of his father. Harper's damning evidence seemed plausible, but nothing about this rogue American was trustworthy. He decided to reserve judgement until they were back on British shores.

Richard breathed a sigh of relief as they moved with caution out into open waters. The tiny lights along the shores of Iran became faint twinkling stars. The first light of dawn was beginning to creep over the horizon. The pilot hit the throttle and the jet boat began to pick up speed, leaning back in the water, lifting the bow before it crashed down onto the waves with a juddering bump. Spray splattered over the boat soaking them all. He licked the salt off his lips and looked at his fellow passengers. Harper and David sat next to each other, leaning up against empty crates which previously had been full of cigarettes smuggled into Iran. He found it amusing that a boat previously loaded with contraband was now returning with a cargo of foreign spies. It was also ironic that the two men in front of him on this boat were sworn enemies, handcuffed together like bosom buddies. Richard couldn't quite believe he was taking them back to London. He studied them both and felt distant from their world. Amira had arranged cuffs to keep them out of trouble and she carried a gun just in case, but Richard decided they were no longer a threat. His father was tired of all this subterfuge. It was for his son to take up the challenge of uncovering the truth behind the conspiracy, where religious loyalties need not create division. As he shook the Ayatollah's hand, back at the camp, he pledged that one day, he would personally deliver the Gospel of Barnabas, ensuring the truth would be revealed.

There was land ahead; a long golden beach, a few palm trees and some low cliffs, pock marked by the sea. He could see a ruined castle and looking back, with the sun up, the sight of the mainland loomed in the distance. They were only a few miles offshore and still in Iran.

'It's Queshm island.' Amira shouted in Richard's ear above the noise of the engines. 'We have to skirt round it before crossing the gulf to Khasab.'

The sea got rougher as they emerged from the shelter of the island. Tankers passed them on all sides, more threatening in the full light of day. They were not the only fast boats doing the crossing in both directions. The vessels were all shapes but always small when paired against the oil carrying giants. Their key advantage was their speed against the lumbering tankers, they could outrun the big boys. Some were precariously overloaded, heading into

Iran, sitting too low in the water, easily sunk if struck by a big wave. Richard tried to convince himself that the boatman knew what he was doing. It was their livelihood and they did these runs every day. A vital lifeline to Iran and the crippling sanctions imposed by the West.

It was less than forty kilometres and yet it seemed ten times longer. He closed his eyes and let the spray drench his face, wishing the journey to end. He opened his eyes intermittently and peered back across to his father, who was being sick. Turning the corner into the lengthy estuary that led to Khasab couldn't come soon enough. The water's calmed immediately and the boat shut down its two outboard motors to a minimum pace. The bow sunk back into the water and the journey became pleasant after the awful crossing. Grey cliffs surrounded them on all sides and radiated the heat from the sun. It was bloody hot. He saw Amira seek protection from her veil, but Richard, Harper and David had nowhere to hide from the burning rays.

Reaching the harbour, the quayside was bustling with activity. Piles of silver waterproof bags, full of goods from Dubai and the UAE littered the quayside. Boats were being rapidly loaded. Despite the chaos, organisation existed generated by a big profitable business. Warehouses lined the docks, their doors open, revealing new cars to be shipped across the Gulf, one by one, with crates stacked with cigarettes. Nobody took any notice of them as they set foot on dry land and walked away from the water. There was no customs post and little attention paid to the fact that they'd just crossed the border between two countries. They passed one warehouse piled high with Nokia and Motorola phones. There was no attempt to hide the illegal traffic. It seems that there was an unwritten rule with the authorities. Iran needed the products to escape the sanctions and Oman remained passionately neutral.

'Where to now?' Richard asked Amira.

'We wait in the coffee shop along the harbour. We relax and wait for our next contact.'

'Who told you all this?'

'The Ayatollah. He is on our side and we promised not to let him down.'

The coffee shop was about half a mile from the harbour. By the time they reached it, perspiration was dripping off their bodies and soaking through their shirts, leaving tide marks of sweat. They gulped down copious quantities of ice-cold water which the café owner brought to them without comment. On a small gas ring Richard saw a large pan bubbling away, filled with rice and chicken. His hunger pangs could no longer be ignored. He ordered a portion by pointing at the pan and never thinking how it might be paid for. The owner of the café served up the food and sprinkled raisins and pine nuts on top. He seemed to have been given instructions because he never queried payment. The food looked delicious and he began to eat without resting until he had finished. His father was still suffering from sea sickness and could not stare at the food for fear of being sick again. Harper hadn't thrown up but had been close to doing so. He'd clearly lost his appetite. Amira nibbled at flat bread and relished the thick syrupy coffee. They waited. They hadn't slept for hours and the mid-day heat was taking its toll even with the shelter of the café awnings. Richard fell asleep.

The female voice in his ear sounded familiar. He wondered whether he was dreaming, frustrated that he could no longer hear Becky's voice, as if all the women he knew in the world were competing to erase her memory. 'We are ready to go,' the voice said.

'Ready to go where?' He blinked at the woman staring down at him.

It was Nadia.

'Hello Richard.' She looked pleased to see him again. There was an air of relaxed confidence about her, so different from what he'd seen in London. Dressed in jeans and a blue long-sleeved smock with a silk headscarf revealing her fringe resting on her forehead, she wore Chanel sunglasses and make up like she'd just come from a shopping mall in Dubai. He surprised himself in the way he was distracted by these details.

He wanted to be angry, seeing her standing in front of him, so calm and smug. 'Nice of you to show up now after doing your best to get me killed,' he said bitterly. 'Why didn't you tell me about the virus on the computer stick?'

Nadia's smile dissolved. 'I can explain,' she said.

'Go on.'

'What you don't know you'll never reveal, and you were too close. I did it for your own sake, knowing the Ayatollah would look after you. You must have realised he wants to be leader. His contact with me is part of his grand plan. If it gets out, he'll face execution for treason.'

He still didn't know whether he could trust Nadia. He sensed that he was just an instrument of that plan and was expendable. He looked across the café in the direction of David and Harper. They were both sound asleep.

He replied to Nadia, nodding at the two men. 'One of them is responsible for the murder of Becky. Where did you get the photographs you showed me?' He pointed his finger. 'No bullshit answers, no lies.'

Nadia looked around as if she were checking out who was listening. 'The Ayatollah sent them to me.'

'And where did he get the photos?'

'I don't know.'

'You told me the photos were from contacts in Turkey.'

'I lied. I couldn't tell you about the Ayatollah and the virus on the memory stick.'

Nadia's answer urged him to confront the two men again. He stormed over to where they were sleeping and shook David. 'Wake up' he shouted.

David was not the only one to wake. Harper sat up and stared at Nadia, as shocked as he was that she'd come back. Amira hadn't been asleep but stood up when Richard became aggressive.

'Did you ask Mantazi to stop the Ankara Gospel getting back to Iran? Tell me. Yes or No' he said, staring directly at his father.

David looked bemused by his son's outburst. He remained calm.

'No,' he whispered under his breath. 'It's true I wanted to stop the Gospel coming to Iran because I thought it would inflame tensions between Iran and Saudi Arabia. But I had no authority to order such an operation. I didn't do it. You've got to believe me.'

'Leave it Richard,' Amira said. 'There is a time and a place for this and it's not now.'

But David would not leave it alone. He pointed to Harper. 'Here is the man who arranged it with Mantazi.'

It was Harper's turn to speak. 'Your word against mine.' he said with more than a hint of sarcasm.

David ignored Harper's cynicism and spoke directly to Richard. 'It's simple really. I'm an enemy of the United States and so is Iran. Harper is tasked to destroy the regime with covert action, and he knows that killing both of you in Ankara would do his job for them. On the one hand, Soleimani would be severely pissed off that the chance to bring back the Gospel from Ankara had been thwarted. And on the other hand, the Saudi/Iran peace initiative that Nadia was planning with the Ayatollah would also be dead in the water. Harper was working for the factions in the US administration that think Iran is the pariah state and not Saudi Arabia who they sell a lot of US and British arms to.

'But they killed Becky and not me.'

'Becky had another agenda and I think that messed things up. When we get to England, I'll prove it to you. Harper wanted you both killed but, in the end...'

'I cancelled the hit,' Harper said with a smirk. 'Bullshit. Why would I do that? Somebody else stepped into silence Becky. Someone who had an interest in seeing you alive but didn't give a shit about her.' He pointed an accusing finger at David Helford.

Nadia had been on her cell phone and didn't listen what David had said, or at least he thought that was the case. She ended the call and intervened. 'We need to leave and quick.'

Richard sighed, still no clearer on why Becky had been killed. He allowed his eyes to follow the tarmac road up into the mountains. There were two Mercedes waiting outside. He stood up and began walking towards the vehicles. 'We better go then.'

Harper and David followed and were put in the front car with a driver and two of Nadia's men who were both armed. Nadia, Amira and Richard followed with a driver and one more guard.

Nadia sat in the back with Amira and Richard on either side. The cars drove at speed along the well-made roads, obstructed only by the desert wind blowing sand in swathes across the surface. Richard looked out of the window and contemplated what he wanted to say to Nadia. If she was telling the truth, then she must be working with the Ayatollah in the spirit of reconciliation with Shia Islam and not as a supporter of Wahhabism. It was difficult to believe that she was opposed to the dominant ideology of Islam in Saudi Arabia. What if she didn't oppose it and was working for the GID, the Saudi Intelligence Service, with the mission to disrupt the Iranian regime by pretending to support someone who opposed it. What if she was only interested in defeating Iran then she might be responsible for the murder of Becky. Nothing was conclusive. With reluctance, he decided to say nothing. The journey to Muscat was going to take at least six hours. He closed his eyes and tried to sleep.

A screech of brakes jolted him out of a deep slumber. The wheels of the Merc locked and skidded to a halt throwing them against the front passenger seats. Nadia took time to recover her composure before leaning forward to speak to the driver. She turned back to face Richard.

'It's a roadblock,' she said. 'Let me deal with it.' She straightened her veil and climbed out of the car. He could see the other driver shouting at the guards on the road. Something was wrong.

'I don't like this.' Richard said to Amira.

His hunch was correct. Three men who looked nothing like Omani police appeared from behind the large rocks that were scattered along the roadside. They converged on their car and opened the door. It was him they were after.

He kicked out as they dragged him from the Merc. The blow from the rifle felt like a sledgehammer plunging into his stomach, the pain of previous assaults springing back into his consciousness. He was winded, putting up no resistance. As they pulled him back through the dust, he saw Nadia running towards him. She was waving her hands but the men who held him were not listening. The fake soldiers had gone. The jihadis were in control. They were going to kill him.

At times like this life moves in slow motion. The brain tries to rationalise what is an irrational event. *Why didn't they just do it now? A bullet to the head and no chance to resist. A ritual execution, a beheading because I killed Abdul.*

The chatter of machine gun fire split the air. He felt the man who was holding him go limp, relaxing his grip. Richard crashed to the ground, bullets ricocheting around him. He buried his face into the ground and hoped that the dead body lying next to him would provide some cover.

His father was holding the gun, firing with cool precision, giving the jihadis no chance to return fire.

'Run while I cover you.' David screamed above the noise. The jihadists retreated, his cue to get away while his father pinned the gunmen down. He wondered whether it was enough, but went anyway, hoping that he might live another day. Reaching the car, he found Amira crouching with Nadia, protected by one of her security guards. The men who'd been in the other Merc were hiding like frightened lambs after giving up their weapons to Harper and David. The American hadn't broken cover, unlike David he lay low behind the other car, preparing his weapon.

His father stood alone with a death wish, guns blazing, making it difficult for the jihadis to fire back. His expression was blank and tired. Richard wanted to help but had no gun. The guard near Nadia cradled his but looked too scared to think about using it.

'Give me your gun,' Richard shouted. Nadia nodded and the guard handed it over. It was a Glock 19 which was a blessing as he'd used one before. He clicked off the safety and cocked the weapon, peering around the car where he could see. Harper was firing from the safety of the other Merc but had done enough for David to take cover, dodging behind a rock and reloading. Wasting no time, David advanced towards the target, zigzagging through a jumble of rocks, letting out short bursts from his automatic rifle.

David didn't see the threat behind where he was running. Another jihadi had broken out from the rear and was preparing to fire. Richard moved into the open and fired three rounds. The bullets bounced all around the jihadi, but none found its target. Richard cursed, and ducked behind the car again. His father reacted with ruthless efficiency, diving to the ground and rolling over, killing the man with two shots direct to his chest. The two jihadis he'd been trying to take down took the diversion as their opportunity. They came out, their guns burning death. Richard fired again, luckier this time, bringing down one of the men with a wound to his leg. Reacting, the other man turned his gun away from David for a second. The moment's hesitation proved to be his last mistake. A bullet from David's rifle struck the man through the side of his head. The other man lay helpless on the ground, blood gushing from his leg. David didn't look when he shot him as well.

Richard stared at his father with a growing sense of horror at the way he'd executed the men without a conscience. Harper walked towards them, still pointing his gun. Amira, Nadia and the guards stayed hidden while the three men stared at the dead lying at their feet.

David sighed. Fatigue was stamped across his face. 'Kill or be killed. Him or me.' he said with an apologetic glance sensing Richard's shock at his clinical method of killing. 'You either live or you die. It's your choice in this game.'

Richard ground his teeth, realising there was no point moralising. The men who attacked them would have shown no mercy. His father was right. He turned away and stared at the foothills of the mountain range. A glint of sunlight reflected sharply back from about one hundred metres. It was bright, forcing him to close his eyes. His eyes were still closed when David came at him, throwing himself over his body. The power of the tackle, sent him flying, falling backwards onto the ground. His father landed on top of him, a dead weight, crushing the air in his lungs.

There was no anger in his scream. Only pain.

Chapter Thirty-One

The Road to Muscat, Oman- September 23rd, 2005

Blood was seeping through his fingers. He couldn't move, pinned down by his father's weight. Signs of life, draining away. Low weary groans from the man he despised. The same man who had saved his life.

The sniper hadn't finished. Harper came to their aid, dragging his father away when the American's body reared up, his face contorted in pain. A splatter of blood spurted from his stomach where a bullet had ripped through his back and out the other side. For a moment, Harper continued pulling until David was clear of Richard. It was the second bullet that made him crumple. Harper sank down onto his knees, terror in his eyes as if he knew the second wound was fatal. He slumped forward, blood, bone and brain dripping from the hole in his head. Richard's stomach turned at the horror of Harper's injuries; bile and vomit rose in his mouth. He knew he'd be next and was only alive because his father had taken the bullets for him. He lay on the road exposed to the sniper's gun, frozen with fear, transfixed by the way they'd tried to save him even though he hated what they stood for. His stupor was broken by the sight of more bullets tearing into the prone bodies of the two men. The firing stopped for a moment. He sensed the gunman reloading and took his chance, rolling away from more bullets pounding into the road where he'd been lying a second ago. He found his feet and grabbed Harper's gun, running for the safety of the car. Amira was crouched at the rear observing the carnage a few feet away. Back in Yazd, she'd been calm and in control, but seeing Harper hit by a bullet in the head had flipped her over the edge. She had no weapon and looked helpless without one. Nadia sat on the ground, shouting into her satellite phone over the sound of gun fire. She was furious and panicking at the same time. Her security guards were running away, abandoning them to their fate.

Richard glared at Nadia. 'Who knew we were here?' he said panting through gritted teeth.

She didn't reply, continuing to talk on her phone. She wasn't expecting this, he thought, but maybe she knew it was coming. Two more shots blew up the tyres and he heard the ping-ping of more shrapnel finding its way into the car's body work. It was only a matter of time before he'd strike the fuel tank and they'd have to follow the guards and run like hell.

He sat on the road propped up by the car and took deep gulps of air. His shirt was covered in blood, his father's blood. Or did it belong to Harper?

Harper was dead. The firing had stopped. The sniper no longer wasted his ammunition on the bodies on the road. Richard had no tears for the American, but he wanted to save his father, if he was still alive. He checked his gun, trying to slow down his breathing. The moment he emerged from behind the car, the shooting would resume. He'd be a sitting duck but had to try. He handed Harper's gun to Amira.

'When I say, keep firing for all your worth in the direction of the sniper. Don't get yourself killed but draw his fire away from me while I go and get him.'

Amira nodded, nervously taking the gun, and checking the magazine. 'There aren't many rounds left,' she said. 'We've not got any more ammo.'

Richard sighed. The only cover available was his father's body. He rehearsed how he would pick him up. A fireman's lift would be too difficult. He'd have to drag him across the road and hope for the best. He looked at Amira and then at Nadia.

'Help is coming.' Nadia said.

'How long?' asked Richard.

'It could take twenty minutes.'

'I've got to get to him. He might not have long to live.' He signalled to Amira. 'Are you ready?'

'Yes.'

David Helford was only ten feet away, but it might have been ten miles. It would take the gunman a few seconds to realise there was somebody else to kill and take aim. He hoped to reach his father by then and begin to drag him to safety.

Richard stepped out from the cover of the car and ran, only a few steps, from one side to the other and then hitting the ground heavily and crawling the final few feet.

He counted to three and waited for the onslaught.

Silence. There was no more shooting. He continued to expect the worst, but the silence remained. His father's face was turned towards him and he remembered the eyes of Masood on the train.

Dead man's eyes.

He noticed a quiver in his father's lips and at that moment forgot there might be a gunman. He had to hear what his father was saying.

'Don't move me. Save yourself,' the old man whispered.

Blood was dripping from the corner of his mouth. He struggled to speak. Richard could see the desperation on his father's face, struggling to find the words. 'M...M...Mossad,' he said at last. 'In M...M...M Six.' The dying man coughed, and more blood came from his mouth. Richard realised he was lying in a pool of his father's blood. There was no more time.

'What do you mean?'

'... didn't kill Bec...'

'Did Harper?' Richard raised his voice, desperate to know what his father knew.

'Sorry...S...Son...I love you...'

The old man had no more to give. His body jerked into a spasm as the last drops of life leaked away onto the desert floor. Richard bowed his head, involuntary tears flooding his eyes.

The sniper had gone and sent his father and Harper to Hell.

Chapter Thirty-Two

Tigan, Essex, England, AD1105.

Although the drawbridge is down, two soldiers bar my way. One is older and fatter and seems to be in charge. I think it is a father and son as their faces appear similar. 'What is your business here, stranger?' asks the father.

'My name is Robert de Valognes – son of Sir Peter de Valognes. Let me through. This is my home.'

It was probably an exaggeration to call these men soldiers. They were farmers who had been given a battle axe and told to guard the keep. If they were relatives, as I suspected, they'd put their lives on the line to look after their family. If they could do that well, they would be better protectors of the gate. A simple logic, but with these two I am not sure the theory will work. I could see they were nervous, their hands twitching against the handle of their axes. The older one moved closer and began to stare me out. His breath smelt of ale and onions. He looked me up and down, stepping back to avoid the reach of my sword. Something was registering in his thick skull, a flicker of recognition.

'We heard that Robert was dead or a deserter to the Crusaders cause,' he said with a sneer.

'Do I look dead to you?' I replied. 'I am here and want to see my father - take me to him.'

'It is him,' said the older man, looking down at Masood who was gripping my hand tightly. 'And this is his little bastard, I suspect, born of an Arab woman, I would guess.' He nodded, turning to the younger man for approval. 'Yes, it is him. A blight on his father's great name.' He turned to

look me in the eye and bared his teeth in a gesture of disgust. 'A pox on you for whoring with the enemy.'

My patience was wearing thin. I let go of Masood and drew my sword, assuming a battle pose. 'Who's first?' I said. 'Let's see who the deserter is. Let me enter in peace or I will make my own way and you will suffer the consequences. The choice is yours.'

The commotion brought other people into the bailey. People were shouting and one voice stood out from the crowd. After all these years away, I still recognised my younger brother – Michael. He ran towards me, pushing through the guards who'd blocked my way, embracing me with the warmth of a brother who loved me despite what had been said about my cowardice.

'It's wonderful to see you Robert, it's been so long. Where have you been?' he said. 'We thought you were dead.'

'It is a long story that's taken nine years to complete. It's a miracle that I am here to tell it.' Masood was clutching at my tunic, a worried expression on his face. 'This is Masood,' I said. 'His parents are dead; I am his guardian. He has no one else.'

Michael squatted down on his haunches and held out his hand to Masood. I appreciated the way he welcomed the boy without any question.

'Where is father and mother? Are they here? I have some explaining to do. It will be difficult for them to understand. I hope my father will hear me out.'

'He has cursed you many times and of late refused to allow your name to be spoken.'

I sighed and allowed my brother to take my hand and lead us both up the stone staircase and into the Great Hall which was situated halfway up the tower. My mother must have been told of my arrival. She was waiting to greet me, her arms outstretched, tears streaming down her face. 'I thought you were dead,' she wailed.

My father sat on his chair where he always received visitors. He did not say anything and did not rise. Instead, he stared through me as if I were not in the room, his legs outstretched, hands gripping the armrests of his seat. He was the Lord of the Manor and I was his serf not his son. I walked slowly towards him, my boots banging on the oak floorboards that formed the ceiling of the floor below. Masood, Michael and my mother waited at the other end of the hall. My father continued to say nothing, even when I stood before him. I bowed and knelt on one leg. My head remained lowered and I waited for what seemed like an age until he spoke.

'Are you a coward?' His voice echoed around the room.

'No, my Lord,' I replied.

'Have you brought the name of Valognes into disgrace?'

'No, my lord...I fought for two years in the Holy Land. I killed many Arabs in the name of Jesus Christ. After the battle for Antioch, God told me that I should not fight. Just like Christianity, Islam is the religion of Abraham. They revere Jesus and the Virgin Mother in their holy book. We should live in peace and worship God together.'

My father rose to his feet. He drew his sword and swung it above me. I raised my head in defiance, exposing my neck to the cutting edge of his blade. I did not flinch or quiver like the coward he thought I was. If he wanted to separate my head from my shoulders, then at least I could look God in the eye in the next world. My mother screamed.

The sword came down beside me, splintering the wooden floor, but not my head.

'Are you defying the decree of the Holy Father by refusing to fight?'

'I am following the orders of God himself who does not want this war.'

'The Pope is the messenger of God. If you defy him then you defy God himself.'

It was my turn to get angry. I stood up and walked towards him. 'The Pope is just a man like the rest of us and is appointed by men. He is not St Peter who was appointed by Jesus Christ.'

My father was an old man. He was overweight and red in the face from too much venison and wine. He was calm now, but I could see his anger prevailed.

'You are no longer my eldest son. When I die Michael will inherit this castle and the lands around it.'

'I have no need of your wealth and I am happy that Michael takes my birth right.'

'If it weren't for your mother and brother, I would have killed you for the disgrace you've brought on the family name. Instead, I will sign over Great Oaks to you and a bag of silver pennies minted in Colchester. As long as I'm alive, I forbid you to set foot in this castle again.'

'Thank you, father.'

I bowed and walked backwards, out of respect, to the entrance of the Hall. My father had returned to his chair and slumped into it. There were tears in his eyes which pleased me because it showed that he did love me whatever I had done to displease him. When I reached the end of the hall, I turned and took Masood's hand. My mother was weeping. My brother shook my hands and stepped back when I tried to embrace him. I understood it would be a mistake for him not to follow the wishes of my father. I nodded and left the Great Hall.

The people stood in silence, lining the bailey on both sides leading to the drawbridge. I bowed my head out of respect for them, acknowledging I was the banished son.

The sun was shining. I was not disappointed with the outcome. I hugged Masood and told him we would walk to Great Oaks and begin a new life.

Chapter Thirty-Three

Muscat, Oman- September 24th, 2005

Richard didn't bother to search the dead jihadis bodies. He knew they wouldn't carry identification. He stared down at their faces and wondered whether they were Al Qaeda. They had the look of Afghan Mujahedin and were not dressed like Taliban although they'd have to wear something less obvious in Oman. Whoever they were didn't matter. They came to avenge the death of Abdul and he was the target.

He relived the moment when his father saved his life. The crunching tackle, positioning himself to take the bullet meant for him. The last words of his father still rang in his ears:

He tried to shut it out of his mind and focus on how the shooting happened. *How the hell did the bastards know we were in Oman?*

They must have followed them over the Straits of Ormuz. Al Qaeda operating in Iran seemed unlikely but possible. There was no time to travel from Afghanistan. He was sure somebody had tipped them off. He turned to face Amira, who was kneeling in front of the bodies of Harper and his father. She was praying, distress and worry lined her face, tears running down her cheeks. Nadia was pacing up and down by the car, refusing to look.

'Who did you call, Nadia? Somebody knew,' he said.

'I called my people in Riyadh. They swear it wasn't them.'

'Who else?'

She hesitated and turned away.

He stepped closer and grabbed her arms, raising his voice. 'Who else? '

She glared at him, pushing him in the chest. 'How dare you. Let me go,' she shouted.

He released his hold. She walked away a few steps before turning back, staring at him, hesitating before speaking. 'If you must know...It was Rowena...your boss.'

The news hit him hard. He felt sick. At first, he couldn't find the words. He struggled to accept what she was saying. 'You're lying,' he said. His attention was diverted by the sight of three police cars and a van roaring down the highway, lights flashing. 'Are you telling me you've been briefing her all the time of my movements?'

'Yes - but not on everything.'

'But you told her where we were?'

'Yes.'

Richard did not reply. He was too angry to say something he would regret later.

The police cars screeched to a halt. Several officers jumped out and stood to attention waiting for the Captain's orders. They wore brown uniforms with berets and designer sunglasses. Every aspect of these men was immaculate. Roadblocks were set up and the policemen got to work.

The Royal Omani Police cleared up the mess of bodies as if they were clearing a jack-knifed lorry that had just spilled one hundred bags of rice over the road. There was no forensic examination or painstaking search of the crime scene. No careful clearance of the blood and brain spewed across the highway. The body bags were loaded into a police van which drove off without waiting for the rapid investigation to be completed. The remaining police swept the debris from the road onto the sand and let nature claim the evidence. The Captain surveyed the scene with an air of confidence that he already knew who was behind the attack. Nadia was following him, asking a stream of questions he did not answer. He waved her away like he was swatting a gnat. Richard had a sneaking admiration for the way they were dealing with the incident. He understood that the priority for the police was to sweep this under the

Persian carpet. In other words, give it to the Iranians who could call the foreigners spies and get some propaganda value. Omanis preferred a lower profile, leaving the big guns to get embroiled in Middle Eastern politics. That didn't mean the Omanis weren't involved. They just preferred to be more discreet.

It took just over fifteen minutes after the police had arrived, before they resumed their journey to Muscat, driven fast with sirens wailing and blue lights used to maximum effect. The captain travelled with them, leaning over the front passenger seat to ask in broken English what they'd been doing in Iran and who was trying to kill them. He wiped his brow and turned up the air conditioning. 'It's too damn hot to play silly games and pretend we don't know this is the work of Al Qaeda,' he said. 'It helps nobody and besides, we'll all die in this heat.'

'I wish I knew who was trying to kill us, do you?' said Richard, flashing a puzzled glance at the captain. 'We've been doing archaeological research.' He flashed his Professor Lewis Raymond's false Passport at the policeman. He didn't ask to see the documents of the two women and showed little interest in his passport.

'They are Sunni terrorists, who will not be tolerated. They were trying to kill you for no other reason than you were foreigners. The perpetrators will be captured, you have my personal guarantee. I am sorry you have been through this horror in my country. May I suggest that next time you come to Oman you do not use the Straits of Ormuz. It is a dangerous stretch of water and full of undesirables who might bring you harm.' He coughed and popped what looked like a mint into his mouth. 'We'll drop you off at the British Embassy. The bodies will be in the morgue until you are ready to claim them. You will tell the Americans…?'

Richard nodded.

The Captain turned to face Nadia before continuing in a much more serious tone. 'I know exactly who you are.' He looked at her with distaste. 'You are Nadia Zabor of the GID. You were not granted permission to enter Oman therefore you are here illegally. We will overlook this offence in the interests of diplomacy. You are not welcome in Oman and will be taken to the airport and put on the first flight back to Riyadh.'

Nadia said nothing and Richard hadn't ruled out that she had tipped off the gunmen. The Captain seemed to have the same hunch. He might have agreed with him, except for one thing. She was scared and surprised when the shooting started.

The British Embassy were not pleased to see them. They'd arrived in the middle of a party entertaining local dignitaries. An official said the station chief would see them in due course. They'd have to wait. Richard decided not to kick up a fuss. It would do no good and he wanted to talk to Amira first so they could get their story straight. They were ushered into a windowless room with a couple of low armchairs and given nothing to eat or drink. Fortunately, there was a water fountain in the corner. He poured Amira a tumbler full and then drank several glasses himself in quick succession. She drunk a little and then sat on one of the easy chairs and put her head in her hands. He was physically drained. The relief that they were safe opened emotions in him that he had kept locked away. He wept, unsure whether it was Becky, his father, or both that he was grieving for.

Amira moved to console him. 'It's not your fault,' she said. 'It's mine.'

At first, Richard didn't register what she was saying. He was too engrossed in his own thoughts. 'What did you say?' he said at last.

'It's my fault.'

'What do you mean, it's your fault?'

'It was my fault Becky got killed. I didn't know that the men were going to kill her, but I was instrumental in sending them on their mission.'

Richard's mouth dropped open. 'You...' he whispered. A part of him wanted to shout out but disbelief muted his rage. 'Oh my God. Why didn't you tell me this before now?'

'Your father wouldn't let me. He was comfortable for you to channel the blame in his direction and away from me. Now he is dead there is no more reason to keep quiet.' Amira's eyes were filled with tears. 'I'm so sorry Richard...It wasn't meant to be like this, I swear.'

Richard looked at her and smiled faintly. 'Perhaps we should go back to the beginning,' he said calmly.

She took a gulp of water. 'I'll try. It's a long story and I may have to break off if the embassy staff come.'

'Start now,' Richard said bluntly.

She cleared her throat. 'Your father - David - got me into Iran after I helped him get away from the Israelis. 'We switched boats and the Israelis bombed the ship they thought your father was on killing innocent sailors.'

'Mossad's subtlety in covert ops was never one of their strong points,' said Richard.

'No, it wasn't, but it helped me gain credibility with the clerics because I was trusted by David. My mission was to try and open discussion with factions of the clerical elite. Ways out of the sanctions, bringing Iran back into the international fold. All that sort of stuff. I pretended I was a professor assisting your father with the investigation into the scroll you found on Crete.'

Richard nodded. 'I know all that,' he said. 'Go on.'

'As you know the scroll gave us proof of a conspiracy by Paul and the Roman Catholic leaders at Nicene to deny the Gospel of Barnabas its rightful place in the canon of holy scripture. The study with your father led me to the

University of Teheran and the Ayatollah who you've met. He had the ear of the president.

'The Ayatollah was desperate to see the Ankara Gospel and was working unbeknown to me with Nadia to bring it back to Iran. The IRG also wanted it back because it would prove Shia rights to the Holy Prophet's ascendancy. Both your father and I wanted it stopped because the Gospel would cause divisions within the two branches of Islam and jeopardise any peace initiative. I approached Mantazi and asked him to stop the Ankara Gospel getting back to Iran. I didn't tell them they should kill anybody. I just wanted them to use their contacts in Turkey. The men he chose were Sunni hit men within the IRG who were affiliated with the MEK when they fought with Saddam's army in Iraq. They were Al Qaeda sleepers who knew all about what had happened to Abdul and wanted to avenge his killing. They wanted to make you suffer by killing someone close to you, someone you loved.'

He didn't know what to say. The door opening broke the impasse. Two men walked in, both wearing lightweight linen suits. He guessed that the man in the black suit was the Ambassador whereas the scruffy desert suit belonged to the station chief.

I'm Christopher Richardson-Blythe, British Ambassador and this is the Head of Station.' No name was offered. Richard and Amira shook hands with the two men.

'I am sorry to hear about the shooting today,' said the Ambassador. 'The Omani authorities want to keep it quiet. They don't want to admit to having Sunni terrorists on their shores and who can blame them. I expect they will catch the perpetrators before nightfall. Their methods are rather more ruthless than our own dear police.'

Richard nodded.

'I've agreed to a news blackout and the UK Government is aware. I'll leave you in the capable hands of this gentleman.,' the Ambassador said, offering his hand once more to Richard, but not to Amira.

'Let's go and find somewhere more comfortable,' the station chief said when the Ambassador had gone.

'Does the Ambassador know who we are and who the British guy and American guy who were killed were?' Richard asked.

The station chief chuckled. 'He knows nothing. 'My name's Pearson by the way.' He led them into a new rather more plush office with a view of the embassy grounds. 'I've got a conference arranged with Rowena at Vauxhall Cross. We'll take you both to the airport shortly after that.'

Richard's mind was racing, wondering what he would say to Amira when they were on the plane home. He glanced furtively in her direction. She seemed to understand his awkwardness. He decided to stay quiet about what Nadia had told him. He wanted to catch Rowena out. There was a large video conference facility in the room.

Pearson shook his head. 'London wants a phone call.'

Richard wasn't surprised. How could Rowena look him in the eye and tell him she wasn't involved in the hit.

The speaker phone crackled and sprang into action. Rowena was already on the line. 'Richard - so pleased you're safe. I'm sorry about your father.'

'No, you're fucking not, Rowena. Don't bullshit me.'

'Ok…Ok…I get it…you're still in shock.'

'The bullet was aimed at me. My father saved my life.'

Silence crackled across the line. He would have loved to see Rowena's face squirm.

'Are you sure?' she said.

'Course I'm fucking sure and I'll tell you something else Rowena. Somebody in the know tipped them off.' He paused to let his bombshell sink in. He could almost smell the uneasiness. 'There were only two people who could have told them where we were. One was you and the other was Nadia from the GID. Are you in contact with Nadia?'

'I can't answer that question,' Rowena responded feebly.

'I'll take that as a yes.' Richard waited for her to respond but nothing came. He was getting quite a lot of face pulls from Pearson, shocked by the insubordinate way he addressed Rowena. Richard no longer cared if they reported him or not. He could not forget what his father had said.

Pearson interrupted, 'We have agent Amira Al Marami from the CIA here with us. She was also present at the time of the shooting. She is a British citizen. I think you know each other.'

'Yes, I do, thank you Pearson.' Rowena paused, choosing her words carefully thought Richard. 'Hello Amira…I'm sorry to hear about Agent Harper. It's a sad loss to the Agency.'

Richard and Amira exchanged annoyed glances. He'd expected better from Rowena.

'I am more annoyed than sad,' Amira replied.

Silence again. The speaker phone exaggerated the sounds of Rowena shuffling papers and tapping her keyboard. After a couple of minutes, she spoke. 'Are you suggesting that I had something to do with the deaths of Harper and your father, Richard?'

'Why didn't you tell me about Nadia?'

Rowena ignored the question for the second time and tried to change the subject. 'Amira. How was your mission to improve relations with Iran?'

Richard was losing his temper but gritted his teeth when Amira raised her hand, a signal to back off.

'We have established contacts which we are not at liberty to divulge. Some progress has been made but they were hampered by Agent Harper's covert operations to promote regime change. He was supplying arms to the MEK.'

Richard looked at Amira and said. 'In support of Agent Amira's mission, I believe that we are close to finding the true Gospel of Barnabas. I would like to give that to the Iranians to complement the scroll discovered in Crete that was given to them by my father.'

'You think it is in Britain, don't you?' Rowena said.

Richard was incredulous that Rowena knew anything about where the bible might be. 'Who briefed you Rowena? How do you know what I think?'

Rowena again avoided the question. 'If it is on British soil then it belongs to the United Kingdom. You will not be able to hand it to Iran. Is that clear?'

'As clear as mud. As clear as the part you played in the deaths of my father and Harper.'

Rowena was angry. 'I will ignore your accusations as I know you have been through a considerable trauma and are in shock. But if you seriously think I could be involved in tipping off Al Qaeda then you have taken leave of your senses. I have spent my life fighting Osama Bin Laden, I am not about to go and join him. This call is terminated, and I will speak to you when you are back in London.'

The phone line cut, and the drone of the dialling tone filled the room until Pearson punched the button to switch off the speaker.

'Have you taken leave of your senses?'

Richard grunted. 'I think dear Rowena is about to find out.'

Chapter Thirty-Four

Great Oaks Wood, North Essex- October 1st, 2005

The moment Richard saw the wood, he knew he was in the right place. The perimeter was circular covering approximately one hundred and twenty acres of densely packed trees. He imagined Robert de Valognes riding his horse along the track that had been built by the Romans. The wood had been left to its own devices with little sign of coppicing in recent times. Lichen rose up the sides of ancient yews and new growth emerged from oaks, jagged and cut off in their prime by lightning strikes. There was only one part where man appeared to have intervened. A clearing was evident forming a triangular wedge into the heart of the forest. He remembered the words of St Thomas.

Split wood, I am there. Lift up the rock, I am there.

Oaks bordered the clearing, converging at a single point - the sharp end of the wedge. The tree at the pinnacle was very old. It stood battered and regal, a huge girth of at least ten metres, indicating a life that went back centuries. Richard felt sure Robert de Valognes must have witnessed this oak tree in its first flush of youth. He was less sure about the other oaks on either side. There was no doubt that they were old but not old enough to be seen by Normans. He knew the icon Masood had given him on that bombed out train back in July was linked with this place. The three oaks inscribed on the silver case that protected the icon were trees that had been planted in this wood. He was sure of it.

Before coming to the wood he'd spent two days in the British Library in the Rare Manuscripts Reading Room piecing together the story of Sir Peter de Valognes.

Initially, he had been thrown off course by the name Tigan which appeared at the top of the knight's journal, a name he could not find in old maps of Essex. Further research revealed that the word meant *enclosure*. A plural word suggesting two settlements, one of which appeared to relate to the Great Oaks enclosure. His breakthrough at the British Library was when he discovered Sir Peter had disowned his son Robert and banished him to a section of land that was surrounded by the ancient wood. Information was sketchy but it appeared that Robert had started an order of monks dedicated to St Barnabas. He knew he was onto something when he discovered that the Norman church in Great Tey was also called St Barnabas. The church had been built in the 12th century after the Valognes settlement was no more, but it was an unusual saint dedication for a Christian church. He'd contacted the vicar but there seemed to be no record of why the church had been given that name.

He broke into a run, drawn by an irrational desire to touch the oak. Amira was with him, but he felt alone. He had been like that ever since they got back home. A sense that there was nothing left now his father was gone. It embarrassed him that he was grieving for a man he harboured so much hate for. It embarrassed him that he thought more about the man he despised and less about Becky. He trusted no one now and for the first time he began to feel the same disillusionment that his father had felt.

But where were the three oaks?   And where was the rock?

He walked back along the open area staring at the floor, searching for signs of the settlement. A few man-made stones lying hidden in the long grasses would have signified that somebody once lived here. He found nothing.

Raising his head, he looked at Amira. 'I'm certain it's here but I've no idea where,' he said. 'I want to search this area with a metal detector. There must be something left by the people who lived here.'

Amira wasn't listening. She was pouring over a folder which contained photographs of the icon. She nodded to herself, closing the document and started walking into the forest, disappearing into the undergrowth. Richard followed, straining his eyes to see her in the darkness. There was no distance between them, but the forest canopy blocked out nearly all the light. In between the trees, giant ferns searched for a glimpse of the sun, benefitting from the boggy vegetation which his feet were sinking into.

'Amira,' he shouted. 'Where are you? I can't see you.'

A scream caused the crows to squawk in the trees.

'Over here, Richard. I've fallen into a pond. My feet are stuck in the mud. Over here…I've found something.' Her voice was more excited than scared.

He followed the sound. She seemed only a few feet away, but he still couldn't see. 'Where are you? Keep calling… I can't see you.'

A few feet ahead he could see bullrushes, and reeds - tell-tale signs of the presence of water. He waded into the reeds, feeling the cold-water seep into his shoes, his feet difficult to lift, clogged in the mud. His next step generated a splash as he sunk above his knees into a putrid muddy pond.

Amira was clinging onto a large boulder. She was up to her waist in water, a foul smell, stirred up by her helpless movements. 'I can't move,' she said. 'I'm sorry…I saw the inscriptions on this rock and forgot where I was. I went blindly towards them. Do you see the carvings in the stone?'

Richard paddled through the water, making sure his feet were clear of the mud before taking the next step. There was no doubt that the inscriptions were writing, rather than a sculptural relief but in the poor light it was impossible to determine what was been said. 'We need to get you free and then we'll look at what this is.' He moved closer to her and put his arms around her waist, joking with a mischievous smile. 'Not the most romantic place to get intimate. I don't rate your perfume or is it me who has just farted?'

Amira didn't smile. 'I can't joke,' she said. 'Not when we are this close to where the Gospel must be hidden.'

He felt the same and didn't know why he had made the crass remark. It was a coping mechanism because he couldn't face the disappointment of not finding the Gospel. 'I'm going to pull you and when I do, try and free your feet,' he said.

He counted to three and pulled, gripping the boulder to give him extra leverage. Amira strained, gritting her teeth as she tried to heave herself free. It was no use.

'I'm going to go under water and free one leg at a time,' he said. All his clothes were wet. Kneeling wouldn't make him wetter, but it would help him get low enough to dig her feet out. The water rose to his chest as he sunk down. The bottom of the pond seemed flat as if it were man made. It didn't seem natural. He lowered his hands into the water and recoiled as he touched something hard. It felt like metal. Reassured, he grabbed the object with both hands and tried to free it from the mud. It came away easily. As he lifted the object out of the water, Richard and Amira gasped. They were staring at a cross, caked in mud and silt. There was no sign of any corrosion. He pulled away the mud and detritus wrapped around the shaft and let out an excited shriek. It was remarkable – made of the most precious metal of all – gold. An altar piece that would have stood centre stage. Something priceless.

Richard held the cross high into the air and watched as a thin shaft of light reflected a sparkle onto the water. Amira was laughing. 'Oh my God look at that. It's incredible. You've found the spot,' she said. 'The Gospel must be here.'

The excitement of finding the cross made him forget that Amira was still stuck. Amira didn't want to remind him. She couldn't take her eyes off the beautiful object. 'It must be a thousand years old...I can't believe it,' she said. 'I suppose you'd better get me out of here.'

Richard placed the cross carefully on to the boulder and put his hands down into the water a second time. With the cross removed there was more opportunity to move the mud away from Amira's ankles. It seemed that there was just one small area of mud where Amira was trapped. He realised that he was on a flat surface – not something produced by nature - a man-made stone floor. They would have to drain the pond.

It took another half an hour to free Amira and by the time they got back to the car, they were exhausted. They were both dripping wet, their clothes saturated and caked with mud. 'We've got to get out of these clothes before we do anything else,' Richard said. 'We need to race back to London. I am going to report the find to Rowena and get her permission to hire one of those machines that suck out sewage. It will be perfect for this job.'

Vauxhall Cross -October 1st, 2005

Six hours later, Richard and Amira were seated at a circular table in Vauxhall Cross staring at Rowena. In the centre, the magnificent 11th Century cross they'd just found, acted like a sacrificial peace offering to the enemy before they commenced negotiations.

'The cross must go to the British Museum and anything else you find on the site stays in this country. Is that clear?' Rowena said.

Richard did not like being told what to do, especially from Rowena. It may have been clear but that didn't mean he was going to obey Rowena's edict. Richard had done everything he could to avoid Rowena since he got back to London. His father's body had still not returned from Oman and he blamed her for his death. After all, she'd openly said that David Helford should be eliminated. He dreaded when his father would be brought back to the UK and he'd have to arrange a funeral. He still hadn't told his mother, not that she retained any further feelings for her estranged husband.

Rowena remained silent throughout the debrief that followed. She never interrupted once which was so unlike her usual abrupt and confrontational style. He'd revealed that Becky's death was orchestrated by a Sunni Al Qaeda rogue cell operating within the IRG. It was highly unusual for this to happen in the Shia dominated state, but it seemed they were a specialist hit squad who could be used within Qods in covert action without drawing attention to itself. Ironically, Brigadier Mantazi's links to the MEK had helped embed the cell into Iranian Qods operations. Richard explained that intelligence on this group and its links to Afghanistan were non-existent, but it seemed likely that they were committing a revenge killing after Richard had been responsible for the death of Abdul. There was still some suspicion that the cell was being run out of Riyadh by Nadia Zabor, a GID officer, but it had not been proved. He understood from Nadia that she had been working for HM Government, but this was denied. When Richard said this, he studied Rowena's reaction and had not seen a flicker that HMG might be lying through its teeth. Wrapping up, Richard said there were no warnings about the hit in Ankara but went on to say he strongly believed it was the same cell responsible for the attack in Oman. He said the first bullets were aimed at him in keeping with the revenge theory.

'First kill the loved ones and then kill the man,' Richard said.

He paused and wondered what Rowena was thinking. If only he could figure out what she was up to. He decided to follow her, to see where it would lead.

'The lorry will be delivered first thing tomorrow morning to the edge of the wood.' He pointed to the wood's location on the map. 'We've ordered a small enough machine to get it along the byway and into the wood. We've also squared the arrangement with the Woodland Trust.'

'Good,' Rowena said.

Clapham Common Northside, London October 1st, 2005

Richard followed Rowena from Vauxhall Cross to Clapham Common Northside. After leaving the tube station, it was easy to keep close as she hurried along the road, lost in her thoughts, oblivious to anybody who might tail her. He walked along the edge of the common directly opposite, keeping a close eye out for something that might explain why she was there. Without warning she turned into the drive of a large Edwardian terrace. There was a bench within sight of the house. He sat down and watched, pulling up his hoody and leaning forward as people walked past, ignoring him as if he didn't exist. He didn't know what to expect but something told him that she was shaken by what they had discovered in Great Oaks Wood. His explanation of who was responsible for the murder of Becky didn't seem to ring true with her either and he wanted to know why. It was only a hunch, but Rowena knew more than she was letting on.

When the door opened, he saw another woman. Rowena kissed the woman on the lips, not a long kiss but still very intimate. They exchanged smiles. Richard had seen the woman before on the island of Folegandros. Maia Zevi –

sister of his father's Mossad lover. Sister of the woman his father had stabbed to death.

Chapter Thirty-Five

Great Oaks Wood, North Essex- October 2nd, 2005

The water had gone. The sewage removal lorry had done its bit. Richard stood in the depths of a man-made pit lined with York stone except for the small circle of mud that Amira had been caught in. He felt sorry for the frogs frantically hopping around and vowed to refill the pit as soon as they were done.

The shock of seeing Maia with Rowena played on his mind. His boss was playing ball with Mossad but the men who killed Becky and his father, not to mention Harper were not Israelis. He needed to confront her about it but how? He couldn't own up to watching her house. Amira distracted his thoughts, calling him to take hold of the equipment she was passing down. They had brought shovels to clear the muddy ditch because there was no sign of anything on the stone covered area. It seemed to have some importance because it had been fenced off by a rectangle of stones embedded in the ground. He set to work with the spade, shovelling the mud clear of the central point. Amira joined him and together they dug the ditch deeper. It was dirty work, but they encountered little difficulty moving the soil, as it had not solidified and remained wet from the pond water.

They were about three feet down when they found something. Richard was getting frustrated and had slammed his spade into the sodden earth. His spade hit stone, stopping his thrust downwards. He adjusted his shovel's angle and cleared the earth away. A stone frame supporting a wooden oak trap door was slowly revealed. Richard tapped the wood expecting it to disintegrate but it was in good condition, preserved over the centuries by the thick covering of Essex clay. A rusted copper ring handle attached to the door showed that there was something behind, but Richard remained pessimistic that it would be stuck fast. With some trepidation he picked up the ring and securing his foothold tried to raise the door. It wouldn't budge.

'We need to get rope and use the truck to pull it free.' he said. It was fortunate that the lorry carried enough rope and after a delay of twenty minutes they were ready to pull the trap door free. After tying the rope to the copper ring, he prayed that the nails would hold after all these years buried in the mud. He watched the rope tighten as the truck moved slowly forward. There was a groan and then with a clatter the wooden door lifted and bounced as it bumped across the stone floor of the ditch. The oak door must have been over two feet thick, caked with mud, but miraculously remaining intact.

He shone his torch into the hole. Worms and beetles were rushing around in a frenzy, reacting to the light that had appeared after centuries of darkness. As far as he could see, the trap door revealed a shaft dropping about ten feet. At the bottom he hoped he would find a tunnel. There was no ladder, so he untied the rope that had been attached to the door. Wrapping it round his body a couple of times, he began lowering himself into the hole. Amira stayed at the top providing some light to his descent. The walls of the ditch were dripping with water, but the clay seemed mercifully solid. He noticed that the builders had embedded flint into the mud to give it added solidity. At the bottom, his feet sank up to his knees in water. He breathed a sigh of relief when he saw a tunnel leading off to the right. He shone his torch and estimated that it was around five feet high and around three feet wide.

'There's a tunnel,' he shouted up to Amira. 'I'm going in.'

His torch barely penetrated the darkness as he moved, picking out every bit of ground before edging another step forward. The musty smell of long trapped subterranean air cloyed at his lungs forcing an involuntary cough. A faint echo captured the sound suggesting a larger chamber ahead. He struck a match to check for oxygen. There was some air although the flame did not burn vigorously before it went out. A trickle of water dripped on his face making him stop and tap the wooden supports that had been used to shore up the tunnel. They didn't look safe, but he knew he couldn't turn back now. He walked on another few feet, crouching as he went, noting that the ground beneath him had become stonier as if someone has laid a bed of gravel. A few more feet and the gravel gave way to a stone parapet with a few steps leading down. Richard flashed his torch all around. He had entered a carefully constructed chamber with a low vaulted ceiling which reminded him of a crypt in a church. Immediately in front of where he stood, his torch picked out a plinth about three feet high. He moved his light over the surface and did not register what he was looking at. He flicked his torch back again and this time he lingered. A stone coffin was resting on the plinth, carved with a coat of arms which he recognised belonged to the Valognes family. He might have expected a carving of the knight's face and body, resplendent in the battledress of a Crusader, but this man was no longer a hero.

There was no lid to the casket. A skeleton lay on the stone bed.

He didn't shiver or cry out with the shock of seeing the remains. It was like meeting an old friend and he remembered the skeletons he'd seen on Crete. He joined his hands together and did the sign of the cross, a tribute to the man he'd seen come alive in his journals. It was Robert de Valognes, the man who had gone to the Holy Land and become disillusioned with the battle against Islam. The real prize was the Gospel of Barnabas but for some strange reason, he did not see any compelling need to look for it. A sense of calm and contentment descended on him. He shone the torch more closely at the remains and saw gold coins in the eyes and mouth. Something for the next world he thought. The knight's sword lay beside him and he wondered how many people had been slain with it. He surveyed the rest of the bones and lingered once more on the skull. The back seemed to have shattered as if it had been smashed with an axe. Maybe Robert de Valognes had been murdered which might explain why Akila's son Masood had left England and headed to the Middle East. Next, he examined the plinth. The Crescent Moon and Star, sign of Islam, was the first thing he noted carved into the stone alongside the shield of St George, a symbol of his Crusader heritage. Above the two symbols was an inscription, calligraphy which he'd seen before in Iran, the letters that appeared on many mosque walls -the sign of Allah – the first lines of the Holy Koran. Richard contemplated the significance of this unification of motives. The knight had incurred the wrath of his father and fellow citizens by converting to Islam. After standing perfectly still for a moment, in quiet contemplation, Richard walked around the plinth. At the side, he spotted a recess and on a stone shelf a jewel encrusted box, fashioned in what looked like silver. He had no doubt he'd discovered what he was looking for.

His hands were shaking when he slid back the catches. Emeralds adorned the box and Richard remembered the stones on the icon's case. They were also emeralds and he wondered whether they'd come from the same source. The leather binding was plain and undecorated. The book was indeed holy and needed none of the finery he'd seen in other bibles. He didn't remove the book from its box, but his hands continued to shake as he closed the lid and returned the catches to where they'd been for a thousand years.

When he got back to the end of the tunnel, he looked up and wondered how he'd climb the ten feet to the surface while holding the box. He shouted to Amira, but she did not respond. He shouted again, but there was still no answer. His suspicions were immediately aroused. Something was wrong. The rope was still dangling and when he pulled, it tightened. He was wearing a fleece and decided to wrap the box in the garment and attach it to the rope. Tying the rope securely around his waist, he began to ease his way up the shaft. He sensed there would be a reception party as soon as he poked his head through the hole, but there was nothing he could do. He was sure Maia would be waiting.

It wasn't Maia. It wasn't even Rowena.

A gun was pointing at Amira's head.

'Hello Nadia,' said Richard. 'What a pleasant surprise.' He pulled himself out of the hole and sat up to face the Saudi woman. Amira was breathing heavily but remained calm. 'I thought you and Amira were working together in league with the Ayatollah.'

'I thought that too,' said Amira. 'After all that we've done working for peace.'

'Shut up,' Nadia retorted, nudging the gun into Amira's head. 'I respect you Amira, I don't want to kill you. But you and the Ayatollah are naive about peace ever existing between Iran and my country.'

'All this stuff about Words of the Faithful is just hot air?' said Richard.

'No. It's genuine. This is my own agenda which is why I want the Gospel of Barnabas? I care about the superiority of Islam as a Sunni. The Gospel speaks for Islam not Shia or Sunni.'

Richard nodded. 'Makes sense, but why were your men in the mountains trying to kill me and not my father?'

'Revenge,' Nadia replied. 'I loved Abdul and you killed him…We met when my husband met him in Dubai and became lovers. He was a good man who had been destroyed by the Americans killing his family in a fruitless attempt to get rid of Osama Bin Laden.'

'But if you wanted revenge, why not kill me when you captured me in Cyprus? Instead, you promised me and Harper a million bucks each.' He gestured to the box Amira was still holding. 'Do I get $2 million now that Harper is dead?'

Nadia let out a sarcastic laugh. 'I never intended to pay you a dime.'

'Thought so. You lied to me from the start.'

'The time to kill you wasn't in Cyprus. My revenge was personal, and I couldn't let it jeopardise my mission. I needed you to go to Iran and carry the memory stick and cause the disruption, while at the same time winning the Ayatollah's trust.'

'So, you've taken me for a fool, and you were right. I knew it was wrong to trust you.'

'You saw the woman before you saw the GID agent.'

'A big failing of mine.' He smiled looking directly at Nadia.

'My mission was to maintain the special relationship between Israel and Saudi Arabia in our united front against the Shia Clerics of Iran,' she replied. 'The United Kingdom are also our allies and I wanted to be seen to cooperate.'

'Which is why you've been briefing Rowena, I assume.'

'What if I did? I may have wanted you dead in Oman, but I was nothing to do with Becky's murder.'

'I don't believe you.'

'Enough.' Nadia shouted. 'No more questions…just give me the Gospel and I'll be on my way. Give it to me and there will be no bloodshed.'

He had no intention of giving up the Gospel to a bunch of Saudi fundamentalists. He played for time. 'One last question, Nadia, the attack in Oman wasn't what you were expecting was it? You didn't arrange it even though you wanted me dead- did you?'

Nadia glared, tightening her finger on the trigger of her gun. 'I arranged it, but the idiots went too far and killed Harper and your father.'

Richard grunted. 'You didn't care about Harper…Your men beat him up in Cyprus.'

'Saudi Arabia is an ally of the United States. The death of a CIA officer would get me in trouble with my masters. He wasn't supposed to play the hero.'

'Killing a British officer isn't as important as a US guy.' He let out a cynical laugh. 'But if you'd killed me, you wouldn't have got your hands on the Gospel.'

'Not true. All the research in Iran was given to me by the Ayatollah and in the UK – Rowena was helping me.'

'She wouldn't allow you to take the Gospel out of the country.'

'We'll see about that.'

'Except I found it.'

Amira took her chance. She elbowed Nadia in the ribs and ran. Nadia fell backwards but recovered quickly and fired. The bullet struck Amira from behind and she fell forwards, blood streaming from a shoulder wound. He leapt on to Nadia, throwing all his weight into her body. His advantage was short lived. He gasped as a boot struck his ribs. She had not come alone. Two heavy weights. His head was spinning but he heard her shouting in Arabic. 'Get the box.'

Dazed, he pulled himself to his feet. They were running towards their Range Rover, carrying the box containing the Gospel. The car's engine roared into life as the driver hit the throttle. The rear tailgate was open and Nadia jumped inside. The car waited for a few seconds, revving its engine. It moved forward without warning, wheels screeching, sending clouds of dirt into the air. They were coming straight at him. He waited, diving on the bonnet at the last moment. His timing wasn't perfect. He bounced and, as the driver jerked to the left, he let go. His body lurched off the bonnet, crying with pain as he hit the ground. The Range Rover was reversing at speed heading in his direction.

The explosion threw him off his feet. The vehicle somersaulted through the air in a ball of fire. Debris went everywhere, burning the grass and burying pieces of shrapnel into his jacket. He was too close to avoid the fall out. His hair was burning. Instinctively, he rolled over, smothering his scalp with his arms. His thick hair was singed, and his jacket in shreds, but he didn't notice. Only one thing mattered.

'The Gospel. They've got the Gospel.'

He ran towards the Range Rover, watching helpless as Nadia and her heavies floundered like burnt embers in a raging fire. He saw the silhouette of Nadia for a second clinging to life before the flames consumed her. The heat was unbearable. He collapsed onto his knees and passed out, overcome by the fumes.

He awoke to the sight of Rowena crouching beside him, dabbing his face with a wet cloth.

'Are you alright? They were going to kill you…We had to do something.'

'Did you Rowena?' The pain ignited his anger. He pushed her away and pulled himself up. The car was a burnt out shell. There were people gathered around – Policeman no doubt.

'Special Branch,' said Rowena.

'Did they find anything?'

Rowena shook her head but said nothing.

A paramedic had joined them. 'We better get you to a hospital to sort out those burns,' he said. .

'Have you found Amira? She's wounded,' he asked as they lifted him onto a stretcher.

He twisted his head from side to side. Something continued to trouble him. He tried to focus and remember what Rowena had said.

We had to do something.

There was another woman beside Rowena.

'I had to do it,' the woman said. 'It was my last mission. No more killing. I swear. The truth is not always the right answer.'

The face was blurred but he knew who it was. She spoke again. 'Proving that Jesus is not the last messenger helps no one…There is no God but God. Remember that and we will live in peace.'

He knew Maia was right. Her voice was vaguely distant, drowned by the ringing in his ears, playing back the explosion in his head like a stuck record. She stared directly at him while Rowena looked at Maia. Her eyes were distressed, expressing a loss of trust for the woman by her side. They'd seemed happy when he saw them last night.

Not anymore. Something had changed.

Chapter Thirty-Six

London, Vauxhall Cross, October 19th, 2005.

'I resign.'

The letter lay on Rowena's desk unopened. She picked up the envelope and holding it by the edge, as if it were a piece of soiled toilet paper, dropped it into the bin by her desk.

'You don't just resign from the Secret Service. I won't accept it.'

'I'm not going to work for an intelligence service that has no loyalty to its employees. You kept me in the dark about your contacts with Maia in Mossad and Nadia in the Saudi GIS. I could have easily been killed and you wouldn't have given a shit.'

'That's not true and you know it.' Rowena replied, angrily rising to the challenge of Richard's temper. 'We saved your life. We put you first and damaged the whole operation. I've no idea how we are going to square this with the Saudis.'

'It should be easy. Nadia wasn't the flavour of the month. Her extracurricular activities, with Words of the Faithful, trying to unite Islam was a push too far. It didn't help her case with the Saudi Royal family who don't tolerate dissent. I think they'll be glad to see the back of her.'

Rowena nodded. 'You may be right. Sale of arms is important to the British economy.'

'And it doesn't matter who those British arms kill.'

Rowena shrugged. 'It's not for us to make judgements. All that remains is your father was a traitor and we needed him eliminated. You openly hated him and yet I knew you wouldn't kill him. We had to try other ways. We couldn't tell you because you wouldn't have gone along with it. You were the bate to catch him and in the end it worked.'

'But you would have let me die in the process.'

'To repeat what I just said. We saved your life. I didn't know Nadia was going to try and kill you. You should be grateful.'

'But what about Becky? She was collateral damage that you didn't care for.'

Rowena bowed her head and looked saddened by the mention of Becky's name. 'I didn't want her to die, that was never part of the plan.'

Richard erupted. He leant over the desk and stared directly into Rowena's eyes. They were only a few inches apart. She averted her gaze and he knew she was hiding something. 'What do you know? Tell me now before I do something I might regret.'

She stood up and walked around her desk. Her back was facing Richard, her arms were folded, she stared ahead to the window and the view across the Thames.

'You won't face me, will you?' he shouted. 'What do you know?'

'She turned around and there were tears in her eyes. Her mascara was running down her cheeks mingling with tears. 'Not here Richard. Come to my apartment at 8pm tonight and I'll tell you, I promise.'

Rowena's apartment was on Falcon Wharf, South of river, walkable from Vauxhall and not far from the heliport at Battersea. Richard hung around the area all day, choosing to visit Tate Britain rather than do any work in the office. He'd resigned, whether Rowena was going to accept it or not. This was a way of showing he no longer wanted to work for MI6. There was nothing for him to do even if he felt he could work. He thought about Becky all the time and his father and felt alone. He spent several minutes in front of the Pre Raphaelite painting of Ophelia by Millais, transposing the innocence and misunderstood face for Becky's until an annoying woman, deliberately blocking his line of sight, forced him to move on. Holman Hunt's work depicting strayed sheep trapped in the bracken on the edge of a cliff also resonated with the way he felt. One foot wrong and he would be over the edge. After leaving the gallery, he wandered along the river, taking time to gaze at the running waters and let his mind go blank. It was just like he'd felt when they buried his father in the same cemetery where Becky lay. Apart from him, only his mother attended. There was no eulogy and only a few prayers. His father had died wanting to change the world and left it with the world turning its back. He felt numb, not knowing whether to grieve or feel relieved that the stigma of his father had finally left him. He could get on with his life but had nothing to get on with.

The loss of the Gospel of Barnabas troubled him deeply. There was a story still to tell the world that genuine Christian religious texts had been left out of the Bible to manipulate the Western view of religion. He wondered what other secrets were still to be found in the Monastery in Iran. He thought of Fatima still searching for manuscripts in the cellars below the church. Who would listen to her now?

Rowena's apartment was on the third floor. He buzzed the bell and when her voice crackled over the intercom, he said, 'I'm here,' without introductions. He took the stairs, needing time to prepare himself.

She was waiting on the landing and went back inside. He followed shutting the door gently. He had to stay calm whatever she said. The aggression he'd shown earlier would get him nowhere nearer the truth.

Her apartment was modern, an open plan layout with contemporary steel kitchen units and grey leather sofas. He thought of his own place looking plain and unwelcoming.

How could she afford such luxury? Floor to ceiling windows made the best of the river views providing access to a balcony. A sliding door to the outside space was open, allowing the noise of a helicopter taking off to drown her voice. He could see the twinkling lights of the London skyline and party boats sailing up the river with music blaring. Rowena pushed the door shut and their conversation became hermetically sealed. The formality of her work attire had been abandoned in favour of jeans and an unflattering smock. Her feet were bare, and her hair hung down over her shoulders, no longer tamed by ever present hairspray. She had a drink in her hand which he could see was gin only because there was a large bottle of Gordons on the table.

She poured him a drink without asking and retrieved ice cubes from the kitchen but no lemon. There was a large plastic bottle of tonic on the table which she invited him to add if he wished.

He took a gulp of his gin, preferring it neat, before speaking. 'I need to know for certain why Becky was killed and who did it...Amira thought she was to blame.'

'It wasn't like that. Amira wasn't responsible. It wasn't a Sunni Al Qaeda cell embedded in the Revolutionary Guard.'

Richard stared at Rowena. 'If not them ...Who?'

'Mossad killed Becky.'

The statement came as a shock that made no sense. 'How could Mossad infiltrate Iran?'

'They hire hit men everywhere, even in Iran, ready to act if required. The men who murdered Becky were so deeply embedded that nobody suspected them. They even guarded the President. Killing Becky was bread and butter to them. Except for one thing – their cover was blown as soon as they carried out the hit. They were a suicide squad whose job was to assassinate the President if he did things that don't suit Israel, like declaring war.'

'I can understand that. So why would Mossad sacrifice a team who could take out the president for a minor problem like Becky. She had nothing to do with any of this. If they wanted to hurt my father, they should have killed me. They didn't even kill me when they had the chance in Folegandros. Maia could have easily revenged Dinah's murder.'

Rowena sighed. 'This is hard to say.'

'What? Just get on with it.' He resisted the temptation to shout. 'I've had enough shocks to last me a lifetime. Who cares about another one?'

She poured herself another gin and sat down on the larger of the two leather sofas. 'I don't know how to say this but when you were away in Greece, Becky came to Vauxhall Cross. She just turned up at the office and demanded to see someone who knew you. The security guard pleaded ignorance and directed her away from the building. After she'd gone, he contacted me, showing her picture on CCTV. I recognised Becky from the photo on your desk. I also had her address from your *notification in the event of my death* letter and went unannounced to her flat. She was in a vulnerable state because she'd had a visit from Harper. He'd said some nasty things about you and then she told me your father had called. I comforted her and...' She hesitated.

'And what? Spit it out,' he said, unable to contain his irritation.

'We kissed.' Rowena stopped and looked at Richard.

He gasped. 'You did what?'

'Becky was upset. Originally, I only intended to give her a hug, but she responded more than I was expecting. She kissed me and then pulled away almost immediately and apologised. I told her it was just fine. She left in a hurry, but things developed from there.'

'I don't believe you.'

'Believe what you like. I'm attracted to women. It's not a crime anymore you know.'

'But Becky isn't like that.'

'That may have been true on our first meeting, but things began to change.'

'Go on.'

'Women respond to gentleness and you were distant and distracted. We all need love in our lives. irrespective of gender, or sexual preferences. You weren't there and I was. After our first meeting, I asked her to help me and get Harper to talk. She adopted the role with relish and led him on until he gave her gold-plated material. Harper may be Mr CIA tough guy, but he was putty in her hands. Men are stupid when it comes down to wanting sex with a pretty woman, and what's more she was pregnant to one of his enemies, what could have been more fun?' She paused and reached for a packet of cigarettes in the coffee table drawer. He'd not seen her smoke before, but her hands were shaking, and her nerves seemed to be shredded. She inhaled deeply and turned her head to avoid blowing the smoke in his face.

'She reported back to me every time she saw Harper, including that time when you went to Northern Cyprus. That's when I found out your father was spying for Iran while working for the Israelis. It was a shock but finally I had the information I needed to condemn your father as a traitor. When she told me, I got carried away and gave her a hug. As I released my hands from around her waist, I kissed her instinctively and without thinking. A short peck on the lips was all I had in mind, but she responded with passion I'd not been expecting. The first kiss on our first meeting had been a little embarrassing and had not lasted long. I'd expected we'd say no more about it, but this was our third meeting, and this was different. She wanted more. I stayed the night and we became lovers.'

Rowena stopped and let the shock of what she was saying, work its way into his mind. There was no anger, only numbing disbelief that he could accept her betrayal in a positive light. It was a relief that Harper had been telling the truth. It explained Becky's evasive response when he asked whether she was sleeping with the man he hated as much as his father. Her denial had been half-hearted because her heart was elsewhere. There was no anger because at that moment he discovered something about himself which reflected on him rather than Becky.

He didn't love Becky and never had. The baby she'd been carrying created an illusion of a love that didn't exist. Despite emotional acceptance of his failed relationship with Becky, it did not take away the grief and blame he felt for her death.

'I'm not proud of myself, but I swear to God I didn't know what was going to happen,' Rowena said, slurring her words as the effect of the gin began to kick in. 'Nadia was briefing me and so was Maia. Nadia wanted the two of you to go together to Ankara as a couple to help the handover of the document, making you appear like tourists, less suspicious than if you'd been alone. If I'd known that Becky was in danger, I would have stopped it happening. I would never want Becky dead.' Rowena was crying hysterical sobs that showed her guard had come down. She stubbed out her half-smoked cigarette, bending it crudely into the ash tray. She reached for the gin, but this time swigged from the bottle. Pulling herself together, she mopped her eyes and lit another cigarette. She coughed as the first smoke filled her lungs.

'I still don't get it,' he said after a pause. 'If you cared for Becky, really cared, you could have overruled Nadia.'

He could see his question had hit home, but she held it together.

'The Saudis and Israelis are strange bedfellows, but they are united in their hatred of Iran,' Rowena said. 'I was in the middle, hoping to keep them from falling out.' She sighed and reached for the bottle again. 'I'm pissed...I hate what the fucking Service has done to me. I did care for Becky, but it's not your fault she was murdered. I blame myself for what happened.'

'Why?'

'Maia found out.'

Richard raised his eyebrows. 'So, what happened?' he said, nervous where this was leading.

Rowena poured the last dregs from the gin bottle and groaned with annoyance when only a trickle barely covered the bottom of her glass. She sank back in her seat and put her feet up on the coffee table, swigging the gin in one short mouthful. The drink was taking its toll, but he could see the alcohol had loosened her tongue and everything was going to come out.

'I loved Maia and think she loved me, but our jobs kept us apart. I met her when I was put in charge of liaison with the Israeli Secret Service. She was the contact lead. I liked her straight away because she had a conscience, never approving of Mossad as state-run killing machine. She wanted to quit.

'But if you loved Maia why did you go anywhere near Becky?'

'Loneliness. Maia and I were apart a lot, but I also had a strange compulsion to know more about your life. I suppose I latched onto Becky's unhappiness and that drew us together despite my feelings for Maia.' Rowena looked at Richard, her face crestfallen with grief. 'One night, we were lying in bed together in London, I broke the golden rule and shared an intelligence secret. I told her about the Ankara document, and what we planned to do next. In a fit of stupidity and emotional childishness, I told her about my affair with Becky. I was desperate for her to love me. I wanted her to be jealous and I succeeded. It was a mistake blinded by my emotions which you cannot have in this business. It is unforgiveable. But I swear I never thought she would take such extreme action.' She grabbed Richard's arm pleading with him to understand. 'We had an argument, the night before we met you in the woods and killed Nadia.'

'How do you know for certain Maia had Becky killed?'

'Because I told her. The only other person who knew about Becky was Nadia.'

'Why couldn't Nadia have done it? She wanted me dead, why not Becky as well?'

'Because Nadia wanted to see the Ankara document. Killing her prevented that happening.'

'Where is Maia now?'

'I don't know. She may be still in London, but she hasn't been in touch with me, since the killing of Nadia.'

The pointlessness of it all made him sick. He rushed to the toilet and tried to puke. Nothing came out. It was unreal that something like this could be reduced to a ridiculous lovers' tiff. He left the apartment without a further word and took the path down onto the riverbank. He started walking, his pace quickening until he was running. He headed east along the river, not stopping until he reached Vauxhall Bridge. He looked up at the MI6 building, so ostentatious, a vain apology for secrecy. He knew that the Official Secrets Act would prevent him from saying anything about Becky's death to her parents and her brother Edward.

There was still a problem. The person responsible for her death was still alive.

Maia. Why had she done it? Jealousy seemed a poor excuse.

Amira was waiting on the bench in front of Tate Modern. He remembered the meeting in the restaurant when she seemed so full of life and contradictions after Masood had been killed. She wore a sling to support her injured shoulder and a veil to cover her hair. She winced when he hugged her. 'I'm sorry,' he said. 'Does it hurt?'

'I'd laugh if it didn't hurt so much. But don't worry, I'm okay. Nadia didn't shoot to kill I'm sure of that.'

'That's good news. I was worried about you. It must have been difficult hearing what Nadia said.'

Amira sighed. 'Yes, it was hard. I trusted her and she betrayed me, but I remain optimistic.'

'You are not the only one who trusted her. I was a bloody fool.'

'I liked her.'

'But you worked so hard for peace, and she spoiled it. What an achievement it would be if the international community welcomed back Iran from its exile as a pariah state.'

'I haven't given up. I'm still in touch with the Ayatollah.'

They sat in silence and stared at the river traffic, which would always fill empty time. 'You know I can't stop thinking about Harper. He was such a sadistic bastard and yet in those last moments, he stepped forward and took the bullets, trying to help my father who he wanted to kill.'

'You will never understand someone like Harper,' she replied. 'It's a game to him and as adversaries, I suppose he admired your father's resilience. He didn't want to give the jihadists the satisfaction of killing you both. That was his job.'

Richard looked down at the floor. ' I suppose you are right. Pathetic macho men, they were both as bad as one another.' He looked at his watch and stood up.

'Your father was a good man. Stupid but good...you should remember that.'

He forced a smile. 'You know. It wasn't your fault Becky died. Rowena told me the hit men were Mossad agents deeply embedded in Iran. Maia was responsible for the hit. Mossad did it. Nothing to do with you.'

Amira's eyes widened with evident relief. 'But why would Maia order something like that? She had principles and wouldn't kill an innocent person like Becky.'

'That's just the point. Was Becky innocent? I met Maia for the first time on Folegandros. She never looked like killing me so why a few days later would she murder Becky?'

'I agree. It seems strange.'

'Rowena told me she was having an affair with Maia when she also got intimately involved with Becky. She thinks Maia killed her in a state of jealous revenge.'

Amira eyes widened. 'Becky. Are you sure?'

He turned to face her. 'I don't believe it. There is some other reason this happened. The murder of Nadia was a score settler – payment for Becky's murder.' As he spoke, his mind caught Maia's eyes, pointing the gun but not firing in Folegandros. She was protecting him.

'She didn't fire the gun. I was dead meat and of no use to them, but she didn't fire. She didn't want to kill me. I must see her and find out why.'

Amira took hold of his hand. 'I agree. It doesn't stack up. I'll do my best to find her for you.'

Chapter Thirty-Seven

Bishop Auckland Castle - Six months later

Six months had passed, and Maia still hadn't found him. He'd lasted only two weeks on his mother's farm, finding it difficult to deal with her new lease of life, shacked up with Joe, her farm manager. When he protested, pointing out Joe was half her age, she hit the roof, reminding him that he had always been there when her son had failed to visit. He had to admit she had a point and at least Joe would keep the farm in some sort of order. All in all, Joe was reliable and grounded.

Unlike himself.

London wasn't any better. After a few days, feeling more depressed in his dingy flat, still seeing signs of Becky everywhere, he retreated, filling his car with books, and driving North. He rented a cottage in the Yorkshire Dales, near Reeth, a place he remembered from his school days boarding at Barnard Castle School. He set about clearing his mind of the past, kidding himself he was happier reading, going for long walks and being alone. The memory of Becky continued to haunt him. After all this time he still didn't know the truth.

In his dreams he was always running, watching himself, chasing after something through the mountains of Iran and Crete. Sometimes it was his father and sometimes he saw Becky. They were waving at him to follow and he did so until they disappeared. On worse nights he had nightmares, watching the Range Rover explode in flames. Nadia's last seconds as she burned alive. After all those years buried with the knight, the Gospel was destroyed in minutes. Maia set the charges. She destroyed the Gospel, but he blamed himself for bringing it back to the world.

Whatever, he felt about Maia, he had to see her and find the truth.

'I don't know where she is,' Rowena said when she finally agreed to take his call. 'Leave it alone, Richard. It's over. You've left the Service. Time to move on.'

He'd taken for granted the surveillance capabilities of his former employers. Without them, finding her was impossible. Phone calls to Amira in the States, provided little solace, only reassurance that she would come when the time was right.

He couldn't wait for ever. Rowena had given him three months' notice which helped. He'd fallen back on his savings, but they were disappearing fast. Just as Rowena had said, he needed to let it go or do something.

He chose the latter. On a day trip to York, he bought a computer, and connected via dial up to the internet. He joined Facebook and called himself Barnabas Helford, describing himself as a lover of Hafez poetry and the gnostic gospels. His first posting left his identity in no doubt:

Loved meeting you in Folegandros. Hope to see you soon.

It was a long shot, but if Amira was to be believed, then Maia would know where to find him.

He was right. The reply appeared the next day

Meet me at Bishop Auckland Castle in The Long Dining Room. 11th April, 14.00.

I will wait fifteen minutes. Don't be late.

He double checked the date. 11th April was tomorrow. It was a strange choice of location. Near where he was living was a good thing, but why somewhere so obscure. He trawled the internet for answers, cursing the time it took and getting nowhere. In desperation, he called the local library in Richmond. The librarian was eager to help, ringing him back after less than five minutes of research.

'The Long Dining Room has some controversial art on its walls,' said the librarian, a note of triumph in her voice.

'A series of thirteen paintings by Francisco de Zurbaran known as Jacob and his Twelve Sons.'

'Why are they controversial?'

'They were painted at the time of the Spanish inquisition.' The librarian paused as if she was expecting him to fill in the gaps. She continued when Richard remained silent. 'Zurbaran risked his own life painting symbols of Judaism at the time the Spanish inquisition was determined to destroy the Jewish religion.'

'You've been extremely helpful. Do you have a book that has pictures of the paintings?'

The librarian chuckled. 'This is not the British Library, you know. I got all this from Encyclopaedia Britannica.'

At least, he understood the reason why Maia had chosen it. A reference to everything he'd been fighting for. Jacob was an important figure in all the Abrahamic religions. She was a Jew and these paintings personified the persecution of her people. It all made perfect sense.

The next day couldn't come soon enough. As he entered the dining room, he saw her standing alone studying one of Zurbaran's works. He thought it must be Jacob. The father of all those sons. Did he tell them lies like his own father had done?

He walked over and stood beside her. 'A controversial subject for a Christian bishop to purchase, don't you think?' he asked.

She continued to stare at the painting. There was no acknowledgement. Her answer was matter of fact; how she might have spoken to any stranger sharing a moment in front of a masterpiece. 'It's a story that resonates with all the Abrahamic religions,' she replied. 'Maybe that's his point.' The tone of her voice faltered a little. 'We all regret the lies of our fathers.'

'I agree. Religious leaders have always manipulated the story of God to serve their own purposes, like the rejection of the Gospel of Barnabas by Paul. They forget, there is no God but God.'

She turned to face him. The edginess in her eyes he'd noticed on the first day they met on Folegandros had gone. Seeing her standing in front of him, very much alive, triggered all those memories he could not forget. 'You destroyed the Gospel and perpetuated the lie.' His voice was laced with bitterness. 'Hello Maia. Why have you taken so long to speak to me? I thought I could trust you to do the right thing and low and behold you are still working for Mossad.'

She did not answer, choosing to move onto the next painting. She checked the name. It was Simeon, dressed in animal skins.

'Cursed be their anger, for it was fierce; and their truth, for it was cruel: I will divide them in Jacob and scatter them in Israel.'

'You didn't come here to quote the bible at me. Did you?'

'It's from Genesis – a reference to the murder by Simeon and Levi of Shechem who raped Jacob's only daughter – Dinah.' She stared at him, locking onto his eyes. 'Do you remember Dinah? Was your father Shechem?'

'Of course, I remember Dinah. I also remember Becky. Legend says she was killed on your orders.'

Maia turned away and whispered. 'If only you really knew Becky.'

'What don't I know?'

She said nothing, moving onto the next painting. They were alone apart from two other people out of ear shot.

'Why have you agreed to see me now?' Richard asked. 'After all this time.'

'You need to know the truth.'

'It's too late for that.'

One of the other visitors was staring in their direction, pulling a face to register disapproval that they were talking loudly.

'We need to talk, but not here.'

'There's a Deer Park outside the castle grounds. We can walk by the river.'

Daffodils danced in the breeze, washed by rain which greeted them as they stepped outside. The trees were overflowing with blossom, glistening with the health of an English spring. They walked down to the river, flowing fast among the trees. The sun waged a battle against the dark showery skies throwing shimmers of light across the water. 'If only Tel Aviv were like this,' she said.

'Don't suppose you want to defect. Do you? Can't see Rowena supporting your application.'

She struggled to suppress a smile. 'I couldn't think of anywhere worse to work than MI6. I would rather tend a flock of sheep and live a peaceful life.'

'But you don't do you? Instead you continue to work for a bunch of murderers.'

She ignored his comment and continued. 'It's about Becky. You want to know the truth, don't you?'

'Go on.'

'She was a spy who worked for us.'

His face turned grey. He stepped backwards and banged his fist into a tree. 'Tell me you're joking.'

'She worked for us from the beginning. It was nothing to do with you. She wasn't spying on you, although she did give me some useful tips on Rowena. Getting together with you was just a coincidence. We recruited her for another reason.'

'What reason?'

'Did you know one of her best friends at school was Asma Akras. She's Assad's wife. She was born and raised in London, you know, to Syrian parents. They used to meet up for lunch when she was in London. Always at the Dorchester. She kept us up to date on what Assad was thinking. She also got close to Nadia to help us. Nadia got wind of it. She was furious. That's why she was murdered. Nadia could not allow her to be friends with Assad's wife.'

He turned his back on Maia and tried to think. He knew she was telling the truth but couldn't bring himself to accept it. 'What the fuck are you saying. Prove it to me.'

'Think back to Folegandros. Do you remember me pointing the gun at you?'

'How could I forget?'

'I didn't kill you because Becky would have never forgiven me. We even let your father get away on her instructions.'

Richard shuddered. He let out a sarcastic laugh. 'That's bullshit, and you know it. My father killed your sister and another Mossad agent. There was no way you were going to let him walk free.'

'It's true our original intention was to take him out, but Becky convinced me otherwise. You remember Becky told you she spoke to your father. She realised that he could do more damage to Iran if he were allowed into the country.'

'But you bombed the Istanbul Star. If you knew he wasn't on that boat, then why sink it?'

'Two reasons. It created a smoke screen for a time allowing your father and Amira to get into Iran without MI6 trying to stop him. It also pleased the Iranians that Israeli forces were trying to take him out. It gave him credibility.'

'But you killed innocent sailors.'

Maia laughed. 'The sailors were smuggling parts for the centrifuges as part of Iran's nuclear programme. There was nothing innocent here. They deserved to die.'

Richard sat down on the wet ground and put his head in his hands. 'Becky was right. He caused a stir.'

He laid down on the grass and felt his hair go damp. Water dripped from the trees onto his face. 'So, who told Nadia about what Becky was up to?'

'She made the mistake herself. Unfortunately, Becky was never trained in the craft of spying. She was a natural at keeping secrets, which is why you never suspected, but she didn't realise Nadia would be tracking her phone. A call to me from Cyprus was intercepted. That's why Nadia insisted you take her to Ankara. She had people there to carry out the hit. Sending you to Iran to hunt down your father for her murder, could only work in her favour.'

'But the photos? What about those men meeting my father?'

'Your father knew them, but the photos were set up. Those men didn't carry out the murders.'

He put his head in his hands and groaned. 'Why are you telling me this now? After all this time.'

'Because it is not over Richard.' She took hold of both of his hands and pulled him to his feet. 'It's time to stand up for truth. Those paintings we've just seen show how my religion has been vilified, not by Muslims but by Christians. There must be a unified belief in God. The truth needs to be out. I killed Nadia to avenge Becky, but I never intended for the Gospel to be destroyed. I believe in what your father believed in. You should do it for Becky and the child she was carrying. It is what she would have wanted.'

There was a sincerity in her expression, something he had never seen when Nadia pleaded with him. 'Why do you care what Becky thinks?'

'Because I loved her.' Her eyes were watery with tears. 'I thought long and hard about this which is why I have taken so long to contact you.'

'What are you saying?'

'I have got something to give you.' She paused and took a sharp intake of breath. 'The Gospel was not destroyed. I rescued it from the wreckage.'

Richard's mouth dropped open. His mind went blank. He was speechless.

'It was miraculous, as if God wanted this to happen. Nadia put the casket in a hidden compartment below the boot, to assist with smuggling the Gospel out of the country. It protected the silver chest from the intense heat which ultimately preserved the Gospel. The explosion threw the compartment clear of the wreckage. I found it quite by accident.'

'Or divine intervention,' said Richard, allowing himself a smile. 'That's incredible news.'

'As an Israeli, I had a duty to preserve it for my country. The implications for Islam could have been huge and my government would not have liked that. I have wrestled with my decision for six months.'

'So what have you decided?'

'I have decided that God and truth should come first before my government. I have also resigned from Mossad.'

She handed him an envelope. 'The Gospel is in this safe deposit box in London. I am relying on you to find a way to recover the scroll you discovered in Crete and to unite it with the Gospel. It needs to be released as a piece of academic research which encourages peace in the Middle East. That should be your life's work, Richard – for Becky, your father, your child and the world.'

She let go of his hands and turned away. 'Nobody knows except you and I, that the Gospel was not destroyed. Use that secret wisely.' She stared at him and smiled. 'Goodbye Richard. Face the world again. It's what Becky wants.'

He watched her go. The weight of guilt had been lifted. The Lies of Our Fathers were still hidden from view. He had to expose them. He had to tell the world the truth.

THE END

Epilogue

The Zagros Mountains, West of Yazd- six months later

Fatima had prayed to God that one day she would find something truly remarkable in the thousands of documents at the monastery. The monks must have been great scholars studying everything from astronomy to the philosophy of Plato and Aristotle but there had to be more about their theology and the debate about the apocryphal gospels. There had to be something about the Gospel of Barnabas. The Ayatollah had told all her all about the Gospel's destruction and the betrayal of his Saudi Arabian contact – Nadia. The loss of the Gospel only made her redouble her efforts to find an answer. It was true, she admitted to herself, it was not just an academic interest that drove her on to find something new in the treasure trove that had become her life's work.

One thing she was certain about was that the monk, whose notebooks she had, was Akila's son Masood. He'd written the notes about the Gospel and where to find it for his own benefit because one day he would send the information back to England. She felt certain that there would be something else that might explain the originality of the Gospel and the possibility that other copies might exist.

Something led her back to St Thomas.

Recognise what is right in front of you. The father will oppose the son. Nothing hidden will fail to be displayed.

When Thomas left the Monastery, he travelled to India to preach the Gospel. There was nothing new in that assumption. The book he'd chosen was the Gospel of

Barnabas and not the Gospel of Luke. A theory that had just been proven by the answer *right in front of you.*

A letter between Barnabas and Thomas. At first, she ignored the message. A cryptic message hidden in the text. The words of Thomas revealed the answer. Jesus had survived the crucifixion, cut down from the cross before he was dead. He had gone to ground and headed for India. Thomas was determined to follow.

Fatima looked up at the dark desert sky. The nights were still bitterly cold. She'd walked in Barnabas footsteps and now Thomas begged attention. What really had happened to Jesus of Nazareth after his crucifixion on Mount Calvary? If these two saints would accompany her then she would live forever in their presence.

She prayed to God that the Englishman she'd met would help her find the answer.

To be continued in the third novel in the Barnabas trilogy
The Wilderness of Truth

Contact me on https://jonathanmarkwriter.com
Twitter: @jonmark1956

Afterword

Although this novel is a work of fiction, it addresses some real themes which I hope readers will find interesting. I wanted to explore the question of why religious conflicts exist between the major religions of Judaism, Christianity, and Islam, when in reality they all emanate from the same Abrahamic source. I also think there is considerable evidence to support the conclusion that religion has evolved over the centuries from a variety of sources, including Plato and Zoroastrianism, which are centuries older than the Abrahamic religions.

With regard to Christianity, ideas were formed initially by Paul in his Letters which are a significant part of the New Testament. There is a sense that our view of Jesus Christ has been formed by Gospels that were chosen by the Church many years after his death. In my novel, I speculated about Gospels that existed, but were not selected for inclusion in the Bible by the Council of Nicaea in the fourth century AD. These unselected documents are known as the Gnostic Gospels, many of which were found by the Dead Sea at Nag Hammadi in 1945. I wanted to focus on the Gospel of Barnabas and the Gospel of Thomas.

The text of the Gospel of Barnabas is regarded as a forgery, but there is no doubt Barnabas existed and is often revered by Christians where many churches are dedicated to his name. He is referred to several times in the Acts of the Apostles who named him Barnabas, meaning 'Son of Encouragement'. His real name was Joses which is the Greek derivation of Joseph. He worked very closely with Paul and set up a church in Antioch. Despite this, we know he fell out with Paul and might therefore have a different view of what Christianity was all about. The Gospel of Barnabas is controversial as it promotes an Islamic view of Jesus, which has not been accepted by Christians. Muslims do accept Jesus, known as Isa in the Holy Koran, as a

311

prophet, but do not believe that a human being could ever be the Son of God. It is possible that Barnabas shared a contrary view to that promoted by Paul.

In my novel, I ask the question, what if an original version of the Gospel of Barnabas did exist? The story I am relating is not without foundation. In 2000, a leather-bound text written in Aramaic, the language of Jesus, was discovered by Turkish police during a raid on a smuggling operation. The text is held in the Museum of Ethnography in Ankara. It is believed to date back to the 5th century AD and could be the Gospel stolen from the grave of St Barnabas in Cyprus, where he was born and executed by the Romans at Salamis.

This idea that documents which promoted a contrary view of Jesus is given more credence by the Gospel of Thomas where an authentic version was found in the Dead Sea scrolls. It is a series of sayings of Jesus rather than a biography. Many of the sayings are mystical rejecting the idea of Jesus being the Son of God. Thomas, famous for being the apostle that doubted the resurrection of Jesus, is known to have journeyed to India to preach. Today, there is a branch of Christianity related to St Thomas in Southern India around Kerala. Its traditions follow an earlier version of Christianity not recognised by the Western version created by Paul. The followers of Thomas built a monastery over his grave which is now a place of pilgrimage for Christians and Hindus. The mystery of Thomas will be a theme in my third novel in the trilogy called *The Wilderness of Truth,* set in Southern India.

A large part of this second novel in the trilogy is set in Iran. A sub plot in the story explores the schism between Shia and Sunni Islam. I speculated in the story about what might happen if the centres of Sunni (Saudi Arabia) and Shia (Iran) were to resolve their differences. In many respects this conflict between factions of Islam can be compared to the divisions within the Abrahamic religions.

My story is asking the question, why do these conflicts in religion exist when there seems to be many points of common interest? These beliefs can be summarised as a belief in a superior being who we choose to call God.

While researching my novel, I visited Iran to experience first-hand this beguiling country, as a centre of Shia Islam and also a country rich in history and culture. Iran is often labelled as a pariah state, the bad boy of the Middle East. I think this is unfair. It is a country full of contradictions which celebrates the poetry of Hafez, the rich history of Persia and the Zoroastrian festival of Nowruz, while supporting a dour and authoritarian political regime.

Iran is the centre of Persia and the origin of Zoroastrianism. This ancient religion which predates Abraham is instrumental in defining the concepts of Good and Evil and laying the foundations of religion as we know it today, irrespective of which religion you follow. As the German philosopher Nietzsche said, Zarathustra, the founding father of Zoroastrianism, invented morality. It defines the universality of religion.

I don't believe I have any detailed understanding of the problem of diverse religious beliefs, but I hope, in this story, I have inspired interest in what is a complex and fascinating subject. If I have, may I suggest that you turn to the true experts in this field. For that reason, I have listed the following excellent books which influenced my thinking.

A History of God by Karen Armstrong -Vintage Books 1999
A History of Christianity by Diarmaid MacCulloch – Allen Lane 2009
Iran – Empire of the Mind by Michael Axworthy – Penguin 2007
The Gnostic Gospels by Elaine Pagels - Phoenix 1979
Heirs to Forgotten Kingdoms – Gerard Russell– Simon & Schuster 2014
The Crusades by Thomas Asbridge – Simon & Schuster 2010

Printed in Great Britain
by Amazon